To Alok

"This

it."

MW01533890

Rend Your Heart

Sharon Westra

Sharon Westra

PUBLISH AMERICA

PublishAmerica
Baltimore

ISBN: 1-4241-4382-9
PUBLISHED BY PUBLISHAMERICA, LLLP
www.publishamerica.com
Baltimore

Printed in the United States of America

Dedicated to

Ashley Farnsworth
who, in her own words, loves Sara Brooks the best!

Acknowledgements

There are a few people who helped shape this book and I thank them from the bottom of my heart:

Corey Whaley, for patiently explaining the world of car racing to me. His enthusiasm and knowledge of the sport helped tremendously.

Lil Clary, for kindly sharing—in great detail—the experiences she went through from a riding accident which resulted in a ruptured spleen. I may not have used many specifics, but the information helped me understand what it would be like and, for at least a few pages, I lived with the medicated pain, confusion and slow recovery.

Rachel Adeline, who diligently read the manuscript and thoroughly filled out critique sheets. It's quite evident that Rachel truly cares about the main characters and it was not only helpful, but fun to see their world from her perspective. Thank you, Rachel, for investing the time.

My husband, Paul. When I was ready to put the manuscript on the shelf in my closet and let it stay there permanently, he made suggestions and encouraged me to face the daunting rewrites. I probably would have given up if he hadn't believed in me and this book.

Beth Jones, whose honest editing kept me evaluating and re-evaluating. Beth not only edited, she was my "brain-storming" friend, who helped figure out several scenarios and kept me going when I was ready (oh, so many times!) to give up. Thanks for everything, Beth.

I would be remiss not to mention that I received much inspiration from the songs of Sara Evans and one particular song of Rich Mullins. I must have listened to his song "Growing Young" over a hundred times while writing this book.

"Rend your heart, and not your garments.
Return to the Lord your God,
for he is gracious and compassionate,
slow to anger and abounding in love…
—Joel 2:13

CHAPTER 1

There is a time for everything, and a season for every activity under heaven.
—Ecclesiastes 3:1

"It's not going to be easy," Jim predicted, leaning against a light pole.

Sara shielded her eyes from the intense afternoon sun and looked into his face, trying to read his expression. "You mean staying together in spite of the distance?"

With a slight shake of his head, Jim reached for her hand. "No, I mean going through day after day without seeing you and listening to your stories. I know I'll be miserable; it's just not going to be easy."

Sara pressed her lips together and fought to hold back the tears, but they dribbled down her cheeks despite her efforts. She turned slightly away from the glare of the August sun and stared across the street, looking at nothing in particular. This was not the way goodbyes were supposed to be. If she was writing a novel, she would certainly not have the young couple saying goodbye on the sidewalk of a frontage road where vehicles whizzed past every few seconds. Oh, no, if Sara Brooks was writing the scene it would take place at a train station, with the hero waving goodbye from the window of the passenger train. Or on the shore of some remote beach with the surf crashing wildly against craggy rocks and the wind whipping the heroine's long hair while the hero's boat drew away from shore.

Sara swiped at her tears. Of course, if she was writing this story there would be no goodbye, because she would have found a better solution for her characters. She would not have them on the verge of a separation simply because the girl had decided to go to college in a town three hundred miles away from her boyfriend's university. Oh, no. If she'd been scripting this plot, she would have had the hero declare his undying love accompanied by a marriage proposal and had him follow her—

"Sweetheart..." Jim's voice broke through her daydreams, bringing her back to the stark truth. This was *not* a romance novel; this was real life. Hers and Jim's, and, like it or not, this was the path they had chosen.

She looked into his eyes. "I'm going to be miserable, too. Please don't forget about me, Jim."

"Never." Despite the traffic, and the children playing in a yard next door, Jim pulled Sara into a hug. He did not normally display his affection in public, but this business of saying goodbye was harder than he had thought it would be. All during the past year, when they were both attending Midwestern Christian University and Sara talked about giving up on nursing to pursue her real dream in the field of hospitality management, Jim had been very supportive. Even when he realized it meant her going to school in Milwaukee while he stayed to finish his senior year in Minneapolis. It had seemed then—and still did—like a viable solution, but that didn't mean it was easy.

"Do you think we should go back?" Sara's voice was muffled against Jim's T-shirt, which was now damp from her tears.

"I guess." The others were waiting at her parents' house: Sara's family, his cousin Katie and her new husband, Wayne. Katie and Wayne had driven from Minnesota with him to attend a friend's wedding with Sara; now it was time to head back. Jim's classes started Tuesday, Sara's on Thursday. The separation they had been dreading for months was finally here.

No sense putting off the inevitable, Jim told himself. Holding tightly to Sara's hand, he headed down the sidewalk. When they reached the house, they shared a bittersweet kiss. Then, resolutely, Jim stepped away. "I'll say goodbye to your family and tell Wayne and Katie that it's time to go." His words belied his actions, for his feet would not move. He stood still and drank in the sight of Sara, with her petite build and her wild mass of curls—how he loved that hair—and her blue eyes, brimming with tears.

Sara looked back at him, her eyes traveling over his features: the dark brows, hazel eyes behind dark-rimmed glasses, and the straight nose sporting a sprinkling of freckles. She recalled when they met. It was while he was still attending the community college in his hometown and had come to MCU to visit Katie. She had brought him up to their dorm room and Sara had come out of the bathroom, having just washed her hair. She was surprised to find company in the room, but Jim's lazy smile had put her instantly at ease and had even set her heart fluttering. Now here they were…a year and a half later…saying these miserable goodbyes.

"Just go, Jim," she whispered, knowing it was not going to get any easier. She followed him toward the door, but stopped short of going inside. She waited only a few minutes until he returned with Wayne and Katie.

Katie, Sara's best friend of all time, gave her a tearful hug. "Oh, Sara. I'm going to miss you so much. Promise you'll come visit."

Sara nodded. "I will." Leaning closer, she added, "Don't let Jim forget about me."

"Never, I promise." Katie climbed into the automobile while Wayne waved to Sara over the hood of his little black car. Sara returned his wave and tossed out a goodbye before turning to Jim, who was leaning against the trunk of the car.

"Sometimes even the right decisions are hard ones," he said.

Sara gave a slight shake of her head. "Let's not discuss it anymore, Jim. I can't…"

He put his arms out for a final hug and kiss. "I love you, sweetheart."

She nodded against his shoulder. "I love you, too." Sara forced herself to step back and allow him to climb into the car, but she could not stand there and watch them drive away. "Goodbye," she called, then went into the house and fled to her bedroom, where she dove onto the bed and gave full vent to her tears.

Sara moped for three days, but as she brushed her hair Wednesday morning, she told herself to pull it together. It was going to be a long year, but feeling sorry for herself and missing Jim to the point of crying was not going to make it better. This was going to be their life for at least the next nine months and she needed to accept the fact that their relationship was reduced to e-mails, phone calls, and the occasional weekend visit. It was what it was, and Sara, as much as she missed Jim, did *not* want to miss out on life.

After all, tomorrow marked the start of fall term and she could not wait to begin! Her lifelong dream was finally at her fingertips. If only she hadn't wasted three entire years going through MCU's nursing program. Of course, if she hadn't done that, she never would have met Katie or Jim. She never would have found her Prince Charming. And that was her other lifelong dream. To marry a prince—oh, not a real prince, but the prince of her heart, the man of her dreams, the hero of her life story. And she was sure that man was Jim...

If only Jim would say something about getting married. They'd been dating for over a year and a half and he had never once—in all that time—said anything about being together forever. But of course, he would. This year. Before he graduated in May. Sara stared at her reflection in the mirror. "He will, Sara Brooks. He will and until then, you'll study hard and make the most of living here."

Here: Milwaukee, Wisconsin. Home to her older sister, Morgan, and her husband, Mark, and now Sara. Since Mark was often out of town with speaking engagements as a counselor for families of troubled teens, Sara helped Morgan with their three young children in exchange for room and board and a small stipend.

Tossing her hairbrush onto the mirror-topped dresser, Sara turned and glanced around her room. It was so *big*. Compared to living in the dorm her freshman year and the small basement apartment she had shared with Katie last year, this room was absolutely castle-size. The architect labeled it a bonus room; Mark and Morgan planned for it to be a family room when their children got older, but for now, it was Sara's home—furnished with a daybed, a dresser, a nightstand, a rocking chair, a small TV with a built-in DVD player, a utility-sized fridge and even a microwave. The bed was covered in a green-checked comforter and matching curtains fluttered in the morning breeze. Green and blue throw pillows decorated the bed. A spider plant hung by the window and a lacy fern graced the top of her dresser.

As much as Sara loved the comfortable and spacious room, the best part was living with her older sister. In the Brooks family, the eldest was Morgan, twenty-seven, and married now to Mark for seven years. They had three children: Courtney, Nicholas and Tucker. Then came Sara's brother, who lived in Florida. Next was Sara, twenty-one, and lastly, Nicole, a junior in high school. Growing up, Morgan had mothered them all and then stepped naturally into her role as a true, bona fide mother. With her own children to care for, Sara felt confident that Morgan would finally see Sara as a child no longer, but as a sister and friend on equal ground.

Feeling better than she had in days, Sara fairly skipped downstairs for breakfast. Entering the kitchen, she found Courtney at the table eating oatmeal while playing with a hand-sized doll.

"Good morning, buttercup!" Sara tousled the little girl's messy curls, that so resembled Sara's own wild locks. "Where's your mom?"

"Giving the baby a bath." Courtney shoveled a spoonful of cereal into her mouth as she made the red-haired doll swoop overhead.

"And Nicholas?" Sara asked as she began filling the coffeepot with water. Her niece just shrugged. "Aunt Thara? Are you going to cry today?"

Sara twirled to look at her niece. "I have been doing a lot of that, haven't I? No, baby, I am not going to cry today."

"I'm not the baby!"

"Oh, that's right. You are a very big girl now, almost four years old and big enough to be Momma's helper." As the coffee started its steady stream into the glass pot, Sara grabbed a carton of yogurt from the refrigerator and took a seat across the table from her niece.

Morgan entered the room, eight-week-old Tucker cradled in her arms. "Good morning, sis."

Sara laid her spoon on the table and held her hands up for the baby. "Oh, let me have that little guy." Sara buried her face against the baby's body and drew in the fresh, sweet smell of baby wash and powder. "Mmm...you smell good enough to eat; yes, you do."

Morgan tossed Sara a grin before placing a bagel in the toaster. "My, but you're cheerful this morning."

"Aunt Thara'th not going to cry today," Courtney spoke up in all seriousness.

"Is that so?" Morgan raised her eyebrows at Sara.

"Yes, Courtney speaks the truth." Sara settled Tucker in the crook of her arm and resumed eating her yogurt. "Morgan, I know I've been awful since Jim left, but as of today, that's going to change. I'm determined to make the best of it. I mean, it's the way things are and I can't keep carrying on like I have been."

"I'm very glad, Sara, really." Morgan breathed a prayer of thanks that her sister was coming out of her funk.

"I mean, I knew when I made plans to come to MATC that I was embarking on a two-year program while Jim still has a year to finish at Midwestern..." Sara's voice trailed off as she once again envisioned an altered scenario. This time the young couple stood on top of a cliff overlooking the ocean—like in a Victorian romance novel. Sara's long skirt would be billowing in the gusty wind and her curly tresses fluttering around her face. Jim would declare his undying affection and she, holding her head high, would say adieu… *Adieu—of course!* That's what she should have said. Instead of blubbering in the driveway like a baby, she should have been poised, cupped Jim's cheek and whispered, "Adieu…"

"Earth to Sara. You were saying?" Morgan asked, carrying her bagel to the table.

At the sound of Morgan's voice, Sara came back to the real world, wishing life could be as dramatic as in romance novels. "Oh…just that I decided to make the best of this separation. It was my choice to come here and I really am so thankful to be living with you and so terribly excited to get started on my hospitality degree."

Courtney pushed her empty bowl away and announced that she was finished.

"Go put on the play clothes that I laid out on your bed, sweetie," Morgan instructed. "We're going to meet Gracie and her mom at the park this morning."

Courtney scampered off, doll in hand, while eighteen-month-old Nicholas toddled into the kitchen, still in his Spider Man pajamas. He held a scruffy blue teddy bear and had lipstick smears across his cheeks. Morgan and Sara chuckled when they saw him.

"So, that's why things were so quiet. I see you got into Mommy's makeup again." Morgan rose to wipe his face and asked Sara if she wanted to come along to the park.

"Sure…I don't have anything else to do."

After taking care of Nicholas, Morgan reached into a cupboard for a mug and poured herself a cup of coffee. "Do you want some too, Sara?"

"Please." Sara watched her sister draw a mug from a cabinet, then cross the kitchen to the coffeepot. "The mugs should really be in the cupboard above the coffee maker."

Morgan turned, a puzzled expression on her face.

Sara shoved her empty yogurt container aside. "I mean, no offense, Morgan, but so often I look in the wrong drawer or cupboard for something. I mean, honestly, haven't you ever realized that your kitchen is not efficient?"

Morgan set the coffee cups on the table and scooped Nicholas onto her lap, her eyes traveling around the kitchen. "Actually, yes, many times, but, Sara, you have to remember I was nearly eight months pregnant when we moved in. Mom helped by taking Courtney and Nicholas, and friends helped unpack, but they would only put stuff where I told them. Literally, Sara, I was so exhausted and tired of making decisions by the time we unpacked the kitchen that I just tossed the stuff in any old place. I figured once the baby was born I'd rearrange things." Morgan took a sip of coffee and shook her head. "I'm never going to get around to it—at least not until Tucker's in kindergarten!"

"That's why you should always unpack and organize your kitchen first. That's what Katie and I did."

"Where were you when I needed you?"

Sara looked at Morgan's cupboards, envisioning where things should go. Mugs above the coffee maker, spices next to the stove. "I could do it for you."

"Classes start tomorrow, Sara. You'll be way too busy."

"It's not that difficult. I'll do it today. You don't mind if I skip going along to the park, do you?"

"In order to get my kitchen organized? Not at all."

"I always say, 'There's no time like the present.'"

Morgan chuckled. "That's Grandma that always says that. Along with, 'Don't put off till tomorrow…'"

"Right." Sara jumped up from her chair, bumping her mug and spilling some coffee onto the table. "I'll get right on it." She held the baby out to Morgan. "Do I have complete freedom?"

"I have complete confidence in your finished project. Just help me dress the boys and we'll get out of your way."

Sara knew that the best way to tackle the kitchen was to take everything out of the drawers and cupboards and start fresh. She found a few empty boxes in the garage that she filled with cookbooks, hot pads, groceries and the contents of Morgan's pencil and junk drawers. Stacks of dishes, pots, pans, mixing bowls, well, everything else, covered the table, counter tops and floor. Sara stood next to the stove and used the small space between the burners— the only flat surface in the entire room left empty—and drew a map of the kitchen on a flattened, brown paper bag. "Spices here," she muttered penciling in *sp* on the appropriate place.

The phone rang—jarring Sara's concentration. With hopes high that Jim was calling, Sara made a mad dash toward the phone, which sat on a built-in desk on the other side of the cluttered room. In her rush, she knocked over a partially open bag of white flour that had been sitting precariously on a stack of cookware. As the ten-pound sack toppled over, flour spewed out. Jumping over the entire works, Sara landed barefoot in a loose layer of flour. Slipping, she grasped for the table, knocking over a stack of Tupperware in the process.

"I'm coming!" she hollered as she counted the fourth ring. Breathless, she picked up the receiver. Her heart plummeted as she realized the voice on the other end was not Jim's, but that of Mark's secretary. "Yes, I'll tell her," Sara said, after listening to the message.

She dropped the receiver back into its cradle and leaned against the desk. *Oh, Jimmy…why couldn't that have been you? Why don't you call me at…* Sara glanced at the clock above the kitchen sink…*at ten o'clock in the morning to tell me how much you miss me? Why, for once in your life, can't you do something spontaneous and call out of the blue to say that you love me…to tell me you'll wait for me…no…* Sara sniffled as, against her resolution, tears pricked her eyes…*to ask me to marry you…*

18

CHAPTER 2

In his heart, a man plans his course,
but the Lord determines his steps.
—Proverbs 16:9

Jim Hoffman clicked open his e-mail, happy to see one from Sara in his INBOX. That girl could send three a day and always have something new to say. Smiling, Jim wondered what was on her mind now. She had already sent a message this morning before classes.

Jim,

My professor for my hospitality law class looks just like Mr. Dykstra—you know, from the MCU library! Same thick moustache and owlish eyes. He even talks the same, with that stilted accent. I wonder if they're cousins... Maybe there's a conspiracy to infiltrate Northern Midwest Campuses with misplaced Dutchmen or something...

Sara

Jim chuckled. Sara was forever dreaming up stories. She said that someday she wanted to write a book—the great American novel. Although she openly admitted it would be hard to compete with Margaret Mitchell's *Gone with the Wind*. But if anyone could do it, Sara Brooks could.

Jim closed his e-mail. He would write her later, before bed, when maybe he would have something to say. His e-mails always seemed boring compared to hers. When they were together they could carry on lengthy conversations—about almost every topic under the sun—but when it came to phone calls, e-mails and letters, Jim was at a loss.

Anyway, there was only so much to say about his classes. This semester they centered on small business management and operations, accounting, marketing, and taxes. Not exactly the kind of stuff that made for interesting stories. However, *he* found them interesting. After all, he needed to learn everything about owning a small business, because he planned to open his own bike shop someday.

Growing up, Jim's family had made several trips from Minnesota to Washington State to visit relatives. Twice they had extended their vacation with driving tours down the coasts of Washington and Oregon. On the second of those trips, Jim's career dream was born. He loved the look and feel of the small coastal towns, which were so different than what he was used to in the Midwest. In one such town in Oregon, he stood in front of a tourist shop that sold kites, wind chimes, souvenirs of every kind, and rented bicycles. Listening to the surf crash against the rocks, he made up his mind right then and there, that when he got older he was going to live in a town like that and not just *rent* bicycles, but repair bikes and sell them, plus all the paraphernalia that went along with biking. He would cater to tourists, but he'd be there for the locals, too. After all, they would be his meat and potatoes during the winter months.

Jim just needed to decide how, when, and where this was all going to happen; of course that's what senior year was about. And it looked like he would have plenty of time for making plans. His work study job—clerking in the college bookstore—only amounted to twelve hours a week and his social life was practically nonexistent. Two of his roommates from last year had graduated, Wayne had gotten married, and the two new roommates, Craig and Gary, were hardly ever home.

That left Andy, a friend and roommate from last year, but he had picked up an extra class and was busy researching mission opportunities. Andy had decided to teach people in a third world country about agriculture so they could better support themselves. With his farming background, his business classes, and his genuine love for people, Andy was a perfect fit for this type of undertaking. His girlfriend was also excited about the prospect, but she would follow Andy anywhere. They had grown up together and had known from a young age that one day they would marry. In fact, Andy had confided in Jim that he was planning to propose to Greta this fall. He wanted to get married next summer and leave for the mission field as soon as possible.

Jim flopped down on his bed, thinking about how much he missed Sara. He ached with loneliness for her. He reached over his head to where he kept a framed five-by-seven picture of her. She had the most expressive blue eyes and the wildest, curliest light brown hair and she was all fun and drama and…well, she was everything that he was not and they complemented each other.

Someday, like Andy, Jim would plan a proposal of marriage—but there was no hurry. He had career goals and plans to make; besides, he was sure Sara was not ready for marriage either. She had two years of school and then she would want to use what she learned. She longed to work for a big hotel and organize conventions and other events.

Wait a minute. In the small coastal towns on the West Coast, Jim didn't remember seeing many big hotels. That was big city stuff. Like Seattle, Portland, Eugene… Who would hold a convention in say…Florence, Oregon? Sand dune buggy riders? Jim pursed his lips. Ooh, boy, planning their future was going to be more complicated than he had thought. He was not going to ask Sara to move to a little coastal town where the best she might hope for would be to cater a mayor's luncheon.

The phone rang, scattering his thoughts. He pushed himself off the bed and headed to the kitchen, where he picked up the phone. "Yeah? Hello?"

"Jim! Oh, you're home! I'm so glad."

"Sara." His face lit up. "I was just thinking about you."

"I've made the most amazing discovery."

Jim grinned. Everything with Sara was always over the top. "What's that?"

"Oh, Jim, it's fantastic! I don't know why it didn't dawn on me weeks ago. I mean, I've had my schedule forever. I don't have any Friday classes. Not any! Not this semester and it doesn't look like next semester either. Isn't that great?"

"I guess…" Jim opened the fridge and pulled out a can of Pepsi. "That'll free you up to help Morgan."

"Help Morgan? Jim! This means I have a three-day weekend every week! We can visit each other all the time."

"Every week?" Jim sounded doubtful. "You're not serious. I mean, that sounds great in theory, but it's not very practical."

The wind taken out of her sails, Sara dropped onto the rocking chair in her bedroom. "Are you saying you don't want to see me every weekend? Wouldn't you like that?"

"It's not a matter of liking it. It's not even a matter of wanting to be with you. Man, Sara, how can you even question me about that? It's the practical side of things."

"What things?"

"Well, for one, you're supposed to be around to help Morgan. That's why you're getting room and board."

"Well, yes, I know, but Morgan doesn't need me every weekend. Just when Mark is out of town. That's usually midweek, only now and then on the weekends."

"Well, what about the gas? It's three hundred miles. And where would you stay? I know you and Katie are best friends, but I don't think Wayne wants an extra person around every weekend when he and Katie are still newlyweds."

Growing defensive, Sara rose from the chair and marched over to the window. "It's not like I would be at Katie's that much. Wouldn't I mostly be with you?"

"Well, yeah, but unlike you, I do have Friday classes. *And work.* I work in the bookstore every Friday from three until six. And Saturday mornings from nine until noon. I agreed to take those shifts, which nobody else wanted, because you're not here and I have nothing else to do."

After a lengthy silence, Sara said, "It sounds like you don't want me to come visit. When did you think we'd get together?"

"In October, when I have my reading break, and then Thanksgiving and then Christmas." Saying it aloud didn't sound like much, Jim realized, but what could he do about it?

"I thought you'd be excited about my news. I guess not…I guess…" Sara quit talking and pinched her nose. She would not cry on the phone.

Jim was at a loss for words. He was just trying to be practical. Sara had told him more than once that she needed him to do that. She knew, fully well, that she could go off on a tangent too easily and needed his matter-of-factness to bring her back to earth. "Come on, Sara. This doesn't mean I don't want to be with you. I was just thinking about you. Thinking about our future."

Our future? Jim never talks about our future. He talks about his future and my future, but he never puts them together. Maybe he's thinking about marriage… As she stood at the window, Sara was no longer looking at her sister's neighborhood. She was envisioning herself and Jim standing on top of Maple Ridge with the breeze ruffling through the leaves in their full fall colors—deep reds, brilliant oranges, radiant golds. Jim was holding out an engagement ring and telling her he couldn't live without her—

"Sara? Are you still there?"

"Oh, yes, I'm here."

"So, this weekend thing? Are you mad at me?"

"No," she sighed. He was right. She had not been very practical. "I understand, but your reading break is five weeks away. Do we have to wait until then? I miss you so much."

"I know. I miss you, too. Why don't you call Katie and see if it works for you to stay over one of the next two weekends? You can drive over Friday morning and we can have most of the weekend together."

"I'll do that."

She asked how his classes were going, but he had just e-mailed her about them last night and could not think of anything new to say. After asking a couple of questions, Sara gave up. *Goodness! Getting Jim to talk on the phone is like pulling teeth!* So she told him about her classes. She was sure her favorite class was menu planning and design and her most difficult was hospitality law. Jim settled down on the apartment's threadbare brown couch and listened. She had already e-mailed much of this information, but the way she talked was captivating. Her stories were always upbeat and entertaining.

When Sara could not think of anything else to say about her classes, she told Jim how Nicholas had written on the hallway wall with a marker and she had spent twenty minutes washing it off. "He's a little rascal," she said, laughing. *And someday, I want one just like him.* She would never dare say that to Jim though, not unless he brought up the subject of marriage and a family first, but she could not stop herself from thinking it. As her dialogue wound down, Jim inserted that he should go, promising to call her Friday night around eight. She told him she would e-mail Katie and try to set up a weekend visit. He was about to say, *"I love you,"* when the apartment door opened and Gary walked in. Jim caught himself just in time and simply told Sara, "Goodbye."

Remembering her musings of last week, Sara softly and romantically said, "Adieu, Jim."

"Sara, are you coming along with us to Mom's for dinner tonight?" Morgan looked up from the pile of towels she was folding.

Coloring at the table with Courtney, Sara shook her head. "I wasn't planning on it. You probably won't be home by eight o'clock, will you?"

"Probably not. Why? What's happening at eight o'clock?"

"Jim said he'd call then."

Morgan suppressed a smile. "Don't you think he'll call back if you're not home?"

Sara tossed her mane of curls. "Well, of course he would, but I don't want him to think his call wasn't important. Besides, I've been counting down the hours. *I* don't want to miss it."

At seven forty-five, Sara laid down her textbook. She did not want to be in the middle of reading when Jim called. She gave herself a critical look in her mirror. Her hair could use a brushing and her lips some lipstick. As Sara ran the brush through her hair, she chuckled. *It's not like he can see me. Too bad we don't have those picture phones…* She tossed her brush down and reached for a tube of Misty Mauve lipstick.

She glanced at her watch. Eleven more minutes. She filed her nails. Nine more minutes. *Cappuccino!* Sara filled a mug from her bathroom sink and put it in the microwave to heat. What a great idea of Mark's to put a small microwave and fridge in here. It gave her a feeling of independence. After all, living with her sister's family was not exactly being on her own, which Sara felt very ready for. Although, if truth be told, she'd rather be living with a husband…

The microwave dinged and Sara stirred the packet of instant coffee into the large MCU mug while her thoughts envisioned a little house where she and Jim lived as newlyweds. She would not be waiting for his phone call…they would be snuggling on the couch, each drinking a cup of cappuccino—well, Jim wouldn't. He didn't like coffee. He would have hot cocoa or a soda.

Sara glanced at her watch: 7:58. She took her cup and the phone and settled down on her bed. Her heartbeat was slowly increasing as she anticipated hearing Jim's lazy voice. Her eyes roamed to his photo on her nightstand as she took slow sips of her hot drink, every now and then glancing at her alarm clock. 8:01. 8:04. 8:06. *Come on, Jim, call…* 8:10. Sara laid the phone on her green-checked comforter and scooted to the edge of her bed. She set her half-empty cup of coffee on the nightstand and walked to the window. *Maybe Andy or one of the other guys is tying up the phone. I wish I could convince Jim to get a cell phone.* She knew what Jim thought of cell phones though. A luxury item, an unnecessary expense, an inconvenience.

At 8:20, Sara began to get irritated. *Why did he say eight o'clock if he didn't mean it? Doesn't he care? What is he doing? Should I call him?* She would hate for him to think she was checking up on him. For that matter, she would hate for him to know that she was waiting impatiently—as if she had nothing else to do but sit around and wait for his promised phone call.

By 8:40, she was worried. *What if something's happened? Something must have happened!* She reached for the phone and determinedly punched in the number for Jim's apartment.

"Yeah? This is Gary."

"Hi, Gary," Sara greeted sweetly. She hadn't met Jim's new roommates yet. "Is Jim there?"

"No, do you want to leave a message?"

"No, that's okay. There's no message." Sara dropped the phone onto her bed. *I might as well have gone along to Mom and Dad's. Jim Hoffman, are we in love or not? Do we have a future or don't we?*

Sara couldn't help but think about Katie and Wayne. They had been married in May. Sara had lived with Katie for two years, watching enviously as Katie and Wayne fell deeply, passionately, inextricably in love. And it wasn't just them. The girls from her old youth group were all engaged or married. Russ, Jim's old roommate, had married in August and recently, Amie, another friend from MCU, had sent Sara a copy of her engagement announcement. *And I just know that Andy and Greta will be announcing their engagement soon. I'll be the only one left…*

The phone rang. Sara grabbed it before it could ring a second time, drawing in a deep breath to compose herself. "Hello?"

"Hi. It's me."

8:54. Sara heard the garage door open as Mark and Morgan pulled into the driveway. "How are you?" she asked.

"I'm good."

Sara paced back and forth from the bed to the dresser and forced her voice to sound casual. "So, what've you been doing?"

"Wayne and Katie had Andy and me over for supper. She said it's all arranged for your visit next weekend. She wants us to come for supper on Friday. I said she could count on it."

"Oh…" Disappointed that Katie had been the one to tell Jim the good news that she was coming for a weekend visit, and not really sure how she felt about spending the first evening with him in the company of Katie and Wayne, Sara didn't know what to say. Nothing about this phone call was going the way she had anticipated. "So, that's where you've been."

"Yeah, sorry. I couldn't really get away by eight, but I figured it didn't really matter when I called. I mean, we just talked Wednesday and I don't have anything new to say. How about you? Anything much happening over there?"

"Well, I was going to tell you that I'm coming next weekend, but I guess you already know that now."

"I can't wait to see you. Do you think you could get here between one and three? That's my break between class and work."

"Work?"

"Yeah. Don't you remember my schedule? Monday, Wednesday and Friday from three until six. Saturdays from nine until noon."

"I remember." *Aren't you going to take time off when I'm there?* Sara didn't dare ask. She hated to be demanding, but she couldn't help but wonder if this relationship meant as much to Jim as it did to her.

"Sara? Are you okay?" Jim straddled a kitchen chair. "Did something happen?"

"No, nothing happened."

"Well, are you mad at me or something?"

"No, I'm not mad." That was true enough. She was not *mad*, just…just… "We need to see each other." If she could look into his eyes, she would know how he felt. If he still loved her.

"I can't agree with you more. I miss you."

"You do?"

"Of course I do. What do you think? I'm counting the days until next weekend."

Just like I was counting the minutes until our phone call. Tears filled Sara's eyes and dribbled down her cheeks. "Me too, Jim. I need to be with you."

"Sara? Are you crying?" Man, he felt helpless. There *was* something wrong. He knew it.

Sara drew in a quivering breath and held it a moment. "Are we doing the right thing, Jim? I mean, it's only the beginning of this separation and I'm not sure if I can handle it."

"Sara, just hang in there. Trust me. We'll get through this."

"Will we? I hope so, because more than anything, I want to stand beside you…" Sara remembered the vision she had dreamed earlier of the two of them on the top of Maple Ridge. She would bide her time. He was bound to bring up the subject of marriage during one of their visits this fall—surely by Christmas.

Her mood brightening, Sara settled onto her bed. She reached for her cappuccino, took a sip, then spit the now cold coffee back into the mug. She chuckled, realizing she'd been a fool for the better part of the last hour, questioning Jim's commitment to her. She had something many girls didn't have. A down-to-earth, well-meaning boyfriend who loved her.

CHAPTER 3

"For I know the plans I have for you," declares the Lord, "plans to prosper you and not to harm you, plans to give you hope and a future."
—Jeremiah 29:11

Sara thoroughly enjoyed the trip to Milwaukee to visit Jim. She felt so grownup—taking a five-hour road trip all by herself. She could play whatever music she wanted, not to mention singing along as loud as she pleased. The September sun was shining, there were those wispy clouds high overhead that just made a girl's imagination soar, she was wearing a brand-new burgundy ribbed shirt, and she was on her way to spend the weekend with her boyfriend.

Stopping at the last traffic light before Jim's apartment, she studied herself in the rearview mirror. With a practiced hand, she finger-combed a few stray locks into place, then dug into her purse for a tube of lipstick. She flicked the lid off too hard and it flew out of her hand and rolled under the passenger seat. *Bother…* Just as the light changed, she pursed her lips and put the tube of Enchanting Pink lipstick to her mouth. Critically, she examined the results in the mirror as the man behind her honked his horn. *All right, already! Some people are so impatient!*

Approaching Jim's building, Sara scanned the small lot for his car. Not spotting it, she glanced at her watch. 12:22. *That's just great; I made too good of time. He won't be home from class for at least twenty minutes.* Deciding to backtrack a mile and grab lunch, she pulled back onto the boulevard.

There was a long line at the drive-through window of the taco place. It looked busy inside too, so Sara decided to wait for her turn outside. She refused to let the slow-moving procession sour her mood. It took almost half an hour before she was back at Jim's apartment, but at least his vehicle was in the lot.

Stepping out of her car, she slung her purse over her shoulder, then grabbed the colas and the bag with the burritos and crispy potato rounds. She was about to slam her door when she remembered the box of cookies and bars she had baked for Jim and his roommates. Temporarily setting the glasses of cola on the roof of her car, she stretched across to the passenger seat for the shoe box of baked goods. Spying her empty, disposable coffee cup, she grabbed that too. Cradling the box in her arms, she retrieved the colas and precariously balanced them on the lid. With hands and arms full, she advanced toward the cement stairwell.

"You would have to live on the second floor," she muttered. With careful steps, Sara climbed the stairs, then stood outside the door without a free hand to knock. Pausing for just a heartbeat, in which Sara regrettably realized she was not going to be able to throw her arms around Jim for the romantic reunion she had been anticipating, she called his name and gently kicked at the door.

In a moment, the door opened and Jim stood before her. He was dressed in blue jeans and a short-sleeved tan-and-green collared shirt. He grinned, his eyes resting on her face. Man, but she looked great—as always. Time seemed suddenly suspended. "You made it."

"Yes, I'm here." Banal, trivial words that stated the obvious and belied the excitement they felt. Her hands trembled and the cups of cola wobbled on the lid of the box and she could feel the bag of burritos beginning to slip through her fingers. "Jim! Grab the bag."

He tugged the paper sack and the coffee cup out of her hand. "You're really loaded down."

"Besides lunch, I have a box filled with goodies for you." She lifted the box slightly to draw his attention to it. "Ooh…" One of the glasses tilted and dribbles of cola dripped down her new shirt. "Oh!"

Jim tried to rescue the glass, but the lid popped off and the brown cola streamed down Sara's top. She tensed as the cold liquid soaked through to her skin. Hastily, Jim set the bag of burritos on the ground, tossed the empty coffee cup aside and took the box from Sara's hand. "I'm sorry, Sara."

Looking down, she tugged at the sticky, wet shirt. Her new top—the one she had chosen with such care for this reunion with Jim—was a mess. Slowly, she raised her blue eyes to Jim's face. He was trying to hide a smile, relishing how good being with Sara was. In spite of the crazy things that always happened to her, or maybe because of them, he was overcome with love for her. Lowering the box to waist level, Jim leaned forward and kissed Sara's pouty lips. "I'm glad you're here."

Sara nodded. "Me too, but I'll have to change now."

"Yeah. Let's just set this down…" They stepped inside and put everything on the table. Then Jim followed Sara down to the car and waited while she dug through her bag for a clean shirt. She pulled out a black tank top and a lemon-colored polo shirt and eyed them critically. Deciding to wear the polo, she tossed the tank top into the backseat and bumped her head in her rush to rejoin Jim.

He chuckled and reached for her hand. "You can slow down now; you're here."

Sara blushed, wishing her heart would beat normally. She was just so anxious to spend every minute with Jim.

They ate lunch, then sat and talked for a while. Andy came home and greeted Sara with an enthusiastic bear hug. She opened the box of goodies and offered it to him.

"Don't mind if I do," Andy said, then devoured two gooey chocolate-caramel bars. "I knew there was something missing this year, Jim. It's Sara and Katie's cooking."

Jim reached into the box and drew out a bar for himself. Winking at Sara, he said, "Well, I think it might be just a little bit more than their cooking."

Sara blushed. This was great—being here with Jim and Andy, and tonight spending the evening with Katie and Wayne. As much as she loved going to MATC and enjoyed living with her sister, Sara could not help but feel that *this* was where she belonged. This was her world and when she was with Jim, everything seemed right.

Jim rose from the table and reached for Sara's hand. "Let's go for a walk before I have to leave for work."

"Okay."

The young couple walked hand in hand down the boulevard, Sara entertaining Jim with her stories. They laughed often, enjoying being together…and in love. When they neared the apartment on their return, Jim spoke about his plans for their weekend. "You can hang out here for a while and then head over to Katie's. She should be home from work by three thirty; I'll meet you over there later. Tomorrow after work, I thought we could hike to Maple Ridge. The weather's supposed to stay nice."

"Maple Ridge?" A vision floated through Sara's mind of her and Jim standing on Maple Ridge like they had earlier in her daydreams. In that fantasy she had been wearing a skirt, but realistically, a hike demanded jeans or shorts and her black tank top and tennis shoes. "That sounds perfect."

They reached Jim's stairwell just as Andy was coming down. "Hey, Sara. I have a study group, but maybe I'll see ya later. Thanks for the goodies."

"You're welcome; goodbye." Sara waved and followed Jim into the apartment.

"So," Jim said. "Will you be okay here by yourself?"

"Yes, Jim. It'll only be thirty minutes or so." Sara glanced around the apartment. "I could do some cleaning for you."

"You don't have to do that."

"Really, I'd like to. Besides, I saw the state of your bathroom. Trust me, it needs cleaning."

Jim grinned and planted a kiss on her cheek. "Whatever makes you happy. I'll see you later." Just before he shut the door, he stuck his head back inside. "The cleaning supplies are under the sink."

Sara chuckled and headed to the bathroom. She opened the window and, whistling, gathered the cleansers and rags and set to work. Several minutes later, she rinsed the tub after giving it a good scrubbing. Turning off the water, she realized someone was speaking in the other room. She grabbed a towel to dry her hands and headed out of the bathroom, ready to meet Gary or Craig. She stopped near the dining room table, realizing it was only the answering machine.

Sara was about to turn back to the bathroom, when she heard the words *jewelry store.* Her breath caught in her throat and she took a step toward the machine, her ear cocked to listen.

"*…your engagement ring is in. I know how anxious you've been for it to arrive. We'll be open until eight o'clock tonight. Our Saturday hours are from nine until six.*"

Engagement ring! Sara clasped a hand over her heart. *Oh…I should not have heard that message. I'm never going to be able to act natural now…* Overcome with excitement, she twirled around in circles. *It's just like in my dreams…a hike to Maple Ridge…*

31

Suddenly the door to the apartment opened. Sara stopped mid-twirl, terribly conscious of the neon-green light blinking on the answering machine, and looked to see who was entering. "Er—hello…?"

Taken by surprise, the young man looked up, then relaxed. "You must be Jim's girl. I'm Craig."

"Hi, Craig. Yes, I'm Sara. I was just…" she glanced back at the bathroom. "Um, doing some cleaning, but I'm about done. I'll be out of your way in a sec."

"That's fine. It's no problem if you need to hang out here. I'm not staying long."

Sara looked at her watch, hoping to escape before Craig decided to listen to the message. "Actually, I should be on my way over to my friend's house anyway. Jim's meeting me there later. I'll just put this stuff away…" Sara backed into the bathroom and hurriedly shoved the cleaning products back under the sink. "Nice to meet you, Craig," she called as she grabbed her purse and dashed out of the apartment.

Now that was a close call, Sara Brooks. She rushed down the steps, realizing what a great story this would make, and she couldn't tell anybody. Not even Katie. Well, maybe someday. Someday when she and Jim were happily married she could tell Katie how she had overhead the message from the jewelry store and nearly been caught by Craig.

The drive from Jim's building to Katie and Wayne's small basement apartment went past in a blur. Pulling up to the curb of the house, Sara couldn't even remember driving there. *Just think…by the time I go to bed tomorrow night, I'll have a ring on my finger. I wonder what style Jim picked out…* Sara's imagination ran away as she sat in the car daydreaming for several minutes. Suddenly, Katie stood at her door, rapping on the window.

"Hello? Sara?"

"Oh!" Giggling, Sara opened her door. "Hi."

"I just came out to get the mail and saw you sitting here. What are you doing? Didn't you think I was home? My car's right in the driveway."

"Oh, Katie!" Sara threw her arms around her best friend. "I've just been thinking. I guess I lost track of time."

"I guess!" Katie laughed. "It must have been some serious subject."

"I'll tell you about it later." Sara stepped back and held Katie at an arm's length, looking her friend over from head to toe. Katie's long blond hair flowed loose down her back and her green eyes glittered in merriment. "Let me look at you, Mrs. Wayne Anderson! How's married life treating you?"

Katie blushed. "Very well. Come on, we have so much to talk about."

Sara grabbed her large duffle bag. "I've already had to change my top." Laughing, she followed Katie into the basement apartment, telling her about her clumsy reunion with Jim.

Katie shook her head. "Why am I not surprised?"

Sara dropped her bag next to the couch and circled the room, taking it all in. "Katie, I love what you've done with the place. It looks really nice." She crossed the room to where a large framed print of a sunflower hung above Katie's antique bookshelf. "This is pretty. It reminds me of all those flowers Wayne used to give you."

"That's why we got it," Katie explained, a dreamy look in her eyes.

Sara turned to study her friend's face. "You and Wayne are so lucky. You have the most romantic relationship. You guys have your own flower and your own song. Jim and I don't have anything like that."

"You and Jim are very sweet together, Sara. Come on, we can talk in the kitchen. I'm going to make cheesecake for dessert. Want to help?"

The next two hours passed swiftly as Katie and Sara talked about everything under the sun while preparing dinner. Before they knew it, Wayne was home from work. He walked around the corner to the kitchen, grinning. "I can hear you two all the way out to the street."

"Oh, you cannot!" Katie flashed her husband a smile.

He drew close to give Katie a kiss on the lips. Sara averted her eyes, wishing Jim would kiss her in public like that. "Sara," Wayne greeted. "It's good to see you. Maybe now we can get a smile out of Jim. He's been so solemn lately."

Sara blushed, thankful for Wayne's kind words. She watched as he snitched some of the fruit Katie was slicing for salad and she tenderly slapped his hand away. *They're so great together*, Sara mused.

"Want some coffee, Sara?" Wayne asked, pulling the pot from the coffee maker and filling it with water from the tap.

"I'd love some."

Katie put the last pieces of sliced banana into the fruit salad, then joined Wayne and Sara at the table and the three friends talked until Jim arrived. He entered the room with cheerful greetings and handed Wayne a black zippered sweatshirt. "Here, I remembered you left this at my place last week so I stopped home a minute to grab it."

Sara sat up straighter, wondering if he had taken time to listen to the phone message. She squirmed in her seat, but Jim didn't say anything else and she didn't dare ask. Obviously, if he had listened, he had not taken the time to go to the jewelry store before coming here.

Katie asked Wayne to set the table while she dished up the chicken and potatoes. Sara made herself useful by pouring glasses of water. Dinner was enjoyable as lighthearted dialogue flowed easily, but Sara had a hard time focusing. The spoken words on Jim's answering machine kept replaying across her mind.

Over dessert Jim announced, "Well, I guess he's finally going to do it."

"Who? Do what?" Wayne questioned.

"Andy—propose to Greta."

Sara stopped her fork midway to her mouth as her breath caught in her throat.

Wayne grinned. "That so, huh?"

"I guess. When I stopped home there was a message for him on the machine saying his engagement ring is ready at the jeweler's."

"Andy!" Sara exclaimed.

Jim looked at her. "Why are you so surprised?"

Before Sara could respond, Katie said, "Jim, you shouldn't be sharing that information. It's private. Isn't that right, Sara?"

"Andy…?" Sara whispered, trying to absorb the information that the message she had overheard had been for Andy not Jim.

"It's hardly a secret. He's been talking about it for weeks now." Jim turned to Wayne for support. "Isn't that right?"

Wayne shrugged and put another bite of cheesecake on his fork. "More like months."

Andy…Greta…she'll be the one wearing the ring… For the next few minutes Sara was unaware of the conversation going on around her, oblivious to the fact that the subject had been changed until Katie rose to clear the table and asked if Sara was going to finish her cheesecake.

Sara looked mutely into Katie's eyes and shook her head. Surprised to notice Sara's blue eyes clouded with unshed tears, Katie leaned close and softly asked if she was okay. Sara gave a slight shrug of her shoulders and stole a look at Jim. He was playfully arguing some baseball stats with Wayne. Her heart ached with love for him…to stand with him forever as a couple…to conquer mountains together…to accomplish their dreams…

Jim laughed at some obscure point Wayne made, his hazel eyes crinkling in humor behind his dark-rimmed glasses. Katie squeezed Sara's shoulder, a subtle way of offering to have a private chat if Sara needed. But Sara didn't want to talk to Katie about this. There was no way she was going to admit how foolish she had been. Determinedly, Sara squared her shoulders and said, in a clear, loud voice, "Andy and Greta married! How wonderful."

Wayne looked at her. "I'll say it again, it's no big surprise."

"Everyone seems to be getting married." Sara chanced a quick glance at Jim. Would he take the hint?

"Not quite *everyone*," Jim said matter-of-factly as he rose and carried his plate to the sink.

Sara's heart sank. *Everyone except us.* She looked down at her hands, at the finger that needed an engagement ring. Looking up at the others, Sara pasted a smile on her face. If waiting was what was required of her, waiting was what she would do. She just hoped she wouldn't become an old maid waiting for Jim.

CHAPTER 4

Be self-controlled and alert. Your enemy the devil prowls around like a roaring lion looking for someone to devour.
—I Peter 5:14

"I have no life!" Sara declared as she entered the living room and flopped onto the couch. "I mean, here it is, Friday night and what am I doing? Reading bedtime stories to a four-year-old. Granted, *Rapunzel* is terribly romantic, but if I have to read that book one more time, I'm going to scream."

Rocking the baby, Morgan rolled her eyes at Sara's histrionics. "I can take it from here, if you want to go out."

"Go where? With whom?"

Morgan shrugged. "Haven't you made any friends at school?"

"Not really. It's not at all like when I went to Midwestern. I mean, that was so different, living in the dorms and eating in the caf and basically spending all my time on campus. There're so many people you get to know and somebody is always up to doing something. But here I just go to class and then come home."

"Well, I agree, Sara, you should have more to your life than childcare duties. Maybe you should join the singles group at church."

"Singles! I'm not a *single*; I'm in a relationship with Jim."

"It's not a dating service, Sara."

"Well, then why do they call themselves *singles?*"

"Maybe because they aren't married, that makes them single—like you."

"Oh. Well, maybe I could try it, but I've seen their bulletin announcements. They only do something once or twice a month. That's not very often. I need something more than that." Sara rose and went to the front window. It was that dusky time of evening when the sun was just about to disappear below the horizon and everything was coated with a muted shade of pinky, purpled gray. Sara's thoughts wandered back to the story of Rapunzel that she had read to Courtney. She grabbed her thick hair, pulled it out, then let it drop, dreaming about a Prince Charming coming to her tower bedroom and calling for her to come out. The prince, of course, was Jim...

"I've an idea," Morgan spoke up. "I never use my membership at the health club anymore. Why don't we switch it over to your name and then you could take aerobics or something. I think they even have dance classes. That would be fun, don't you think?"

Sara turned to look at her sister. Morgan's idea was worth considering. The social aspect of a class full of people was especially appealing. "That'd be fun! Are you sure you don't mind?"

"Not at all. Honestly, Sara, I haven't gone to the club since I was pregnant with Nicholas, but Mark keeps making the payments. Let's go tomorrow, get you enrolled and check the class schedule."

"It sounds great. Do you think they teach ballroom dancing?" She was already visualizing her and Jim in evening wear, waltzing outdoors under the moonlight on a warm summer night.

"All right, if you'll just sign here." The club employee laid a contract in front of Sara. She picked up a pen and dutifully signed her name with Nicholas dangling across one of her legs. Tucker whimpered in Morgan's arms and Courtney did a ballet dance around the lobby.

Sara could hear music coming from the upstairs aerobic room, could feel the beat of it pulsing in her veins and sense the upbeat energy radiating from the people as they made their way through the lobby. High energy permeated this place and Sara couldn't wait to become a part of it.

"Here's a list of the classes you wanted." Sara's attention was drawn back to the woman sitting across the desk and she accepted the offered program. "You can start at any time; there are no signups or anything."

Sara took a moment to study the schedule. "Perfect…" There was an aerobics class offered on Mondays and Wednesdays from three to four. She could easily make that since her college classes were finished by two o'clock. "And your dance classes?"

"We're just getting into that so we only offer a couple. We have ballroom dancing on Tuesday evenings and line dancing on Thursday nights."

"Okay. Well, I'll just start with the aerobics for now and then see. Thank you." Sara rose and picked up Nicholas. "I guess I'll start on Monday. Is that okay?"

"Certainly. On your first time you might want to come in a few minutes early, meet your instructor and find out what the class is doing."

Sara nodded. Arriving early would be simple if she came directly from school. Maybe the club could become her after-class hangout. She could bring Jim here when he came to visit. They could use the pool and the hot tub and maybe… Turning back to the salesperson, Sara asked, "Do you ever sponsor dances on the weekend?"

"No, I'm afraid we only do instruction."

Sara nodded. It was just as well… She would never get Jim to a dance anyway.

Sara stepped from the campus building where her classes were held and headed toward Highland, where her car was parked. She was looking forward to going to the health club and participating in her first group fitness class. This really had been one of Morgan's more brilliant ideas. There were bound to be other young women working out whom Sara could become friends with.

By the time she had driven to the club, checked in with the receptionist and changed from her jeans into workout clothes, she was only ten minutes early for class. She entered the aerobics room to find a man stretching. He flashed her a warm smile in welcome. She nodded in greeting and made her way to what she assumed would be a back corner for class. Following his example, Sara began some stretching routines.

"You're new," the man had a fluid, pleasant voice.

"Yes, I was hoping to meet the instructor before class starts."

"That's me; I'm Dean." He approached Sara and offered a hand.

"Hi, I'm Sara."

"You'll want to bind that up," he said, motioning to Sara's thick, free-flowing mass of curls. "We get pretty active in here."

"Oh—I didn't…" Sara patted her new warm-ups where pockets would normally be.

"Here." Dean walked across the room and reached into a small plastic container. "There's some in here; you'll want a sweat towel, too. Normally you'll get one from the front desk." He handed her the rubber band and a towel he had taken from a small stack.

"I guess I'm not very prepared."

Dean shrugged. "You're just new; you'll learn the ropes. I take it you've never been to a group fitness class before."

"No, I'm a rookie."

"Be sure to stretch your hamstrings—like this." Dean demonstrated and Sara copied his movements, studying his face as she did. He had a distinguished look with his glasses and stylishly clipped black hair. She could better picture him in a suit and tie than his athletic apparel.

"You're not what I expected. For a teacher, I mean."

"No? Why's that?"

Sara shrugged. "I don't know. I'm not sure what I expected, but it wasn't you."

Dean chuckled. "Is that a nice way of saying I'm too old for this?"

"Not at all." Although he had to be nearing thirty. "You just seem...well..."

"Out of place?"

Sara blushed, then flashed him a dazzling smile, unable to come up with the right words.

"Would it make you feel better if I told you that teaching aerobics is only a side job? That in my real life I'm a freelance photographer, but that doesn't make enough to pay the bills so I teach aerobics on the side?"

The door opened and two women entered, prepared with sweat towels dangling from their fingers. "Hello, Dean," they greeted territorially as they staked out a spot in the center of the floor. Dean greeted them, his attention compulsorily removed from Sara.

The door opened repeatedly as more people trickled in for class. Sara finished stretching as a young woman claimed the spot next to her.

"Hi, I'm Sara," she greeted cheerfully.

"I'm Kelly," the other woman responded as Dean turned the music on. For the next hour, Sara concentrated on following the aerobic steps. Keeping to the beat was no problem as her natural ability for timing and rhythm took over, but learning all the twists and turns would take a little practice. At the end of the hour, Sara felt great. Tired and sweaty, but great.

There was some chatter as the members of the class toweled off and waited in line for the drinking fountain. Sara talked with Kelly for a few minutes, then looked for Dean, but he was deep in conversation with another man so she slipped out of the door and down to the locker room.

After a quick shower, Sara let her hair down and changed into the jeans and striped polo shirt she had worn to school, then stepped into the lobby and headed for the juice bar. There wasn't an employee behind the counter, so Sara turned and watched the television in the upper corner of the room while she waited for the attendant to return.

"Sara Brooks! In the flesh."

She whipped around at the sound of her name being spoken by a deep, caressing voice and found herself staring into the darkest pair of eyes she had ever seen. No, she had seen them before, and the chestnut brown hair, and the dimpled chin, and the classic movie-star features. As handsome as Gavin Manes had been in the ninth grade, he was stunning now. Self-consciously Sara smoothed a hand over her hair, only too aware of the tendrils along her face that were damp from perspiration.

"Gavin. You work here?" She felt short of breath. Gavin was here. In *her* gym. She couldn't believe she was seeing him after all these years.

"More or less." He leaned over the counter, studying every inch of Sara, then whistled under his breath. "My, my, girl, but you grew up into a beauty."

Sara blushed. "I had no idea you were living in Wisconsin again."

He winked at her. "I've been back for a while. How come I've never seen you here before?"

"I just joined." Sara's mind was simply spinning with Gavin Manes, the forbidden heartthrob of her early teen years, standing here, face to face. She leaned against the counter for support and dug into her purse

"Put your money away. This one's on me, for old times' sake. What'll it be? Mango Madness? Citrus Cooler?"

Sara dropped her purse onto the counter and studied the menu posted above Gavin's head. Unable to focus, she said, "I'll just start at the top and work my way down."

Gavin chuckled and turned to look up at the posted juice choices. "Berry Bonanza." He pulled a plastic glass from a stack below the counter, filled it with crushed ice and proceeded to mix Sara's beverage with a practiced flair. Setting the drink in front of her, he said, "I guess that means you plan to come often."

Sara nodded. "I'm taking aerobics."

"Dean's class?"

"Yes."

"Good, that's during my shift. Just a sec." Gavin stepped away to wait on two others while Sara sipped her juice, watching him furtively. He was so handsome, and his thick dark hair was impeccably in place. "So, Sara," he said, returning to her end of the counter, "I think I owe you a date."

"A date?" She hated to hear the squeak in her voice.

"Now don't tell me you don't remember." He had a way of looking at her that distracted her beyond measure, but of course she remembered! As if she could forget how they had met on the second day of their freshman year of high school and flirted with each other all during first semester. He had asked her out, but her parents stood firm on their rule that she could not date until she was sixteen. So they sat together at chapel and ball games, holding sweaty hands under cover of a jacket, bemoaning the fact that Sara would not turn sixteen until March of her sophomore year. She had never felt that her parents were more unfair than when she had been dying to go out with Gavin Manes. Then his dad had been transferred to Arizona and Gavin had moved away two weeks after Sara's fifteenth birthday. They had never seen each other again, but a little corner of Sara's heart had always held on to the memory of a dark-haired, dark-eyed youth who lived life on the edge and had been her first love.

"Don't worry about it," she said. "It was a long time ago."

Gavin studied her face with that all consuming look he had. "Some things are worth waiting for."

Sara laughed. "As if you've been waiting for me all this time."

"I think a part of me has. What do you say? Friday night?"

"I couldn't." Sara shook her head, thinking of Jim. "I'm dating someone."

"It figures. A girl as beautiful and fun and smart as you…" Gavin let his words trail off, but they left Sara feeling very special. "It's my bad luck. First you're too young, now you're spoken for."

"Well," Sara shook her curls and reached for her belongings. She had to get out of here. She needed to call Jim and pull herself into the present, not back in ninth grade with a sweet-talking, fun-loving boy. "Thanks for the juice. I guess next time it'll be Citrus Cooler." As she said it, Sara warned herself that maybe she had better not stop for juice again. Her memories of Gavin were dangerous—a little like playing with fire.

"Wednesday. Four o'clock. I'll be expecting you." Gavin winked and watched Sara slip away from the counter and head out the door without a backward glance. *So she has a boyfriend, that just makes it a little more challenging.* Gavin was always up for a challenge, especially where women were concerned. And Gavin Manes was used to getting what he wanted.

CHAPTER 5

Show me your ways, O Lord, teach me your paths;
guide me in your truth and teach me.
—Psalm 25:4-5

Sara walked toward the campus parking lot with a lilt to her step. Class had been especially interesting today. The instructor shared humorous anecdotes about what *not* to do in regards to food and beverage service. He had done it with a fake French accent and had the entire class chuckling. Still smiling, Sara unlocked her car door and climbed in.

Pulling onto the boulevard and heading toward the health club, Sara felt a tingling in her veins and a warmth creeping into her stomach. She tried to tell herself it was not because she would see Gavin again. *I mean, he means nothing to me. Nothing.* It had all been a long time ago and even then, it had really been nothing. Just a few months of innocent flirtation. Just a few times of sitting next to each other in chapel and at basketball games, and one time at a school-sponsored movie night in the gym.

Why should her stomach have butterflies now? Gavin Manes was just a tiny piece of her past, which had nothing to do with her present, especially since she was practically engaged to Jim. Wasn't she? Then why hadn't she told her sister she had seen Gavin? When Morgan had asked about aerobics class, Sara had told her about meeting Dean and Kelly, but had not said a word about Gavin.

It's just because it's unfinished business. Like a romance novel left incomplete. If Gavin had never moved away, our puppy love would have run its natural course and eventually we would have each moved on to someone else. Still…there was something about seeing Gavin so unexpectedly and knowing he would be there again today that made Sara both excited and anxious. She shook her head, causing her curls to bounce on her shoulders. *I don't have to talk to him. If it's going to make me uncomfortable, I just won't talk to him.*

Sara pulled into a parking spot in the club's large lot, grabbed the duffle bag with her gym clothes and hurried through the entrance. She didn't even glance at the juice bar, but checked in at the front desk, grabbed a sweat towel, and went directly into the locker room to change, then up the steps to the aerobics room. The room was empty so she stretched then wandered around looking at the pictures on the walls. After several minutes, Dean entered with a cheerful greeting.

"Back for more? I'm glad I didn't scare you away."

Sara grinned. "I loved it. It was so much fun."

"Good." Dean headed over to the CD player, Sara trailing behind him.

"So, are you really a free-lance photographer or did you make that up?"

"I am. What about you? What do you do?"

Sara told him that she was taking classes at Milwaukee Area Tech College for a degree in hotel and hospitality management. He listened while he stretched, motioning for her to warm up while she talked.

"That's great." Dean liked how much spark and enthusiasm Sara spoke with and knew he would enjoy spending time with her. "So, I'm just going to come right out and ask…are you seeing anyone?"

Sara's mouth practically dropped open in shock, but she quickly recovered. "Yes. His name is in Jim and he's in college in Minneapolis."

"A long-distance relationship. That can be tough." Dean found himself slightly disappointed that Sara was not free, but also a little relieved because at twenty-six, Sara might think he was a little too old for her.

Sara did not say anything else because the door opened and three people entered. Instead, she turned and walked to the same back corner she had stood in the first day, pondering the question Dean had asked. *He was just being nice. Surely, someone like him wouldn't be interested in someone like me!* Sara couldn't help but smile and she couldn't wait to tell Morgan. *What a riot!*

After class, Sara took her time in the locker room. She brushed her hair, washed her sweaty face and reapplied her makeup. Not that she planned to talk to Gavin, but just in case... Slowly she opened the locker room door, looked across the lobby and spied Gavin behind the juice bar. He was handing an older man a glass of juice, smiling and joking with the him. *Oh...* Sara felt her knees go weak. *Why does he have to be so movie-star handsome?* Just then, he turned and saw her standing in the doorway. His face lit up in pleasure and expectation.

"Sara? Ready for your Citrus Cooler?"

She drew in a deep breath. *After all, what harm could it do to talk to him? I talked to Dean. At Midwestern, I talked to other guys all the time. It's really no big deal.* Sara approached the juice bar, set her duffle bag on the floor and slid onto a barstool.

Gavin prepared her drink, stirring it for an extra long time before setting the Cooler in front of her. With a wink, he said, "I fixed it extra special, just for you."

"Thanks." Sara handed him some money and took a sip from her straw. "Mmm...this is better than the Berry Bonanza. What's your favorite?"

Gavin leaned over the counter and in a low voice drawled, "That would have to Pineapple Passion."

"Oh." Sara blushed a little, flustered, and said, "It'll be awhile before I get to the P's."

Gavin winked again, then moved down the counter to take another order. He was kept busy mixing drinks for a few minutes so Sara sipped hers slowly and subtly watched him from the corner of her eye.

After he had waited on the last customer, he wiped his hands on a towel and came to stand in front of Sara. "So, this guy you're dating...it can't be too serious. I don't see a ring on your finger." He deftly lifted Sara's left hand, held it for just a moment to make his point, then released it.

Sara tried to ignore the tingling in her fingers that came from Gavin's touch. "Oh, well, no, we're not engaged yet, but we will be. I mean, we've been dating for almost two years."

"Two years? Wow. That's a long time to date someone."

"Yes, it is..." The thought flashed through her mind that Wayne and Katie had dated less than a year, Aimee and Ryan only six months, Mel and Russ only a few weeks...

"Sara," Gavin drew her attention back to the conversation at hand. "So, what's the guy waiting for?"

"Well, he's in school. I guess, uh…" Sara felt an unreasonable irritation that Jim had put her in this position.

Gavin made a tsk-tsk sound and raised his eyebrows. "Kind of makes you wonder…" Nonchalantly he took a step away. "I've got to get back to work, Sara. I have some supplies to order. I'll see you Monday, though—won't I?"

"Uh—" Dazed, it took Sara a moment to respond. "Yes. Monday will be…" she looked up at the menu above his head. "Cranapple Crush day." Immediately she clamped her lips closed. *Crush*…like the crush she used to have for Gavin, and he for her. Unsettled, she looked his way and he winked before picking up a supply order form and bending over his work.

"So, how was aerobics?" Morgan asked as Sara entered the kitchen.

"Did Jim call?" Sara countered, reaching for the phone.

"No. Were you expecting him to?"

"I'll be in my room." Sara headed for the stairs, dialing Jim's number as she went. She closed her bedroom door as she listened to the phone ring once…twice…three times. *That's right*, she suddenly realized, *Jim's at work.* The phone was answered and Sara recognized Andy's voice on the other end. She could not bear to talk to Andy, *Mr. Engaged Andy*, so without saying a word she clicked off the receiver and sat dejectedly on her bed.

Katie… Sara punched in the number for Katie's apartment. When she heard Katie's sweet voice say hello, she dissolved into tears.

"Who is this?" Katie asked.

"It's me…Sara."

"Sara! What's happened? Why are you crying?"

"I don't know. It's just… Oh Katie, I love Jim, but sometimes it's very confusing. Have you ever wondered about how your past affects your future and if things had happened differently you could be living a whole different life now?"

"You know perfectly well that things in my past *totally* affected the way my life is today. What's going on, Sara?"

"Do you really think God has our lives under control? Never mind, I know what you're going to say." Sara crossed the room and mindlessly straightened the items on the top of her dresser. "Katie, after you fell in love with Wayne, did you ever…I mean…do you ever…"

"Sara, I'm not sure what you're getting at, but my heart is committed to Wayne. I've never regretted it, never doubted it."

"But do you ever look at other men? I mean, would you ever think another guy is…say…handsome?"

"No, I don't go around looking at other men, but if a very good-looking man crossed my path, I might notice that he's handsome. No one could capture my eye like Wayne does, but I'm not naïve enough to think he's the only good-looking man on the planet. But, Sara, what I do with those thoughts is what counts. No matter how handsome some guy might be, I'd never ever entertain thoughts of getting close to him. I can't imagine even being tempted, but if I was, you can believe that I'd run the other direction as fast as I could."

Sara had been chewing on her lip as she listened to her friend. "That's what I thought you'd say. Of course, it's different for you. You're married."

"Sara, did you meet somebody?" Thinking of her cousin, Katie's heart sank to her toes.

"There's this guy at the club…"

"Oh, Sara."

"I love Jim, Katie, but this guy is so…so…" *alluring!*

"Be careful, Sara. Please think about what you're doing."

"I'm not *doing* anything, Katie. He's just so attractive."

"Well, looks aren't everything. Jim is rather cute himself and he's salt of the earth, Sara, salt of the earth."

"I know, but he hasn't…well…" Sara could hear the speculation in Gavin's voice again. *Two years…kind of makes you wonder…*

"If this guy is messing with your heart, maybe you should stay away from the club," Katie advised.

Stay away from the club? Sara felt a strange tendril of disappointment run across her heart. "It'll be okay. I'm probably just blowing this all out of proportion. Don't say anything to Jim, okay?"

"Don't worry; I'd rather die. Wayne just got home, Sara, so…"

"I'll let you go then, 'bye." Sara laid the phone on her bed and scooped Jim's picture up from her nightstand. "I wish you were here. I wish I had your ring on my finger, then I wouldn't have to fight off advances and wonder."

As Sara drove to the club Monday afternoon, she reflected on the three great phone conversations she had had with Jim since her misgivings the other afternoon. Last night they'd talked for a long time and laughed at the silliest stuff. And the best thing was, Thursday afternoon he was coming for the weekend. He had a two-day reading break and had even managed to get the weekend off from work. Sara could not wait to see him!

Convinced that Jim had a firm hold on her affections, she merely waved

47

to Gavin as she dashed across the club's lobby and into the locker room. *See,* she told herself, *Gavin doesn't necessarily make my knees go weak.*

She entered the exercise room to see Kelly in the center of the room warming up.

"Hi, Kelly. You're early."

"I have the day off today."

The girls chatted as they warmed up, then sat cross-legged on the floor while they waited for class to begin. Kelly told Sara about her job as a reading aide in a local grade school. Her husband was a fifth grade teacher in the same school. *Isn't that convenient,* Sara thought. Kelly was only a couple of years older than Sara, but had been married for two years already. *Isn't anyone single besides me?* Sara wondered. The church's single group came briefly to mind, but she quickly pushed thoughts of it aside as Dean asked if everyone was ready and turned on the music.

After class, Sara invited Kelly to have a juice with her, but Kelly said she had an errand to run and would see Sara on Wednesday. Sara waved, chatted with Dean about their weekends, then went down to the locker room and took a quick shower. Leaving her hair in a ponytail, Sara took care to apply mascara, lipstick and a spritz of body splash. Slipping onto the stool she was beginning to consider hers, she greeted Gavin.

He turned from stacking glasses in the cupboard, a smile lighting his face. "Well, hi. I was beginning to think you'd left without getting your juice."

"What? And miss Cranapple Crush day?" Sara flashed Gavin a smile, convinced she could chat with him as simple friends and nothing more. After all, in three more days, Jim would be here. Maybe she'd bring him to the club and introduce him to Gavin. Then everything would be out in the open, Gavin would no longer question her relationship with Jim and she would no longer feel guilty for talking to Gavin.

"I like it better down," Gavin said, opening the bottle of cranberry juice.

"What's that?"

"Your hair."

"Oh," Sara felt behind her head and patted her ponytail. "Well…" She could not think of a witty comeback. Why did Gavin make her feel so tongue tied?

"Here you go, Cranapple Crush…" The way he looked at her as the word *crush* rolled off his tongue made Sara blush as if he meant something else. As if six years had not passed since they had crushes on each other. He kept his fingers on her glass for a moment longer than necessary, then crossed his arms in front of his chest. "So how come this boyfriend of yours never comes into the club with you? If you were my girl, I would be here."

Sara turned Gavin's words over in her mind, trying to figure out if what he said was an insult or a compliment. Not sure how he really meant it, she explained that Jim was going to college in Minneapolis.

"Ah…one of those long-distance relationships, but how come you're here if he's there?"

Sara told him about transferring to MATC and living with Morgan and helping with the kids and the housework. He leaned over, his elbow resting on the counter only a few inches away from her. "It must be a drag on the weekends."

"Sometimes, but Jim is coming this weekend, so that'll be nice."

"Well, maybe some weekend when Prince Charming isn't here, you'll let me take you out." Gavin held his hands out in front of Sara. "Nothing to it. Just two old friends sharing a pizza or something."

That sounds innocent enough, Sara thought, *and fun.* "Maybe."

Gavin's dark eyes flashed. "Sara, you always did walk the straight and narrow. I swear, the closest thing you ever did that came anywhere near going over the edge was letting me hold your hand during chapel. Remember?"

"I remember." Sara also remembered how his simple touch had always sent shivers up and down her spine.

"I bet you a hundred dollars that your boyfriend is a plain old Joe leading a boring life. I bet he takes you to dinner and the movies and that's about it."

"Well, where would you take me?" Sara feigned indifference, but secretly, she was curious.

"Let's see," Gavin boldly reached behind Sara and pulled the ponytail holder from her hair, freeing the light brown locks to tumble around her shoulders. "Maybe dancing or to the races. You ever been to the races, Sara?"

She wanted to be angry at him for taking such liberties with her hair, but something about the way Gavin was looking at her made her throat constrict and she could only shake her head in answer to his question.

"There's nothing more exciting than the races, with all the noise and the speed and the people cheering. I know you'd like it. Ever do any racing of your own?"

"Me? Race a car?"

Gavin shrugged. "I've done it lots of times. Not at the speedway, just the dirt drag way over by Cooper's Corner. You ever hear of that?"

"No." *Surely I've led a sheltered life.*

"I'll take you sometime. Would you hold my colors and cheer for me?"

"Hold your colors?"

Gavin nodded. "Yeah. We always have someone—preferably a girl—hold our flag near the finish line. Sometimes my sister does it for me."

"Your sister. That's right. Allison," Sara said, remembering that Gavin had a twin sister. "She lives here, too?"

"We share an apartment."

"Oh." Suddenly Sara remembered that back in ninth grade she hadn't much liked Allison Manes. "I should probably go."

"My loss," Gavin said. "This was nice. No interruptions today."

"Yes, it was nice. I'll be back on Wednesday."

"I'll look forward to it."

Tuesday evening, Mark came home from the office with the news that a storm was brewing. "Is there anything out in the yard we should bring in?" he asked Morgan.

"I'm sure there are toys out there. Could you take a look?"

"I'll help," Sara offered. She followed Mark outside and took note of the dark clouds gathering to the north. The wind was beginning to gust. She picked up a pair of Courtney's forgotten flip-flops, a rag doll, and Nicholas's cowboy hat. Mark stacked a couple of patio chairs, stating it was probably time to put them away for the winter anyway.

An hour after supper the storm hit in earnest, the wind howling around the house rattling the windows, rain drumming against the roof. Sara stood at the window in her upstairs bedroom, watching the tree branches bending and swaying in the force of the wind. She knew that Mark had built a fire in the living room and Morgan would be making hot chocolate, but Sara yearned to sit out the storm with Jim. She leaned her forehead against the cold windowpane and wondered what he was doing and if the storm would hit Minnesota as well.

The next afternoon, Sara dashed for the shelter of the health club. It was still raining, although not as hard as last night. When she checked in at the front desk and reached for a sweat towel the receptionist asked her to wait a minute. "I have a phone message for you somewhere…here it is," she said, handing Sara a scrap of paper.

Sara glanced at the scrawled note, which stated that she was to call her sister. "Thanks, Sheila." Sara detoured to the juice bar where she set her backpack on her stool and dug into her purse, wondering why Morgan had not called her on her cell phone. Pulling it out, she soon realized her battery was dead. "Gavin, can I use a phone?"

Pouring juice, Gavin nodded and pointed to a phone at the end of the counter.

"Morgan? It's me, what's up?"

"Why don't you answer your cell phone?"

"The battery's dead."

"Well, Jim's been trying to reach you all morning. He's on his way to work and wants you to call him there just before three o'clock, when his shift starts. Here's the number; got a pen?"

"Just a sec," *Jim!* Sara dug in her purse for a pen and she grabbed a paper napkin. "Okay, I'm ready." Trying not to tear the napkin, she jotted down the number, then thanked her sister and hung up.

Glancing at her watch, Sara dropped her duffle bag to the floor and perched on the stool. Waiting a few minutes to ensure Jim's arrival at the bookstore, she dug her calling card from her wallet and ran through a number of different reasons why he would be trying to reach her.

"It's Katie," she announced randomly to Gavin.

"What is?" he asked.

"There must be something wrong with Katie. Can I use that phone again?"

"That's what it's there for."

Sara dialed the number for the campus bookstore and waited impatiently while a woman went to find Jim.

"Sara?" Jim sounded out of breath when he came on the line. "Where've you been? I've been calling all day."

"I went shopping before class and I didn't know my cell battery was dead. What is it? Are you okay? Is Katie okay?"

"We're fine. Did you guys get that bad storm yesterday?"

"Yes, but it didn't end up to be as bad as they predicted."

"Well, it was pretty wild over here. My dad lost a ton of shingles off his roof. It was in bad shape before and now most of the back side needs to be repaired. It can't wait. Since Wayne and I don't have school the rest of the week, Dad asked us to come down and help fix the roof. It's probably going to take three days. We're driving down tonight after work so we can get started first thing in the morning. Sorry, Sara, I really need to go help my dad, but that means I can't come see you."

"Oh." Sara rubbed her forehead, disappointed, but concerned. "Are they okay? Your dad and mom?" Mr. and Mrs. Hoffman lived just outside the city limits of Albert Lea, a town ninety miles south of Minneapolis.

"They're fine, just not the roof. Well, Dad's worried about things, with the rain and all, but that's supposed to quit tonight so we should have clear working weather. I just feel bad about our weekend. I was looking forward to being with you and seeing where you go to school and the club and all."

Sara felt like spouting off that this wasn't fair, but it wasn't Jim's fault and it couldn't be helped. She noticed Gavin watching from behind the juice counter so she turned slightly away. "I'm disappointed, too, Jim. I really need to see you. Desperately."

"I was hoping you'd go to my parents' too, so we can salvage at least some of our weekend. I'll be on the roof all day, but it'll be too dark to work after supper. Katie's coming, too—after work on Friday."

Sara felt the tears forming. Four days at his parents' house—while Jim spent the days on the roof—could not possibly live up to the weekend she had planned for them here. But it was better than nothing. She ached to see him. Sara glanced at Gavin. He was still watching her, warming her with his steadfast gaze. Yes, she needed to see Jim. "I'll talk it over with Morgan. I'm sure it won't be a problem. I had cleared my schedule anyway, to be with you. Why don't you call me after you get there tonight and I'll let you know when I'm coming."

"Good. I'll do that. I have to go now."

"Okay." Sara lowered her voice and started to whisper that she loved him, but before she finished she heard the click of Jim's phone. Slowly, she hung up the club phone and returned to her stool to retrieve her purse and backpack.

"Bad news?" Gavin asked.

"Not bad exactly, just disappointing."

"I've got just the fix. Hold on." Gavin turned away to get some juice for Sara. She slid onto her stool, no longer in the mood for aerobics class. It had already started anyway. She could hear the music coming from upstairs. Gavin returned and with a flourish presented her with a glass of purple juice topped with creamy foam. "Grape Grandeur for the miss."

"Thanks." Sara smiled at him.

He smiled back. "So, you know what they say about bartenders."

"Not really, I don't go to bars."

"What do you call this?" Gavin swept a hand down the counter. "Anyway, bartenders make great listeners if you want to talk about it."

"I don't know…" Somehow talking about boyfriend woes to another man didn't feel right. She could call Katie tonight and cry on her shoulder. Katie would be alone anyway, if Wayne was going with Jim. Hmm…it would be the first night Katie and Wayne would spend apart since they got married. Maybe Katie would want some sympathy from Sara.

"You know what, Gavin? I really don't want to talk about it."

"That's all right by me. We can talk about other stuff and get your mind off your troubles. Tell me about your classes."

So Sara talked and Gavin listened, every now and then breaking away to wait on a customer. While she talked, Gavin reaffirmed his desire to date Sara. He wasn't looking for anything permanent; however, he did like a pretty, spunky girl to spend his weekends with and he was between girls right now. Besides, he'd never quite forgotten about Sara Brooks. She had plagued his dreams a few times back in high school, even months after he'd moved away.

Forty-five minutes later, Sara ran out of things to say. Gavin grinned, teasing her. "Finished already?"

"Yes," Sara blushed. "I know I gab too much."

"I don't think so." Gavin leaned over the counter, placing his face mere inches from hers. "I find you absolutely fascinating."

"Oh, well…" A flush of pleasure warmed her inside.

"If I made you a refill would you stay and talk some more?"

Sara shrugged. "What would we talk about?"

"Hey, girl, we have over six years to catch up on. We could probably find a thing or two."

She smiled. "Probably we could."

Gavin retrieved Sara's empty glass and turned away triumphantly. He was already making her forget about whatever had been bothering her. Every time Sara left the club, Gavin wanted her to leave with warm feelings. He wanted to make sure she came back and not just for aerobics.

"So how is it that you and Allison ended up here after moving to Arizona?" Sara asked, accepting the fresh glass of juice Gavin handed her.

"We weren't there very long. Dad's transfer was a bust. Mom hated it there. Before my junior year we moved to Ohio. Allison and I finished high school there, then my dad got restless again. We moved back here, and," Gavin shrugged, "here I am."

Sara noted that the aerobic music was no longer playing. It seemed strangely quiet in the lobby without the pulsing beat throbbing in her veins, even with the ping of racquetballs and occasional grunts and shouts from the nearby court. Kelly came down the stairs from class, surprised to see Sara at the juice bar. They chatted a few minutes, Sara explaining about the phone call that had made her late. They said their goodbyes, with promises to see each other Monday.

"Well," Sara said. "I guess that's my cue. I should go too."

"I wish you'd stay," Gavin said.

Sara laughed. "I've been here an hour already."

"You haven't finished your refill."

Sara pushed the half-full glass of grape juice across the counter. "You can have it."

"But I have an hour left on my shift and you make the time go by so fast."

"Gavin, I can't stay here for another hour."

"Why not? Is there some place you have to be? Someone to see?"

Sara hated to admit that her social life added up to a few phone calls a week with Jim, a couple with Katie, e-mails and her time here at the club. A sister, brother-in-law, one niece and two nephews hardly counted. Neither did her nightly date with Rapunzel, Cinderella and their princes. But to say she had somewhere to go, when really she was only going home to help Morgan make dinner or play with Nicholas and Courtney... When the thought of staying here and talking with Gavin presented the most fun she had had (with the exception of aerobics class) since...since she had gone to visit Jim and Katie three weeks ago.

"I can't stay here with you," she said decisively. "I have a boyfriend, remember?"

Almost forgot, didn't you? "This isn't a date, Sara. Just harmless, innocent conversation. Two old friends, catching up."

Sara wavered. *What am I thinking? Tomorrow I'm driving to Jim's parents' house. I can't stay around here talking to another guy for an hour.* "Sorry, Gavin. I'm going out of town for the weekend, I should go home and pack."

"I thought your boyfriend was coming here."

"We had a change of plans. I'll see you Monday, okay?"

"I'll be here."

CHAPTER 6

Cast your cares on the Lord and he will sustain you.
—Psalm 55:22

As Sara pulled off Interstate 90 at Albert Lea and turned north, a glance at the clock told her it was a little past six o'clock. Jim's mom had promised to hold supper until she arrived, but Sara hoped for a little time alone with Jim before they had to join the family at the table. She was so looking forward to this reunion! There would be no spilled soda down her shirt this time! Of course, with Wayne and Mr. and Mrs. Hoffman there, it would not be the wild, romantic reunion that romance novels were known for. Everyone might even be gathered in the kitchen waiting for her and she would have to greet Jim in front of them all.

Sara sighed. *Why does my life have to be so boring? Why couldn't I be arriving by train and Jim could come to the station to pick me up? He could be waving a colorful scarf as the train pulls into the station...* Suddenly, she remembered what Gavin had said about Sara waving a flag with his colors. In the muddled mess of her mind, she was no longer sure if it was Jim or Gavin waving a scarf as she dismounted from the train. Oh, she knew she was going to see Jim, but a vision of Gavin, with his dark features, winsome smile, and flirty eyes danced in her mind.

Her heart rate quickened as she imagined Jim waving goodbye from one end of the train station while Gavin, waiting at the other end of the platform, waved a green-and-white flag as she approached. But wait; shouldn't she be headed toward Jim, not Gavin? But Jim didn't have a flag. Didn't he want to wave her colors for all the world to see? There was Gavin, asking her to stay…Jim, saying he couldn't come…

"No…" she moaned. "It's not Gavin… It's Jim I need."

The Hoffmans' driveway came into view. Light spilled from the front rooms. Sara pulled into the driveway, jerked the car into park, threw open her door and ran for the porch. "Jim!" she called, bursting into the hall.

He was loitering in the kitchen, waiting for her arrival, while Wayne and his parents watched the evening news in the family room. Now he met her at the entrance to the hall, surprised at the force with which she threw herself into his arms.

"Oh, Jim, hold me tight."

"What's the matter? You seem scared or something. Is someone following you?"

Vehemently Sara shook her head, then nodded, then shook it again. "Just hold me."

He pulled her tighter against his chest, so tight she almost felt as if she was being crushed. *Cranapple Crush*… "Oh, Jim." She pushed herself away and stared at him with wild eyes.

"Okay, Sara, you're scaring me now. What's happening?"

She put a hand to her throat and drew in a gulp of air. "It's like a bad dream. I had this vision…some guy…"

"A dream?" Jim was confused. "While you were driving?"

"He haunts me."

"Who haunts you?"

She couldn't say Gavin's name, couldn't admit to Jim that she was slightly attracted to someone else. That she wasn't so much scared as confused.

Mrs. Hoffman entered the kitchen. "There you are, Sara. We thought we heard your car pull in."

"I think I left it running." Dazed, Sara headed back out the way she had come. Casting his mother a bewildered look, Jim followed Sara, his heart thumping wildly in his throat. Sara was always high drama, but this…this was crazy.

She sat half-in half-out of the car, staring blankly at the dashboard. Jim reached in, turned off the ignition and pulled out her key. "Sara, are you going to tell me what's going on?"

Embarrassed, she pressed her lips together and looked at him. "I must have fallen into a half-sleep while I drove. I had been wishing that we could have an exciting and romantic reunion, just like in romance novels, but my mind was playing games and there was this guy luring me away from you."

"What guy?"

"Just a guy. I wanted to walk in the house and have you sweep me off my feet—like when Rhett Butler came home and claimed Scarlett O'Hara—"

"Sara. Listen, your arrival was not like a romance novel. The way you charged into the house was more like a scene out of *Wuthering Heights*, with Heathcliff obsessing over Cathy. You scared me half to death."

She reached for his hand and gave it an apologetic squeeze. "I'm sorry, Jim. I scared myself, too." She climbed out of the car and stood tentatively at his side.

Jim placed his hands on either side of her face and looked deeply into her eyes. "Are you okay now? There wasn't really anyone chasing you?"

"No, it was just my imagination working overtime."

"You're sure?"

"Yes. Now I'm sure. You have a settling affect on me."

He looked into her eyes for a moment longer. Life with Sara was certainly never dull. Why she wanted to add any more excitement, he could not understand. "Okay then." His eyes twinkled. "I can pick you up and carry you into the house like Rhett Butler if you really want."

"That's okay, but next time I'm coming on the train."

After supper, Jim knocked on the open door to the bedroom where Sara was staying. Leaning into the room, he said, "I've come to steal you away."

Sara flashed him a smile. "Where are we going?"

"To town. The last time we were here you said you wanted to see all the places where I used to hang out."

"I'd love that, but what about Wayne?"

"He's fine here by himself. He brought a book to read and he'll probably call Katie."

"Are you sure?"

"This was supposed to be our weekend, Sara. Let's try to salvage some of it. Grab a coat and we'll get out of here before Dad decides he's in the mood for a game of cards."

Sara reached for her black jacket and followed Jim down the stairs. Once seated in the car, Jim took a moment before backing out of the driveway to grasp Sara's hand and plant a kiss on her mouth. "I'm glad you came. I've been looking forward to it all day."

"Me too. I miss you like crazy all the time."

"Yeah. The feeling's mutual."

Jim backed onto the dark country road. "All day on the roof, Dad was cracking jokes and telling stories to keep us going. Wayne would sing or hum, but I was just thinkin' about you."

Sara scrunched her shoulders up; it felt so good to be with Jim. "You're sweet. So, where are you taking me?"

"You're on a magic carpet ride and the tour's just about to begin."

Sara giggled. Jim was funny when he was relaxed like this. Approaching a curve, he slowed to about five miles per hour. "See that?" He pointed to a bend in the road. "That's where I slid into a snow bank the first winter I had my license. I was driving Jason and me to school. It was slippery and I was inexperienced, driving too fast for the conditions and…" Jim chuckled. "Showing off a little, too. You know, big brother stuff. Anyway, we hit a patch of ice and I spun out of control."

"Were you hurt?"

"Just my pride." Jim increased his speed and continued toward town. "Did about five hundred dollars' worth of damage to Dad's Ford."

"Was that your only accident?"

"Just the one. How about you? Ever have one?"

Sara laughed. "You're kidding, right?"

"No, what's so funny?"

Sara laughed harder. When she could catch her breath she said, "Let's see…there's the time I tore the driver's door off my dad's truck, the time I got the Toyota hooked on another car in a parking lot, the time I backed into my uncle's Jeep and the time I ran over the dog."

"Oh." Amusement glittered in Jim's hazel eyes. "At least I've been forewarned." He made a couple of turns, then pulled to a stop in a residential district and pointed to a driveway across the street. A basketball backboard with the net missing rested above the garage door. "I played more games of ball in this driveway than any place else. My pal Danny lived here. Our middle school is just four blocks away. We got into the habit of coming here to shoot buckets after school. Rain or shine, except for basketball season. Then we'd have practice at school. In ninth grade, we got our brothers started. To keep peace we paired up with each other's. I'd play with Tim; he had Jason."

"That explains the basketball skill."

Jim nodded, lost for a moment in the memories.

"Whatever happened to Dan?" Sara asked as Jim pressed the accelerator. "Do you still see him?"

"He joined the Marines. He's stationed in California."

Jim drove slowly past his old middle school, then continued down the avenue until he reached the elementary school he had attended. He turned into the carpool circle and put the car in park, his headlights illuminating the playground. He had not been down this street in years, yet everything looked the same.

"What a great playground," Sara said. "What was your favorite?"

"The merry-go-round."

"Mine was the swings." Sara unbuckled her seat belt, opened her door and scampered for the swing set.

"Wait!" Jim called, laughing. He hurried around the vehicle, slammed the car door Sara had left open, then sprinted for the swings. He jumped onto the seat next to Sara and, pumping vigorously, was soon swinging as high as she was. Carefree and laughing, they raced to see who could go the highest, then Jim slowed and grabbed the chain of Sara's swing.

"Remember in grade school," Sara said, "if you could swing in tempo like this with someone then that meant you were going to marry that person?"

"No, I never knew that."

"Oh." Sara sighed. If Jim was ever going to take the bait, that had been a perfect opportunity and as close of an invitation as she was ever going to give him. Oh well…she would evaluate his response—or lack of one—later, she didn't want anything to ruin their evening right now. Sara leapt from her swing and ran for the merry-go-round. Jim caught up to her as she climbed aboard.

"Push us, Jim!"

He took hold of the iron hand railings and ran in a circle, pushing the merry-go-round ahead of him. After completing two cycles, he vaulted onto the floorboards and sprawled at Sara's feet as they spun. Sara's curly hair streamed behind her as she put her face into the wind.

"I thought these things were outlawed!" she hollered.

Jim shrugged and struggled to stand, bracing his legs against the hand railings. "It was always our goal to stand up, no hands."

Laughing, Sara rose to her feet, but lost her balance and grabbed Jim for support. They toppled over and sat on the floor of the carousel as it slowly rotated to a stop. Dizzy, Sara half crawled, half fell, onto the damp grass. Jim dropped to her side, short of breath.

"What a rush," he finally said. "Sara, you're crazy."

She rolled onto her back. "Oh, Jim, look at the stars."

He leaned back on his elbows and tilted his head to the heavens. "Amazing." They sat quietly for several minutes looking at the sky, each thinking their own thoughts. Sara figured this little adventure was almost worth writing about—if she ever did write that romance novel—while Jim smiled to himself over Sara's playfulness. Left to himself, he would take life too seriously.

"This isn't the end of the tour, is it?" Sara asked, suddenly sitting up. "I want to see some more things." She was delighted with this side of Jim. He rarely focused on himself and she did not want it to end.

"All right." He stood and helped her to her feet. "Let the tour continue!"

Ten minutes later, he pulled into the parking lot of a gas station that had a restaurant attached. "This was the most popular place in town. It probably still is. Come on." Jim held the door and let Sara enter first. The café was decorated with black and white tiles and red Formica tabletops. An old-fashioned jukebox playing an old Beatles tune was in one corner and signs and placards from the fifties decorated the walls.

Sara took it all in with a big smile. "So this was your hangout. Did you have a favorite table?"

Jim nodded and led the way toward an empty corner booth. They shrugged off their jackets and slid onto the red vinyl benches across the table from each other. "I recommend the Turtle Sundae, but everything's good."

Sara studied the menu, while Jim looked around the place. "Man, I haven't been in here for three years. It hasn't changed a bit. I used to come here all the time."

A waitress brought glasses of ice water and took their order. They both ordered the sundae Jim had suggested. Sara put her hands on her lap and studied Jim's face. "So tell me more," she urged.

He shrugged. "We'd come here after ball games and stuff. I had one friend, Tad, who never got tired of switching the sugar and salt. He thought it was so funny. None of my buddies dated much, but we would sit in this corner booth and pick out the girls we'd ask out if we were brave enough."

"Really?" Sara's blue eyes glittered in amusement. "What kind of girls did you pick out?"

Jim blushed. "I don't know. I wasn't a very good judge of what kind of girl was right for me. Not at first anyway. There was this one…in tenth grade. She was pretty and soft-spoken and sweet. Finally, I got up my nerve and asked her out. We came here and it didn't go very well. You know me, I don't always talk very much. She was worse. I guess she was really shy, but I didn't know that when I asked her out. So we sat at that booth over there and hardly said two words to each other. It was agonizing. After I brought her home I decided that quiet girls were not for me." Jim laid his hand, palm up, on the table in an open invitation. "I needed someone like you."

Sara chuckled and laid her hand in Jim's palm. "Thanks a lot. A girl of gab, that's me."

The waitress brought their turtle sundaes and Sara's eyes grew big at the sight of them. "Jim," she said under her breath as the woman walked away. "We should have shared."

His eyes sparkled. "No way. I'm eating all of mine." They ate a few bites in silence, then Jim said, "It's your turn. I told you about my first date, now I want to hear about yours. You probably had tons of boyfriends."

"I did not. Only a couple."

"So tell me about your first date. The first time some cocky kid asked you out, what was it like?"

"The first?" Sara's heart froze.

"Yeah, the first time somebody said, 'Sara, will you go out…?' How did you feel, what did you say?"

Sara let the spoon rest in her bowl. Her stomach was turning a somersault and her heart was pumping too fast. *Just be calm…* "I was fourteen."

"Fourteen!" Jim almost choked. He swallowed the bite of nuts and banana in his mouth, then said, "Man, Sara, fourteen?"

She shook her head. "Don't worry. My parents wouldn't let me go."

"I'm glad. How old was the guy?"

"He was fourteen, too. We were freshmen." Sara had a memory of how crestfallen Gavin had been when she had to inform him that she was not allowed to go.

"Man, Sara. I figured you were popular in high school, with lots of friends—both girls and guys—but I never thought you'd started dating so young."

"I didn't start so young, Jim Hoffman. You asked me to tell you about the first time a boy asked me. That's when it was. I didn't go. I didn't go out until after I turned sixteen."

"So did he respect that and wait? Or did he follow you around and try to get you alone with him?"

Sara clasped her hands together under the table. "What are you saying, Jim? Are you accusing me of something? Because Gavin was very sweet and it was all very innocent."

"Gavin, is it?" Jim snorted. How did they get here? Why had he asked Sara about old boyfriends? He could not stand hearing about it. He couldn't stand to think that any other guy had ever had designs on her, although he knew of course they had. No girl as pretty and spunky and outgoing as Sara would make it through four years of high school without being popular with the guys. But for some stupid reason Jim could not leave it alone. "So when you were old enough? Then you went out with this guy? How long did you date him?"

"We didn't date at all. He moved away. My first date when I was sixteen was with my minister's son. Does that make you feel any better, Jim? We went out a total of three times. Then I didn't date again until midway through my junior year. Do you really want to know all this?"

"No, I don't." Jim pushed his bowl away. He had not quite finished his sundae, but he was no longer hungry. "I guess I don't want to take a trip down the memory lane of your love life. As far as I'm concerned, it's a closed book. I'd rather not ever hear about the other guys you used to have a thing for. Fair enough?"

All thoughts of introducing Jim to Gavin vanished. If Jim didn't want to know, Sara wouldn't tell him. The reason for his irrational jealousy over some unknown guys in Sara's past did not dawn on her. If it had, she would have taken reassurance in the fact that it only meant he loved her and wanted to claim her for his own. As it was, the exchange with Jim left her feeling slightly agitated with him and strangely protective of Gavin.

Friday, while Jim was working on the roof with his dad and Wayne, Sara spent the morning doing homework. In the afternoon she helped Mrs. Hoffman bake cookies and cut up apples for sauce. Katie arrived from Minneapolis around five thirty while the men were cleaning up and Sara was setting the table. Jim's mom was putting the finishing touches on supper.

"Sara!" Katie entered the kitchen from the back hall and spun her friend around. "It's so good to see you! Hi, Aunt Sylvia." Katie added, reaching to give her aunt a warm hug. "It's so great of you to have us all."

Mrs. Hoffman chuckled. "With Harley getting all that free work out of the boys, it's nothing. I'm glad you could join us for the weekend. And Sara and I, well…" Jim's mom laid a hand on Sara's arm. "I can't tell you how much I enjoy getting to know her better. She's very special."

Sara blushed, but smiled.

"I agree," Katie said. "That's why she's my best friend. And someday, Jim will make her my cousin."

Sara's blush deepened and she shook her head at Katie, trying not to let Jim's mom see.

"It's all right, Sara," Mrs. Hoffman said, turning back to her supper preparations. "I know how young minds work. Katie, I have you and Wayne in the guestroom if you want to bring your bags up. Sara, why don't you help her? Supper will be ready in about fifteen minutes."

Sara grasped Katie's arm with one hand and picked up her suitcase with the other, dragging Katie behind her up the stairs. "I can't believe you said that in front of Jim's mom."

Katie smiled. "Lighten up, Sara. What's so wrong with it? Like everyone in this house doesn't assume you and Jim are going to get married someday."

Sara set Katie's overnight case on the floor of the guestroom and looked sternly at her friend. "We don't know that for sure, Katie."

Katie shoved the suitcase out of the way with her foot, then leaned against the dresser. "Has something happened?"

"No, I just... You know that Jim has never, I mean *never*, mentioned marriage to me. I don't need you to go blabbing about it in front of his mom."

"Okay." Katie held up her hands. "I'm sorry." She watched Sara perch on the edge of the bed and begin to mindlessly pick at the knots of Aunt Sylvia's homemade quilt. Brooding silence filled the bedroom. "You *have* met someone else, haven't you? That phone call the other day... Oh, Sara, how could you?"

"I haven't..." Sara shook her head. "I haven't done anything."

"Who is he, Sara?" Katie waited for a moment, but Sara didn't answer. "I can't believe this. Tell me it's not true."

Sara raised misty eyes to her friend, her best friend, and knew she could never confide her confusion to Katie. She might be her best friend, but she was Jim's cousin. They had grown up together and after all, people always said blood is thicker than water. "It's nothing, Katie. I am not involved with anyone else. It's just that I'm not and never have been one hundred percent sure about what Jim is planning."

"You need to talk to him."

"No, Katie. It's for Jim to bring up when he's ready."

"Then until that happens you need to rest in God's plan. Just rest assured that God is working everything out."

"Is He? I'm not really sure anymore. Choices come along every day that we're forced to make."

"Yes, but then you seek God's will and guidance. He shuts doors and opens doors and—"

"Maybe sometimes He opens two doors at once and then He leaves you to pick."

"God never leaves us. Sara, that's blasphemous!"

"It's so easy for you, isn't it? Being a minister's daughter and all."

"Well, you were raised in a Christian home. You should know all this stuff, too."

Sara thought of Jim and Gavin and the awkward triangle she was in. If God had a plan for her, it sure was obscure. "Honestly, Katie, I can't believe you always have an answer for every situation. Have you already forgotten the unsure times you faced even where Wayne is concerned?"

"No, I haven't, but I learned that I need to stay in tune to God and His Word."

"I don't need you to preach me a sermon. Man, Katie, sometimes you have a holier than thou attitude."

Katie bit her lip and forced the tears to stay put. She was at a loss for words. She and Sara had never had an argument like this before. Hearing Wayne come out of the upstairs bathroom, Katie quickly laid a hand on Sara's arm. "I'm sorry, Sara. I'll pray for you."

"If you think I need it," Sara shot out, squeezing past Wayne as he entered the room.

Tears dribbled down Katie's cheeks as Wayne walked into the room. He looked from Katie to Sara, who was disappearing into her bedroom. "What happened? Did you girls have a fight?"

"Sort of. She's mad at me and she's really mixed up right now—about God and Jim and everything."

Just then Jim hollered up the steps that supper was on the table. Katie drew in a quivering breath and muttered under her breath that she couldn't appear at the table with weepy eyes.

"Go wash your face; I'll go down and stall a little."

Katie slipped into the bathroom while Wayne headed down the steps. He passed Jim going up. "Katie's in the bathroom, she'll be down in a few minutes."

"Is Sara up here?"

Wayne nodded, then continued down to the kitchen.

Jim knocked lightly on Sara's door. "Hey, did you hear? Supper's on."

Sara opened the door. "I heard; I'm coming."

"You okay?" Jim asked.

"I'm fine. How was your day on the roof?"

"I'm stiff and sore, and famished."

The family gathered around the table, having only to wait a minute or two before Katie joined them. After prayer, the serving dishes of fried chicken, mashed potatoes, green beans and fresh applesauce were passed in relative silence. Once the men's initial hunger had been curbed, Mr. Hoffman gave a report on the day of repair work. "We'll have a shorter day tomorrow," he predicted. "Should finish by early afternoon. I hope that rain they're forecasting holds off until we're done."

"What do you kids have planned for tonight?" Jim's mom asked.

"I don't know, but I'm bushed," Wayne said.

"We don't have to go anywhere on my account," Katie said. "We could stay home and play games or watch a movie."

"Your father and I have a discussion group at the pastor's house. We're on a committee about redecorating the church."

Jim's dad groaned audibly. "Is that meeting tonight? What time?"

"Seven thirty. We should be finished by nine."

"All right, then I'm coming home and going to bed. My old knees can't take all this time on the roof."

Jim and Wayne pointed out that they could finish without his help. They knew what to do, but Mr. Hoffman would not hear of it. "I might not be as spry as you boys, but I can still put in a day of work."

Second helpings of food were passed as talk moved on to other topics. When the meal was finished, Jim's dad retreated to his leather chair for a quick catnap while the women cleaned up. Jim and Wayne took the basketball outside and stood in the semi-darkness of the driveway and shot a few hoops without expending much energy.

Jim moved under the basket to catch the ball that Wayne put up. He dribbled a couple of feet out, then held the ball and twirled it between his hands. "Is something going on with the girls? They hardly spoke at supper. I don't think they said two words to each other."

"I guess they had an argument."

Jim whistled under his breath. "Man…what about?"

Wayne shrugged and motioned for Jim to toss him the ball. "I'm not really sure."

Katie came out of the house, a bag of garbage in her hands, and headed for the trash can, on the far side of the garage. Banging the lid back on the can, Katie wiped her hands together, strode purposefully to the center of their court and looked Jim full in the face.

"You have to talk to Sara, Jim."

"Why?"

"Because she has some issues that you should know about. I mean, do you have any idea that she thinks God doesn't care about her?"

"She doesn't think that."

Wayne wandered over and stood behind Katie. "Katie, I think Jim knows Sara as well as you do, if not better. If she wants to talk to him, she will."

"I'm not so sure about that. She said she doesn't think she has a heart relationship with God. I'm very concerned about this."

Suddenly the backdoor slammed. They turned to see Sara standing on the porch, staring at them. "Katie Anderson!" She stepped down and approached the others. "I can't believe you're out here talking behind my back."

"I'm not talking behind your back." Katie felt Wayne place a hand on her shoulder and give her a warning squeeze. "Well, I'm not gossiping anyway. I'm just telling Jim that he should talk to you."

"What gives you the right? I told you something in confidence, Katie. *Confidence.* If I want to talk to Jim about it, then I'll do so. I don't need you interfering."

"Sara," Jim took a step closer, "Katie's just worried about you."

Sara's jaw dropped open. "And you're taking her side?" Whipping around, she turned her back on the others and took two steps toward the porch, then twirled back around. "I know she's your cousin and all, and now Wayne is too and it's just this cozy family threesome where I'm the outsider, but aren't I special to you?"

"Well, of course." Jim crossed the distance between them in four long strides. Lowering his voice, he said, "Sweetheart, if you'd just tell me what's going on… Wayne said you and Katie had a fight."

"I don't want to talk about it, but apparently Katie does. Why don't you ask her?"

Katie's hand covered her mouth. Wayne shuffled his feet. Jim looked despairingly from Sara to Wayne to Katie and back again. In the meantime, Sara marched toward the porch.

"Where are you going?" Jim called after her.

"Home. I'm going home, Jim Hoffman. Just try to stop me!" She yanked the door open and rushed up the stairs, making it safely to her room before the tears exploded. All the while, she was thinking, *Try to stop me, Jim. Please, try to stop me!*

Frantically, Jim looked at Wayne. "What do I do?"

Wayne shoved Jim forward. "You'd better go talk to her."

Jim took off for the house and scaled the stairs three at a time. Outside Sara's room he paused to catch his breath, then, slowly, without knocking, nudged the unclasped door open. She was lying on the bed, shaking with tears. Gently, he sat on the side of the bed and laid a hand on her back. "Sara, you can't go. It's dark and you'd hardly make it home before midnight."

Sara stiffened, then her voice came, muffled and quivering. "Is that the only reason you don't want me to go? Because it's *late*?"

"No," *here I go again, putting my foot in my mouth,* "I don't want you to go, period. Sara, this was supposed to be our weekend. None of it's the way we planned, but we were making the best of it. If you go now, then, well… Sara, I was planning on you staying until Sunday afternoon."

"Do you really care?"

"Yes. Don't you? I mean, don't you care about us anymore?"

Sara rolled onto her back and looked at Jim. Their eyes met and held in a steady gaze. Long moments passed. Jim felt sweat beginning to trickle down his back, fearful because her answer was so slow in coming. Sara was convinced that she had always cared more about their relationship than Jim did. She was the one waiting for a marriage proposal while he…while he… She couldn't think about that now. Not with Jim's eyes boring a hole into her soul. "I care. I'm just scared sometimes."

"Scared of me?"

"No, just…" Sara struggled to sit up and lean against the headboard. "Life, I guess. I mean, where are we heading, Jim?"

He brushed stray locks of hair from her face. "That's what I'm trying to figure out. When I do, I'll tell you." Sara wondered if his cryptic statement meant that he was still trying to figure out if they were going to get married. "I love you, Sara. Isn't that enough for now?"

She wanted to shout *NO!* at the top of her lungs. She needed more from him, but she would not—not now or ever—pressure him into an engagement. "I guess."

"So, you'll stay? I mean, it isn't fair to me—to us—if you leave because you and Katie are having a disagreement. Can't you girls work it out? I mean, honestly, Sara, she wasn't saying anything mean about you. She loves you. She's concerned is all."

Sara chewed on her bottom lip, in the preoccupied manner she had. Katie was the best friend she had ever had and despite a little bit of jealousy that Katie was already married to a guy who absolutely doted on her, Sara loved her, too. "I guess I can tell her I'm sorry."

Jim sighed. "Good. And hug and be friends again?"

Sara smiled. "What are you? My mother?"

"No. Definitely not." He placed a hand behind her head and drew her close for a kiss, which turned into two. "Now, before we go back downstairs, is there anything else you need to talk about? Katie seems to think that I don't know what's going on deep in your heart."

Sara shook her head, her emotions were worn down and she did not feel up for a heavy discussion. Besides, there were too many issues to sort out. Some other time they could talk about her questions concerning God, but Sara would never admit that she wasn't sure if Jim ever planned to make her his wife, and the nagging daydreams about Gavin would have to stay buried forever.

CHAPTER 7

Therefore…fix your thoughts on Jesus…
—Hebrews 3:1

Before the night was over, Sara and Katie tearfully made up from their argument and when they said goodbye on Sunday afternoon, Sara apologized one final time.

"It's okay," Katie said, hugging her friend. "Friends forever, right?"

"Forever," Sara agreed.

As Wayne and Katie pulled onto the road, Jim casually draped an arm around Sara's shoulders and suggested taking a walk before Sara left also.

They strolled leisurely down the country roads in the chilly October weather. Sara thought it was almost like a storybook romance, walking hand in hand with Jim while occasional leaves floated down around them. The brilliant autumn colors were almost at their peak and the air was so brisk that little puffs of steam rose from their breath. The wind gusted now and then, causing the leaves to swirl in mad little circles and Sara's curls to fly into her face. When they were nearly back to the house, Jim detoured from the road and trudged across an open stretch of long grass to an orchard. He led Sara a few rows in, then turned north.

"We'll be out of the wind here," he explained.

Sara looked at the canopy of leaves overhead. She had never imagined how dreamy walking through an orchard could be. Maybe she should say goodbye here, and *this* time she would serenely say *Adieu.* She was determined that at least once they were going to have a truly romantic goodbye. Reaching the back corner of the Hoffman yard, she stopped and faced Jim. "I'll just say goodbye here."

"You don't want me to walk you up to the house?"

Sara shook her head.

"Why not?"

Sara shrugged. "It's more romantic this way."

Jim chuckled and placed his arms around her. "And we must have our romance, mustn't we?" He kissed her then, long and deeply. "Man, Sara, you're really something."

"Just say farewell, Jim," she instructed softly, gazing into his eyes. "Because I'm going to say adieu and then I'm going to gracefully walk away."

His eyes glittered in humor. He took a step back, reached for her hand and kissed it. "Farewell, Sara."

"Adieu, Jim." Sara took her first few steps backward, holding her arm out toward him, then she turned to walk toward the house. All would have been perfect if she had not tripped over a protruding tree root. Jim quickly stifled his laughter. Sara resisted the urge to turn around. *Grace, Sara, depart with grace.*

Now, halfway home, she felt good about the way everything had gone. They had made the best of the time they had had. Jim had been so sweet all weekend, so comfortable and talkative. She had enjoyed herself very much. One of the highlights was when he had given her the tour of his old hangouts—except for those few tense minutes in the restaurant when he had asked about her first boyfriends.

Jim didn't have anything to worry about where Gavin or anyone else was concerned. Jim was her guy, her beau—Sara liked the sound of that, her beau—and Gavin was simply an old friend—an intriguing and handsome old friend, but simply a friend.

Monday afternoon Sara pulled into a parking spot in the club's lot and hurried into the lobby. She had stayed after class to talk to her professor and now she only had a few minutes to get changed and ready for aerobics. She didn't even bother to look for Gavin behind the juice bar, but rushed straight for the lockers.

She entered the exercise room just as Dean was about to start. "No warm-up today," she groaned under her breath to Kelly.

"How was your weekend?"

"Wonderful. Fabulous. How was yours?"

Kelly shrugged. "I cleaned my windows. It wasn't very exciting."

"Oh." Sara did not say anything else, but realized that maybe her life wasn't so boring after all—at least not when she spent weekends with Jim.

After class, they talked a few more minutes, then walked downstairs together and parted ways. Kelly headed for the parking lot and Sara the women's locker room. When she was finished in the bathroom, she made her way to her customary stool at the juice bar and looked up to the posted menu to see what she was having today.

"Guava Grapple! Who thinks up these names anyway?"

"Probably some rich dude in a suit. Some of them are pretty ridiculous, aren't they?"

Sara's eyes shot from the menu to the man behind the counter. "Who are you?"

"John."

"Where's Gavin?"

"He called in sick. I think he has the flu."

"Oh." Just now, the thought of sitting here drinking juice didn't hold any appeal if Gavin wasn't going to be on the other side of the counter. "I guess I'll take mine to go."

John raised his eyebrows as he filled a plastic glass. "Another one of Gavin's groupies, huh?"

Sara flicked her curls behind her shoulders. "I don't know what you're talking about. I'm just in a hurry."

John smiled, muttering under his breath. "Yeah, right. And I'm King Arthur." Aloud to Sara, he said, "Here you go. That'll be $2.75."

Sara traded him three dollars for the drink and slipped off the stool. Driving home, she tried to rationalize why she was so disappointed that Gavin wasn't there. After all, he was just a friend.

On her way through the lobby Wednesday afternoon, Sara shot a quick glance toward the juice counter to see if Gavin was back. There he was, grinning and complimenting an older, gray-haired lady on how fit she was. *He sure does have a gift for making people feel good*, Sara thought as she headed for the locker room.

After class, when she perched on her stool, Gavin wasted no time coming over to say hello.

"I heard you were sick," Sara sympathized. "Are you feeling better now?"

"I am. Thanks for asking." He leaned over the counter and said in a low voice, "You know, I was so sick I could barely see straight. Anything less would not have kept me away from work on a Monday."

"And what's so special about Monday?" Sara asked, glancing up to the posted juice list.

"It's the day you come for aerobics."

Sara's blue eyes flew from the menu to his face. It was obvious from his eyes and the look on his face that he was serious. This was not meaningless flirtation. Sara's heartbeat quickened. "I bet you've said that to at least a dozen females today."

Gavin solemnly laid a hand over his heart. "You're the only one, Sara. Honest."

A faint blush rose to her cheeks. Growing uncomfortable under his steady gaze, she glanced away. "You shouldn't…" Sara's voice trailed off. Why did he unnerve her so?

"Shouldn't what? Desire to spend time with a beautiful girl?"

"But I'm…" Feeling vulnerable, she looked into his dark eyes. Thoughts of Jim scattered like leaves in a gusty wind.

"You're an unmarried, attractive, energetic woman, that's what you are and I look forward to seeing you. I meant it, Sara. It's only because I was so weak and couldn't see to drive that I wasn't here the other day."

"I missed you, too." Sara gasped. She shouldn't have said that. He was messing with her insides big time.

Gavin's dark eyes flickered and a smile teased at the corners of his mouth. With a steady arm, he reached across the counter and briefly touched her chin. "Relax, Sara. I won't tell anybody."

"You're laughing at me."

"No, I'm not. Now, what are you having?"

"I had the Guava on Monday." She looked up to the menu. He followed her gaze. "Kiwi Kiss," she whispered, her heart beating in her throat.

"Ah…" Gavin met her eyes and winked. "Kiwi *Kiss*, I like this one." He turned away and put crushed ice into a glass. Trying to compose herself, Sara straightened her shirt and dug through her purse for a tube of lipstick. Gavin finished preparing her drink then held it an arm's length away. "I'm sure glad I wasn't sick today. I would have hated to miss my kiss."

"Your kiss? What are you talking about?"

"I never serve a Kiwi Kiss without giving the real thing."

"But…you can't—"

Gavin leaned over the counter and planted a kiss on her cheek. Setting the glass of light green juice in front of her, he said confidentially, "The little old ladies really like this one."

Sara wrapped her hands tightly around her glass to steady them. "I can imagine."

Gavin laughed and his dark eyes flashed. "Sara, Sara. You're still walking down the straight and narrow, aren't you?"

"It's a safe place to be."

"And how fun is that?"

"I have fun."

"Excuse me." A man on the other end of the counter cleared his throat. "I'd like a Pineapple, please."

Gavin winked at Sara and went to prepare the man's drink. When he came back to deposit the bills in the cash register Sara said, "What if he had ordered the Kiwi? Do you kiss the men, too?"

"Uh—no! I have my standards."

Sara laughed. "You're just a big ol' flirt!"

Gavin clutched his heart. "You wound me." He picked up a bottle of disinfectant and sprayed a portion of the counter, then wiped it with a cloth. "Hey, remember when we were talking about the races? It's almost the end of the season. I want you to come with me Friday night."

"Gavin, I cannot go out on a date with you."

He shrugged. "So, it won't be a date. You can pay your own admission. You can meet me there, if that'll make you feel better. I want you to come. It's fun, Sara."

"I don't know…"

Gavin crossed his arms over his chest and leaned against the cooler. "Does this boyfriend of yours expect you to sit home every weekend and not have any fun?"

"Of course not. He wouldn't do that."

"Well, does he have something against official, sanctified races?"

"Probably not."

"So, okay. Why can't you go to the races with me? I'm not making a move on you, am I? And the Kiwi Kiss doesn't count."

Considering it, Sara sipped her drink. It was true, what Gavin said. It's not like he was asking her out to some candle-lit restaurant. There would be hundreds of people at the racetrack. Gavin was just an old friend, and of course Jim did not expect her to sit home with preschoolers every weekend.

"I'll go."

"Good. Do you want to meet me there?"

"I don't know. Where is this place?"

"Down in Kenosha County, just north of the Illinois border."

"In that case, I'll ride with you."

"Fine. Meet me here at five. We'll grab something to eat on the way."

"What should I wear?"

"Jeans. A warm coat. Gloves. Maybe a hat. We'll be outside."

"Okay." Sara pulled three dollars from her wallet and slipped off the stool.

"How was the Kiwi?" Gavin asked, picking up the singles.

"I liked it. It was light and refreshing."

As she made her way across the parking, she brushed her fingers across the cheek Gavin had kissed. "I liked it a lot—maybe a little too much."

When Sara entered the club on Friday, Gavin was nowhere to be seen. Noticing that it was John behind the juice bar, she wandered to the far side of the lobby, hoping to stay out of his line of vision. She did not want him to know she was meeting Gavin. Not after the remark he had made on Monday. She only waited a couple of minutes until Gavin came out of the men's locker room carrying a heavy denim jacket. He had changed from his work uniform into faded jeans and a flannel shirt. Sara could not help but notice that even in old, scrubby clothes, he was breathtaking handsome.

They exchanged greetings, then Gavin led the way to his car. It was an older model Chevy with rust spots. Sara had assumed he would own a top-of-the-line sports car, but then, how much could he make, working behind a juice bar? Sara realized she knew very little about Gavin. Well, there would be time tonight to ask him questions.

Waiting in line at a drive-in hamburger place, Gavin asked Sara how difficult it had been to get out of the house and away from the kids.

"I'm not exactly the live-in nanny. I don't have to be there all the time."

"So it's cool with your sister that you're going with me tonight?"

Sara shrugged. "She's fine with it." Of course, Sara had just told Morgan that she was hanging out tonight with a friend from the club. She had not said who it was and if Morgan assumed it was Kelly, well, Sara was not going to set her straight.

Gavin and Sara purchased admission tickets and made their way to seats in the grandstand. The wind was whipping across the track so Sara zipped up her jacket and pulled on her gloves. She was surprised at all the action happening on the track. Mechanics and drivers were scurrying around working on the cars and the ground crew was busy packing the dirt track.

"Are you warm enough?" Gavin asked, tugging the collar of his jacket up.

"Yes, just confused. What are they all doing? You're going to have to explain everything."

Gavin was in his element. This was his twelfth visit to a speedway since the beginning of June. "The drivers and mechanics are prepping their cars and doing warm-up laps. Soon they'll start the time-ins and then it's going to get noisy." Patiently, he gave Sara a quick education on the world of racing.

Once the time-ins got underway, Sara could not believe the speed of the cars as they competed for placement. And Gavin had been right. It was noisy—actually, that was an understatement. It was downright deafening.

"They must be going ninety miles an hour," she yelled to Gavin.

He chuckled. "More like a hundred and twenty."

She stared at him. "They're crazy."

It made her nervous to watch and yet she found her heart pumping faster with the challenge and excitement of each race. When the cars lined up for another race Gavin told her to choose a favorite to win. She already had her eye on a sky-blue car that had done well in the preliminaries. She pointed it out to Gavin.

"That blue one; number thirty-seven. It's my favorite."

"Smart lady, it's got a real shot. Wait here; I'll go buy some drinks."

It was almost twenty minutes until Gavin returned with two plastic glasses. He chuckled when he saw Sara sitting with her hands over her ears. Dropping into his seat, he handed a frothy glass of beer to Sara. Pushing it away, she said, "No thanks. I don't drink alcohol."

"It's only beer."

"I know. I don't want it. I never drink."

"Never?"

"My great-uncle on my dad's side was an alcoholic. He could never keep a job and when he was drunk, he was mean. He died from liver failure and, well…I never ever want to go down that road and put my family through what his went through."

"Sara, you don't become an alcoholic from drinking a little beer."

"How do you know what a first beer will lead to? I bet Uncle Marty didn't know."

Gavin studied her face. She was serious. "Okay. Sorry. You hold these and I'll go back and get you a cola."

"No, you don't have to. You were gone so long the first time, I don't want you to miss anything."

"That's because I ran into some buddies of mine. I won't be more than five minutes this time."

Gavin hurried down the steps, berating himself for his blunder. Obviously, Sara and what's-his-name did not live life on the edge. If he wasn't careful she'd go running back to Mr. Perfect Straightlaced Boyfriend. Gavin reached the front of the line, purchased a cola and quickly made his way back to their seats.

"See," he said with a charming grin. "Five minutes, tops."

"Thanks. I'm sorry you had to go to so much trouble."

"It's no big deal. You don't mind if I…?" he asked, lifting his glass.

Gavin's drinking did make Sara a little uncomfortable. People in her circle of friends didn't drink alcohol, but if he only had one…and didn't get drunk… "Just don't pressure me to go against my convictions."

"I'd never do that. It's cool. Look, they're lined up for the next race."

Over the next hour, the cars raced lap after lap, seemingly gaining speed with each circuit. They ran in tight groups, almost bumper to bumper. The arena was extremely noisy and smoky from the engines, but Sara enjoyed the high energy and excitement that permeated the speedway, to say nothing of Gavin's company. His laughter was contagious and he took time to explain what was going on. Finally, it came down to the final laps of the night. Surprisingly, Sara's blue car was still in.

In a quiet lull while the cars were lining up, Sara said, "Which one do you want to win?"

"The yellow. I've seen it before. It has a pretty good track record."

Toward the end of the race, with the yellow car moving into first place and Sara's blue one battling for third, Sara grabbed hold of Gavin's arm as she squealed and cheered with the other spectators. In the final seconds, the audience seemed to hold their breath before the winning car reached the finish line, then they exploded in cheers and applause. Gavin's yellow took first; Sara's blue car came in third.

Laughing, Gavin pulled Sara into a hug as she danced up and down in an excited jig. "Swe-et!" he whistled.

"Oh!" Sara laid a hand on her heart. "My heart is going a million beats a minute!"

"It's the adrenaline rush," Gavin explained. "Come on." Warning her to stick close, he led the way out of their row.

She grabbed a handful of his denim coat and followed him down the steps and into the crowded hallway. He walked around the backside of the bleacher seats and approached a group of people that stood off to the side.

"Way to go, Manes." One of them handed Gavin an envelope. "And is this the lucky lady?"

Gavin casually looped an arm across Sara's shoulders and drew her forward. "This is Sara. Sara, these are the guys. And Allison. You remember my sister, don't you?"

Sara nodded politely at the others and said hi to Allison, who merely smiled in return. Gavin waved the envelope. "Thanks, guys. Maybe I'll see ya next week." He turned to go, taking Sara with him.

"You'd better be here," one of the guys hollered after them. "Next weekend is the last race of the year!"

"We'll be here," Gavin answered with a wave. Glancing at Sara as they made their way toward the parking lot he said, "So, what did you think?"

"It was a lot of fun, but I think my ears will be ringing for two days."

"Yeah, it is noisy. I guess I should have brought earplugs for you."

Outside the gate, Gavin opened the envelope. He drew out several ten-dollar bills and handed three of them to Sara.

"What's this?"

"Your winnings."

"My winnings?"

"Yeah. I placed a bet on the blue car for you."

"But I didn't even win."

"I know. That's why you only got thirty bucks. This is what the winning pot looks like." Gavin fanned out the remaining tens.

Sara did not know what to say. "But...Gavin...betting? Is that even legal?"

He shrugged. "It's just a little harmless wager. No biggie. I do it all the time."

Sara held the tens out toward Gavin. "I can't take this. I—"

"Relax, Sara. You earned it. You picked the blue car and it placed."

Sara stared at the money. He laughed and tugged on her elbow to resume walking. "Sara, you need to let go a little. It's a friendly little game. No one is forced to risk anything. It's good, clean fun."

He reached the car, unlocked the passenger door and opened it for Sara.

She started to climb in, then stopped. "Wait. I should drive. You had those beers."

"That was hours ago. I'm fine."

Sara debated. She had no idea how long it took alcohol to work its way through one's system. Gavin seemed fine, but his reflexes could be slow. "Really, Gavin. I think I should drive."

"It was only two beers, but I guess if it'll make you feel better you can drive to the diner down the road. We'll get something to eat and have some coffee. Fair enough?"

"I guess so."

At the diner, they sat in a booth in the corner. Sara laid her prize money on the table. Shivering, she said, "The one thing I didn't like, besides all the smoke and the noise, was the cold. It's freezing outside."

Gavin chuckled. "That's three things, but who's counting? So, what do you want to eat?"

"Something hot."

Sara ordered a bowl of French onion soup while Gavin asked for a chili dog with fries. While they waited, they drank coffee and talked. The service was slow and it took nearly half an hour for the waitress to bring their order. The French onion soup turned out to be extremely watery and Gavin's fries were excessively greasy. They joked about new names for the diner, like *The Greasy Spoon* or *The Watering Hole*. All the while, Sara could not help but notice how intently Gavin looked at her. After they polished off the last of Gavin's fries, he flagged down the waitress and asked for the bill.

Sara shoved the tens across the table. "Use this to pay."

"You really don't want that money, do you?"

Sara shook her head. "I don't think I believe in gambling."

"You don't *think* you do? Don't you know?"

Two months ago, she would have spouted off that she was adamantly opposed to it, but ever since Gavin had reentered her life, she found herself confused over many things. Besides, she did not want him to think she was judging him, and she certainly did not want to come across as some Goody-Two-Shoes. She had accused Katie of acting "holier than thou" and she did not want Gavin to think of her that way. She looked at him and simply shrugged.

He winked at her. "Sara, you're one of a kind, you know that?"

The way he said it made her feel positive he meant it as a compliment, and the way his chestnut-brown eyes bored into hers made her spine tingle.

"So," he continued, "want to come with me again next Friday?"

"I'm not sure. I had a lot of fun, but…" What Jim would think, she could not imagine.

"It's too much like a date, huh?"

Sara nodded.

"I could get a few others to come with us. It'd be no big deal. Just a bunch of friends hanging out together."

"I guess that'd be okay, but don't place any more bets for me, okay?"

Gavin laughed. "It's a deal. I'll make arrangements with my buddies. Meet me at the club at five again, okay?"

"That'll be fine." There was a strange feeling in her gut and a voice in the back of her mind telling her it was not a good idea, but Sara wanted to have fun. She wanted a social life beyond aerobics, and if she and Gavin were with a group of people, then another outing with him would not constitute a date. The fact that there was no way she'd tell Jim or Katie or even Morgan about it did not penetrate her consciousness.

It was past midnight when Sara got home. The porch light greeted her. She worked her key in the lock and quietly entered the house. Light shone from the kitchen so she walked softly in that direction, hoping Mark or Morgan were not waiting up for her. The room was empty, with just the light over the kitchen sink left on. Sara turned it off, then tiptoed upstairs. In the dim light coming from the Winnie-the-Pooh nightlight in the hallway, she could make out two Post-it notes stuck to her door. She pulled them off and entered her room, flicking on the light as she did. Tossing her purse on the bed, she looked down at the notes stuck to her finger. *Jim called—8:30* read the first one. The other: *Jim called again—10:30—Call him when you get home,* M.

Sara shot a glance at her alarm clock, wondering if Jim wanted her to call him this late. *Is he waiting up?* Debating, she shrugged off her jacket and tossed it onto the rocking chair, then reached for the phone. It only rang once before Jim answered. Sara felt a twinge of guilt that he must have been waiting by the phone for hours while she had been out with Gavin.

"Hello," she said. "I wasn't sure if it was too late to call. What's up?"

"Just our regular Friday night phone call. Did you forget?"

"No…but didn't Morgan tell you that I went out with a friend tonight?"

"Yeah, she did. I just didn't figure you'd be out all night."

"Oh. Well, we stopped for a late-night snack." She hoped Jim would not ask too many more questions. "What've you been up to?"

"Not much. Andy and I watched the World Series and played some cribbage, but I've just been missing you. I kept thinking about last Friday and how we spent it together."

Was that really just last week? Spending time with Gavin totally threw Sara's sense of reality for a loop. "That *was* fun." Sara picked up her jacket and hung it in the closet, then turned on her bedside lamp and turned down the covers of her bed. She couldn't think of anything to talk to Jim about.

"So," Jim said, breaking into the silence, "is this your friend from the club? What did you say her name is, Kelly or Christy or something?"

"Kelly takes aerobics with me." Sara was careful not to lie. Desperate to turn the conversation away from her evening activities, she told him that Kelly worked part-time in an elementary school, then asked how Andy was doing.

"He's fine. He's actually pretty involved helping Greta with the wedding plans. More than Wayne ever did with Katie."

"That's nice…" Sara had never been at such a loss for words. This was the most pitiful conversation she had ever had with Jim. Ever had with anyone, for that matter. "I'm pretty tired, Jim. I think I'll say good night."

"Oh…" Jim could not disguise his disappointment. This was so unlike Sara. She was always up for talking—no matter the hour. "Okay… Shall I call you tomorrow night?"

"Sure. That'll be good. 'Night." Feeling empty, Sara slowly set the phone down. She rubbed her forehead and moaned, knowing she had just blown off Jim because she had spent the last seven hours in the company of another guy. She climbed into bed, realizing that she didn't know anything more about Gavin's life than she had at the start of the evening—except the fact that he drank beer and gambled.

CHAPTER 8

God has said, "Never will I leave you; never will I forsake you."
—Hebrews 13:5b

Tuesday night, Sara poked her head into the kitchen to say good night to Morgan, who was perusing recipe books.

"Good night, Sara. Oh, say," her sister called before Sara could disappear around the corner.

"Yes?"

"I read in Sunday's bulletin that the singles group is going ice skating Friday night. That sounds like fun. I thought it was something you could do."

"I could…" *If I wasn't going to the races with Gavin.*

"Would you like me to call the leader for you?"

"No, Morgan. I don't need you to arrange my social life for me."

"Well, I just thought since you don't really know anyone…"

"Thanks, but I can take care of myself, okay?"

"All right, good night."

"'Night."

Late Friday afternoon, Sara bundled into layers. First a tank top, then a turtleneck, then a bulky cream-colored sweater and two pairs of socks. She grabbed her winter jacket, a scarf and gloves and bounded down the steps to the kitchen, where Morgan was mixing a meatloaf.

"Goodbye, you little munchkins," she said, hugging Nicholas and Courtney. "Auntie Sara won't be able to read stories tonight, so I promise tomorrow I'll read double."

Morgan patted the meat into a glass loaf pan and smiled at her sister. "You're so good to those kids, Sara. Aren't you eating supper here?"

"No, I thought I'd grab something out."

"Are you dressed warm enough for the ice rink?"

"I'm layered," Sara answered, tousling Nicholas' hair. "Don't wait up."

As she backed out of the driveway, she told herself that omitting details and skirting around issues was not lying. Besides, it really was none of Morgan's business if she went ice skating with the church's singles group or to the racetrack with a different group of singles.

When Sara walked into the club a few minutes after five o'clock, Gavin's face lit up in pleasure. He turned to the two girls standing next to him. "Allison, Mandy, this is Sara."

The three girls exchanged greetings. Allison was as blond as Gavin was dark, with short, straight hair. Mandy's hair was almost jet black and long—her braid fell halfway down her back. Both girls were taller than Sara.

"Allison and Mandy are going to ride with us," Gavin explained. "We'll meet everyone else at the track. Come on."

He led the way to his car in the back parking lot and opened the front passenger door for Sara. She wondered whether sitting in the front next to Gavin would make things seem too much like a date, but before she could decide, Allison and Mandy claimed the backseat. Sara flashed Gavin a smile and climbed in. He winked and shut her door. Despite Sara's reservations, he planned to create a date-like atmosphere and pursue Sara. He didn't have any doubts about reaching his objective; he'd only ever struck out with a girl once.

When the foursome arrived at the racetrack, they met up with a group of four guys. Gavin rattled off names: Jared, Scott, Moose and Robbie. Sara mentally made notes to remember which name went with which person. Moose was built like a football linebacker; Robbie was his opposite—thin and short. Jared was the one Allison had talked about on the ride over as having just dumped his girlfriend, and Scott was the one Mandy sidled up to, sliding her hand through the crook of his arm.

Moose used his height and build to weave a path through the spectators milling around and led the group to seats in the grandstands. Sara found herself sitting behind Allison, Mandy, and Scott and between Moose and Gavin. Moose was so big that his shoulder and arm took up part of Sara's space, so she found herself crowded against Gavin. *At least I'll stay warm this way.* The way Mandy cuddled next to Scott in the seats in front of her, Sara figured she would stay warm too. *It's disgusting,* Sara thought, *she's practically throwing herself at him.*

"Warm enough?" Gavin asked huskily in her ear.

"So far," Sara smiled at him. "I dressed warmer this week."

"Yeah, but it's colder. I think I noticed a few snow flurries on the drive down."

"Really?" Sara lifted her face to the sky. Dark clouds were overhead, but she did not notice any flakes. "Will they stop the races if it starts to snow?"

"It'd have to really be coming down. This is the last weekend of the season anyway."

Gavin and Sara talked intermittently during the warm-ups and preliminary races. Even though they were with a group of six others, Gavin made sure that Sara stayed focused on him. He was glad he had subtly arranged to have Moose sit on the other side of Sara since it forced her to sit close.

After an hour or so, Jared stood and announced that it was time for a beer run. Sara's heart froze. Surely not all of them were going to drink? She did not want to be the only one that didn't—they wouldn't understand the reason and they'd probably think she was a baby.

"Who's going to help me?" Jared asked.

"I will," Allison offered, rising from her seat and easing past Mandy and Scott.

"Sara and I will get our own," Gavin said, laying a gloved hand on Sara's knee. He lowered his voice and said in her ear, "I'll take you down in a few minutes and get you coffee or hot chocolate. We can watch the hot laps down there."

"Thanks, Gavin." Sara was touched at his thoughtfulness. *Maybe no one else will even realize I'm not drinking.* Sara was so concerned with fitting in that the thought of taking a stand for what she believed in did not even cross her mind. Of course, her principles had never been challenged before. Her high school and college friends had been non-drinking groups, so she had never really had to face a situation where beer was offered and the others were all drinking.

When Gavin spotted Jared and Allison returning with cardboard drink carriers filled with glasses of beer, he rose from his seat, tugging on Sara's arm. She followed him to ground level and trailed behind as he made his way to the concession area. Turning, he asked what she wanted.

"Hot cocoa, please."

Gavin placed the order for one beer and one hot chocolate and paid for their beverages. Taking a sip of his, he motioned Sara to follow him to a vantage point near a fence, where they could watch the races while they had their drinks.

"It's a little warmer down here," Sara commented.

"That's because we're protected some from the wind."

By the end of the second round of hot laps they had finished drinking their beverages. Gavin tossed the empty glasses into a nearby trash can, but did not make a move to return to their seats. "Let's stay down here for a while where it's warmer," he said, standing close against Sara's back. "Have you picked a car to win yet?"

"I'm not sure I should tell you," she teased. "I don't want you placing any bets on my behalf."

Gavin chuckled. "I tried that once already. I don't think I'll do it again anytime soon."

They laughed and Sara ended up pointing out an orange car just as the flag went down for the start of the next race. Gavin's response was lost under the roar of the engines and cheers from the crowd. Sara still couldn't get over the speed and how close the cars came to each other as the drivers passed each other and jockeyed for positions.

Sara kept her eye on the orange car, silently tallying its laps until she lost count. Out of the corner of her eye she noticed a black car come from behind at a dizzying speed. Trying to pass, it got too close to Sara's favorite and in a split second it was actually driving over the top of the front tire of the orange car. Sara gasped and held her breath as, for a moment, the two cars were locked together, then, with a tremendous screech of brakes, the orange car began to slow down. The black one disengaged from the other, but in the process it flipped over and skidded across the track and with a crash of metal, smashed into the fence on the far side. The driver of the orange car managed to keep his coupe upright, but it spun out of control, doing a couple of three-hundred-and-sixty-degree turns before it also crashed into the fence.

Sara grabbed the fence for support and Gavin instinctively clutched her arm, silently willing the drivers to emerge from their cars. Medics rushed to the scene and several mechanics and other drivers ran over and stood in a half-circle near the wrecked cars. Race cars were still whizzing past, seemingly unaware of the drama unfolding near the fence.

The driver of the orange car surfaced and without assistance walked away amid cheers from the crowd. The spectators quickly quieted, however, as medics continued to work to remove the other driver from his auto.

"It's taking so long," Sara fretted after a few minutes.

An EMT approached with a spinal board, and every minute seemed an eternity until the medics finally extricated the driver from his car and placed him in the pit ambulance.

"I'm scared for him, Gavin," Sara whispered. "Will we ever know if he's okay?"

"Yeah, they'll make an announcement pretty soon." Realizing he was still holding tightly to Sara's arm, Gavin rested both his hands on her shoulders. She slightly relaxed her hold on the fence and leaned against his chest as she silently prayed for the driver. It seemed like forever until the ambulance left.

"Now what?" Sara asked.

"We'll just wait." Gavin rubbed her shoulders. He had seen accidents before. He knew the announcers would give them some information.

It wasn't long until a pronouncement came over the loudspeaker. *"We are sorry to announce that driver G. Griffin died in the accident. In his honor, and due to pending investigations, we will be closing the track. We ask that everyone leave in a timely matter as police wish to secure the scene."*

Sara began shaking and tears trickled down her face. Resting his chin on her shoulder, Gavin placed his arms around Sara, thankful to have someone to hold. He had been to too many races to count and had seen accidents before, but this was the first time he had ever witnessed a fatality.

"Gavin…it's the most awful thing!"

"I know." He tightened his hold on her, breathing in the lilac scent of her shampoo. "I'm sorry, Sara. I'm sorry I brought you here."

"It's not your fault." She raised her face so she could look into his eyes and assure him that she did not blame him.

"I'm still sorry." With gloved fingers, he cupped her chin and brought his mouth to hers for a kiss—a desperate, needy kiss. Nerves raw, Sara did not fight his advances.

When Gavin lifted his face, he saw Allison, Mandy and the others approaching. The entire group seemed fazed. Gavin whispered for Sara to wait, then walked over to Allison and pulled her slightly away from the group.

"Are you okay?" he asked.

She nodded. "I'm fine."

"You sure?" Gavin asked. He was shook up himself, but Allison had always been the tough one.

"I'm sure. Mandy wants us to hitch back to town with Scott and Jared. That won't upset your little group date, will it?"

"No." Gavin shook his head. "Not after all this." He watched Allison rejoin the others, exchanged waves with his buddies, then sidestepped back to where he'd left Sara standing by the fence. Tentatively, he placed an arm around her shoulders. When she did not shrug it off, he left it there and began walking toward the parking lot. "Allison and Mandy are going to ride home with Scott. That okay with you?"

Sara nodded. *What does it matter after all we've been through tonight?* They walked in silence to the car. Gavin opened the door for her. "Don't worry about the beer, Sara. I'm sober."

"That's good." She held out her hands. "I'm still shaking. I couldn't possibly drive."

He took her hands in his. "I know. I kind of feel the same."

"I'm not ready to go home."

"Me either. Let's go to the diner for a while."

When they arrived, Sara made her way to the restroom while Gavin secured a booth and ordered hot coffee for both of them. Sara scrutinized her face in the mirror, first dabbing at the runs of mascara with a damp paper towel and then detangling the mess the wind had made of her hair. Performing these ordinary tasks calmed Sara's nerves more than anything else had.

She joined Gavin at the booth, tossing her gloves on the table and her jacket onto the bench before sliding in across from him. The gum-smacking waitress followed Sara with a pot of coffee and filled their mugs while asking if they'd heard about the accident at the speedway.

Gavin nodded. "We were there. We don't want to talk about it."

"Oh. Well, sorry." The waitress turned and flounced back toward the kitchen, disappointed not to hear a firsthand account of what had happened.

Sara wrapped her hands around the hot drink. "I still can't believe it."

"It isn't normally like that."

"I know. I was there last week, remember?"

"Yeah, I just feel bad. Here I practically begged you to come and then this happens."

"I'm not blaming you, but I don't think I'll ever go back."

"I suppose not."

There was so little to say. It was simply comforting to sit together, sipping their coffee and trying to put the accident behind them. After two refills, they decided to go home. It was a long, quiet drive back to the city. When they finally arrived at the club's parking lot, Gavin pulled up next to Sara's car. "Do you want me to follow you home? Make sure you get there safely?"

"That's sweet, but I'll be okay."

"I think I will anyway."

"All right." Sara opened her door, but did not make a move to climb out. As awful as the fatal accident had been, strangely, she did not want the evening to end. She did not want to leave Gavin—the only person who would ever understand what she had witnessed.

Sensing her mood, Gavin moved closer, placed a hand behind her neck and kissed her lips. Drawing back slightly, he said, "It won't seem so bad in the morning."

"I don't think I'll be able to sleep."

"Do you want my number? In case you need to talk about it?"

"Maybe. I don't know."

He opened a cubbyhole between the bucket seats, pulled out a scrap of paper and a pen and printed his phone number. "Here. Call me anytime."

"Thanks. Goodnight, Gavin." She tossed a leg out, then looked back at him. "I don't blame you in any way."

He nodded, then reached over and planted one more kiss on her lips. "Goodnight, Sara."

"Goodnight. I'll see you Monday."

He waited while she started her engine and let her windows defog, then he followed her out of the lot and all the way home. When she pulled into the driveway, he beeped his horn and drove off. Sara locked her car and quietly entered the house, hoping to avoid Morgan and Mark. She hurried upstairs to her room and firmly closed the door. Without bothering to turn on a light, Sara shed her coat and gloves and dropped into her rocking chair.

Three things were foremost in her mind: tonight she had seen a man die; she had willingly let Gavin kiss her; and there was nobody she could ever talk to about either of these events.

CHAPTER 9

And call for help when you're in trouble—
I'll help you, and you'll honor me.
—Psalm 50:15

    Sara tossed and turned and could not get to sleep. Every time she was just about to drift off, the scene from the racetrack replayed in her mind. She would see one car colliding with the other, see it flipping, sliding… She could hear the squeal of breaks, the crash of metal, the screams from the crowd, from herself. Then, the pall of silence. The tense waiting, the driver being extricated from his smashed car and finally, the ominous voice of the announcer, …*driver G. Griffin died…* For the umpteenth time, Sara rolled over and buried her head under her pillow. She would never forget…

    Sara tossed off her covers and wandered to the window, created a slit in the blinds and peered out. The snow had started—small, tight, swirling flakes. She wondered what the driver's family was doing right now. Did he have a wife, children? Or was he younger—with a fiancée? Parents, sisters, brothers?

    Oh, God, was he saved? Sara breathed the prayer, then involuntarily shivered and retreated to her bed, yanking the covers tight around her chin. She closed her eyes to pray, but the picture of the paramedics pulling the dead driver from the scene invaded her mind, pushing all prayers aside.

I have to talk to somebody or I'll go crazy...but if I tell Morgan or Katie or Jim they'll want to know how come I was at the races and who I was with... I can never mention Gavin's name. Never.

Sara flicked on her bedside lamp and opened the small drawer of her nightstand. She took out the scrap of paper with Gavin's phone number. Staring at the digits he had written in block lettering, she wondered if she should ask Gavin if he thought the driver was saved. But...was Gavin even a believer? Sara had no idea. They had never talked about spiritual issues; for that matter, they had never discussed any serious topic other than her great-uncle's alcoholism—and that only briefly. Except for tonight's tragedy, everything with Gavin had been light...and fun...and flirtatious...and... *I can't call him!*

Sara dropped the paper as if it was burning hot. *I let him kiss me.* The first kiss—at the track—was, perhaps, understandable given the circumstances, but the other two times, in the car...why she had practically *invited* his kiss. Sara sank into her pillow and moaned. *How could I have let him kiss me? It would kill Jim if he ever suspected that I...that I...*Sara fingered her lips. She couldn't deny that Gavin's kisses had been... *Stop, Sara! Don't even go there. It was unusual circumstances, that's all it was.*

Determined to put the night behind her, Sara turned off her lamp and tried to sleep. Half an hour later, she was still awake. She stared at the red numbers of her alarm clock. 4:19, 4:20, 4:21. Desperately, she rose, got her cell phone and, climbing back under the covers, dialed Katie's number.

The phone rang six times before a sleepy Wayne answered.

"Wayne!" Sara cried in a loud whisper. "I need to talk to Katie."

"Sara? Are you all right? Is anyone hurt? Dead?"

"No—yes. Please, Wayne, just let me talk to her."

Wayne rubbed a hand over a chin rough with whiskers. "Do you know what time it is?"

"Yes. Please, I just need to talk to her."

There was silence as Wayne carried the phone to the bedroom, then muffled words, then finally, Katie's worried voice asking Sara if she was all right.

"Oh, Katie." Just hearing the caring voice of her best friend, brought tears to Sara's eyes. "The worst thing..." The tears began streaming down her cheeks, making it impossible for her to speak.

"Sara! Tell me now! What's happened?"

"I…" Sara sobbed into the phone.

"Tell me you're okay. Tell me Morgan and the children are okay!"

"We're all okay." Sara gulped down her tears and fought for control. "I just needed to hear your voice. I just… I witnessed a car accident tonight and…well, the driver died and…"

"Oh, Sara, how awful. Were you alone?"

"No, there were other people around, but it was horrible. The screeching and the squealing and…" *and Gavin kissed me…and I liked it. Oh, Katie…what am I going to do?*

"Sara? Are you still there?"

"Yes."

"So, were you involved? Did you have to file a police report? Will you have to be a witness in court?"

"No…" Katie didn't get it. There was so much more here than the accident…there was Gavin and those kisses… "I miss Jim, Katie. I can't keep doing this."

"Jim. Of course." Katie shrugged at Wayne, who had turned on the lamp and sat at her side. "Of course you miss Jim."

"When we're together it's fine, but this separation is hurting us. What if…what if…"

"Sara, listen to me. Jim loves you. I know he's miserable without you. He's never going to forget about you, never going to do anything to hurt you, never—" The rest of Katie's words were lost under Sara's resumed weeping. Katie cast a look at her husband. Moving the receiver slightly away from her mouth, she said, "I don't know what to say. She's desperate for Jim. I guess she's afraid he's not going to stay with her through this separation."

"She's crazy. Let me talk to her." Wayne took the phone from Katie and firmly commanded Sara to listen to him. "Jim adores you, Sara. This is just middle-of-the-night paranoia talking. You've got to get a grip."

Katie yanked the phone out of his hand. "You can't talk to her like that."

"Listen, Sara," Katie soothed. "You can trust Jim. Just hang in there. Thanksgiving will be here soon and then you'll be together again."

Thanksgiving…I can make it until then. "You're right, Katie. I know it in my head." *Even though this is more than middle-of-the-night paranoia. This is a wonderfully handsome man that is stealing my breath away.* "Don't tell Jim that I called. Please don't let him know how crazy desperate I am."

"Sara, you should talk to him about this. He should know how hard this is for you."

"No! Promise me, Katie. Make Wayne promise, too."

"I promise," Katie said, remembering the fight she and Sara had had at Jim's parents' house. "We won't say anything."

"Thank you."

The girls said their goodbyes, then Katie clicked off the phone and set it on her nightstand.

"Another display of Sara's dramatics," Wayne said. "Was it really worth calling in the middle of the night?"

"I don't know," Katie said, hugging her knees. "There's something very wrong. I just don't know what it is."

Sara waited until nine o'clock the next morning before she resolutely picked up her phone and dialed Gavin's number. When a woman answered, she was surprised, until she remembered that Gavin shared an apartment with his sister.

"Oh, Allison. It's Sara. Is Gavin there?"

"Yep, right here." Allison, standing in the kitchen in her pajama bottoms and an oversized sweatshirt, handed the phone to her brother. Gavin pushed aside his bowl of cold cereal and said hello.

"Gavin? It's Sara."

Gavin shot his sister a victory sign. "Sara, how are you?"

"I didn't sleep much. Did you?"

Gavin shrugged. "Not too bad."

Nervously, Sara paced her bedroom floor. "I called to say that I can't see you anymore."

"Whoa, girl. Don't tell me that."

"But it's true. I can't."

Gavin could almost strangle himself. He'd moved in too fast with those kisses. He knew she had wanted them, but that was in the wake of the tragedy and the dark of night. This morning, she was back to reality. "Come on, Sara, we've got a good thing starting. Don't end it now."

"I can't start something with you, Gavin. I'm practically engaged to someone else."

"Practically doesn't mean anything. You want this as badly as I do. I know you do. Can't you feel what's between us?"

Sara's heart was pounding too strongly. Why did he have to make this so difficult? "It's the wrong time, Gavin. It's too late for what might have been."

"Maybe where you're concerned, but from where I stand, it's just the beginning."

"No, Gavin. I'm not going out with you again—not even in a group."

"I want you to tell me that to my face. Monday, after I get off work. Hang around after aerobics and wait for me. If you still feel the same, then tell me to my face. I deserve that much, Sara. After all, you let me kiss you."

"I'm sorry I did that, I shouldn't have, but all right. I guess you have a point. We'll talk about it on Monday."

"I'll see you then." Gavin clicked off the phone and set it on the table.

"What do you see in that girl, anyway?" Allison asked. She had been leaning against the counter, listening to Gavin's half of the conversation.

"She's hot, in case you haven't noticed."

"Maybe, but she's not your type. The Sara Brooks I remember from high school was Miss Prim and Proper and extremely talkative. I remember nicknaming her Chatty Cathy."

"What do you know? She's fun to be with."

"She's also very innocent."

"Yeah," Gavin agreed, "but that's part of the fun. I can show her the world."

Allison stared at her brother. "You almost sound like you're falling in love."

Gavin faked a choking cough. "No way. That's not in my cards. I'm just looking for a good time."

"Well, I don't remember you ever putting so much effort into hitting on a girl before. You're a goner, Gav."

"Naw, it's all just a game—a challenging, intriguing, passionate game."

Jim called Sara Saturday afternoon. He apologized for not calling the night before, but he had driven down to his parents' house for his dad's birthday dinner. By the time he got back, it was eleven thirty and he figured Sara would be in bed. She didn't tell him she had been out as well, she figured the less said about last night, the better. Maybe, the less said, the sooner she could forget about the crash and Gavin's kisses.

Jim told Sara everything was set for his roommates' reunion over Thanksgiving weekend. "It'll be cool, Sara. Russ and Mel are coming and even Andy and Greta decided to spend the weekend up here with us, instead of with their families in Iowa."

"Are you sure this is what you want to do?" Sara asked, visualizing how little privacy she and Jim would have amid seven other people.

"Of course, we've been planning this since last year. You know that.

Don't you think it'll be fun to be with the whole gang again?"

"Yes, but if we went to one of our parents' we'd have a lot more time alone."

"I know, but there'll be time for that later. Come on, Sara. This will be great. Katie's planning on you and Greta staying there. Russ and Mel can stay here since Craig and Gary will be gone."

"It will be nice to see them all, it's just that I need to be with you, Jim."

"We'll be together. It's going to be great."

"You keep saying that."

"Well, it will be, especially with all our friends here."

The discussion moved on to other things, but Sara found herself preoccupied and unable to concentrate. She would not be able to totally relax until Gavin was out of her life—he and his kisses.

Of course, it would help tremendously if the next time she saw Jim he asked her to marry him. *Wait a minute! What better time than Thanksgiving? Maybe that's why Jim is so excited about this. All our friends… Oh! It would be perfect. Jim can propose and then we can announce it while everyone is together.* Sara lost herself in her daydreams. The more she thought about it, the more she was convinced that this was exactly what Jim was planning.

"Sara, are you still there?" Jim's voice broke into a stillness that had lasted for several seconds.

"Oh. Yes. I've…um…been thinking about Thanksgiving weekend. You're right, it's going to be perfect. Do you want to take a private hike up to Maple Ridge after dinner?"

Jim chuckled. "Maybe. Let's wait and see what the weather's like first."

After they said goodbye, Sara flopped onto her bed. It would be wonderful. Russ and Mel would come from South Dakota, Greta from Iowa, and Peter would drive over from St. Paul. They'd all be there to celebrate Jim and Sara's good news. After all, everyone except Peter—who might forever remain single for all the interest he showed in women—was either a newlywed or engaged. They would all be thrilled.

The idea of Jim proposing to her in less than two weeks kept Sara starry-eyed for the rest of the weekend. Thoughts of Gavin and his ardent kisses receded to the background as she dreamed up different scenarios for how and when Jim would say the magic words.

Monday afternoon, as she pulled open the front door to the health club, she did not even feel tempted to toss a wave to Gavin. She would do nothing—*nothing*—to give him the slightest idea that she was not committed to her current relationship. Engaged women did not go around talking and flirting with, let alone kissing, other men. As soon as Gavin's shift was over, she would end what ever it was they had. It could hardly be called a relationship. A friendship, perhaps. Whatever, Sara would end it and she would not let herself be sidetracked by Gavin's flashing dark eyes or his seductive smile.

When she arrived at class, she approached a couple of women she had not talked to previously. She would not rely on Gavin for a social life. She chatted and laughed with the women, even though they were at least a decade older than she was. When Kelly arrived, she and Sara retreated to their customary corner.

"What's got you in such a good mood?" Kelly asked.

"Just love," Sara answered dramatically, swooning a little as Dean switched on the music. She and Kelly exchanged smiles, then focused on the aerobic exercises. As Sara twisted, bent and did knee lifts, her blood pumped through her veins in time to the beat of the music. She felt energetic, strong and attractive. So what if Gavin desired her? So did Jim, and her heart was already given to him.

"Want to stay and have juice with me today?" Sara asked Kelly as they toweled off. "My treat." If she was there with Kelly, it would not allow Gavin much opportunity to flirt and possibly break down her defenses.

"All right. I guess I have time."

The girls chatted and laughed for nearly an hour before Kelly pushed her glass across the table. "That was good, and this was fun, but I need to get home and fix supper."

"I'll walk out with you," Sara offered, jumping off her stool and grabbing her things. She followed Kelly to the parking lot, then stood talking with her for a few more minutes until Kelly got into her red Jeep and drove away. Sighing, Sara walked slowly across the lot to her own car, opened the door and tossed in her duffle bag. She looked back toward the club and decided to wait for Gavin out here.

She started her engine so the heater would run, turned the radio on low and opened her hospitality law textbook to chapter seventeen, noticing they were nearly at the end of the book. She was glad. She had learned a lot, but this had not been her favorite class and she was ready to move on to something more exciting. She read several pages, but found her eyes drawn repeatedly to the door of the club. She could not see through it from this angle, but she could picture Gavin inside. He'd be flirting and laughing, with his dark eyes flashing and his hand unconsciously combing his dark hair into place.

Shoving her book aside, Sara reached into her purse and pulled out her wallet. She flipped it open and stared at Jim's photo. "I love you," she whispered, "but you're far away and..." She wondered if he was ever tempted by other girls. The idea brought a feeble laugh, then she gulped. Maybe that was why he hadn't proposed yet... *Don't be ridiculous, Sara. Jim? With another girl? Anyway, he's going to propose next week.*

A tapping on her window made Sara's heart jump to her throat. Looking up to see Gavin peering in, she snapped the wallet shut and shoved it into her purse, then opened the door.

He stepped back so it could swing wide, then squatted onto his haunches at her side. "I was afraid you'd left."

"I've been out here doing my homework." She retrieved the textbook from the floor and set it on the seat next to her.

Gavin chuckled. "Yeah, right. So, that's him, huh?" He pointed to her purse. "The guy you're breaking my heart for."

Sara fiddled with the straps of her purse. "Better you than him," she murmured.

"What was that? I couldn't hear. Will you get out of the car and talk to me, face to face?"

Sara drew her key from the ignition and did as he asked. She followed him to the side of the building, where he leaned against the cement block wall and grasped her hands so she had no choice but to stand close and face him.

"It was the kissing, wasn't it?" Gavin asked.

Sara tried to tug her hands out from his, but his grip was firm. "Gavin, please."

With a hint of annoyance, he dropped her hands. She shoved them into her coat pockets, then looked into his face. "What was that?"

"The kisses. They scared you off. I thought you wanted it too, but I guess I moved in too soon, too fast."

"Yes, you moved in where you weren't wanted." A gust of cold wind spiraled a lock of Sara's hair across her face. She shivered and, not daring to take her hands from her pockets, tossed her head to remove the hair from her eyes.

"Don't give me that. In the car, you wanted me to kiss you."

"It was a mistake, Gavin. I made a mistake. It was the night..." Sara knew the excuses sounded feeble—even to her.

Gavin hunkered against the wall, the breeze blowing into his open jacket. "Can't we go somewhere warmer to talk about this?"

"No." She was resolved to resist his charm. "We'll talk here. It shouldn't take very long. It might have been the kisses that prompted me to reach this decision, but the fact is that I'm practically engaged."

"We've been over this before. Practically doesn't count. I want my chance with you."

"We're from two different worlds, Gavin."

"So what? Man, Sara, you're like a shooting star. I'd like to ride through the skies with you."

"I'm flattered, really, but I already have someone taking me on a magic carpet ride. I'm going to see him next week for the holiday. We're going to have a beautiful visit and I don't want to feel guilty because of you."

"Because you're attracted to me?" Gavin paused just a moment, before adding, "Admit it, Sara, you are and you found those kisses as stimulating as I did."

Sara didn't want to discuss those kisses. "I'm not going to go out with you ever again. I'm not going to stop at the juice bar unless Kelly is with me."

Gavin leaned close and dropped his voice. "Just answer me this, if what's-his-name didn't exist, would you give me a chance?"

"His name is Jim," Sara whispered. Gavin was too close and he was too good looking. She took a step back. "Don't ask me that, Gavin."

"It's true, Sara. You feel this attraction every bit as much as I do." He ran a finger gently down her cheek, then abruptly stepped aside, leaving her breathless. It was not his style to beg. "All right; you win. I'll leave you to him, but remember, I'm here. Winter is on its way with its long, cold nights. I don't think you'll find much comfort in a long-distance phone call, so…" Gavin shrugged. "You'll know where to find me." He turned and walked away. *Let her mull that over for a while*, he thought as he headed toward his car without a backward glance.

Sara watched him leave with a smidgeon of regret. This was what she wanted, wasn't it? Then why did she feel so unsure? Gavin had a way of bringing her to the heights of passion just by the look in his dark eyes, the sound of his voice and the engaging mannerisms he used so easily. He lifted her up—even against her will—then let her plummet back to earth. Not wanting him to see that he left her feeling mystified, she hurried toward her car. It was strange how she felt. After all, she was the one who had told him they could not have a relationship. But for some reason she could not define, every encounter with Gavin left her breathless.

Sara draped yet another sweater across her bed. She wanted to plan precisely what she would wear for the entire Thanksgiving weekend, starting with her arrival tomorrow night. While Sara rummaged through her wardrobe, Courtney, dressed in Sara's black high heels and one of her skirts, danced around the bedroom. Nicholas, lipstick smears across his chubby cheeks, climbed onto Sara's bed and began jumping. When he came close to the edge, Sara scooped him up, kissed his tummy and placed him on the floor.

"Now, stay down. Here," she reached into a dresser drawer and tossed out some mittens, gloves, a stocking cap and winter scarves, "you can play dress-up like your sister." Smiling, she watched as he picked up the stocking cap and struggled to pull it onto his head, then she turned from her nephew and perused the clothes in her closet again. The sleeve of her ivory corduroy jacket caught her eye. "Perfect..." she breathed, withdrawing it from the closet. "I can wear this on the drive down. It'll be just the thing for greeting Jim at the door and it'll work great for a walk up Maple Ridge. What do you think, Courtney?"

Sara held the coat in front of her and faced her niece. Courtney stopped dancing long enough to look at her aunt. "You'll need a hat," the little girl stated.

Sara laughed. *Here I am, taking fashion advise from a four-year-old.* "I think you may be right, and I think this one might do the trick." She tugged the cap off Nicholas' head. It was an ivory knit, with flecks of red and navy. Somewhere, Sara had gloves to match.

Nicholas let out a wail when he realized his hat was gone. "Goodness!" Sara said. "It's hard enough for a girl to plan her engagement wardrobe without all your fussing. Why don't you go watch some TV or something? Where's Mommy?"

"Baking," Courtney answered in her matter-of-fact way.

Sara draped a scarf around Nicholas' neck and put a pair of mittens on his hands. They went all the way up to his elbows. "There you are, little prince, go down and show Mommy." *Little prince...* Gavin's face flashed across Sara's mind. Immediately, she pushed the vision aside. She was proud of the way she had avoided him for the past week. She had merely smiled at him as she came and went to aerobics. She had not bothered to stop for juice. Now, hanging her jacket up, she admitted to herself that she missed it. Not the juice so much, but the hour spent in Gavin's lighthearted company. It was a sacrifice she was willing to make though—for Jim. For the right to be Jim's fiancée.

Sara sank onto her bed, the crazy juice names floating in her brain.

Cranapple Crush, Kiwi Kiss... She had never even made it to Pineapple Passion, Gavin's favorite. Maybe next week, after she had the security of Jim's ring on her finger, maybe then she could go back for juice. Gavin wouldn't come on to her if she was engaged. She would just need to flash that diamond in his face. It would tell him—tell the whole world for that matter—that she belonged to somebody. That there was a man who wanted to make her his wife and spend eternity next to her side. That was all she really wanted. To have a ring on her finger and stand with the man of her dreams, on top of the mountains, next to the raging sea, or out in the middle of the sandy desert, forever and ever, until the sun and the moon were no more.

CHAPTER 10

Come to me all you who are weary and burdened, and I will give you rest.
—Matthew 11:28

Forever and ever… Sara was saying to herself as she pulled into the small parking lot of Jim's building. She and Jim together, forever and ever. The litany faded from her mind as she scrutinized the only open space in the lot. It was going to be a tight fit. Determined, she scrunched up her nose and concentrated on getting her car between an oversized black pickup and a small, dented Toyota that was several inches over its lane marker.

Halfway in, Sara knew she was stuck. If she drove forward one inch she would add another dent to the Toyota; if she backed up she was sure to put a scratch on the truck's beautiful paint job. Sara sighed, admitting that she needed to run up and ask Jim to help her park. *One more romantic reunion hits the dirt!* Frustrated, Sara cautiously opened her door as far as she dared. *Great. Just great.* She might be a size four, but there was no way she could squeeze through a five-inch gap. She pulled the door shut, climbed over the console between the bucket seats and managed to slip out the passenger side. *At least I have the wherewithal not to lock the doors with the car running,* she thought as she sprinted for the steps and Jim's door. Knocking, she realized it was probably not very smart to leave the car running in this neighborhood. Just because she could not move the car in or out didn't mean some punk couldn't do it in the mere seconds her back was turned. Jim opened the door with a smile, ready to receive a hug, but Sara turned abruptly and flew back down the steps.

At the bottom of the staircase, she turned and hollered. "I can't get my car parked!"

Jim hurried after her. When he caught up to her, he chuckled. "Got yourself in a pickle, huh?"

"It isn't funny, Jim."

"It is, sort of. I mean, look." He gestured toward her car, wondering why some girls were even allowed behind the wheel of an automobile.

"Aren't you going to fix it?" she challenged. "I mean, you can, can't you?"

In a flash, Jim squeezed his almost six-foot frame into the car through the narrow opening on the passenger side, slid over to the driver's side and maneuvered Sara's car nicely into the allotted parking space. He emerged, triumphant, with a smirk on his face. "I don't know, can I?"

Laughing, she ran to him. "You made that look so easy!"

"It was easy," he agreed, embracing her.

"Not to me. I must be missing the part of my brain that does spatial stuff."

"Some girls are like that," Jim grinned, teasing her. "You never did tell me how you took the door off your dad's truck."

"Let's just say...it was something like this."

Jim laughed. Sara hadn't been here ten minutes and the whole world seemed brighter. She naturally brought laughter and lightheartedness and, well, craziness with her. Not to mention beauty. Man, but she was beautiful. He should tell her... "Hungry?" he asked instead. "You didn't stop to eat on the way, did you? I thought we'd go out."

Hungry? Food was the farthest thing on her mind right now. This was very possibly her engagement night. "I don't know. What time is it?"

Shivering, Jim suddenly realized he was standing outdoors on a November evening without a coat on. "You have to know what time it is to decide if you're hungry? It's after seven. I'm starved. Come on." He grasped her hand and hurried upstairs to the warmth of his apartment.

"Where is everyone?" Sara asked, looking around while Jim got his winter jacket from his room.

"Greta's here already, but she and Andy went out somewhere. Craig and Gary left for the weekend. Russ and Mel aren't due in until late tonight. Ready? Let's go."

"Wait." Sara could not go out to dinner—not if Jim might use this opportunity to ask her to marry him—dressed like this, with her hair uncombed and day-old makeup on. "I should change into a skirt and—"

"Why? You look great. Really great." The sincerity in Jim's face and voice and the love in his eyes melted Sara's heart. There was something in the way he said it that made her feel loved and cherished. He did not say things the way Gavin would. Gavin's compliments left her feeling giddy, breathless, and desirable, but Jim's warmed her from head to toe, from outside to inside, and made her feel serene and attractive not just in looks, but in character as well. *I wish I was that way. Noble in character. I wish I truly was the way Jim sees me.*

Jim placed a hand on her back and propelled her toward the front door. "Come on. We're wasting time. We've got places to go, things to do."

Turning, she glanced at him, her eyes traveling quickly to his pockets. "Do you have everything you need?"

"Yep." Jim ushered her down the stairs. "We're going to make up for that weekend we didn't get when I had to help fix the roof. This will be a weekend to remember."

It's true! He's going to ask me tonight. Mrs. Jim Hoffman. Sara Hoffman. She tried the names out while Jim pulled onto the road and headed toward the freeway. *Jim and Sara Hoffman.*

They went downtown to a small, family-owned Italian restaurant, where there were real linen tablecloths and tapered candles on the tables. Occasionally, bursts of good-natured ribbing came from the kitchen, but the young couple concentrated solely on each other. *It's a night for dreams to come true*, Sara thought. *Fairy-tale stuff—starlight, full moon, Prince Charming at his best, candles, romance.*

She and Jim talked and laughed easily together. Although they covered several topics, Jim steered clear of his post-graduation plans. Listening to Sara's silvery laughter and watching how her blue eyes sparkled in the candlelight made him wish he was ready with a plan of action. A plan that included marriage in the not-too-distant future, but he had not made much headway figuring out where he and Sara should spend the next part of their lives and he wasn't sure if they should get married soon after she graduated or if they should wait a year to get on their feet.

Sara would be so nice to come home to. She's beautiful and bubbly and needs taking care of.

"Penny for your thoughts," Sara said, tapping his hand.

He folded his hand around hers. "I was just thinking how especially alive you seem tonight. All sparkly and…and…" Jim could think of no adjectives to describe her.

"Oh." *What is he waiting for?* "It's just the same old me. You probably forget what I'm like in between visits."

"Never, Sara. I don't ever forget. I dream about you constantly."

"You do?"

"Yes." Jim leaned over his empty dessert plate and whispered, "I dream about your kisses."

Sara blushed. "My kisses?"

"Yes." Subtly, Jim waved to the waiter and asked for the bill. He realized he hadn't even received a hello kiss in all the commotion of parking her car.

Sara rested her fingertips lightly on her lips, regretting that she had ever let Gavin near enough to touch her lips. And why did thoughts of him have to invade her romantic dinner with Jim?

Jim stood, gallantly pulled back Sara's chair, and helped her put on her corduroy jacket before he donned his black coat. Once they were outside, Jim placed an arm around Sara's waist.

"Want to take a walk and enjoy the city lights?"

"I would." Sara tugged on her gloves and put her cap on, then slipped her hand through Jim's arm and snuggled against his side. They walked for several blocks before crossing the street and coming back.

"It's beautiful out," Sara commented as they approached his car. "All frosty and clear. We should come back at Christmas and see the stores with their holiday decorations up."

"It's a date." Jim took a roundabout way home, driving to the top of a hill, where a large, old church was situated. He parked in the lot and turned off the headlights. Spread out before them was the city in all its dazzling lights. "I discovered this place and have been wanting to show it to you."

"It's breathtaking."

"Yeah. I like it up here. You can't see any of the city filth or recognize the poor neighborhoods. Just the skyscrapers and the lights. It has an equalizing effect."

"Why, Jim Hoffman. You're just as much of a romantic as I am."

Jim chuckled. "Hardly. Sara Brooks, you're in a category all by yourself."

Later, as they drove home and it became clear that Jim was almost back to the apartment and had not yet asked the all-important question, Sara felt her stomach begin to ache with disappointment. *Oh, Jim…there would be no better time. The night's been so romantic…*

"What are you waiting for?" Realizing she had stupidly stated her question aloud, Sara clapped a hand over her mouth.

Turning the last corner before his building, Jim cast a quick look at her. "What? Waiting for what?"

Sara shrunk down on her seat, wishing she could hide inside her coat. "To take me to Katie's." It was the only thing she could think of. She could hardly blurt out, *TO ASK ME TO MARRY YOU!*

Jim glanced at the clock in his dash. "You want to go there now? I thought we'd hang out at my place for a while. I don't know where Greta and Andy are, but somebody should be here when Russ and Mel arrive."

"Oh."

"Besides, aren't you going to drive yourself to Katie's? You should be able to get your car out now that I put it in straight."

"I guess I forgot." She could just kick herself. *What if he's been planning to do it here, when we went inside? Now the mood's been broken.* "Okay, I'll come up with you and wait for Russ and Mel."

"Good." Jim grinned. "I'm in charge of tomorrow's stuffing. I was hoping you'd help chop celery and onions."

Later, Sara lay in bed on a futon in Wayne and Katie's little spare room that they had turned into an office. She could not believe that her hopes had been crushed. Jim had not asked her to marry him. She had no ring on her finger. What's more, she was surrounded by couples that were either engaged or recently married.

When Sara left Jim's apartment and arrived at Katie's, she unknowingly came upon Andy and Greta kissing good night at the door. Andy had quickly stepped aside and stammered an apology. Greta had slipped into the house right behind Sara, but that didn't dismiss the fact that Greta's face was glowing. Her face would glow! Their wedding was only seven months away. A tear trickled down Sara's face as she enviously thought of Greta, sleeping in the other room on Wayne and Katie's couch, with Andy's diamond ring sparkling on her finger.

"There's always tomorrow," Sara whispered to encourage herself. Tossing onto her side, she thought, *Who am I kidding? If Jim was planning to ask me this weekend, tonight would have been perfect.*

For the friends who reunited at Jim's apartment, Thanksgiving day was special. Although thoughts of family and home crossed their minds at various times during the day, most of the group lived too far away to go home for a four-day weekend. They would see their families at Christmas. In the meantime, this gathering of friends was like a family. They had become close over the past few years. Andy, Wayne, Jim, Russ, and Peter had lived together for varying amounts of time. As romantic relationships developed, one by one the girls were drawn into the group. First Greta, then Katie; Sara was next, and lastly Mel. Peter was the only one who remained unattached. The four women teased that they were going to find a wife for him. He just shook his head and ignored them. He was deep into theology and Greek and had no time for—or interest in —a relationship.

After dinner, Sara looked out the window, hoping to snag Jim away for their walk to Maple Ridge, where maybe, just maybe, he'd pop the question. Unfortunately, the temperature had warmed slightly and it was raining. Unless they went for a drive, they were cooped up here. Sara turned and looked at the guys collected around the table. Wayne and Andy were arm wrestling and the others were gathered around watching. Jim would want to stay here with his buddies...

Sara joined the other girls in the kitchen, where Greta and Katie were paging through Mel's wedding album.

"Look at this," Katie pointed. "It's Greta catching the bouquet. What a great shot."

"Mel, could I have a copy of that?" Greta asked, her dark eyes shining.

Sara always thought that whenever Greta's attention turned to Andy, she got a mysterious, smitten look on her face. Like she and Andy shared some great secret. Like theirs was the romance of the century. Just because they had known each other since they were babies, had dated since they were sixteen, and had known forever that they were going to get married... Sara sighed. If only she and Jim had known each other that long... She turned around and let her gaze rest on Jim. *Who am I kidding? Jim's not ready. He might never be ready. I could end up waiting for him to propose until I'm thirty. I'm going to become an old maid waiting for him...*

It felt absolutely suffocating in that kitchen with Greta, Mel and Katie all discussing their weddings. Didn't they realize that Sara was floating in no-man's land? Katie, at least, should know better, but no...the other girls kept talking about their dresses, flowers, music, and cakes until Sara could no longer stand it. Turning abruptly, she marched to the living room.

The arm wrestling had broken up. Russ was channel surfing, looking for the football game; Andy and Jim were seated on the couch, with Wayne sprawled on the floor in front of them. Peter had dragged a dining room chair over to the corner and was perched on that. Sara went over, sat on the floor at his side and asked about seminary. She listened steadily, inserting questions frequently for thirty minutes while the other guys watched football and her girlfriends talked weddings in the kitchen. Although she rarely delved deeply into the Scriptures and had never before given one thought to the Greek or Arabic languages, right now, Peter was the safest company. No girlfriend, no plans to get married, just a plain old Joe.

Mel came from the kitchen with her bridal album tucked under her arm and stowed it away in a suitcase. Katie announced that she would make a pot of coffee and Greta came to stand behind Andy, that serene and mystifying look in her eyes again.

"How about a game of charades?" Sara suddenly asked, motivated to find something to do that would lessen the chance of more wedding talk.

"Women against the men," Mel laughingly agreed.

Russ turned down the volume on the television set. Andy and Wayne pushed back some of the furniture while Jim hunted down a tablet and pens. Soon a rousing game of charades was in full swing. Sara threw off her moping spirits and totally got into the game. It was so easy with Mel's constant laughter, the guys' playful arguments, and the fact that Sara truly was in her element in the middle of a good game of charades. It meshed so well with her flair for the dramatic. The game lasted for over an hour, with the girls winning.

"Where's that coffee?" Wayne asked.

"And the pies Russ and Mel brought? Isn't it time for pie?" Andy asked.

"I think the losers should wait on the winners," Mel declared.

"Consider it done." Russ rose, dragging Andy after him.

Over pie, coffee and hot apple cider, they continued to reminisce, while every so often someone commented on how fun it was to be together again.

"We're not going to be able to come next year," Andy said. "Greta and I, well, it looks like we might be going to Kenya. We'll have language studies first, but," he shrugged. "We won't be able to come here."

"Wow. Kenya…" Katie said, dreamily looking at her husband.

There were other comments and questions about the proposed mission work, then Peter asked Jim where he would be next year. It was an innocent question. One people often asked those about to graduate.

Jim looked across the room to Sara, but she averted her eyes while her heart started racing like the cars at the speedway. *What will he say?*

"I'm not sure," Jim calmly stated.

Not sure! Not sure? How can he not be sure? Couldn't he even admit that he would be wherever she was? Was he seriously still thinking of going to the West Coast and putting two thousand miles between them? Was he not going to stand by her side? Was he not going to ask her to marry him?

Sara could picture Jim's graduation. He would stand there in his cap and gown; his mother would take pictures. He would want to pose with Sara—he might even hold her hand—and then they would all go out for dinner. Jim, Sara, his parents, his brother, his sister and her family, aunts, uncles…and Sara would sit there knowing it was the end. She was simply Jim's college romance. Once graduation was over, Jim would smile, say he had a good time, wish her the best and move on. Move on…move away…and Sara would be left with nothing but memories. Keepsakes of a two-and-a-half-year relationship…but no engagement ring.

"It's sad to think that our lives are going in so many different directions." Katie's voice broke into Sara's poignant thoughts. "Bit by bit, year by year…we'll move farther away from each other."

Sara stared at her. *Katie! Can you not see that I'm dying here? Must you talk so of moving away? Can't you say something to Jim? That surely he's going to…to…*

"We've got to keep in touch and every few years have a Thanksgiving reunion," Greta suggested.

Hello! Sara inwardly fumed. *What's going to happen to me? Are you going to invite Jim to the reunion, or me?*

"Wouldn't it be great if we could form our own community and stay together?" Katie pondered. "Peter could be our minister, Mel and Wayne the teachers and Greta could cut hair."

"Yes," Russ agreed, smiling at the thought of his friends all staying together through the years. "I could run the radio station and Andy could be our resident farmer."

"Katie can be our nurse; Jim can operate the local store and Sara…Sara…" Andy looked across the room at her. "Sorry, what are you studying again?"

"Sara will plan all our parties and decorate our homes!" Katie said, tossing a genuine smile toward her friend.

"It sounds like a great time, but there will need to be other people," Mel pointed out. "Otherwise Wayne and I won't have any children to teach. Even if one of us has a baby soon, it'll be years before they reach the upper grades."

"That's true." Russ glanced at the other couples, then added, "I wonder who will be first. To have a baby, I mean."

"Probably you and Mel," Wayne spoke up. "After all, you two had the shortest courtship. You went from 'How do you do?' to 'Will you marry me?' in about two weeks."

Mel's laughter filled the room. "It wasn't that fast!"

The conversation went on, but Jim tuned it out. His eyes were on Sara. *My bets are on us,* he thought. *We'll surprise them all and have the first baby. Last married; first to be parents. Man, but Sara is going to make one terrific mother.* He knew she would be the kind of mom to get down on the floor and play with her children and she wouldn't even scold the boys when they came inside with their clothes covered in mud. *Boys...* Jim gulped. *How about at least one girl that looks just like Sara with wild, crazy curls and eyes as blue as a summer sky...*

Sara sat with her eyes on her lap. Not only was the conversation totally uncomfortable, Jim kept staring at her. He had the strangest look on his face. Sara could not meet his eye. *Whatever is he thinking?* A pit started growing in her stomach. At first, it was an itty-bitty cherry pit, but then it grew. As Sara's thoughts grasped desperately at the meaning behind Jim's look, the pit in her stomach soon became watermelon size. It was clogging her throat. Jim was not going to propose this weekend; he was going to break up with her! All this talk about staying together with their friends was causing him to realize that he had better do it soon. Sara started swaying on her chair. She could not breathe. *Oh...God...* She had been so foolish to think he was going to propose!

Sara bolted from her chair and ran for the bathroom, slamming the door behind her. Tears streaming down her face, she vomited. Afterward, she rinsed her mouth, took a hand towel off the rod, slumped to the floor and wept bitter tears.

There was a knock at the door and Jim's worried voice.

"I'm sick," Sara managed to answer.

"Can I come in?"

"No. I've got the flu or something." *Or something...* Fresh tears flowed down her face.

"Come on, Sara."

"Go away. I'm sick."

In the hall, Jim looked at Katie. "Do you think it was the food?" he asked.

"Oh, I hope not."

Jim stepped around Katie to the living room. "Is anyone else feeling sick?"

There were head shakes and negative answers. Andy looked up from his second serving of pie. "It's probably just the flu."

Katie knocked on the bathroom door. "Sara? Can I come in?" She waited for an answer, but when none came she slowly opened the door and peeked in. Sara sat with her back against the tub, her face buried in a blue hand towel. The room held the faint sour smell of vomit. Katie entered the room and pulled the door shut. Kneeling at Sara's side, she put a hand on her friend's head and gave her a hug. "I'm sorry you're sick. How miserable. Did it just come on sudden like?"

Sara nodded. The watermelon-sized pit was still sitting in her stomach. It was never going to go away. Jim didn't want her. When was the last time he had said *I love you?* Sara couldn't remember. Was he in it just for fun? If she could not have Jim for all time, then she did not want him at all. Sara drew the towel away from her face. "Can you take me home, Katie? To your place?"

"Of course." Katie rose and helped Sara to her feet. "How's your stomach? Should we get a bucket for the car?"

Sara just shrugged. She had no idea what her body would do next. She only knew she felt weak and lovesick. She let Katie usher her into the hallway, where she stood at a loss. She could not think; her body could barely function. Katie went to retrieve their coats, purses and a bucket while Sara leaned against the wall for support. Suddenly Jim was there, standing in front of her with a worried look on his face. He placed his hands on her arms and murmured soothing words. Sara turned her face away. She did not want to look at him. It hurt too badly. She would throw up again if she let herself look into his eyes—his traitorous eyes.

She tried to stand up straighter, to look stronger than she felt. Katie brought her coat and Jim helped her into it. She didn't really want his help. Why was he being so considerate? Katie draped an arm around Sara and escorted her out of the apartment. Vaguely, she heard the others say goodbye and wish her well, but she could only offer a feeble wave. Wayne already had the car started. Jim climbed into the back with Sara while Katie sat in front. Sara let her hand lie limply in Jim's, but leaned away from him against the door.

"You don't have to come," she told him.

"I want to."

"I'm just going to go to bed."

Jim shrugged. "I'll stay anyway."

I don't want you to... Tears slipped down Sara's face and dripped off her chin. *Just go away...far away...*

Jim reached over and wiped a tear off Sara's face. "I'm disappointed, too, but the main thing is for you to get better."

She pushed his hand away from her face. *Don't touch me... I just want to die in peace.*

Sensing Sara really did not desire to talk, Jim sank back, and unconsciously tapped his finger against the bucket he held on his lap. *Best laid plans...* he thought. *Every single one of our weekends seems to go haywire.*

At Wayne and Katie's, they settled Sara onto her futon in the extra room. Jim stood in the doorway for a moment, asking if she needed anything.

Grimly, she looked at him. *I can't begin to tell you what I need, Jim Hoffman. If you don't know by now, then you're never going to know.* Instead of saying the words that were crying out to be said, she simply shook her head.

"I'll be out here," Jim said. "Just holler if you need me."

Need you? Need you! I'm dying for you!

Carrying a Mexican-woven blanket, Katie slipped quietly into the room as Jim left. She laid the blanket over Sara, then pulled out the desk chair and sat at Sara's side. "I'm heating water for tea."

Sara struggled to sit. "I think I just want to go home, Katie."

"That's a long way to drive when you're not feeling well."

"I don't care. I just want to go home."

"But you'll probably be better by the morning. I thought we could go shopping tomorrow."

Another tear slipped down Sara's face. "Katie, I can't stay here. I just want to go home."

Katie patted her friend's leg. "You must feel really cruddy to cut your weekend with Jim short."

"Jim." Sara drew in a big quivering breath. "I think I've been kidding myself about Jim, Katie. I think...I think..."

The teakettle started whistling, its piercing scream reached the girls in the spare room. Katie glanced toward the partially open door and hollered for Wayne to get the kettle. Then she reached for Sara's hands. "What were you saying about Jim?"

Sara shrugged, battling her tears. "I don't think it's going to work."

Katie could only stare at her friend. Sara looked back at her with unflinching eyes. "Your sickness has gone to your head, Sara. Jim is crazy about you. He's sitting out there worried sick because you have the flu. The flu! Imagine how he'd be if you had something serious."

"It's not what it seems," Sara whispered. "We're not what we seem."

Katie rose and shut the door. When she returned to Sara's side, she nudged her friend over and perched on the side of the mattress. "Don't you love him anymore?"

Sara cast a desperate look at Katie. Fidgeting with the fringe on the blanket, she shrugged. "I don't know."

"Oh, Sara."

Sara grasped Katie's arm. "I do—it's just—I need... I don't know."

"It's just the sickness talking," Katie said. "You're not thinking straight because of the flu."

Sara sank back on the futon. She could not talk to Katie. She could not tell her that it was not the flu making her sick. Sara had never known that someone could literally be lovesick, but now she knew. "Ask Wayne to start my car for me, okay? The keys are in my purse. I'm going home, Katie."

"I wish you wouldn't."

"My mind is made up. Will you help me get my things together?"

"Sure, I'll be back to help in a minute." Sighing, she rose and went to the living room, where she announced to Jim and Wayne that Sara planned to go home. Katie retrieved Sara's purse from the coffee table and fished out her car keys. Tossing them to her husband, she said, "She wants you to start her car."

"Going home?" Jim stared at Katie as Wayne got up from the sofa and headed outside. "Now? Sick? With two whole days left of the weekend?"

Katie stepped in front of Jim and pinned him to the couch with a look. "Last month, at your dad's house, did you talk to Sara like I told you to?"

"Yeah. We talked. What's up?"

"I don't know. You tell me."

Jim craned his neck to look behind Katie toward the bedroom, where Sara must be packing. "Tell you what? Everything's fine between Sara and me. We had a fantastic time last night. We've never been closer."

He rose from the couch, pushed his way past Katie to the doorway of the spare room and watched Sara cram a few things into her suitcase. "Hey, Katie said you're going home. You shouldn't drive if you've got the flu."

Sara paused, her pajamas wadded in her hands, and stared at Jim. *That's right, don't tell me that I shouldn't go because you'll die of loneliness or because you need me. Just tell me I shouldn't drive because I'm sick. Just like at your parents' house. Then it was because it was too dark and late; now I'm too sick. Why has it taken me so long to see that you don't really love me?* Ignoring all the things that demanded to be said, she shoved her pj's into her suitcase and told him she would be fine.

"Then stay."

"I feel awful, Jim. I can't stay here. I need to go home."

Jim glanced at his watch. She'd probably make it home by ten thirty, but he'd worry the whole time. "Please wait until morning. See how you feel then."

Sara closed her suitcase. "I'm going now."

"Well…" *This can't be happening.* "Call me when you get there. Do you have your cell phone? Call me on the way and let me know how you're doing."

Sara clenched a hand over her stomach. If Jim didn't stop talking in trivialities she was going to be sick again. It was becoming so painfully clear that he was never going to commit to her, that this was simply a college romance. The awful realization was kneading a hole in her stomach.

Jim could see that Sara was miserable. "I'm serious, Sara. You shouldn't be driving. Why don't you climb in bed and let Katie and me take care of you?"

Sara needed time to think. This weekend that had begun with such anticipation and romance had fizzled away to shredded hopes and disenchanted dreams. "I want to go home, Jim. My stomach hurts. I think I have an ulcer or something."

"Sara…" Jim felt completely helpless. Why was she being so stubborn? She wasn't thinking straight, but he could hardly force her to stay. "If you're feeling that bad, how are you gonna drive three hundred miles?"

Sheer willpower, she thought. "Don't worry about me anymore, Jim. I can take care of myself."

Helpless to change her mind, Jim followed her into the main room, where Katie hugged Sara, with instructions to call as soon as she got home.

Sara simply nodded and stumbled up the steps to her car. Jim helped her place her suitcase in the backseat, then drew her into an embrace. "I'm sorry," he said softly in her ear.

Sara nodded, her head tapping against his as she did. "Me too." So this was it: the beginning of the end. It was unromantic and lacked drama just like the rest of her life. Where was the passionate argument, the anger, the resolute agreement to part ways? That's how it always happened in books, not just this… A simple, albeit painful, realization that she was living in a one-way fairy-tale dream. One from which waking up was excruciating agony.

Sara stepped out of Jim's arms and climbed into her car. Wayne had turned the heater on and it was toasty warm inside. With a willpower she didn't know she possessed, she shut the door and drove away. In a few days, when her stomach stopped reeling, she would need to figure out where they would go from here. If she should be the one to make the break, or if she should continue to wait for Jim to drop the axe. For now, it took all her concentration to not look back, but to steadily drive away from Jim and all her dreams. Away from the romantic life she wanted and into the dark, rainy night. She was just a Cinderella with no glass slipper, a Sleeping Beauty without a prince, a Rapunzel with short hair.

CHAPTER 11

"…for it is time to seek the Lord…"
—Hosea 10:12b

By the time Sara reached Stillwater, Wisconsin, her eyes were swollen, her throat dry, there was a nasty taste in her mouth from vomiting and her stomach ached with a deep-seated, wrenching pain. She pulled off the interstate and stopped at a gas station. She filled her car with gas, then used the restroom and grabbed a bottle of 7-UP from the cooler.

"I'm glad you're open," she said to the clerk. "Being Thanksgiving and all."

"Going far?" he asked, barely glancing at her.

"Milwaukee."

"Well, have a good one," he said as he handed Sara her change.

Have a good one, Sara muttered as she pushed open the glass door and dashed through the rain to her car. *What a joke. Have a good drive? A good night? A good life?* She pulled back onto I-94, twisted the top off her bottle of pop and took a long sip, hoping it would settle her stomach. *Do you have any idea what my life is? This. A lonely five-hour drive on a holiday. A holiday! Not going toward something magnificent, but away from it.*

She imagined the story she could tell Courtney:

Once upon a time there was a girl who went off to college and met the most wonderful boy. He wasn't flamboyant or rich or heart-stopping handsome, but he was kind, a good listener, a steadfast Christian and in an understated way he loved to have fun. The girl fell head over heels in love and dreamed of a future as his bride. She dreamed how together they would climb the highest mountains, ford fast-running rivers and then, after they had accomplished everything they had set out to achieve, they would lie peacefully on the shores of island paradises. The girl thought the boy loved her, too. She assumed he dreamed the same dreams, but the years passed and he never said, Will you be my wife? One day, the girl came to the stark realization...the stark realization...

Fresh tears dribbled down Sara's cheeks. She would have to tell Courtney that she wouldn't be able to finish the story. It was just too sad. Sara could just as well imagine her niece's questions:

Is there a wicked witch? Did she put a spell on the boy? Is that why he doesn't ask the girl to marry him? Maybe it can be broken with a kiss.

I don't think a kiss is going to help...

Sara drove on, mentally and emotionally numb. She didn't want to write stories in her mind anymore. She could not stand to think about her love life and what a shambles it was in. She had started the holiday weekend soaring on air, had spent the day plummeting and now...there was nothing left.

Around eight forty-five, her cell phone rang. It was Jim. Of course it was Jim. He would at least have to pretend that he cared, until he said the fateful words, *I want to break up.* "Where are you?"

"Eau Claire. The rain's turning to sleet."

Jim still could not comprehend why she had gone. Katie was certain that Sara must really be sick—*really sick*—to want to go home so badly. *Sometimes you just need your own bed,* Katie had said. Jim wanted Sara to know how much he missed her, how disappointed he was that their weekend was shot, but he didn't want to make her feel worse. And he didn't want her to think he blamed her. After all, she couldn't help getting sick. So he said nothing about what was really on his heart and instead told her to drive carefully.

Inside her mind, Sara shrieked, *Don't you miss me? Don't you love me anymore?* However, she simply said, "I will."

By the time she got to the Dells, it was snowing. Sara lowered her speed, gripped the steering wheel and forced herself to concentrate on the road. To take the curves slow and easy. After all, there was no hurry to go home. Everyone would be in bed. They were not expecting her back until Sunday...

Wait. I can't go home! What have I been thinking?

Mark's parents were visiting. They were staying in Sara's room. Even if Sara snuck in and spent the rest of the night on the couch, in the morning Mark's father would probably insist on making reservations at a hotel for the remainder of their visit and giving Sara her room back. Morgan and Mark would not appreciate that.

Not only were there houseguests, Morgan would demand an explanation for why Sara had come home so early. There was no way—*no way*—Sara was going to admit that she was convinced Jim was about to break up with her. No way on earth she was going to try to explain that she was actually lovesick. And she could not fake the flu. Big sister Morgan, who was so sensible, would never understand. And she would not appreciate Sara needing extra attention when Mark's parents were visiting. *I can't go home...* Disappointment seeped into her bones.

Unless I go home to Mom and Dad's. Sara would have to make a decision soon, because she was almost to the Madison exit. *What will I tell Mom?* The thought of crying on her mother's shoulder was tempting. Dad would probably get righteously angry and call Jim on the phone, then chew him out for messing with his baby's heart and demand an explanation for Jim's actions. Mom would understand about two invested years wasted on a boy who does not want to make a commitment. Sara would be coddled and protected and... *I can't do that to Jim. I can't let Dad call him up and yell at him. And I can't go back to being Mom's little girl. Not if I'm ever going to stand on my own two feet and have them accept me as an adult.*

Sara drove on past the Madison exit. She could not go home to her parents' house. At least not until this thing with Jim was settled. One way or another, she owed Jim that much. And Madison had nothing else to offer. She really had no high school friends left there. They had either moved away or Sara's connection with them had dissolved during her college years.

As she got closer to Milwaukee, she realized she was in a tough spot where friends were concerned. She only had a handful of MCU friends outside of the Katie-Jim group and she could not go stay with any of them. They lived too far away and were too busy with their own lives.

The people she was closest to—her best friends—were the people she had just left. *Why did I not realize when I started dating Jim that I was risking my friendship with Katie? She's the best friend I have ever had and now I can't even talk to her.* Tears gathered in Sara's eyes again. She had never needed Katie more and had never felt so far from her.

So, where does that leave me? I have no friends now. None. Okay...there's Kelly. Sort of. Kelly was really more of an acquaintance and Sara did not even know her last name. She didn't have a phone number and no way of looking one up. The few people she had befriended at MATC were also only on a first-name basis. Never before in her life had Sara felt so utterly alone. There was no one she could talk to; no place she could go.

The only friend she had left—the name she had so faithfully avoided until now—was Gavin. But really, how good of a friend was he? She barely knew him, after all. Granted, she was attracted to him and he had made it perfectly clear that he was attracted to her, but he was not someone she could go running to for a place to stay. She could cry on his shoulder over her messed up love life, but she could never go there and spend the night at his apartment—never.

"I'm going to have to get a hotel." Sara stated aloud. "Even though I don't have much money. I'll use my charge card. Dad always said it was for emergencies. This certainly is an emergency."

Approaching the city, she watched the advertisements for a Super 8 or something similar that wouldn't cost too much. Within ten minutes, Sara pulled into the nearly empty parking lot of a two-story motel. Making her way inside, she couldn't believe this was happening.

"Only in some dumb book nobody would want to read," she muttered as she moved toward the front desk.

"May I help you?"

Sara rented a room for two nights—she would decide about Saturday later. Maybe she could go home by then. It would be the last night of Morgan's company. Sara would insist on sleeping on the couch. If she arrived late enough, what could they do?

Sara trudged down the hall to her room, trying to see some hope for her situation. Trying to make sense of the fact that this was Thanksgiving—the holiday Jim had pleaded with her to spend his way—and she was alone, in a strange motel, spending money she did not have to spend.

After opening her room door, she flicked on the light, dropped her suitcase to the floor, locked the door and flung herself onto the bed. She wanted to cry, but the tears were used up. *Gone. Dried up. Just like my love life.* Sara struggled to a sitting position and looked around at her surroundings. It was a pretty basic motel room: one bed, a nightstand, a built-in dresser with a mirror, one chair, a large TV. Sara scooted to the edge of the bed, stood up and walked over to the mirror, where she studied her reflection. Her eyes were red and puffy from crying and there was a streak of mascara down one cheek.

"Miserable, Sara. You're really pitiful."

Resolutely, she dug her cell phone from her purse and called Jim's apartment. She figured that he should be grateful she was being considerate enough to call. After all, she didn't really owe him anything when he wasn't kind enough to be honest with her about his feelings—or should she say his *lack* of feelings.

"Oh! Hello," she said, surprised when Jim answered so promptly.

"You made it home then?" he asked, concern filling his voice.

"Yes. I'm exhausted and I'm going to bed."

"I'm sorry. Are you feeling any better?"

"No." *I'm never going to feel better! I hate what you've done to me. To us.*

"What do you think?" Jim asked helplessly. "Is it the flu?"

Sara's hand clenched the phone. *How could he act so innocent? Does he really not have a clue?* "I guess. My stomach is in knots; my head and eyes hurt." *My heart is breaking!*

"I'm sorry," Jim repeated. "It's been a bummer."

"I couldn't help it that I got sick."

"I know; I'm not blaming you." *But did you have to leave?* "I'll call you tomorrow to see how you're doing."

"Call my cell, not the house phone," Sara said, not wanting to admit that she wasn't at Morgan's.

"Sure, okay. You'd better call Katie; she's worried about you."

"I will. Goodnight, Jim."

There was a pause before Jim forlornly said good night and clicked off his phone. *I love you, Sara… Why didn't I tell her?* Jim hastily redialed her number, but it was busy. *She's probably on with Katie,* he reasoned. Disappointed, he hung up. *I'll tell her tomorrow.*

Sara stared at the phone in her hand, wondering if she could ever have a normal conversation with Jim again. Sighing, she pressed Katie's number.

"It's me," Sara said when Katie answered. "Where you in bed?"

"No. I couldn't go to sleep until I knew you made it safely home."

"I did."

"How are you feeling? Is your stomach any better?"

"I don't think so. Now my head hurts."

"Well, go to bed and hopefully you can sleep it off."

"I will. Listen, Katie, thanks for being such a great friend. I've never been as close to anybody as I've been with you. I know there's been stuff lately that, well, that I haven't really been able to share, but it isn't because I don't value our friendship. It's just something I have to figure out."

"Oh, Sara. You know you can tell me anything."

"Yeah…well, listen I'm going to hang up, I just wanted to let you know I got back all right."

"Okay, well, go sleep it off. I'll talk to you later."

"Goodbye, Katie." Sara dropped her phone onto the dresser. It was difficult to keep secrets from Katie, but Sara had no idea how to explain about Jim. Until things were resolved, she would have to stumble along by herself.

She went into the bathroom, washed her face, then decided to take a shower. When she got out, she put on her pajamas, grabbed the remote and climbed into bed. She flicked through the channels, settling on a rerun of *I Love Lucy*. This show always made Sara chuckle, but not tonight. Lucy's problems seemed trivial and ludicrous compared to her own. There was a great big aching hole in her heart and Sara had never felt so lonely in her entire life.

She just needed somebody to talk to. She wondered what the front desk clerk would think if she came downstairs and poured her story out to him. *Maybe front desk clerks are like bartenders…maybe a lot of lonely people stop in the lobby to talk to them. Like they do with Gavin…*

Sara glanced at the phone on the night table. She could call Gavin just to hear a friendly voice. Just to reassure herself that she wasn't totally alone in the world. She needed somebody to care about her. Somebody who was on her side. Somebody who wouldn't demand any answers. Realizing she was describing the way Jim used to be only made fresh tears run down her cheeks. Wresting one of the pillows from under the bedspread, Sara tossed it angrily onto the floor. "I will not cry any more tears over you, Jim Hoffman! I won't! And someday—someday, you'll see—I'll find somebody who loves me. Loves me and wants to be with me forever."

Her mind made up, Sara grasped the room phone and dialed the number for directory assistance.

"Milwaukee, Wisconsin," she informed the operator. "Gavin Manes."

"I have a listing for G and A Manes on Trenton," the voice crackled over the phone lines.

"That must be it," Sara said, then, listening to the recording, she muttered, *Yes, yes,* to the question about having it automatically dialed.

"Hello?"

Sara froze for a split second, wondering if calling Gavin meant a stab in the back to Jim.

"Hello?" Gavin asked a second time.

"Gavin." In a trembling voice, she added, "It's Sara."

"Sara? Aren't you in Minneapolis?"

"Not anymore. I uh—I—" She had no idea what to say.

"So you're home?"

"Not exactly. I'm in a hotel here in Milwaukee."

"A hotel! Sara, what—" Suddenly it dawned on him. She must be having major boyfriend troubles. "Are you okay?"

"Not really."

"You must've had a bad trip, huh?"

"Yes," she admitted quietly. "The worst."

"So you want to tell me about it?"

"Not really."

There were a few moments of quiet, then Gavin said, "Did he break up with you?"

"Not exactly."

"You break up with him?"

"No…"

"Well, something must have happened."

"Or not happen."

"Oh." Only two weeks ago Sara had spouted off that she was practically engaged and could not see him anymore, now she was calling, sounding depressed after spending a mere twenty-four hours with her boyfriend.

"It's all very confusing. I'm not really sure what's going on with my life."

"I see…" Gavin's mind was scrambling. Was this phone call her way of handing him an olive branch? Did she want to be friendly now after sending him away? "So, it sounds like you need some time to sort things out."

"Yes," Sara replied, knowing that in a lifetime, she would never be able to sort it out.

"You know, Sara, I don't know what happened over there in Minnesota," he had the fleeting thought that unless it was a breakup between Sara and this Jim dude, he didn't really *care* what had happened, "but it's apparent that your boyfriend let you cut things short. There must be something wrong with him to let you drive away when your holiday weekend was only half over."

Tears trickled down Sara's face at Gavin's words. "So it would seem," she replied weakly.

"I would never treat you like that, Sara. If you were my girl, I can guarantee that you would never leave a planned weekend early. You wouldn't want to and I wouldn't let you."

"You're sweet," Sara said.

"I mean it, Sara." While Gavin speculated if she would say yes if he asked her out, Sara wondered if she should tell Gavin that she needed his friendship. *It's too soon*, Gavin warned himself. *Just take it slow.* "So, what's next?"

"I'm not sure," Sara slowly admitted. "Like you said, I need to sort some things out."

"Do you want me to come over? Or you come here?"

"No, I'm just going to try to get some sleep."

"Okay, well, tell me where you're staying and give me your cell phone number so I can reach you." He jotted down the information she gave him. "It's going to be all right, I promise."

Sara pressed her lips together, hoping Gavin was right. Hoping somehow this mess of her life would get cleaned up—and cleaned up in a hurry. "Thanks, Gavin. Thanks for being there."

Gavin shrugged. Being here for Sara Brooks was just where he wanted to be. "It's nothing. Now get some sleep."

After hours spent tossing and turning, Sara finally fell into a deep sleep. When she woke, she stared at the bright red numbers on the alarm clock until it sunk in that there were only ten minutes left before they would clear away the continental breakfast. Knowing she shouldn't spend money going out to eat, Sara tossed off her blankets, pulled her coat on over her pajamas and ran down to the breakfast room. She grabbed a muffin, banana and a glass of juice and, balancing it all in her hands, carefully walked back to her room. When she got to her door she realized she had forgotten her room key.

With a big sigh and muttering under her breath why these things always happened to her, she made her way back to the front desk. "Excuse me, I've locked myself out."

If the desk clerk noticed the red and swollen eyes—as evidence of a night spent crying—she made no comment, but simply asked Sara for her name, looked up her room number and handed her a new key.

"Thanks," Sara said, accepting it carefully between two fingers of the hand that held her juice.

Back in her room, Sara nibbled on the muffin and drank half of her juice, then climbed back into bed. The few hours of sleep had not been enough and the memory of yesterday afternoon when Jim sat across the room looking at her in that strange way had not vanished and Sara wanted nothing more than to escape into dreamless sleep.

She slept until noon, when the chirping of her cell phone woke her. Grasping for it on the night table, she said a sleepy hello.

"Oh, sorry," it was Jim's voice on the line, "were you sleeping?"

"Yes."

"So you're not better?"

"No, I still feel awful."

"I'm sorry."

How many times had he apologized in the last twenty-four hours, Sara wondered. And what was he apologizing for? That she was sick or that he knew that she knew that he— "Listen Jim, I really don't want to talk now."

"Well, okay…" Disappointed, Jim didn't know what he could do. "I'll call you tonight."

"Tomorrow, Jim. Call me tomorrow." Sara clicked off her phone, wondering if she had ever been that rude to anyone in her entire life and disbelieving she had acted that way to Jim. To Jim, the absolute love of her life. The absolute love of her life, who made her so angry…so…hurt… "I will not cry anymore," she coached herself aloud.

She stared mindlessly at a picture on the wall for the longest time. Her stomach growled, reminding her that she had not eaten much since yesterday's pie. She ate the banana and drank the rest of the juice, then wandered aimlessly around the room, pulling aside the curtains and looking at the lightly falling snow. She turned on the television, flipped through all the channels, found a soap opera she had never seen before and climbed back under the covers.

Without really paying attention, Sara watched the show, then sat through another soap opera without ever figuring out what was going on or who the people were. It wasn't like she cared. Nobody's life could be more pathetic than her own. She could write a soap opera—oh, yeah, how hard could it be?

At two o'clock she flipped through the channels again, watching each one for about five minutes, until at three o'clock she settled on a rerun of *Little House on the Prairie*. She fluffed up the pillows behind her, figuring this would be a safe thing to watch. There wasn't too much romance on the show. Half an hour later, fresh tears were falling down Sara's cheeks. She had forgotten how this show always got to her. The music and the—

Her cell phone chirped again. This time it was Katie. The girls talked for a few minutes, Sara convincing Katie that she was somewhat better, but that she was spending the day in bed. "Don't call back until tomorrow," Sara pleaded. She couldn't deal with all these calls. It was way too difficult.

"If that's what you want. Take it easy now. Don't let Nicholas pester you."

"He won't. 'Bye, Katie." Sara breathed a sigh of relief. The day's phone calls were over. She watched the remainder of the show, then snuggled back under the covers and fell asleep.

CHAPTER 12

I will instruct you and teach you in the way you should go:
I will counsel you and watch over you.
—Psalm 32:8

Thoughts of Sara plagued Gavin all day at work. Based on last night's phone call, there was definitely something major going on between her and Jim. Sara hadn't admitted that either one of them had broken up with the other, but Sara was not acting like a girl who was practically engaged. It would seem that the door she had shut so firmly in Gavin's face a couple of weeks ago was opening a crack.

As soon as John came to relieve him, Gavin hustled out to his car and drove to the motel Sara had said she was staying at. He spotted her car soon after pulling into the lot. He parked next to it, then sauntered into the lobby. Heading directly to the desk, he said, "Can you tell me what room Sara Brooks is in?"

The clerk, an older gentleman, looked at Gavin over the rim of his dark glasses. "I'm afraid it's against company policy to give out that information."

"Oh, come on. What do you think I'm going to do? She told me that she's here."

"Young man, I don't know what you're going to do, but if she told you that she's here, she could just as easily have given you her room number if she wanted you to know it."

"What if I said that I'm her brother?"

"It doesn't make any difference."

"Well, can you at least ring her room and tell her I'm here?"

"Certainly." The clerk picked up a black phone and dialed Sara's room number. Gavin tried to peer over the counter to see the numbers he pressed, but he couldn't quite see the pad.

"Miss Brooks? You have a visitor in the lobby."

There was a moment of silence then the clerk said, "I'm not sure. He said he's your brother."

"My brother!" Sara's surprised voice carried through the lines. "From Florida?"

The stern clerk looked Gavin over from head to toe, taking in the vest that displayed the health club's logo. "I think rather not," he replied.

There was a muffled sound, then the clerk hung up and told Gavin that Sara said she would be right down. With a grin, Gavin wandered several feet away from the desk to stand next to the elevator. It was a brief wait until he spotted Sara heading down the first floor hall toward him. She was still dressed in pajamas with her coat thrown hastily over top, her feet were bare and her hair was as wild as Gavin could ever imagine.

"Gavin!"

"Hey, sis!" Gavin shot a look at the clerk, then hustled to meet Sara in the hall, out of sight of the front desk. "So—" They stared at each other for a moment, then Gavin motioned to her attire. "This is not good, Sara. Don't tell me you spent all day in bed crying over that jerk."

Sara winced. Whatever Jim was, he wasn't a jerk. "Don't call him that."

"Sorry, but, Sara—man." He placed his hands on her shoulders. "Is he really worth this?"

"I don't—I don't—"

"You listen to me now, Sara. You're going to take a shower and get dressed and then you're coming with me. I am not going to let you sit here the rest of the weekend and do this to yourself."

Sara stared at him. It had felt good to wallow in self-pity for a day, but the evening hours stretched ahead and Sara did not really want to spend them holed up in her room all alone with only the TV for company. But could she do this? Could she get dressed and go out with Gavin and pretend that she had her life under control?

"Go on," Gavin prodded. "I'm not leaving here without you. I'll sit outside your door all night if I have to."

The tiniest of smiles appeared on Sara's face. "You wouldn't either."

"Try me."

"I won't be the best company."

"We'll see about that. An hour with the Gav and you'll be smiling again."

"My, but someone has a pretty high opinion of himself."

He had the strongest desire to pull her into his arms and kiss her, but he was concerned about scaring her off. "Come on, Sara. If you know what's good for you, you'll come to dinner with me."

"Dinner?" The hunger pangs in Sara's stomach rejoiced at the word dinner.

"Dinner and games. We'll go to McGrady's."

"I don't know what that is."

"It's on the East Side. They have the best burgers in town and there's an arcade attached."

"All right, it does sound good. You can wait out here."

"Fine, but hurry up. I don't think that desk clerk likes me."

Once they were seated in Gavin's car, he expressed his desire to stop home and change out of his work uniform.

"Where do you live?" Sara asked. Now that she was out of the hotel, she was anxious to get some food.

Gavin explained that his apartment was only a mile from the health club and he shared it with Allison. It was a simple two-bedroom on the ground level of a six-unit complex. The place was old and a little run-down, with frequently stopped-up plumbing, but it was theirs. All during high school they had talked about getting out of the house. On their twentieth birthday, they made the move. He admitted that it was comfortable living with a sibling. They could squabble over food and bills and chores without taking offense and they were used to each other's annoying habits.

"Here we are," Gavin announced, turning into a narrow parking strip. "Come on." He led the way down the walk and, opening the door, ushered Sara inside. "It's not much, but it's home."

Sara glanced around the apartment from the four-foot-square tiled entryway. To the right was a living room, furnished with matching twin love seats upholstered in gold corduroy, a scarred coffee table, a floor lamp sporting fringe on the bottom of its shade, a television with a DVD player, an Xbox, a stereo, and a large set of speakers. To the left was a decent-sized kitchen. The tabletop was covered in marbleized Formica and the four chairs were covered with orange vinyl. Straight ahead was the bathroom, with what appeared to be bedroom doors on each side.

"Very retro," Sara commented.

"With a Salvation Army twist," Gavin said, grinning. "I'm going to take a quick shower. Do you want something to drink while you wait?"

"Sure, do you have any juice?"

Gavin laughed. "I'm the juice man, remember? I get ingredients from the club at cost so I can fix just about anything you want. How far down the menu did you get?"

"I think my last one was Mango Madness."

Gavin closed his eyes and pictured the menu at the club. "The next one is Melon Medley, but I don't have the right stuff for that one. We'll just move on to Pineapple Passion. That one, I can fix."

"Your favorite."

Gavin cocked his head and studied Sara's face. "You remembered."

"Yes."

While Gavin gathered the supplies and cracked ice with his hammer, Allison came home from work, surprised to see Sara. The girls tried halfheartedly to find something to talk about.

"Where do you work?" Sara asked to be polite.

"At Charyl's, downtown. It's a fashionable women's boutique. Ever hear of it?"

"No, if it's downtown I'm sure it's out of my league."

"I know what you mean. Even with my employee discount I can't afford much there."

Gavin handed Sara a glass of icy yellow juice, then with a subtle nod, motioned Allie toward his bedroom. "I'll be right out, Sara," he said, following his sister.

He closed the door behind him and turned toward Allison. "Listen, Sara's going through a really rough time right now. I don't think she should spend any more of the weekend alone, but I promised Shasta that I'd do a fill-in shift tomorrow for part of the day."

"Yeah, so? I can't go to work for you."

"No, but didn't you mention a shopping trip with Mandy? You can invite Sara along."

Allison laughed. "You're funny, Gav. Why in the world would I ever do that?"

"Because I asked you to."

"Gavin, in case you haven't noticed, I stopped doing everything you wanted when we were about twelve."

"I know, but do it as a favor to me. She's in a bad way right now and she could use some friends."

"Never in a hundred years would I choose to be friends with a girl like that."

"You know, Allie, I'm trying to get something going here. Can't you at least pretend? I want her to feel good about life. Well, about me and I want her to be comfortable coming over here and all."

Allison rolled her eyes at her brother. "You're falling for that girl."

Gavin shrugged. "Let's just say I'm intrigued, okay? Now, how about it?"

"It's asking a lot. She's not my type." Allison reached for the doorknob.

"Maybe, but you owe me. You know that two hundred bucks I loaned you to get your tires? If you do a good job of buddying up to Sara, not just tomorrow, but for a while, I'll call us even."

Allison turned and looked her brother in the face to make sure he was serious. "All right, you've got yourself a deal, but only for a few weeks."

"Deal. That's all the time I need."

Allie headed back out to the kitchen, where Sara still stood drinking her juice. Gavin followed, to make sure Allie came through for him. Opening the fridge and pulling out a diet cola, Allie casually said to Sara, "You know, today is the biggest shopping day of the year and Mandy and I usually go, but I had to work, so we're going tomorrow, and if you want, you can come with us."

"Oh—I, um…" The last thing Sara wanted was to go somewhere with Allie and Mandy. She glanced at Gavin, hoping he would come to her rescue.

"Why don't you go?" Gavin encouraged. "It can't be much fun sitting around a hotel room all day and I have to fill in a half-day at the club tomorrow."

Allie cast Sara a curious look and Sara cringed. She had not wanted Allison to know she was stuck in a motel. "Well, I suppose…" After all, Gavin was right. Today had been terribly long and depressing. She couldn't spend another day like that. "Well, all right. I guess I could come."

Allie forced a smile, then turned toward Gavin. *Happy?* she mouthed.

"I'm going to shower," he announced, heading into the bathroom.

"Meet us here at nine o'clock tomorrow, okay?" Allison told Sara, heading to her room to change.

Sara nodded, took her drink and wandered to the living room. She stood at the window and watched the snowflakes thinking everything seemed like a dream. Everything that happened since Thanksgiving dinner—could that really just have been yesterday? It was difficult to believe that she was standing in Gavin's apartment and had agreed to go shopping with Allie and Mandy tomorrow.

"I should have called in sick today." Sara jumped at the sound of Gavin's voice behind her. Placing a hand on her shoulder, he apologized. "Sorry, I didn't mean to scare you."

"It's all right. I was just lost in thought. What did you say?"

"That I should have called in sick and spent the day with you."

"That would hardly have been honest."

Gavin shrugged. "It's no big deal. I've done it before. Who would know?"

"Well...your conscience for one."

Gavin chuckled. "Like I would ever let a little thing like that stop me." Gavin tugged on his coat. "You hungry?"

"Starved," Sara said, heading to the kitchen to put her empty glass in the sink.

"Let's go then."

On the drive to the restaurant, Gavin kept up a banter of humorous surface talk and when he pulled into the parking lot, he glanced at Sara. "I think I detect a smile on your face."

Sara quickly pressed her lips together. It was hard to stay depressed in Gavin's company.

"It's okay, Sara. That's the whole idea. You know, to get you to laugh."

She unbuckled her seatbelt. "I don't really know how to act. It's been an unbelievable week and I've never been through something like this before."

"You don't need to know how to *act*," Gavin said. "Just let life happen. Just enjoy the time with me and let yourself forget about what's-his-name for a while."

"I would honestly like to do that, Gavin. I'm really tired of being depressed."

"Just let it go then."

While Sara and Gavin enjoyed juicy burgers, onion rings and fries, he noticed several guys giving Sara a second look as they passed the table. It didn't bother him. Actually, it boosted his ego to be seen with a beautiful, lively girl. "I can see that everywhere you go you have guys ogling you."

"I don't either." Sara blushed, but was secretly pleased at the look in Gavin's eyes.

Gavin leaned back, his appetite sated. "Ready for a little pinball?"

Sara shrugged. "All right, but you'll have to teach me. I've never played before."

"Never played pinball? Man, where've you been?"

They entered the game room, where music blared over the speakers. Gavin chose a pinball machine, stuck in some quarters, and positioned himself directly behind Sara, placing his hands over hers on the knobs and shooting the pinball into action. Sara held her breath. The closeness of his body and the strength of his arms was thrilling, but it was a little too much, a little too soon. Wiggling, she managed to create a little space between them. After playing a couple of games together, Sara tried it on her own.

"Okay," Gavin said, "you're catching on pretty good."

Sara flashed him a smile and glanced around the arcade. "How about this?" she asked coyly, moving to stand beside a foosball table. She had been a dorm foosball champion when she attended MCU, but there was no reason to let Gavin know that.

"Foosball? Well, okay, but you'll have stiff competition."

"How's that?" Sara asked innocently.

"I've been known to get pretty intense."

"I want to try."

"Suit yourself."

Gavin played a merciless game and Sara subtly let him win two in a row. "Had enough?" he asked.

"Maybe one more. Maybe we should put a five-dollar bet on it."

Gavin chuckled. "I thought you didn't gamble. Now you want to place a bet when all the odds are against you?"

Sara smiled modestly. "It's just for fun."

Gavin exaggerated a sigh. "It's your loss." He pulled out his wallet and placed a five on the side of the game table. "Let's see your money, pretty lady."

Sara laid her bill next to his. "Ready?" she asked sweetly, before dropping the ball into the center of the table. The game was fast and furious, and before Gavin knew what had hit him, it was over and Sara had won. "What the—? Beginner's luck," Gavin mumbled.

"Must be," Sara agreed.

"Let's play double or nothing."

Sara wavered. She'd never bet anything before; she'd only done it to have some fun with Gavin. And now he knew she could keep up with him.

"Come on," Gavin laid another five on the table. "Don't back down now. You started this."

"Oh, all right." *I'd just better win,* Sara coached herself, laying her last five on the table.

Gavin looked up just before dropping the ball into play. "No mercy, this time."

"Right. No mercy," Sara agreed, concentrating as she bent over the table. She laughed with glee as she soundly beat him a second time, then triumphantly picked up the money and shoved it into the pocket of her jeans.

"You little imp," Gavin said, catching on. "I'll just have to teach you a lesson!" Playfully, he charged around the table, but she scampered away. He gave chase as Sara dashed around a second foosball table, then a ping-pong table, and nearly ran in front of two men throwing darts. Gavin caught up with her just as she sprinted out the door to the parking lot. Laughing, he wrapped her in a tight embrace and turned her around to face him. "That was cheating."

Sara giggled. "I did not cheat. I won your money fair and square."

"For someone that doesn't believe in gambling that was pretty tricky."

"So sue me!"

"Sue you? I'd rather kiss you." Gavin planted his lips on hers in a long, penetrating kiss. Sara's knees turned to jelly and she had to rely on the strength of Gavin's arms to hold herself up. When their lips parted, Sara's face was flushed and Gavin was breathing heavily.

"I—uh—" Sara stuttered.

"You ready to go? Let's rent a movie. The night's young."

Dazed from his kiss, Sara didn't say anything on the short drive to the video store, but after Gavin parked the car she turned to him. "You can't kiss me like that."

"Like what? A kiss is a kiss."

A kiss like that is a big deal. "It's just, well, there's still Jim. We haven't officially broken up yet."

"Look, Sara, from my standpoint, you're a free woman. I mean, you came home all upset and you're the one that called me last night, remember?"

"I know. I'm just confused, but at least for now, I am still his girlfriend."

"So show me some proof."

"Proof?"

"Yeah. All I see is a beautiful, spunky girl who's been left to spend her weekends alone. Fair game, in my book."

"I don't have any proof, but Jim transferred schools to be with me."

"Really? Then how come you're here and he's there?"

"Well, that was last year."

"Oh, *last* year. See, Sara, I just don't look at it the same way you do. Supposedly, Jim is in a relationship with you, but I've never seen him here, and every time you go there you come home disillusioned. Until you've got a ring on your finger or something substantial to prove that you're his girl, then I should be given a chance." Gavin eased as close to Sara as he could and said in a low voice, "How do you know you want him more than me? That guy, he's had—what did you tell me?—almost two years. You seem pretty unsure for a relationship that's been going on that long."

Sara had never been unsure of her feelings for Jim, only Jim's feelings for her. "I—uh—" She couldn't think with Gavin's intense dark eyes penetrating her. "I am unsure, I admit."

"So give me a chance, Sara. Without fighting it every step of the way. Just let it happen and see where we end up. That's all I'm asking for—just a chance. A fair chance. I mean, it's only fair to him, too. Maybe he's asking to be cut loose."

Unshed tears clogged Sara's throat. That's exactly what she had been fearing all along. "Maybe that's true, but don't I owe him something?"

"You already gave him two years, Sara. He obviously doesn't think he owes you anything, does he?"

"It doesn't seem that way."

"No, I'd say it doesn't."

The next morning Sara was digging through her suitcase for something to wear when her cell phone chirped. It was Katie checking in. Sara assured her that she was getting better and Katie could quit worrying about her. They chatted for just another minute, then Sara hung up and hurried to get ready so she wouldn't be late for the shopping trip with Allie.

Sara arrived at Allison and Gavin's apartment just as Gavin was scraping the frost off his car window. She walked over to say hello and he flecked small pieces of ice at her. "Is that the best you can do?" she teased.

Gavin grinned. "Well, I don't have time to start a snowball fight right now. Maybe when I get back."

Mandy's car slid to a jerky stop alongside the curb. She jumped out and, with barely a nod toward Gavin and Sara, disappeared into the apartment.

"Hey, Allie," she hollered. "What's she doing here? Your brother's not seriously dating her, is he?"

"Yes," Allie said, coming out of the bathroom. "And not only that, but she's coming along with us." At Mandy's scowl, she added, "It's a favor for Gavin. It'll be okay."

"She's not going to spoil our fun, is she?"

"No. In fact, I think we'll try to loosen her up. I think Gavin would appreciate it."

"I'm up for the challenge. Bring her on."

"Sara!" Allison called, opening the front door. "You ready?"

"Yes," she called.

"Have fun," Gavin said, climbing into his car. "Wait for me here when you're back, okay? I have friends coming over later and you might as well hang out with us too."

"Okay, I'll see you later."

The ride to the mall in Mandy's dented Toyota was harrowing. There was only an inch or two of snow, but it was slippery and Mandy tended to drive with a lead foot, screeching to a halt at several stoplights. Slamming on the brakes, she muttered, "I missed my turn. Allie, anything comin' your way?"

Before Allison could answer, Mandy pulled a U-turn. A delivery truck was just pulling out of the parking lot of a mini-mart and the driver had to slam on the brakes to avoid hitting Mandy's car.

Sara was squeezing the door handle so tightly her fingers were turning white. *Never, ever ride anywhere with Mandy again,* she kept repeating to herself. Clearing her throat, she said aloud, "What's the hurry, Mandy?"

"No hurry. You got a problem with my driving?"

"Frankly, yes."

Mandy glared at Allison. "And you want to be friends with her?"

Allison subtly poked Mandy in the side, then turned to face Sara in the backseat. "It's just that this whole weekend is a big shopping weekend and Mandy and I go every year and try to find some really special things."

"Well," Sara said, "things aren't going to sell out that fast. In fact, it's easier to find what you want when there aren't a dozen people all poring over the same sale table."

"That's a good point," Mandy spoke up, "when you're doing regular shopping, but Allie and me, well, this is our favorite time for picking stuff up we don't plan to pay for."

Allison reached over and gave Mandy a warning slap on the arm. Mandy took her eyes from the road and stared at her friend. "What? You said—"

"Shhh," Allison hissed to Mandy.

"You mean shoplift?" came Sara's amazed question from the backseat.

"You can call it what you want, and don't say you've never done it before."

"But I haven't."

Mandy shrugged and took a corner too fast. "Last year, the best pick I got was a fifty-dollar sweater."

Resigned to the fact that Mandy was going to tell all, Allison sighed. "That was on Boxing Day."

"Oh, right." Mandy looked in the rearview mirror at Sara. "The day after Christmas, when everyone is returning stuff. The clerks are frazzled; it's easy pickings."

Sara could not believe her ears. These two were pros. Regular shoplifters. "Haven't you ever been caught?"

"Never. It's a piece of cake. Look, we do make a couple of legitimate purchases. That way we have store bags, you know. Then, when there's a lot of people around a table it's pretty easy to toss something into your bag. Smaller stuff we put in our purses."

"But what about those alarm thingies they put on clothes?"

"They don't put those on everything," Allison explained. "Only some things. Mostly jeans. We never go for jeans."

Sara couldn't believer her ears. *I wonder if Gavin knows his sister is a thief.*

Mandy pulled into the parking lot of the mall and drove up and down the aisles until she found an open space. "Stick close, Sara. We'll show you how it's done."

"That's okay," Sara muttered following the other two. "I'll pay for my stuff."

For the next two hours, Allison and Mandy hauled Sara through several stores. Afraid of losing them in the swarm of shoppers, Sara kept her eyes on Allie's blond head, but remained a safe distance away. She wanted no part of her and Mandy's escapade and if they *were* caught, Sara did not intend to be guilty by association.

"We're going for coffee," Allison announced to Sara, pointing to Mandy, who was headed out of the department store. "Come on."

Over a small round table in the food court, the girls enjoyed hot coffee and cinnamon rolls. Mandy and Allison showed each other what they had gotten. Sara did not want to know which items they paid for and which they had stolen. She figured, the less she knew, the better.

Later, after a terrifying ride home with Mandy, Sara sat at Gavin's kitchen table with her schoolbooks spread out in front of her. Allison and Mandy had gone to a movie, but Sara had used her homework as an excuse to stay behind. One morning spent with those two was enough.

Sara spent an hour diligently studying before her cell phone rang. Fishing the phone from her purse, she noticed a small piece of cardboard tucked against her wallet. "Hello?" she answered distractedly, tugging out the cardboard. Her eyes grew big when she saw dangling silver earrings attached to it. She could hardly listen to Jim's questions about how she was feeling.

"Awful," she spouted, staring at the jewelry. *How did this get into my purse?* Jim was saying more, but Sara's mind could not take it in. She could only stare at the earrings in dismay. She was a shoplifter!

"Listen, Jim, it's been a lousy morning. I'm not up to talking." *Mandy. She must have put these in here, or maybe Allison. My bets are on Mandy. When? Where?* Sara turned the cardboard over. *Monique's*, it said. *$42.00.* She was going to be sick. "Jim, I've got to go, I think I'm going to vomit again." Sara clicked off her phone, tossed it onto the table and made a dash for the bathroom. Although her stomach churned and she could taste the bile in her throat, she did not throw up.

Sara paced the living room, the jewelry blatantly displayed on the kitchen table, where she had dropped it like a hot potato. *What should I do? I could try to subtly put it back, but if I'm caught they'll figure I'm stealing, not returning. How am I going to explain that it fell into my purse? If I rat on Mandy and Allison, I might be accused along with them.*

This was no funny joke. This was serious business. Forty-two dollars of serious jewelry. *I'll just lay them on Allison's dresser. She can deal with it.* Sara picked up the earrings and studied them. They were pretty. They glittered in the light. Mandy did have good taste, that was for sure. It wouldn't hurt to try them on.

Sara took off the earrings she was wearing—inexpensive little things— and replaced them with the silver earrings. She went to the bathroom and admired them in the mirror. They dangled to just the right length and were eye-catching. Sara tilted her head this way, then that way. *It's not like I took them and I don't actually know that they stole them. It's not the kind of thing you can ask. Say, thanks for the earrings. By the way, did you pay for them?*

Thou shalt not steal. The age-old commandment ran through her mind. A lifetime of Sunday school did little now to help the situation. *After all*, Sara reasoned, *I didn't steal them. I shouldn't be punished for something Mandy or Allison did.*

Ignoring the almost burning feeling in her ear lobes, she returned to her school project. She was laying out sample ideas for a proposed breakfast buffet for a hotel, taking a standard continental breakfast and expanding it to include waffles, oatmeal and hard-boiled eggs. At first, with the weight of the earrings dangling from her ears, it was difficult to concentrate, but this was an assignment that Sara enjoyed and before long she was sketching ideas on paper.

The front door opened and Sara looked up to see Gavin stamping loose snow from his feet. "Hey!" he greeted. "How was the shopping? Did you get anything?"

Sara's hand flew to finger one of the earrings. "No—no, I just window shopped."

Gavin nodded, glad that his sister was fulfilling her part of the bargain. "So you had fun?"

"Well…sure." She could hardly tell him that she had hated everything about the morning from the harrowing ride to the shoplifted earrings. She asked about him about work as she put her project away in her backpack.

Sara and Gavin spent the afternoon watching a movie. They were fixing grilled cheese sandwiches for dinner when Allie came home, Mandy trailing in behind her. The two were arguing about something.

Suddenly noticing Sara for the first time, Mandy stopped mid-sentence in her tirade and blurted out, "Nice earrings, Sara."

Sara blushed. She had completely forgotten she was still wearing them. "Ah… yes."

Mandy reached out and fingered one of them. "Very nice," she repeated, staring into Sara's eyes. "You have very fine taste."

"Yes, well…" Sara glanced from Mandy to Gavin to Allie. Allie was attempting to hide a smile. "I just—just came across them…"

Mandy snorted in laughter, high-fiving Allie, their argument apparently forgotten.

Gavin shook his head, took a cola from the fridge and, with his sandwich in the other hand, motioned Sara to follow him to the living room. Thankful to escape Allie and Mandy, Sara picked up her plate and hurriedly followed him.

"Such a baby," Mandy whispered to Allison. "What does your brother see in her?"

Allison shrugged. "I have no idea."

An hour later, Gavin's friends showed up. Moose carried a stack of DVDs and Robbie a case of beer. As soon as Scott came through the door, Mandy greeted him with a kiss and led him toward one of the couches. The last one through the door was a messy-haired blonde. His eyes rested on Sara, who was standing beside the kitchen table. He whistled, then took a step toward her.

"And who is this?"

"That's Sara. Sara, meet KC. You remember Moose, Robbie and Scott from the races, don't you?"

"Yes."

KC looked her over from head to toe. "Hey, Gav, is she just part of the group in general or is she with you?"

Gavin placed an arm possessively around her shoulders. "She's with me. You can find your own girl."

"Figures," KC muttered.

Sara shivered involuntarily. She did not appreciate KC's open stares or Gavin's possessive squeeze of her shoulders. Technically, she wasn't his girl, but she'd let everyone think so if it kept KC away from her.

Nearly three hours later, Sara sat against the armrest of one of the love seats, Gavin on her other side with one arm resting loosely around her shoulders. She was not enjoying herself. The movie they were watching was rated R and filled with sex and bad language. No one else seemed to mind, but it made her uncomfortable. And not only that, the others had consumed several beers. KC and Robbie frequently told absolutely lurid jokes—which the others all found excessively funny. But the worst thing—as if anything could be worse—was Gavin. He was practically ignoring her and acting foolish with his buddies—showing off and telling his own share of off-color jokes.

She scooted out from under his arm and went to the kitchen for a cola, wondering if Gavin was always like this around his friends or just tonight. Closing the refrigerator door, she turned and almost bumped into KC, who had come up directly behind her. Sara backed up until she was standing against the door of the fridge.

"So," he drawled, "where did Gavin pick you up?"

Sara bristled. She had hardly been *picked up*. Stepping away from him, she said, "I've known Gavin and Allison since high school."

Matching her sidestep, he said, "So where've you been all this time?"

Sara glanced to where Gavin sat, hoping he'd see that KC was practically stalking her and come to the rescue. His eyes were glued to the movie, however, and he didn't notice. "I've been away. I just met up with Gavin again a couple of months ago."

"Funny, he hasn't said anything," KC murmured.

"Move aside, KC," Allison warned, coming into the kitchen and elbowing him. Not that she really cared if Sara was with KC or Gavin or any one of these other guys, but there was the matter of the two hundred bucks. "Sara is much too nice for the likes of you."

Keeping her somewhat trapped, KC opened the fridge and pulled out a beer. "When you've had enough of Gavin," he said gutturally, "I'll be here for ya. I can show you a real good time. Just ask Allie." And with that, he was gone. Back to the living room, where he sat on the floor to finish watching the movie.

Sara turned to Allison. "Ask you? Don't tell me you dated that guy."

"Yeah, it took me a couple of months to realize what a loser he is."

"And you still hang out with him? Isn't that awkward?"

"He's Moose's cousin. They're all friends with Gavin. What can I do about it?"

"I don't know." Sara shivered. "But he gives me the creeps. Thanks for rescuing me."

Twenty minutes later the movie credits ran. Sara glanced at her watch. It was only nine thirty. She had a feeling the others would probably stay for a while, but she really wanted to leave. She could probably go home to Morgan's without upsetting things too much.

"Oh!" Suddenly her hand flew to her mouth. She had totally forgotten about checking out of her motel.

"What?" Gavin looked at her and squeezed her shoulders. "Something wrong?"

"No—well, yes," she lowered her voice, not wanting the others to hear. "I meant to check out this afternoon and go home tonight."

"You can't go home," Gavin said, not wanting to lose her to the real world yet. "I mean, I don't think you're ready for that. Big sister and normalcy and all that goes with it. I think you need another night away and another day with me to help your heart finish healing." The look he gave her—the passion in those dark eyes—made her forget that she had spent the last three hours wondering about his character. "I mean, I have plans for us to spend the day together tomorrow."

"You do?"

"Yes. I think it's only fair to show you that there's a big world out there and you really don't need what's-his-name anymore."

When Gavin turned his full attention on her, she could lose herself in his dark eyes. "And you think I need you?"

"Don't you think so?" He was close enough to kiss her. Fleetingly, she wished he would.

"I'm not sure what I think," she finally confessed. "It's very confusing. Not just thinking about Jim, but being around you."

Robbie loaded a game into the Xbox. Moose grabbed one of the controls and dropped onto the floor, landing on one of Gavin's feet. Gavin pushed him off, knowing the mood with Sara had just been broken.

She rose to her feet. "Well, I think I'll go. Thanks for the—uh—nice time."

"I'll walk you out."

"Nice seeing you all," Sara said politely as she tugged on her coat and retrieved her purse and backpack from the corner by the front door. Gavin pulled on his own jacket and followed Sara outside.

"So, what are you going to do?"

"I guess I'll stay in the motel yet tonight and check out in the morning," she answered, tossing her bags across to the passenger seat.

"Come by here after you check out. We'll make a day of it. Just not too early, I want to sleep in. Say…eleven."

"Eleven…" Sara's voice trailed off.

"Too early? Too late? What?"

"I was wondering about church."

"Church?"

"Yes, it's Sunday tomorrow, did you forget?"

"No, I did not forget."

"Well, you do go to church, don't you?"

"Of course. I'm not a heathen, but I just went on Thanksgiving."

"Don't you go every week?"

Gavin shook his head. *What a waste of time that would be.* Aloud he explained, "I go on holidays. I don't see the point of going more often than that, but you can go if you want to."

"No," Sara said slowly. "I could hardly show up at Morgan's church, so…if you're not going, then I won't go either."

"I'm definitely not going."

"All right then."

Gavin wondered if he should give her a good night kiss. "It's been an awesome couple of days, Sara. I'm looking forward to tomorrow."

"Are you?" She cast him a smile, her eyes looking deeply into his.

Is this the flirty Sara speaking or the insecure Sara? Gavin briefly wondered. He had no idea, he only knew that Sara was a girl of many moods. In answer, Gavin lowered his lips to hers.

Sara accepted his kiss, then whispered good night, climbed into her car and drove away, her heart beating a thousand pulses a minute.

CHAPTER 13

Whatever is noble, whatever is right, whatever is pure, whatever is lovely, whatever is admirable—if anything is excellent or praiseworthy—think about such things.
—Philippians 4:8

The next morning Sara pulled her coat over her pajamas and headed down to the hotel lobby to get some coffee. Watching the dark liquid accumulate in her Styrofoam cup, she thought how strange it was not to be getting ready for church.

For it is time to seek the Lord... A phrase from one of the Bible verses Morgan had taped to her refrigerator door ran across Sara's mind.

I know, Lord, but one missed Sunday is not going to hurt.

...Seek first the counsel of the Lord

All right! I get the message. Drat Morgan and those verses. Her sister replaced the verses every couple of months, figuring it was a good way to memorize Scripture. *It's working,* Sara mused ironically, *and I'm not even trying to learn them.*

Carefully carrying her full cup of coffee, Sara made her way back to her room and sat on the only chair. She was no longer thinking about missing church. Instead, her thoughts wandered to Jim. She knew she should call him even though she had absolutely no idea what to say. Obviously, they couldn't stay in this "beginning of the end stage" forever, but no matter how he had treated her, it was hard to think of actually breaking up with him. There was a lot of sweetness tied up in her thoughts of Jim, a lot of good memories… Despite Gavin and his persistent interest, Sara's longing for Jim went deep. After all, he had been her Prince Charming for almost two years. Two years!

If Jim walked in here at this very moment with an engagement ring and asked me to marry him, I'd say yes, wouldn't I? Wouldn't I? You know you would, Sara Brooks, you know you want that more than anything. But Jim is not going to ride up on a white horse and ask you to marry him. It's time you stop dreaming fairy-tale dreams.

Sara sipped her coffee. *Oh, Jimmy, if you really want to break up, why don't you just get it over with? I can't live this way much longer.* She sighed, regretting that real life is nothing like books. *In a romance novel, I would be engaged already.* Of course, in most books the hero and the heroine don't even like each other in the beginning. The couple that ends up falling passionately in love starts out in conflict, often despising each other—like in *Pride and Prejudice*—but with both Jim and Gavin, sparks had flown immediately. *Hmm…if I was going to end up passionately in love with someone I detest, it would be KC. Ugh!* Despite her aching heart, Sara laughed aloud at the idea of eventually falling in love with KC. The thought was absolutely absurd!

Sara's cell phone started chirping. With a smile still on her face, Sara dug her phone from her purse.

"Where are you?" Morgan's tone was a mixture between anger and worry.

"I—uh—"

"And don't tell me you're at Jim's or Katie's, because Jim called here asking for you."

"Jim called there? What did you say?"

"I didn't talk to him. Mark's mother answered the phone. Now Sara, where are you?"

"I'm at—uh—" Morgan would never understand this. Never. "I'm at Allison's."

"Allison? Who is that?"

"A girl I knew back in high school. We met up a few weeks ago."

"Sara, I'm very confused. I thought you were staying in Minneapolis until today."

"I was, but I got sick."

"Oh, Sara. I hardly know which question to ask first. If you got sick, why didn't you come home?"

"I couldn't come home, not with Mark's parents there. It's no big deal. I'm a big girl, Morgan. You don't need to worry so much."

"I don't understand this at all. Did it ever occur to you to let somebody know where you are?" Before Sara could answer, Morgan was talking again. "Are you coming home soon?"

"Yes, Morgan, this evening—just like I planned all along."

"Good, because Mark leaves in the morning for a four-day trip. Are you better? Are you up to helping with the kids?"

"Yes, Morgan. Thanks for asking." This last part came out sarcastically, as Sara realized it had taken Morgan the entire conversation to find out how she was feeling. "I had the flu, but I'm over it now."

"Okay." Morgan sighed. "Don't ever do something like this again and you had better call Jim. He's worried about you. Didn't you bother to tell him you were staying at Allison's?"

"Yes, Morgan. I'll call him. Goodbye, I'll see you tonight." Sara clicked off the phone, realizing something had gone wrong with her plan if Jim had been trying to reach her at home. She pressed the button to retrieve her messages and missed calls. There were two from Jim—both from yesterday evening. She must not have heard her phone with all the people at Gavin's apartment. She should have kept her purse right beside her instead of in the corner with her backpack.

Oh well, there was nothing she could do about it now. Sara resolutely dialed Jim's number, not knowing what she would say, only that the call must be made.

"Hello?"

"It's me."

"Sara, finally. I was just about to call you again. Where were you last night?"

Sara felt the armor going up around her heart. Jim hadn't even said that it was great to hear her voice; he hadn't said he missed her; he hadn't even asked how she was feeling. Just a demanding "where were you?"

"I'm sorry, Jim. I was watching a movie and didn't hear my phone."

"I called the house. You weren't there. Did you go out or something?" Jim hated the demanding tone he heard in his own voice. He was just so frustrated over this whole Sara thing.

"I was feeling a little better and tired of being housebound so I went over to Allison's for a while."

"Allison? I don't think you've ever mentioned her before. Man, Sara, didn't you even check your messages? Didn't you figure I'd be calling? And if you were feeling well enough to go out, then why didn't you call me?"

"I did call you," Sara lied. "It was busy for the longest time."

"Busy? Who would be on the phone?"

"Maybe Andy and Greta?"

"She's here, remember? We were all home last night. Andy and Greta, Wayne and Katie, we were all here. Nobody was on the phone."

"Oh." *Oops.* Sara had forgotten about Greta being there. About all their friends being there for the holiday. It felt like a lifetime ago that she had gotten ill and left. It felt like she had traveled to an entirely different planet in the past couple of days. *If I'm going to lie, I'm going to have to be more careful.* "I must have called the wrong number."

"More than once?"

"Well, I just kept hitting redial." It was simple to tell a second lie, after telling the first.

Aggravated, Jim paced from the kitchen to the living room window and back. "You could have tried harder."

Angry and hurt, Sara's eyes filled with tears. He had better not blame her for this state of affairs. It was all his doing. "Jim Hoffman! What about you? How many times did you try to call me?"

Jim drew in a deep, calming breath. Why were they fighting? Why were they in this stupid situation in the first place? He missed her so much. Their weekend had been ruined, now they were fighting, and he wouldn't see her again until Christmas. "Sara, please, let's not fight."

"What do you want then, Jim?" *Say it,* she silently dared him. *Just tell me that you want to break up.*

"I don't know, but it's such a long time until Christmas."

They had been making their plans for months. They were going to spend part of Christmas break at each other's parents' homes. They had even planned a ski outing with Jim's brother, Jason. Sara had no idea what was going to happen now, but their plans seemed meaningless. She could not keep pretending that she didn't know where his heart stood. She should just tell him so. One of them had to say something! It was no use acting as if everything was fine. But when she opened her mouth to confront him, she couldn't get the words out. Instead with a sob, she said, "I've got to go. I'm babysitting and Nicholas is screaming."

Before he could say another word, she hung up. Before he could say *anything* he had truly wanted to say. Like how much he loved her and missed her and how he was hoping to get an internship near her next year.

Dazed, Sara dropped the phone onto the table. She could hardly swallow past the lump in her throat. *I lied to Jim. I can't believe I spent that entire conversation lying to Jim. What's happening to me?*

Her phone chirped again. Assuming it was Jim calling back, Sara snatched it up, an apology on her lips.

"It's ten thirty, are you up?" It was Gavin's happy-go-lucky drawl on the line.

"W-what?"

"I thought I'd better make sure you were up. After all the progress you've made, we can't have you backsliding and staying in bed all day."

"Oh, Gavin. Yes. I'm, um, up. I'm a little distracted. I just got off the phone with Jim and I told him bold-faced lies."

Gavin sighed. "What's the big deal? Everybody does that. He's probably lied to you on more than one occasion."

Jim? Lie? Impossible. "I don't think so…"

"I don't know why you do this to yourself."

"What?"

"Call him, talk to him. Seriously, every time you see or talk to him you are so messed up afterward. Why don't you do yourself a favor and break up with him?"

"I—um—" *Because I love him!* That's what Sara wanted to say, but, of course, what did that matter anymore?

"Shake it off, Sara. Forget about him; today is about you and me, remember? Sara Brooks, Gavin Manes, a little snowfall, a little ride in my car, music, laughter… Now, are you coming over?"

Sara sighed. Gavin was right. There would be time to figure the Jim thing out later. When *he* was ready to be honest with *her*. "Yes, I'll be there soon."

When Sara arrived at his apartment, Gavin met her at the door, travel mugs in hand. "We're out of coffee," he explained, leading her to his car. "That'll be our first stop. 7-Eleven."

At the corner market, they filled the mugs with coffee and Gavin tossed a small packet of donuts onto the counter. "Do you have some cash?" he asked Sara. "Otherwise I'm going to have to use plastic."

"A little." Sara pulled out her wallet. She knew she still had those fives from the foosball game, plus a twenty. She'd been careful with her money all weekend. She drew out a five and handed it to the clerk. "That's funny," she said, distractedly putting her hand out for the change.

"What?" Gavin picked up his cup and donuts.

Sara turned away from the clerk and said, "I was positive I had a twenty in here with those fives, but it's gone."

"You probably spent it." He ushered her outside and took a swig of his coffee.

"I'm sure I didn't. I'm sure I had it yesterday."

Climbing into the car, he took another drink, then set his cup down and restarted the engine. "So what are you saying? That one of my friends took it out of your wallet last night?"

"I don't know. That's a possibility."

"My friends aren't pickpockets, Sara."

Just shoplifters, she thought. "I don't know, maybe I spent it." She knew she hadn't, but she couldn't prove anything. It was disconcerting to say the least, but not worth making a big deal out of. She didn't want to anger Gavin or alienate his friends.

Gavin locked eyes with her. "Let's not argue. I just want us to hit the road and have a fun day."

Sara sighed and dropped her purse onto the floor by her feet. There would be no way to figure out what happened to the money. She might as well relax and enjoy her day. "Hit the road, huh?" she asked with a smile. "And what do you have planned?"

"Just a little day trip and a winter picnic."

"It sounds fun," Sara said, thinking that Gavin always knew how to enjoy himself.

Gavin drove south until they reached the town of Racine. "We might as well buy lunch here," he explained, pulling into the parking lot of a supermarket.

They ordered sub sandwiches at the deli, picked up a bag of chips, a package of cookies and drinks. Gavin added a package of gum and paid for the groceries with his debit card. On the way out, they passed a display of apples. Gavin picked one up and continued walking out the door of the supermarket. He tossed the apple into the air before sinking his teeth into it.

"Aren't you going to pay for that?" Sara asked, keeping pace with him as he took another bite.

"It's just one apple," he said, stowing the groceries in the back seat. "And not a very good one at that," he added, hurling the remains into the shrubbery.

"It doesn't matter. You still need to pay for it."

He reached into the grocery sack and pulled out the pack of gum. "Look, Sara, if they didn't expect people to snatch a few, they wouldn't put them right by the exit."

Sara sighed. Evidently he and his sister were cut from the same cloth after all.

"You coming?" Gavin opened his car door.

Sara glanced back toward the supermarket. *I should go in and offer to pay for an apple, but then, they weigh them and anyway, I don't want to get Gavin in trouble.* "Yes," she said, climbing into the passenger side of the car.

She accepted the stick of gum he offered, then looked around for a place to put the wrapper.

He chuckled and held out his hand. "Give it here." She laid the paper in his palm and he chucked it overhead to the backseat. "Are you always so perfect? Don't you ever push the limits?"

"I was raised with high standards. It's ingrained behavior."

"It's a rigid way to live," Gavin commented as he pulled onto the street. "The world is not going to fall apart if you snitch an apple or don't put garbage in a trash can."

"That kind of stuff makes me feel guilty."

Pulling up to a stop sign, he stared at her. "Guilty? For that stuff? You are in a bad way."

Sara raised her shoulders and cast him an innocent smile. "You think I'm terribly old-fashioned, don't you?"

"Sort of, but it's nothing we can't fix."

That same afternoon, Jim sat moodily on the couch in his apartment. After the holiday weekend, life was slowly returning to normal. Except it did not feel normal to Jim. Nothing felt right. He rose, went to the kitchen and picked up the phone. He dialed Sara's cell number and listened to it ring three times before it transferred to her voice mail. Wearily, he hung up without leaving a message.

Exploring an antique store in the middle of a small tourist town near Lake Michigan, Gavin and Sara heard the chirping of her phone. In a steady voice, Gavin said, "Don't answer it."

The ringing of an unanswered phone always unnerved Sara, but she reached for her handset and turned it off. Gavin was right. She did not want any calls from Morgan or Jim or even Katie this afternoon. She was trying to forget for a while.

They were standing toward the back of the store in a grouping of old signs, lanterns and rusted hand pumps. Pleased that she had not answered her phone, Gavin placed an arm around Sara's waist and drew her close.

"Can I kiss you again?" He had never asked permission to kiss a girl before, but he was doing a lot of things differently this time. He'd scared Sara off too many times, he wasn't about to do it again. "You're irresistible," he added, bringing his face closer.

His flattery made Sara's heart beat stronger and her body feel all tingly. Without giving it much thought, she lifted her face and, closing her eyes, let him kiss her. His kiss was slow and deliberate and when he pulled away, Sara swayed for just a moment, trying to regain her equilibrium.

"You're the best," he whispered.

She opened her eyes and found him looking intently into her face. "You're...um..."

"Dazzling you?" he grinned.

"Yes."

They stood there a moment longer looking at each other. Then, attempting to calm her pounding heart, Sara stepped away and poked around among the signage.

"We should get something," she suggested. "To remember our weekend by."

Gavin's dark eyes flashed and he grinned. "I'm not likely to forget."

"Me either, but you know what I mean."

Gavin joined her, sifting through the stack looking for the unusual. "How about this?" Gavin held up an old rectangular sign. The metal was slightly dented and the white background had darkened with age, but the black lettering was still clearly legible. *Lovers' Lane.*

"Perfect!" Sara exclaimed in delight. They headed to the cash register where Gavin paid for the purchase with his credit card.

The clerk, a woman in her fifties, had seen the way Gavin kissed Sara. Smiling at them as she handed Gavin the receipt to sign, she said, "This old sign is just the thing for you two. You seem very much in love."

Love? Sara blushed, knowing it was too soon to think about Gavin and love in the same sentence.

Love! Hardly, Lady! You know the saying: Keep it easy. Gavin shoved his wallet into his back pocket. Watching the clerk wrap the sign in newspaper, he turned on his movie-star charm. "When a guy has a beautiful girl, what's he supposed to do?"

The woman's eyes flew up briefly, then she bent over her work again. "In my day, I knew all about young love, too. My husband's been gone for five years though."

"Sorry," Sara murmured.

"Yes, well…" The clerk put the wrapped sign into a large bag and handed it to Gavin with a wistful smile. "You two have a nice day, now."

"We will." Gavin said, draping an arm around Sara and leading her outside.

Jim could not stay in his apartment any longer. The four walls were crowding in on him. Senior year was not going the way he had envisioned; he was spending far too much time alone. He had known it would be difficult with Sara gone, but he hadn't bargained for this—weekend visits that constantly went awry and unsatisfactory phone calls. Deciding to head over to Wayne and Katie's, he grabbed his winter coat and hustled down to his car. Anything would be better than staring at his four walls.

When Jim arrived, Wayne and Katie were just returning from a walk. Their cheeks were rosy and they looked undeniably happy.

"Hey, bud," Wayne greeted as Jim climbed out of his car. "What's up?"

Jim shrugged. "I thought you might have the game on."

"I can put it on."

Jim fell in step with Katie. "You don't mind, do you?"

"Of course not. We love having you here."

Half an hour later, Katie rose from the rocking chair. She did not understand football and did not really care to. "I think I'll just leave you boys to watch your game. I'll go bake some cookies."

"Double chocolate chip, okay?" Wayne requested.

"Now come on," Jim argued, "how about my favorite, peanut butter? I mean, how often am I here for fresh cookies?"

Katie looked at the pair sitting on the couch and laughed. "All right. I have nothing else to do—I'll make both kinds." She disappeared into the kitchen, where she remained for the next hour, humming and baking. She figured she could send several fresh cookies home with Jim and still have plenty left for her and Wayne. After she placed the last pan in the oven, she set the coffee, and filled the sink with soapy dishwater.

Jim and Wayne had watched the game in relative silence for the better part of the hour, but as sounds increased in the kitchen as Katie began to clean up, Jim cleared his throat and said in a voice that would not carry to the other room, "Something weird is going on with Sara."

"How so?" Wayne asked.

"I don't know. I can't explain it and I don't know what it is, but something is different. Have you noticed anything?"

"I don't exactly see much of her, but Jim, Sara's always been—uh, would *emotional* be a good description?"

"Yeah, I know." The guys were silent for a few moments, then Jim continued, "It's just odd. We have these fabulous times together, like Wednesday night, and then she goes all crazy on me."

"She couldn't help getting sick the other day."

"No…" Jim sounded doubtful.

"What? You don't think she was sick?"

"I don't know. Man, I just don't know what to think. She hardly talks to me on the phone anymore."

Wayne raised his eyebrows. *Sara, not talk? Something is strange there.* Aloud he said, "So, how long has she been acting weird?"

"A couple of weeks—no, a month, maybe longer. Does Katie know anything?"

"I don't think so, although she has been worried about Sara."

Several more minutes of silence followed. The buzzer rang in the kitchen and Katie got the pan out of the oven. Reluctantly, Wayne asked the question that obviously needed to be asked, "Do you think she's seeing someone else?"

Jim's heart froze. He had not yet faced this question and did not like thinking about it. "Do you?"

Wayne rubbed a hand down his thigh and considered the issue at hand. He was not going to spout off lame assurances without evaluating the situation. "Naw," he finally concluded. "Sara is crazy about you. I mean, you two are practically engaged. Katie's always talking about when you and Sara get married."

"Yeah, but I don't get it. We'll have these fantastic times and the next thing I know, she's shutting me out."

"It's probably just your imagination. You know, being separated and all, but I think you should talk to her. If I had something weird like that going on with Katie, I'd just ask her what was up."

"It's kinda hard when I can't even get her to answer the phone. The last time we talked, we had some stupid fight or something, I don't know."

Katie chose that moment to enter the living room with a tray of fresh cookies and drinks. "Ta-da! The moment you've been waiting for!"

"It's about time. We've been drooling over the smell forever," Jim said, putting on a false cheerfulness. "It's enough to drive a man insane."

Wayne took the hint: there was to be no discussing this in front of Katie. He reached for a mug and two of the chocolate cookies, more thankful than ever that he was happily married.

CHAPTER 14

Whether you turn to the right or to the left, your ears will hear a voice behind you saying, "This is the way; walk in it."
—Isaiah 30:21

Tuesday, after her college classes were over, Sara debated whether or not to stop by the club to see Gavin. It was not an aerobics day and he hadn't asked her to, but it stood to reason that they should see each other. After all, they'd spent the entire weekend together. Yesterday, stopping for her customary glass of juice, didn't seem like enough. Would it be too forward if she went to see him?

Before she could make up her mind, her cell phone chirped. It was Morgan asking Sara if she could come right home to take care of Courtney and Nicholas. Apparently, Tucker had been fussing all day and Morgan thought he might have an ear infection. She had an appointment with the pediatrician and would prefer to leave the other two home. "Nicky just went down for a nap," she went on to explain. "I hate to wake him."

That settles it. Sara assured her sister that she was on her way. *It's just as well,* she thought as she pulled into the lane of traffic. Sara knew she wasn't being fair to Jim. They had not officially broken up yet and seeing another guy—even just a casual friend—was not something she should be doing. *A casual friend? Come on, Sara. Casual, platonic friends do not kiss like you let Gavin kiss you.* A butterfly twirled in Sara's stomach at the memories of Gavin's intense kisses. *Imagine! A boy like that falling for an ordinary girl like me!*

And what about Jim, Sara Brooks? Ah...Jimmy. He was backing away—slowly, moving away from her. She had no control over that, but she knew she shouldn't spend so much time with Gavin until Jim came right out and told her that it was over.

Later that afternoon, Sara sat in front of her computer trying to compose an e-mail to Jim, but there were too many things that she couldn't talk about. She could hardly tell him about her shopping trip with Allison and Mandy when she was supposed to have been home sick. And she couldn't in a million years tell him about spending so much time with Gavin over the weekend.

Oh Jim! Sara buried her head in her hands. *What's happening to us? I can't even e-mail you anymore...*

With tears in her eyes, Sara typed a couple of feeble sentences about school, lamely asked about Andy and Greta's mission plans and then pathetically said she had nothing else to say and signed off.

Before going to bed, Jim checked his e-mail. When his INBOX informed him that there was one from Sara, his eyes lit up and he pulled out his desk chair. Anticipating a much needed letter from Sara, he sat down and clicked the envelope icon. It only took a minute to peruse her few halfhearted sentences. Jim's heart fell. Something was wrong. This short, cold e-mail was so unlike Sara. Where was the drama? The humor? The detailed stories? The passion? Didn't Sara feel passionate anymore? What was wrong with her? With them? Jim closed his eyes momentarily. He couldn't bear to think about it. What if Sara...

"I'll call her," he stated aloud, needing to hear her voice, to convince himself that Sara was still Sara, still *his* Sara. "It's the illness," he said, heading to the kitchen for the phone. "It just tired her out is all."

Propped against her pillows, Sara sat in bed reading—for the third time—*Pride and Prejudice* by Jane Austin. She chuckled, remembering the thought from the other morning about how Elizabeth and Mr. Darcy despised each other before they fell in love and how she felt about KC. She was still chuckling when her cell phone chirped. Scrambling from bed, she grabbed her phone from the dresser. "Yes?" she said.

"You sound happy."

"Jim!" Sara's voice caught in her throat.

"I'm glad you sound happy. I got your e-mail and well…I thought maybe you're not okay."

Her e-mail. Her pathetic, uninspired e-mail. "Why wouldn't I be okay?"

"I don't know. The illness…?"

"I've recovered." She couldn't stop the edge in her tone. Was he accusing her of something?

"Good. So, you're really okay? You're…um…you are happy, aren't you, Sara?"

"I guess so. I was just reading *Pride and Prejudice*. I was thinking about…about how Elizabeth Bennett and Darcy don't like each other at first…and…"

As Sara's voice died away, Jim perched on the kitchen counter. "I just want you to be happy."

Sara drew in a deep breath. "Honestly, it's kind of hard right now, Jim, when you're…you're…" She couldn't say it. She couldn't admit that she knew how he felt.

"So far away. Yeah, I know."

"It's not just the miles separating us, Jim. Don't you have something else to tell me?" *If only he would say it. Just get the inevitable over so my heart can finish bleeding.*

"I don't know. I'll admit, there is something different." *Different with you. What's going on?* He didn't dare ask…not over the phone. This would require a face-to-face conversation.

"Different?" Sara squeezed her eyes closed. "Yes, Jim, I know. There is something different." *Oh, Jimmy, can't you love me?*

"So you feel it, too?"

"Jim." Sara's voice croaked with longing.

"Sara. We need to talk, but not over the phone."

Here it comes, she thought. People only said they needed to talk before they dropped a bombshell.

"Sara? Are you still there?"

She nodded, then whispered, "Yes." This was it then. This was no longer the beginning of the end, it was the end. They would tiptoe through the remaining weeks until Christmas, making surface talk and obligatory e-mails, but they both knew. This was it. Twenty-two months snuffed out like a candle flame.

"Sara! Say something."

"All right, Jim." Sara could not believe the calmness in her voice. Maybe it was because knowing was better than not knowing. He as much as admitted that his feelings had changed. "We'll talk this all out during Christmas break."

Jim was beginning to panic. Why did her words sound so final? "I don't think we should wait that long. I'll try to get away. I'll see what I can do."

"Fine, Jim." Despite her calm façade, Sara was beginning to tremble. She wanted to tell him that she loved him more than anything and that he was the boy she had always been looking for—her Prince Charming—but that would not make things easier. Besides, he was right, this was a conversation that needed to be conducted in person.

"Sara…" He wanted to tell her how much he loved her and couldn't live without her, but saying it over the phone didn't carry enough weight. He would tell her in person, and soon! He would not wait until break, he'd get there sooner than that. He was beginning to realize that this separation was unraveling their relationship and their future depended on them being together soon. "I'll come see you."

She could not listen anymore. Her heart was truly torn in half. No, quarters. No, it was shredding into slivers. She had lost him. She didn't know how or why, maybe she had never really had one hundred percent of his heart, but now she was left with painful splinters. "Goodbye, Jim."

The next day, Jim sat at the kitchen table, the phone to his ear, waiting for someone on the other end to answer.

"Hello?" A singsong voice greeted after the fourth ring.

"Is Colleen there?"

"Speaking."

"Colleen? It's Jim—you know from work."

"Oh! Hi Jim. What's up?"

"I was hoping you could work my three-to-six shift Friday. I'm trying to get out to Milwaukee to see my girl this weekend. I've got Saturday covered, but you're my last hope for Friday."

"I'd love to help you out, Jim—really, that is *so* romantic—but I have a class until four."

"Shoot." Jim sighed. "Well—"

"Wait! I could come straight from class so you could get off early. Would that help?"

"Yes. That'd put me in a little after nine, which would be great. You sure?"

"For romance, yes!" Colleen gushed. "You have a very lucky girl. Sometimes on Friday, Professor Bakker lets us out early; I'll come as soon as I can."

"Thanks, I owe you." Jim clicked off the receiver just as Andy entered the apartment carrying the mail. He strolled over to the table, flipping through the few envelopes, then tossed the lot on the table. Jim glanced at them, but did not bother to shuffle through them. He had not received regular mail from Sara in at least three weeks. "Well," he announced, "I've got it all arranged so I can go see Sara and get things sorted out."

"What things?" Andy asked, opening the fridge for a soda.

Jim sighed, removed his glasses and rubbed the bridge of his nose. "I don't know. Sara and I have hit a rough patch."

Andy took a seat opposite Jim. "I didn't know you and Sara were having problems."

"Things have just been strained lately. When you were a freshman, did you and Greta have trouble with your relationship? You know, being apart and all."

Andy thought back to when he had left Iowa and the girl he had loved for as long as he could remember. It *had* been hard at first. "We had more fights that first semester than we'd had in all the years before or since. Then after that first Christmas we got into a rhythm of how often to visit and when to call and…" Andy shrugged. "I don't know. We just worked it out. We both knew that at the end of college, we'd be getting married."

Jim nodded. Maybe it was typical for a separated couple to go through some growing pains. "That's it then. This lousy separation."

"Probably. I wouldn't worry too much about it," Andy said, heading to the bedroom.

Jim fingered the edges of the envelopes laying on the table. He had never been one to be envious of others, but right now, he was a little jealous that Andy and Greta had their future settled. Even though they were facing an unknown world in Kenya, they knew where they were going and they were going together.

Wednesday afternoon, Sara sat sipping juice uncertainly. It was nearly four o'clock. Her customary time to go home. Surely Gavin would say something about wanting to see her outside of the club. Hadn't he had a good time last weekend? He had seemed like it, but maybe he had already grown tired of her *rigid living*, as he called it.

Gavin handed a regular customer a Melon Medley in exchange for three dollars. Holding the bills in his hand, he turned and leaned against the counter to watch Sara. He could almost see the wheels turning in her head. She was trying not to be obvious, but he was pretty sure she was pining for another date. Good, that was right where he wanted her. It had taken a little cunning on his part, to play it cool and let her stew in her own mixed-up emotions for a while. He was convinced that things had cooled considerably between her and Jim, but Gavin didn't want to scare her off by coming on too fast. No, he had learned over the years to give a girl just enough to make her want you, then back off until she was practically crazy to see you again.

She looked over at him with a tentative smile. He winked at her, then sauntered over to deposit the bills into the cash register. "I've missed you, Sara," he said under his breath.

She almost didn't hear him. "You have?" Her reply was breathless.

"I've been so busy with stuff, you know."

No, she didn't know. She knew so little about him. "Me too."

"Want to go out Friday? To the movies?"

Don't sound desperate, she coached herself. "I'd love to. What do you want to see?"

"How about *Sub Hunters?*"

"Oh," she sighed in disappointment.

He laughed. "All right, what do you want to see?"

"I think that one with Leslie Donnelly looks good."

"It's a chick flick."

"Well, what else is playing?"

"How about a double feature? There's a paper on the lobby table. Go check out the times for Friday night."

Sara slipped off her stool. Carrying her glass of yellow juice, she joined a man who was reading the business section at the round table. "May I?" she asked, reaching for the rest of the paper. Sara rifled through the pages until she found the movie section. Once she had the information she needed she waited patiently until Gavin finished fixing drinks for two other club members. While he wiped his hands on a towel she told him that they could see his movie at six forty, then hers at nine ten.

"That'll work. Do you want to meet at my place or at the theater?"

"Why don't you pick me up at my house?"

"Your house?" Gavin raised his eyebrows. "You told your sister about me?"

"No, but she and Mark will be gone with the kids to a birthday party."

156

"Sounds good. I'll pick you up at five thirty. We can grab a burger on the way to the theater."

Sara slipped off her stool and pulled on her jacket. "I'll be looking forward to it."

He crossed his arms over his chest and grinned. "Yeah, me too."

Friday evening, Sara and Gavin stood in line at the movie theater. "Two for *Sub Hunters*," Gavin told the clerk, handing over his credit card.

"What about the other one?" Sara asked quietly.

"We can get those tickets later. How about some popcorn?" They decided to share a cola and popcorn. Sara offered to pay and Gavin willingly let her. Carrying the popcorn, he strode purposefully down the hallway, then entered the darkened theater. The previews were already playing, but the theater was barely half full and, to Gavin's delight, the back row was nearly empty. There were only three teenage boys in it and they were sitting on the far end. Sara began walking slowly down the aisle toward the front, but Gavin grabbed her with his free hand and gently pulled her back. "Down here," he whispered, gesturing to the back row.

She went in to the fourth seat and sat down, then set the glass of cola in a cup holder and slid off her coat. "So, you like the back row, huh? I've always been a middle-of-the-theater girl myself."

Gavin cleared his throat and made a big show of placing an arm around her shoulders. "I have perfectly good reasons for choosing the back row and they have nothing to do with the view of the screen."

"Oh." Sara giggled softly and snuggled against Gavin, her heart beating rapidly.

Two hours and ten minutes later, the credits ran across the screen to the movie's theme song. "I totally did not get that ending," Sara admitted. "I never figured out who that guy with the moustache was."

"It's sitting in these back seats," Gavin teased. "You were probably a little too distracted."

"I'll say." Sara reached for her coat. It was true. She knew her face was flushed and her heart was racing too fast. She had never—not even with Jim—experienced a movie in quite this fashion before.

"I'll explain the ending on the way home." Gavin rose and reached for his jacket. "You still want to see the other?"

"Yes, if you do."

"If the backseats are open," he answered with a wink. "Need more popcorn or anything?"

"Yes, and a trip to the bathroom."

"I'll meet you outside door six."

"What about tickets? Shall I get them this time?"

Gavin glanced behind him. "Sara," he said under his breath. "We're not paying for any more tickets. We're already inside. Nobody knows if you go from one movie to the next."

"But—"

Gavin laid a finger over her lips. "No buts. Everybody does it. We paid to come in once, that's good enough. Now hurry up." He gave her a nudge in the direction of the restrooms and headed toward the snack counter.

Sara went into the bathroom, arguing with her conscience. *What's the big deal? Gavin says everybody does this. How would I know? I've never stayed for a second movie before. Maybe they really don't care.* As she washed her hands, she let the hot water run over them for a long time. "You have to lighten up, Sara," she said aloud since no one else was at the sink area. "Everyone is always telling you that." *Everyone? Well, Gavin and Allison.*

She shoved open the door to find Gavin waiting right outside. "I thought we were meeting by the movie door."

He handed her the glass of cola. "I changed my mind. I thought you might have a guilt attack. I know your conscience works overtime." He led her down the hallway and pulled open the heavy theater door.

"Well, I guess I can't deny that," Sara said, this time moving into the back row without needing to be instructed. The house lights were still on and the room was slowly filling, mostly with women, but there were a few men accompanying their wives or girlfriends. After they settled into their seats, Gavin entertained Sara with the plot of a ridiculous movie called *The Innocents* as he ate a good share of the popcorn. She relaxed and chuckled over Gavin's tale, forgetting about the fact that she had just sat down to watch a movie for which they had not paid. As the house lights dimmed for the previews, Gavin quickly wrapped up his story.

"You made that all up," Sara laughingly accused.

Gavin shrugged. "Maybe, but my plot is probably better than this one will be."

"How can a love story not be good? They're my very favorite."

Gavin tossed his arm around her and leaned close. "I'd rather act out a love scene than watch one."

An older woman in front of them turned around to see who was talking. Sara giggled softly and squeezed his knee.

It was three fifty when Colleen breezed into the campus bookstore. "I'm here," she sang as she approached the cash register.

Jim was sitting on a stool behind the counter. He glanced at his watch, then smiled at her. "Great. You're even early."

Colleen tugged off her jacket and gloves. "Are you all ready to go?"

"Yeah."

"And your girlfriend has no idea you're coming?"

"None whatsoever." Jim headed toward the backroom to get his coat.

Colleen's voice called after him, "This is so romantic. She's going to be thrilled."

Jim came back, blushing slightly from all the fuss. "I guess. Well, I'm out of here. Thanks again for filling in."

"Anytime. Tell your girlfriend she is a very lucky girl."

Jim waved and stepped into the gloomy afternoon. The clouds were darkening. It looked like snow. If a storm was moving in, he hoped the bad weather would be at his back. He did not want anything slowing him down. Now that he was on his way, he could not wait to see Sara. To assure himself that everything was fine and the weirdness was just his imagination.

As he put the miles behind him, he thought about how much he needed Sara. She filled his life with sweetness and laughter and sunlight. If it wasn't for her, he'd be living a dreary existence. It was becoming increasingly clear that he should settle down in Milwaukee for a while. Next fall he could propose to Sara and after her graduation, they could marry. She could get a job at a convention center downtown or near the airport. He would work in someone else's shop for a time, gaining experience, maybe squirreling away some equity.

Jim nodded; it seemed like a good plan. Logical, feasible... First, he would sit down with Sara and reason out what was going on, because he had no idea. One day she was talkative and sweet and the next day she was giving him the cold shoulder. Sara had always been insecure, but lately... Jim shook his head. Sara was a complex creature with vivacity, creativity, and chattiness mixed in with moodiness, insecurity and a lack of spiritual depth.

Maybe that was it—a spiritual issue. Weeks ago, Katie had said something about Sara struggling with faith issues. Jim sat up straighter, confident that this was something he could deal with. He had a pretty good understanding of spiritual matters and Scripture. After all, his uncle was a pastor and he had listened to many good theological debates around the dinner table on Sunday afternoons. Sara had once mentioned something about being confused with gray areas, but to Jim it was all black or white. Hopefully Sara's brother-in-law would be home this weekend, then if they came to an impasse, they could bring Mark into the discussion. One way or another, they were going to get to the bottom of Sara's problem. He was not going to leave until this weirdness was resolved.

That decided, Jim felt great. Except that he was hungry. A glance at the dash clock told him it was six thirty. He should have pulled off at a drive-in at Eau Claire. Now he would have to wait until he got to the Dells. Never mind, it didn't matter. Every mile brought him closer to Sara. Just thinking about her brought a smile to his face. *What will she do when she sees me?* Jim chuckled. *Knowing Sara, she'll squeal and throw her arms around me as if she had not just seen me last week. Then she'll go on and on about how romantic it is. Humph. Chock one up for ol' Jimmy boy.*

Jim noticed that the farther east he drove, the less snow was on the ground. The storm he had feared did not come and he was able to make great time. At the Wisconsin Dells exit, he picked up a burger and chocolate shake and ate while he drove. He had the radio on and every love song seemed written for him and Sara.

He drove down Mark and Morgan's road, noticing that most of the houses had Christmas lights up. Ahead, he could see white lights outlining Mark's roof. He pulled into the driveway at precisely nine thirteen. Sara's car was parked on the street. He glanced up to her bedroom window. It was dark. She could not possibly be in bed already, she must be downstairs with the rest of the family. Jim closed his car door quietly, straightened his jacket and jogged to the front porch. Grinning broadly, he rang the bell.

Morgan opened the door, the baby in her arms. "Jim!"

"Hey, there."

"Sara didn't tell me you were coming."

"She doesn't know." Jim shrugged. "It's a surprise."

"Oh, Jim, she's not home."

Jim glanced back to the driveway. "Her car's here."

"She went to the movies. Allison must have picked her up, but come on in." Morgan stepped back from the doorway. "You can wait and surprise her when she gets home."

"Maybe I should move my car so she won't see it when she gets in. Do you think I could park it up the street?"

"Yes. Two houses up, on the other side. That's the Goldsteins'. They won't mind. I'll have Mark call and tell them."

Jim took a step off the porch, then turned back before Morgan closed the door. "I forgot to ask. Can I stay here for the weekend? Because if you don't have room, I'll get a motel. I know you weren't expecting company."

"Of course you'll stay here. We have a sleeper sofa in Mark's office. Go park your car and bring your bag in. We've been to a birthday party and my friend sent cake home with us. I'll make some coffee to go with it."

"The cake sounds good, Morgan, but I'm not much of a coffee drinker. Maybe a cola or a glass of milk."

"Okay, I'll get it ready."

Jim went back to his car disappointed, but reasoning that he should not have assumed Sara would be sitting here waiting for him when she had no idea he was coming. He had encouraged her to make friends. She'd be home in an hour or so and would still be surprised.

When he backed out of the driveway, he noticed the Goldsteins had a little parking strip in front of their house. He pulled into that, figuring that in the dark Sara would never notice his car. He grabbed his duffle bag and jogged back to the house. He knocked briefly, then wiped his feet and entered.

Mark met him in the entry hall. "Glad to have you, Jim. Sara's going to be tickled." Mark gestured to the room on the left. "This is my office. You can set your bag in here." He strode ahead of Jim and turned on a floor lamp next to a sofa which faced the door. On the opposite wall was an orderly desk, complete with a computer and framed pictures of Morgan and the children. Two file cabinets were next to the desk. On the outside wall under the window was a bookcase running the width of the room. Along the fourth wall, under a large painting of a pastoral scene, sat two wing-backed chairs—perhaps Mark used those for counseling sessions. Jim figured that maybe tomorrow he and Sara could sit there and talk.

Jim set his duffle bag down between the sofa and the window, shrugged off his jacket and laid it over the arm of the sofa. "I appreciate you guys letting me stay."

Mark smiled. "We're practically family, Jim. You ready for cake?"

"You bet." Jim followed Mark to the kitchen, where he could smell coffee as it dripped into a pot. On the table was a can of soda next to a large slice of chocolate cake. Mark gestured for Jim to have a seat, mentioning that Morgan was putting the baby to bed. "Aren't you having any cake?" Jim asked.

"No. I had two pieces at the party. I'll have some decaf in a minute." Mark explained that friends of his and Morgan's had twin boys, who were four years old today. They had had a large party, with pizza and cake. "Eight adults and eleven kids. My ears are still ringing from all the noise."

Jim chuckled. Family life. Someday… "Sara said you were in Seattle this week."

Mark nodded, filled a mug with coffee, sat across the table from Jim and told him about the talks he had given at Seattle area high schools promoting abstinence as well as the seminars he had given for parents.

Morgan returned to the kitchen, refilled her husband's coffee cup, got another slice of cake for Jim, then joined them at the table. They talked for quite a while about Mark's work. He said the biggest heartbreak was when teen girls told him they were pregnant. "The youngest one I've ever talked to was thirteen years old."

"Thirteen!" Jim exclaimed. "She's just a child herself."

Mark nodded. "I know. So many of these girls are looking for love. They think if a boy holds them and says the magic words, it spells l-o-v-e. They give their innocence away to some kid who knows nothing about love, is much too young for commitment and walks away as soon as the girl tells him she's pregnant. Too many girls throw their childhood away."

The three talked on, waiting for Sara to come home. Jim glanced at his watch several times. At ten-thirty, Morgan stood up, stifling a yawn. "I'm sorry, Jim, but I need to get to bed. The children will be up early. Just make yourself at home. Mark can show you where to shower. The towels are in the cupboard. The sofa bed just needs to be pulled out."

"Thanks, Morgan. Did Sara say what movie she went to?"

"No, but now that I think about it, she mentioned a double feature. I'm so sorry she isn't home."

"Yeah, that's okay. Surprises, well…" Jim shrugged.

Mark rose and carried the dishes to the sink. "I'll show you where things are. Then you can watch television in the living room if you'd like."

"I'll be okay. I brought a textbook along. Exams are coming up, so I should study."

Before going upstairs, Mark turned off the lights in the kitchen and hall. "I'll keep the outside lights on until Sara comes home, if you could turn them off later." At Jim's nod, Mark said good night. "Glad to have you, Jim. Sara is going to be, too. I'll see you tomorrow."

Jim said good night, tugged his econ book from his duffle bag and tossed it onto the couch. The house was in shadows with the only light coming from the floor lamp and what shone through the window from the outdoor lights. Jim diligently read a boring twelve-page chapter, highlighting a few main points. When he reached the end of the section, he closed the book and laid it on the end table.

It was nearing midnight. *Sara, where are you? Come home, I'm waiting...* Sighing, he rose and wandered around the room, looking at the pictures on the walls, reading titles of the books on the bookshelf. They were mostly theology, psychology, and devotional books with a smattering of fiction. He stopped in front of Mark's desk and picked up the framed photos of the children. Nicholas, the little imp Sara was always talking about, grinned with a mischievous look on his little face. It was easy to see from the picture why Sara was crazy about the little guy.

He walked over to the lamp, turned it off, and slouched on the couch with his legs sprawled out in front and daydreamed about the future he and Sara were going to have. Someday they'd own a home of their own and Jim would have pictures of their children on his desk and maybe one of them could look like him, but the others would look like Sara, with curly hair and sparkling blue eyes and— Jim heard a car pull into the driveway. *Finally!*

Eager to see Sara, he went to the window, opened the sheer curtain a slit and peeked out. Sara was climbing out of an old Chevy, someone else was getting out of the driver's side. Jim feasted his eyes on Sara a moment, then looked to see whom Sara was with. Jim froze. Sara's friend was a guy. *Wait a minute. Get a hold of yourself, Jim, ol' boy. Maybe it's just some guy that drove the girls and he's just being a gentleman and walking Sara to the door. Sure, that's it.*

Not wanting to be seen, Jim stepped slightly back from the window, but continued to peer out. The stranger put his arm around Sara and they laughed over something. Jim felt an icy hand clutching his heart, a vise gripping his gut. He positioned himself at the far edge of the window so he could watch as they climbed the steps to the porch. Jim started shaking. The guy was pulling Sara close and kissing her...and she was letting him. Man! She was more than letting him, she was kissing him back. Jim closed his eyes; he couldn't look. Then, he opened them and stared out the window again. He couldn't *not* look. Jim accidentally tugged at the curtain too hard, causing it to pull at its hooks and tear a little. Stumbling back, he dropped onto the couch.

This explained everything. All the weirdness going on with Sara. This explained it all. How long had she been seeing this guy? They were still out there kissing—obviously, this was not a first date; those were not first date kisses.

The front door opened. Sara lingered a moment in the open doorway. Jim could not make out the words, but he could hear the huskiness in the voices, the teasing, engaging manner in which the final good nights were said. The grip on his gut was twisting, tightening... Jim held his eyes closed until he heard the front door firmly shut. In the light that spilled through the windows he could vaguely make out Sara's shadowy form. As she turned and took a step toward the stairwell, he spoke.

"Who's your friend, Sara?"

His voice, coming through the dark house, startled Sara and she jumped. "Who's there?" She squinted into the shadows of Mark's office. "Mark? Is that you?"

"I asked who your friend is."

Sara took three steps to the doorway of the office, reached in and flicked on the overhead light. "Jim!" Shocked, Sara dropped her arms and stared at him.

"Your friend? The driver of the Chevy?" Jim remained seated, his voice steadily calm in spite of his raging emotions.

Sara took an uncertain step into the room. "That's Allison's brother. He drove."

"And that's all?"

"Yes, that's his car."

"I saw you, Sara. You can cut the charade."

"You—you saw?" Her mind was having a hard time sorting things out. She had just come from a breathless outing with Gavin to find Jim sitting on her brother-in-law's couch demanding explanations in a frightfully even-toned voice. "The kissing?"

"Yes."

"Oh." Sara could not move. She couldn't believe Jim was here! She wanted to throw herself into his arms and have everything be the way it used to be. But there was this matter of Gavin...and now Jim knew. "It's not what it seems," she said.

"I'm not buying that."

"But, really, it's just that—"

Jim put a hand up. "Don't even try, Sara, you're not going to be able to talk yourself out of this."

"Well," Sara said, no longer embarrassed, but getting angry herself, "it's your fault anyway. If you—"

"Hold on. There is no way you're pinning the blame on me." He stood and took a step toward her. "Go tell somebody else, because I am not going to listen to you blaming me for your two-timing."

"I am not two-timing. What an ugly thing to say."

"Not two-timing? How can you stand there and deny it? I saw it with my own eyes. How long has this been going on, Sara? Never mind, I don't want to know. It's all becoming crystal clear now. All the weird phone calls and everything. Did you think I wouldn't figure it out? Do you think I'm a total fool?"

"Yes, you are a fool. We had the most wonderful thing going and you couldn't commit to me. Why do you think I went out with someone else? Why, Jim?"

"I couldn't commit?" Jim's voice rose a notch in volume. "What do you think two years indicates? If I couldn't commit I would have been gone long ago."

"Would you? It seems as if you're just waiting for graduation to dump me."

"Where do you get your bizarre ideas? Am I not the one that transferred to MCU last fall because you were there? Isn't that commitment?"

"That's not commitment. That's convenience!" Sara spat out.

"What do you want from me, Sara? What more could you possibly want?"

Sara's pulse was throbbing in her throat. Here was her chance to tell him what she had been waiting for all these past many months. She took two steps closer, lowered her voice and said, "I wanted us to get married."

"Don't you think that's where our relationship was headed?"

"I used to think so, but lately I—I—well, I decided you have no such intention."

"You decided? This is unbelievable. You decide that I don't want to marry you so you start going out with some other guy?" Saying it, remembering the sight of Sara so willingly standing in another guy's arms, brought a fresh blow to his stomach.

"It's not just any other guy. It's Gavin."

"Gavin." Jim repeated the despised name, wondering why it sounded vaguely familiar. "And he's going to marry you, is that it?"

Sara blushed. She had loved Jim; she did love Jim, but Gavin's sweet words and smooth touch had wormed their way into her heart. "He desires me, Jim."

165

"Desires you? Of course he desires you. You're beautiful, but does he love you?"

"I think so."

Jim stared at her, this lovely woman who had become a stranger to him in mere minutes. Dropping his voice to a whisper, he said, "I loved you, Sara."

Their eyes locked across the room. *Loved. Past tense.* The tears dribbled down Sara's cheeks. What if she had been wrong? "When was the last time you told me?"

"I don't know; I don't keep a journal. Do I have to say it every week?"

"Yes. I needed to hear it."

Jim raked a hand through his hair. "Obviously you need a whole lot more than I can give you."

"Can give or want to give? If you had wanted me like I wanted you, then this wouldn't have happened."

"Here we go again. This," Jim pointed to the window, "was all your doing, Sara. I never said I didn't want to be with you. I never went out with someone else. I never—"

"You never said forever," Sara sobbed. "You never said the words I needed to hear. At Thanksgiving you just looked at me and…and…and I *knew*."

"You knew what?"

"That you wanted out. That you were never going to commit and propose to me."

"You have it all wrong. Just because I wasn't ready to ask you, doesn't mean I was never going to. Man, Sara! I can't believe you did this to us."

"I didn't do this, you did!"

Jim slowly shook his head. "You know, Sara, you've spent your life entertaining people with stories, but this one beats them all."

"I just wanted you to love me. If you can promise that next year we'll be married—"

"So now you're handing out ultimatums? That's not the way relationships work, Sara."

"But Gavin is just, well, you're the one I really want to share my life with."

"Too bad, really. It's a little late for you to figure that out." He retrieved his coat, then brushed past her toward the front door.

Morgan's footsteps were heard coming down the stairs. "Sara! What is going on down here? You're going to wake—" She flicked on the hall light and stopped talking as she saw Jim with his hand on the doorknob and Sara with tears streaming down her face.

Jim glared at Morgan. "I can't believe you covered for her."

"I don't—"

"She doesn't know." Sara stepped between Jim and her sister just as Mark drew up behind Morgan. "Nobody knows."

"Know what, Sara?" Morgan asked, fearful of the answer.

"That your sister's been dating someone else behind my back. Apparently, behind your back, too. Man, Morgan, how could you not know this? She's been living in your house."

"Sara! Is this true?"

At Sara's tearful nod, Mark laid a hand on Jim shoulder. "I'm sorry," he said quietly. "We didn't know."

"Yeah, well," Jim tossed a look back at Sara. "I guess she's a pretty good liar."

"Don't talk about me as if I'm not here. I'm not some child like Courtney. And remember, this is not my fault, Jim Hoffman."

Jim simply shook his head, opened the door and stepped outside. Morgan's voice, in its older-sister, compassionate tone, followed him. "Where are you going, Jim?"

"Home, I guess."

"You shouldn't drive all that way tonight."

Mark put a hand on her arm. "Let him go, hon." He nodded to Jim, who sprinted for the Goldsteins' parking strip without a backward glance. Once he was behind the wheel, in the safety and seclusion of his car, the tears broke through. He stared across the dark street to Mark's house as sobs racked his body. He watched as first the outdoor lights and then the hall light went out. His eyes moved to Sara's bedroom window, but no light came on. He never knew it was possible to love and hate someone so much at the same time. All he did know was that it hurt. His insides were torn up, as if a parasite was eating him alive. Sara's cheating was bad enough, but the blame tossing just added insult to injury.

Jim swiped a hand over his face and started his car engine. "Goodbye to you, Sara Brooks. Thanks for nothing." He drove away from Sara's home in a daze, leaving a big chunk of his heart behind. He turned off the radio, not wanting to hear the love songs he had enjoyed on the trip over. He rode in silence, sharing the nearly deserted highway with truckers and an occasional car.

As the shock wore off, Jim recalled more of their conversation. How dare she blame him for what happened! This was not his fault. He was not the one to step out on Sara and date someone else. Never had he imagined that Sara would cheat on him. Granted, he had known something was wrong, but this was inconceivable.

The memory of Sara in the arms of that other guy—kissing him so willingly—made Jim sick. He feared it was a vision he would carry with him for the rest of his life. He'd be like Heathcliff now, in *Wuthering Heights*, forever carrying a love for Sara like Heathcliff carried for Cathy until the day he died.

As the miles rolled by, Jim realized that certain things should have tipped him off. Things that Wayne and Katie had said. Like when Katie had gotten right in his face and demanded that he talk to Sara. She must have known. Of course! Sara would have confided in Katie. They talked all the time—Jim was certain they talked about *everything*. So, if Sara had told Katie and she told Wayne…they all knew! Katie could not spill Sara's confidences, but Wayne could have. Jim suddenly remembered Wayne asking if Sara could be seeing someone else. Jim had brushed it off, but Wayne must have been dropping a hint.

"Thanks a lot, Wayne. Some friend you are. You could have come right out and told me. You *should* have told me. I would have told you."

Jim approached the city, winter's dawn still two hours away. His anger at Wayne was escalating. After all, whose friend was Wayne anyway? "Mine!" Jim shouted. "Wayne owes allegiance to me, not Sara."

Jim turned off the freeway at Wayne and Katie's exit and drove down the quiet streets to their apartment. After parking next to the curb, he bounded to the door, thumping on it for all he was worth.

A couple of minutes passed, then a bedraggled Wayne, dressed in sweat pants and a wrinkled T-shirt, opened the door. Jim's fist came out and smacked Wayne on the jaw. Wayne staggered back, a hand to his face, his eyes wide in surprise. "Jim! What in the world?"

"You knew I was going there! You let me walk right into that trap!"

Wayne rubbed a hand against his smarting jaw and stepped back. "What trap? What are you talking about?"

Katie came out of the bedroom. "Who is it, Wayne?"

"Your cousin," Wayne answered wryly, still rubbing his chin.

"Jim?" Katie came and stood beside Wayne. "I thought you went to see Sara."

"And you!" Jim's eyes were still blazing. "I understand confidences and all that, but you're my cousin. How could you do this to me?"

Wayne glanced up and down the dark street. Only one light was on in the entire block. "I think you'd better come inside."

"I don't understand," Katie looked from Jim to Wayne, noticing the red blotch on her husband's jaw. "Did you hit Wayne?"

"Yeah, and I'll do it again if I don't get some answers."

Grabbing Jim's jacket, Wayne yanked him inside, then shut the door. "You're out of control, buddy. Katie and I don't have a clue what you're talking about."

"Sara." Jim tossed the name into the air and let it hang.

"Sara?" Wayne repeated.

"I thought you were going there for the weekend," Katie said. "To surprise her."

"I did."

"And you're back already?"

"Yeah. I surprised her all right."

"Take your coat off," Wayne urged. "Katie, why don't you make some coffee, and bring me some ice, okay?"

Reluctant to leave the room, Katie hustled to the kitchen. Coffee would be a good thing. Apparently Jim had been driving all night, and Wayne should put some ice on his chin. The fact that Jim had been angry enough to hit Wayne had Katie rattled. Jim was an even-tempered, mild-mannered guy. Katie quickly made the coffee, grabbed a package of frozen corn from the freezer, and hurried back to the living room.

Wayne and Jim were sitting next to each other on the couch. Jim looked defeated, the sudden storm of hostility having passed. Wayne reached for the veggies that Katie had haphazardly wrapped in a paper towel and set it against his throbbing jaw. Katie perched on the edge of the rocking chair. They both waited for Jim to start explaining.

He looked from one to the other. "So you guys honestly don't know that Sara's been—been—man, I can't even say it."

Katie closed her eyes, her heart plummeting. "She's been seeing someone else."

Wayne and Jim both stared at her in astonishment.

"What?" Wayne asked at the same time Jim said, "So you did know."

Katie shook her head. "No, Jim, I didn't. I just figured it out. Just now. A few weeks ago she told me she met some guy at the club, but then she dismissed it as nothing. She asked me some questions and then she dropped it."

"Why didn't you tell me?"

"There was nothing to tell. She never admitted that she was going out with him. I thought she was having spiritual issues. I told you to talk to her, remember?"

"I remember." Jim fell back against the couch cushions. Silence settled over the room for a few moments as they each thought about Sara.

"Katie?" Wayne eventually asked. "Is the coffee ready?"

Katie nodded. It was only a couple of minutes until she returned with three mugs of strong coffee. Jim reached for one. He did not really like coffee, but these were unreal times. He lifted it mechanically to his lips, took a long sip, grimaced and asked for sugar. Katie fetched some from the kitchen and then settled back on the rocking chair. They drank in silence for a while, then bit by bit, Jim told them what had happened.

"Unbelievable," Wayne whispered.

Katie was unaware of the tears trickling down her cheeks. "Jim, she can't be in her right mind."

"She's been lying to all of us, for weeks now."

There was nothing to say. They finished their coffee in silence, then Wayne gave everyone refills. Halfway through his second cup, Jim spoke up. "I was going to ask her to marry me next year."

"She loves you, Jim. I know she does," Katie insisted. "You two were meant to be together. The four of us were going to go through life together."

Jim shook his head. "Not anymore."

"I'm sorry, bud." Wayne gave Jim a friendly slap on the leg. "It stinks."

"I'm sorry I hit you. I really wanted to smack that jerk up one side and down the other, but," Jim shrugged, "you were here."

"That's okay."

"I wish you and Sara had never started dating," Katie said. "Then you wouldn't be hurting and we could all just be friends."

"I could never be just friends with Sara." Jim got a faraway look in his eyes. "From the very first moment I saw her, through all this time, Sara's been like the sunshine after the rain." Jim's voice faded away for a moment, then he admitted, "I was born to love her."

"She's just confused right now; once she realizes how much you truly love her—"

Jim cut Katie off. "I never want to see Sara Brooks again as long as I live."

CHAPTER 15

And this is my prayer; that your love may abound more and more in knowledge and in depth of insight, so that you may be able to discern what is best and you may be pure and blameless until the day of Christ…
—Philippians 1:7

Mark closed the door behind Jim with a prayer for the young man who had just had his heart broken and his dreams crushed. He did not understand why Sara would reject such an upstanding, fine, Christian man, but Mark had learned years ago that matters of the heart were rarely logical.

Sara mounted the steps in an attempt to escape to her room, but Morgan held her back. "Wait a minute, Sara. I want an explanation for what's been going on. Is it true what Jim said about you dating someone behind his back?"

Wiping away her tears, Sara turned to face her sister and brother-in-law. "It's true that I have been going out with someone, but only a couple of times, and I wouldn't exactly say it's been behind Jim's back."

"Not behind his back? He looked pretty shocked just now."

"Well, okay, he didn't know, but Jim has no hold over me. He's never asked me to spend forever with him. There have been no spoken promises or commitments that I've broken. Really, as far as my relationship with Jim goes…actually, it hasn't been going anywhere. I guess you could say it's been at a standstill."

"So, you felt what, stagnated? Bored with Jim, so you went looking for something exciting?"

"You don't understand at all. I was not bored with Jim and I did not intentionally set out to find someone else. It just happened. It happened because Jim lacks the ability to commit."

Morgan slowly shook her head. "It's true, I don't understand your relationship with Jim. So, even though I don't approve of what has transpired, I guess it's between you and him."

Sara released a small sigh and climbed up two more steps before Morgan's words halted her again. "But there is one thing that does involve me and I will not let it go. That's the lying. Whether I would have agreed with your actions or not, you should have been forthright with me. It bothers me a great deal that you lied to me."

"There weren't that many lies."

Morgan laughed, incredulous. "No? So there really is a Kelly and an Allison? You didn't just make them up to cover your tracks?"

"Of course!" Sara said, sounding insulted. "Kelly is a friend from aerobics and Allison is Gavin's sister."

Before Morgan could respond, Mark laid a hand on her arm. "It's late, Morgan, and everyone is tired. Maybe you and Sara should wait until morning to finish this discussion."

"That is a great idea," Sara said, turning and hurrying up the remaining stairs before Morgan could disagree. She went into the bathroom and washed her face, silently waiting for the others to return to bed.

Hearing her sister's bedroom door shut, Sara opened the bathroom door a crack and peered out. All was dark. She crept to her room and closed the door behind her, but did not turn on a light. The darkness fit her mood.

After changing into her pajamas, she wandered to the window. It was a dark night. No stars twinkled; no friendly moon smiled down at her. She was so confused. She had just come home from a magical night with Gavin and she should be able to relive it as she fell asleep, but then she had danced into the house to discover Jim sitting stiffly on the couch with his sad and shocked eyes. The Gavin experience left her floating on a steady wind while the confrontation with Jim was ripping her heart open.

Her gaze dropped to the sidewalk that led from the driveway to the house. Because of the overhang of the porch roof, she could not see the front door, where she had stood breathlessly sharing good night kisses with Gavin while Jim watched. A lump settled in Sara's throat and tears built up again, threatening to spill. She wondered how much Jim had been able to see from his vantage point downstairs. Maybe he had only seen her and Gavin approach the front door and had not actually witnessed the kissing.

Sara turned and crept softly down the stairs so she wouldn't wake the others. On the landing, she flicked the outside lights on and went into the office. Crossing the room, she noticed the dark outline of Jim's duffle bag in the corner. She looked about quickly to see if he had left anything else and discovered his textbook on the end table. Lifting it, she hugged it to her chest, then positioned herself at the window. Her shoulders sagged. This office window gave a perfect view of the porch. Jim would have seen the whole thing. Sara had to admit that despite everything, Jim had not deserved to see her in Gavin's arms.

"I'm sorry, Jim," she whispered. "I did not mean to hurt you." It was true. No matter what he had done—or not done—in the past couple of months, she had never meant to hurt him. None of this had been her choice—she had only wanted Jim to ask her to marry him.

Sara looked up sharply and twirled to face the couch where Jim had sat such a short time ago. *What if the things he had said were true? That he was planning to propose someday? Aye…we're back to the same old problem, Jimmy. Someday… Someday might never come and who wants to wait for someday?*

Slowly, Sara picked up Jim's bag, brought it upstairs and laid it on the bed. She unzipped it, meaning to set his book inside, but paused when she saw Jim's navy-blue MCU sweatshirt—the one she had given him for his birthday—lying on top. Tenderly, Sara drew it from the bag and pulled it over her head. It was much too big, but Sara tugged it down around her hips. Picking up the textbook, she shoved it inside the duffle bag, zipped the bag and dropped it onto the floor. Then she slipped under her covers, and, sobbing quietly, fell asleep with Jim's sweatshirt next to her heart and dreams of floating on the clouds with Gavin in her mind.

Sara woke to a brightness in the room. Not a sunshiny good morning kind of brightness, but the white brilliance of falling snow. Having left her blinds open, it was easy to see the thick white flakes through her window. Sara sat up and tugged the covers up to her chin, pondering the thought that there would soon be a blanket of new snow covering the ground. It was always so pretty when it was fresh, before footprints crisscrossed it and passing cars made it dirty. Sara wished she could scoop some of it up and blanket her heart. Cover up the nagging guilt she felt over hurting Jim, the dishonesty she had been involved in and the disagreeable parts of Gavin's life.

There was a tap at the bedroom door. Sara called, "Come in," and Morgan, pushing the door open, peeked into the room.

"You awake?" At Sara's nod, her sister crossed the room, carrying two large mugs with holly and mistletoe designs on them. "How about a cup of peppermint mocha?"

"Our holiday tradition!" Sara smiled and reached for a mug.

"I thought it might make a good peace offering. What do you say?"

Sara patted the space next to her on the bed. "I say, yes. I don't want to fight with you, Morgan. I could really use somebody on my team."

Morgan sat down on the bed and glanced around Sara's room. "It's nice up here," she commented.

"Yes," Sara agreed, looking around. "I should put up some Christmas decorations."

"We're going to cut a tree this morning. Want to come along?"

Sara stared into Morgan's eyes. "You still want me to? After last night?"

"Yes, Sara. We're sisters to the end. Now, tell me about what happened with Jim."

"I'm not really sure what happened. It started all sweet and romantic and seemed perfect at first, but somewhere along the way I think Jim stopped loving me. I don't know. Maybe I talk too much or am too wishy-washy for him or—" a sob ripped through Sara's speech and the mug of coffee quivered in her hand. Morgan grasped Sara's cup and held it. "I don't know," Sara repeated, "but Jim has never been very communicative about our future and lately I know he's just been biding his time to break up with me."

"He didn't strike me as a young man bent on breaking up, Sara."

"Well, that's the thing. He hides it so well, but he hasn't said that he loves me in ages and graduation is coming up and he never…" Sara's words died off and she tugged at the edge of the comforter in order to wipe her tears. "It's not something that can be explained, Morgan. It just is. I don't want to talk about it anymore."

"All right." Morgan waited until Sara had her tears under control. She did not believe a thing Sara had said. Jim was a man in love and last night when he left, he was a man very much destroyed by Sara's behavior. However, right now, there was no convincing Sara of that, and anyway, there must be more to this than Morgan could see. She knew that her sister had been in the throes of deep love for nearly two years and would not likely throw it away on a whim. Besides, she had come up here to make peace with Sara. Handing her sister's mocha back, she said, "So, tell me about Gavin."

Sara glanced at her sister, to be certain she was serious, then, thinking about Gavin, she closed her eyes briefly. When she opened them, Morgan detected a distinctly Sara look—dreamy and expressive.

"Gavin is…well…" Sara grinned at her sister. "Gavin is so handsome, just wait until you meet him, I know you'll agree. He's fun to be with, he likes to have a good time and he's daring and adventurous."

"Kind of the opposite of Jim's mellow personality, huh?"

"I guess." Sara shrugged and sipped her mocha. "Gavin makes me feel special. He's always complimenting me and he's such a tease, but he has a way of making me feel like I am the most wonderful girl in the world."

Morgan studied her sister's face. "Sara, you shouldn't need some guy— any guy—to make you feel like you're wonderful. You *are* wonderful, no matter what some guy thinks."

Sara cocked her head and gave Morgan a sly smile. "Don't you feel better when Mark looks at you in that special way and tells you that you're great?"

"Of course I do, but even if he didn't, I'd know that I'm special. I'm a child of the King and I have gifts and talents that have nothing to do with my relationship with Mark."

"That's easy for you to say; you've always been good at so many things."

"So are you, Sara. I'm sure Jim's helped you see that."

Sara did not want to get back on the subject of Jim. It was a painful subject, one best left alone. Sara tossed her head. "We were talking about Gavin, remember? I can't wait for you to meet him."

Deciding now was not the time to press the issue about Sara's low self-esteem, Morgan asked what Gavin did.

"Hmm?"

"For work? Or is he a student?"

"Oh, he works at the juice bar at the club."

"And?"

"And? That's a full-time job, Morgan."

"So, he wants to tend a juice bar for the rest of his life? What does he make there? Minimum wage?"

"Morgan! I don't know what he makes, but I'm sure it's not what he wants to do forever. It's just a stepping stone job."

"Oh, so he is going to school?"

"No." Sara did not appreciate the way this line of questioning was going. She herself had often wondered about Gavin's future career plans, but had never been able to get him to talk about it. For that matter, she had never gotten him to talk about anything serious. "Morgan, I can't possibly know everything about him. We've only gone out a few times."

"I see. Well, little sister, my advice is to take it very slow with Gavin and get to know him. It might be wise to figure out exactly how you feel about Jim, because I don't think we've seen the last of him."

For a split second, there was a flash of hope in Sara's heart, but it quickly faded. Sadly, she shook her head. "Jim's history, Morgan. It's best if I put him out of my heart."

Morgan sighed. "You are a complicated person, Sara dear, and your life seems a little complex right now. I know I don't understand much of this, but I'm here if you ever need to talk."

"Thanks, Morgan."

Morgan rose from the bed, then looked back at Sara. "No more lies, Sara. That's inexcusable. You were brought up to know right from wrong."

Sara nodded, but did not verbally make any promises. Some of the situations she found herself in with Gavin or Allison might need a little covering up, because Morgan, who lived in her perfect little world, would certainly not condone them all. Sara handed her now empty mug to her sister. "So, when are we going tree cutting?"

"In half an hour or so."

"All right. I'll be ready."

Just as Morgan was heading for the stairs, the baby began to cry, so she detoured to the nursery and picked up her hungry son. "I'll feed you just as soon as I check on your brother and sister, okay?" she crooned to the baby while she went downstairs.

Morgan was glad she had made time for the chat with Sara, but now she was behind schedule. Mark was at a brief meeting at the company offices. When he returned, he would be ready to make their annual trek to the tree farm. Morgan supposed she could have asked Sara to help with the children, but after last night, Sara needed some time to herself.

Morgan stepped into the living room. The baby was still squalling, but at least Courtney and Nicholas were quietly watching a Christmas video. The doorbell rang. "What now?" she muttered, trying to shush the baby as she headed for the door. She opened it to a dark-haired young man. He flashed a grin and asked if Sara was home.

"You must be Gavin," Morgan said, as Tucker threw his head back crying.

"She's told you about me?" He was visibly surprised, but pleased.

"Yes, come in." Morgan stepped to the bottom of the staircase and hollered for her sister. "You have company," she said when Sara poked her head around the upper corner.

Sara's eyes flew to Gavin standing just inside the door. "I'll be right down," she declared before darting back to her room to get dressed.

"You can wait in here," Morgan said, leading the way to the kitchen. "You'll have to excuse me, but I need to tend the baby," she explained, disappearing back down the hall as Tucker let out another ear-splitting scream.

Sara quickly changed from her plaid pajama bottoms to a favorite pair of faded blue jeans. She glanced down briefly at Jim's sweatshirt, slightly rumpled from sleep, and decided to keep it on. She grabbed a thick pair of socks from her dresser and slipped them on, then hustled downstairs.

"I can't believe you're here," Sara said. "What did you tell Morgan?"

"I just asked if you were home. It was no big deal; she knew my name."

"That's because I just told her about you this morning, but what if I hadn't? What were you going to say?"

Gavin shoved his hands into his coat pockets. "I was just going to wing it. Say you knew my sister or something."

"You took a big chance. Strange guys just don't come knocking on our door."

"I don't want to be kept on a leash, Sara. Anyway, all's well that ends well, right?"

"I guess." Sara could hardly believe she was standing openly in Morgan's kitchen talking to the most handsome man on earth as if it was an ordinary, acceptable thing. "Did you stop by for a reason?"

He gave a nonchalant shrug as if thoughts of Sara hadn't plagued him all morning. "I was on my way home from a staff meeting and wondered what you were doing. I thought we could hang out or something."

"I'm going with Mark and Morgan to cut their Christmas tree. They always drive out to a tree farm. Do you want to come along?"

"Yeah, okay, but what gives? How did I go from secret boyfriend to tagging along on a family outing just like that?"

Taking a moment to collect her thoughts, Sara brushed her uncombed hair back from her face. "Jim was here when you brought me home last night. We had a big fight and things are officially over between us. This morning I told Morgan all about breaking up with him and about you."

"Finally." Gavin could not keep the look of triumph from his eyes. "Now you can put that behind you. This is great, Sara." Gavin placed his arms around Sara's waist and bent for a kiss—a possessive, demanding kiss. "Tell me this is great," he murmured.

Sara's knees went weak with Gavin's passionate kisses, yet it stirred the memory of Jim's face and her betrayal. She nodded, but could not speak.

"Isn't it?" Gavin demanded. "You do want this, don't you?"

Sara nodded, so unsure of herself. "It's just…last night was so awful. When I came home and Jim was here. He threw accusations at me and I hurt him—terribly."

"You hurt him? After what he's been putting you through? Stringing you along? I'd think you'd be relieved that it's finally over."

Sara nodded again, thinking that she should be glad. Now she could move on…right into Gavin's arms and life. "It's hard to let go, Gavin. We've been dating for almost—"

"Two years, I know." Gavin planted his legs farther apart in an unwavering stance, crossed his arms over his chest and looked Sara up and down. "So where does that leave us? I don't want you pining over him when you're with me."

"No, of course not." Sara's answer came out in a whisper. "I'm turning my world upside down to be with you. It's just…just…the memory of his face and those things he said to me…"

In one swift move, Gavin closed the gap between them and pulled Sara into a tight embrace—just like a Rhett Butler move. "I'll make you forget him," he murmured. Sara's heart pounded. When she was in Gavin's arms he could make her forget anything—everything.

They heard the garage door open, then Mark pull his car in. Gavin stepped away, leaving Sara breathless. Entering the kitchen from the garage, Mark was surprised to see a stranger in the room with Sara. Quickly recovering, he reached out for a handshake. "You must be Gavin," he said, studying the tall, good-looking young man who had usurped Jim's place. "I'm Mark."

"Nice to meet you."

"Yes, well," Mark took a moment to study Gavin. "I hope I have a chance to get to know you." With a nod of his head, he headed down the hall so he could change into jeans for the trip to the tree farm.

Sara exchanged a grin with Gavin about the interruption of their kissing.

"Sorry. So, if you want to come along, I'll talk to Morgan about it."

"Yeah, I do."

She poured Gavin a cup of coffee, then waltzed from the room in search of her sister.

"Come with us now?" Morgan responded in amazement, looking up from diapering the baby. "Sara, just last night Mark and I sat at the kitchen table entertaining Jim, and now you expect us to keep company with Gavin?"

"Please, Morgan. He's here and he wants to come. Can't you do this for me? Can't you make him feel welcome and be nice to him?"

Morgan snapped Tucker's overalls. "Oh, Sara, I suppose so, but this jumping from one boy to the other has my head spinning."

"Thanks, Morgan. You're the best."

"Do you think you could finish getting Nicholas ready, please?"

"Yes." Sara zipped from the baby's room and back down the stairs, thinking that Morgan's head wasn't spinning nearly as much as her own heart. Ducking into the kitchen she informed Gavin that it was fine for him to come along. "I just have to get Nicholas ready. Wait here, okay?"

At his nod, she raced to the living room and picked up her nephew from where he was sprawled on the floor. He fussed because he was watching TV, but Sara promised he could finish the video later. "We have to find your socks and boots and jacket," she explained, hauling him upstairs.

She hurried to her nephew's room, suddenly worried that Mark might give Gavin the third-degree before she could return to the kitchen. After impatiently tugging on Nicky's socks and boots, she hurried to the bathroom to brush both her teeth and her hair. A glance in the mirror reminded her that she had not put her makeup on yet. Jim wouldn't have minded if she dashed off to hunt for a Christmas tree without a speck of makeup, but some instinct told her Gavin would appreciate it if she took a few minutes for at least the basics. "Oh…" she fretted, as Mark called up the stairs to see if she was ready. "In a minute!" Hastily, she applied mascara while Nicholas reached into the tub for his toy boats. "That's a pal, Nicky, you play with those while I get beautiful."

She returned to the kitchen, with Nicholas in her arms, at the same time that Mark came from the living room with Courtney. Gavin rose from his chair by the table and set his empty coffee cup in the sink. Mark glanced at Gavin's feet. "It's snowing pretty hard. Do you want to borrow some boots? I have an old pair."

Gavin looked down at his tennis-shoe-clad feet. "Yeah, that'd be great."

Still lugging Nicholas, Sara followed Mark to the back closet. "Thanks for being nice to Gavin."

"No sense letting his feet get wet," he answered. In a lower voice he added, "I don't know what you've been up to, missy, but I'll give him a fair shake."

"Thank you."

In the van, Tucker and Nicolas sat in car seats behind Mark and Morgan. Sara sat in the middle of the backseat, with Courtney on one side and Gavin on the other. Morgan put on a Christmas CD and quietly told Mark they would get acquainted with Gavin over lunch. Relaxing in the back corner, with an arm casually draped around Sara's shoulders, Gavin was amazed at how much effort it had taken for the family of five to get ready—even with Sara's additional help. This reaffirmed his personal vow not to start a family for years and then when he did, to stop at two kids.

The drive to the tree farm took nearly forty minutes. The snow continued to fall in huge, thick flakes creating a winter wonderland. With a smile just for him, Sara reached for Gavin's hand and pulled it onto her lap. He leaned close and whispered something about desiring to be alone with her later.

"Mommy, that man ith telling Aunt Thara thecretth."

Morgan laughed. "It's all right, sweetie, and his name is Gavin."

Gavin tapped Courtney on the shoulder and when she looked at him with her solemn brown eyes, he gave her a wink. "Someday boys will be telling you secrets."

"Oh, no they won't," Mark chuckled from the front. "At least not until she's thirty."

When they arrived at the tree farm, Mark borrowed a saw from the attendant while Morgan placed Tucker in a pack designed for carrying babies. Sara helped position it on her sister's back despite the fact that Courtney hung on her arm.

"Watch Nicholas, will you, Sara?" Morgan asked.

"I've got him." Gavin scooped the little guy up, tickled him and placed him on his shoulders. Sara beamed at Gavin, grateful that he was fitting in so well with her family. Of course, with his charming ways, how could he not?

The group trudged through several rows looking for the perfect tree. When Courtney grew tired, Mark hoisted her up and carried her in one arm, the saw in the other. After thirty minutes of inspecting trees, Morgan selected one. Mark set his daughter down, then knelt on the snowy ground to cut the tree. Nicholas, watching Courtney jump up and down in excitement, clapped his hands.

"Mark, could I get a small tree for my room?" Sara asked. "I saw some back where we parked."

He grunted his consent, then cautioned everyone to keep back as the tree he was cutting started to fall.

"How about you?" Sara asked, stepping next to Gavin. "Do you and Allie need a tree?"

He shrugged. "I'll pick one up later at the grocery store. They're cheaper there." Actually, last year Gavin had gone after hours and taken one off an outdoor display without paying. It did not make sense to pay good money for a tree that would be up for only a couple of weeks. Not when they were so easy to take and his cash flow was tight.

While Mark paid for the trees, Courtney pointed to a nearby clearing and asked her mommy to make a snow angel with her. "I can't, sweetheart. I've got Tucker in the pack."

"Aunt Thara?"

Sara glanced at her niece and chuckled. She could not possibly refuse Courtney's big brown eyes and pouty smile. "What do you say, Nicholas?" she asked, poking her nephew in the side. He bounced up and down on Gavin's shoulders and clapped his mittened hands.

"Whoa." Gavin tightened his hold on the two-year-old, then lowered him to the ground. Nicholas took off at a toddling run to catch up with his sister and aunt, who were already throwing themselves onto the pristine patch of snow. In an attempt to lay on his back, Nicholas fell and rolled sideways. He flopped onto his back, making a large dent in the snow and kicked his legs. Gavin chuckled at his antics and loped over to the little boy's side. "Like this, pal." Gavin grabbed Nicholas's legs and moved them from center to side and back again, making the angel's robe.

Nicholas giggled. "You angel," he said, flinging his chubby arm out to indicate that he wanted Gavin to make an angel next to him.

Gavin rolled his eyes at Sara, who was laughing, and flung himself backward and spread his arms. Mark finished paying for the trees and stood at Morgan's side, watching his children.

"All right," Morgan said quietly to Mark. "We know he's charming, but is there any substance there?"

Mark shrugged. "I'm not sure yet. Yes, he's a nice guy, but for some reason,

I don't trust him. You remember that old saying: Everything that glitters is not gold?" As a psychologist, Mark was used to sizing people up. Occasionally his first impressions were wrong, but usually he was right and something in his gut told him Gavin needed watching.

"I know the saying," his wife said. "I've already encouraged Sara to take it slow."

"I hope she follows your advice." Mark shook his head. "Gavin seems to have swept her off her feet."

"Yes." Morgan had witnessed many flashing, flirtatious smiles pass between the couple. "Well, I think we should get going. The kids are getting hungry."

"I am too. Why don't you grab some candy canes for the kids while I load up the trees?" He hoisted the large tree and left the smaller one on the ground next to Morgan and strode with the awkward load to the van. Morgan approached the attendant's hut and took two of the free candy canes, then told Courtney and Nicholas they could have them as soon as the snow was brushed off their clothes and they were in the van.

"How about us?" Sara asked, grinning. "Don't Gavin and I get any candy?"

"That's okay," Gavin said, pushing himself off the ground and grasping Sara's arm. "You're all the sweets I need." Laughing, he tossed her down and rolled her in the snow.

Delighted with Gavin's attention, Sara giggled and tossed snow into this face.

"You shouldn't start something you can't finish," he warned.

"You started it." Sara rolled away from him.

He stood over her, pointing at Courtney's angel. "You're ruining your niece's snow angel."

"Oh! Help me up." Sara lifted an arm and Gavin pulled her up. "Thanks." She flung one last handful of snow at him, then ran for the van, screaming as he gave chase. Quickly brushing the snow off her clothes, she scrambled in next to Courtney. Gavin shrugged at Mark and helped him finish tying down the trees. Mark nodded his thanks, then climbed into the van and asked who was hungry for lunch.

The older two children, mouths already sticky from the candy, clamored for their favorite drive-in. Mark chuckled and looked to his wife, who nodded her consent.

Later, over burgers and fries, Mark casually asked Gavin about his work and future plans. Sara held her breath, wondering how he would answer.

"I don't plan to stay at the health club forever, even though I think juice bars are a thing of the future. To make one be successful, I think you'd have to offer something besides juice. Like a bagel or something. I'm checking into it." Gavin shrugged and flashed Morgan his fetching grin. "Someday, I'd like my own franchise."

Sara had never known what Gavin's future plans were and she was glad that he had been able to give a satisfactory answer. She beamed at Morgan, as if to say, *Just like Jim.* Under the table, she reached for Gavin's hand and squeezed it. He flashed her a smile, then turned to ask Mark how often he traveled. He knew that Sara's sister and brother-in-law meant to quiz him on his lifestyle, his background, his schooling and whatever else they could come up with, but he would rather steer the conversation away from himself. Gavin was not used to meeting the families of the girls he dated and, as much as he liked Sara, he did not want to be thought of as anybody's future brother-in-law. *Keep it light; keep it easy.* Moose's old, familiar motto raced through his mind. Granted, it was fun to be with Sara, but she was not going to change his lifestyle. *Easy come; easy go. Keep it that way, Gav, old boy. Families get cumbersome.*

On the ride home, the children slept while Mark and Morgan conversed in low tones. Sara leaned her head on Gavin's shoulder and he softly sang a humorously revised, if somewhat tainted, version of the "Twelve Days of Christmas." She giggled quietly, although she had the grace to blush at the suggestive verses.

"Where did you learn that?"

"Robbie's band."

Sara sat up. "Robbie's in a band? I didn't know that."

"He's the drummer. I was going to ask if you want to go to his concert tonight. They're playing in a little joint downtown."

"That sounds so fun! Katie's husband, Wayne, was in a band—he played lead guitar—anyway, we always went to their concerts. A lot of times they played in the campus coffee shop. I especially love concerts in little places like that. It's so cozy—you know what I mean?"

Gavin nodded. "Sort of. Well, this place downtown just has local bands come in. They can't afford any big names."

Sara glanced at her watch. It was already past one o'clock. "What time is the concert, because I really need to study. I have exams the week after next and I haven't begun to prepare."

"We should leave at seven thirty, but do you really have to study? I thought we'd hang out together all day."

"Yes, I have to study."

He leaned close and kissed her. "You sure?"

"Yes," she whispered. "And Mark can see you in the rearview mirror."

Gavin shrugged. "So? You think he never kissed a girl in the backseat of a van before?"

"Probably not with the girl's brother-in-law watching."

Gavin sat back and, with a wink, promised more to come later.

Her heart rate accelerated. What was it about Gavin that made her entire body quiver?

When they returned to the house, Sara walked Gavin to his car, then went up to her room and diligently pulled out the two textbooks she most needed to study—one on management and the other on hospitality law. Placing the books on her desk, she could not help but notice the picture of her and Jim that sat prominently under her lamp. Sara remembered that it had been taken on her birthday. Tears pricked her eyes. She could not bear to look at the picture so she laid the frame face down. *Oh, Jimmy...*

Focus, Sara. You have to study. She flipped open the pages of one of the books, wondering as she did what Jim was doing today. *Probably studying, too.* Suddenly Sara jumped up from her chair and hurried over to Jim's duffle bag, realizing he would need his book and she'd better send it to him right away.

She went to the hall closet, where Morgan kept an assortment of boxes, wrapping paper and a plastic tub filled with tape and scissors. After examining the choice of boxes, Sara lifted a rectangular one off the shelf and grabbed a handful of tissue paper. Back in her room, she set the book inside the box, crumpled tissue and shoved it into the empty spaces so the book would not slide around during shipping. She started to close the box when she realized she should probably include a note.

Sara took a seat at her desk, pulled a pad of stationery from her drawer and picked up a pen. *Jim—* Wondering what to write, she chewed on the end of the pen and stared at the pale blue stationery. Resolutely, she bent over the paper. *I'm sorry for everything, well, I'm sorry for the other night and, and, and you should be sorry too.*

Sara tore the sheet of paper from the tablet and crinkled it up. *I can't write that.* Deciding to keep the note businesslike, she bent over a fresh sheet and wrote: *Jim, While studying, I realized you would need your textbook, so here it is. Sara.*

184

She reread the brief message and then tore that one up also. Surely, the ending of a twenty-two-month relationship demanded more than *here's your book.* Slowly, Sara picked up the framed photo of her and Jim and set it in front of her. Tilting her head, she studied the picture for a moment, then bent over the pad of stationery once more.

Dear Jim, she penned. *You left this book at the house and I wanted to get it to you right away, because I know exams are coming up and you'll need it to study. I don't know what went wrong between us or even when.* Sara glanced at the photo again, fingering the frame for a moment. *I only know that we had something beautiful, or at least, had the potential for something wondrous. I always dreamed of standing on the highest mountains with you, but I guess that'll never happen now. I don't know…* Tears pricked Sara's eyes. *I only know that I loved you…Oh, Jimmy…* A tear splashed onto the blue paper leaving a dark spot. *I love you still…* Sara sniffed and, swallowing tears, tossed the pen onto the top of her desk and stared at the note she had written, knowing she could never send it. Feeling defeated, she tossed it into her wastebasket. *There's nothing I can write.* How could she say on paper what was all in her heart?

She decided that not sending a note would be best. Jim would figure it out and understand. She sealed the box with packaging tape and neatly addressed it. Lifting the box, she brought it downstairs, where she found Morgan at the kitchen table paging through holiday cookbooks.

"Morgan, do you think Mark could mail this Monday morning? Overnight express? It's a textbook Jim left here and he probably needs it right away."

"No problem." Before Sara could head back upstairs, Morgan called after her. "Oh, by the way, Mom called a little while ago. I think you'd better tell her about Jim, because she's still planning on him coming during Christmas vacation."

"Oh, right…" Sara's heart dropped to her toes. She had forgotten that she and Jim had made those holiday plans. "Morgan, I—"

Morgan cast a look of sympathy toward her sister. "Breaking up is hard, I know."

Sara took a couple of steps toward her sister. "But it shouldn't be. I mean, I have Gavin now and I've known for several weeks that it was all but over with Jim."

"The ways of the heart are complicated, Sara."

"Well," determined, Sara tossed her mane of curls, "I do not want to shed any more tears over Jim Hoffman. My heart has bled enough for him; it's time to move on. I'll telephone Mom and tell her. Maybe Gavin will come for a few days."

"Are you sure that would be wise? You need take it slow with Gavin. I hardly think you're at the stage where you should be taking him home for an extended visit."

Sara bit back a sharp retort. What did Morgan know? She had no idea about the magic that existed between her and Gavin. "I'll talk to Gavin and see what he thinks." She hurried upstairs, determined to concentrate on her homework now that Jim's book was taken care of.

CHAPTER 16

Trust in the Lord with all your heart and lean not on your own understanding.
—Proverbs 3:5

Jim woke up groggy after a few hours of fitful sleep. For a split second, he wondered where he was, then he remembered. Groaning, he closed his eyes again, but found no solace in the darkness of his mind, because the sight of Sara in the arms of that other guy was stamped indelibly across his brain. Slowly, he rose to a sitting position and reached for his glasses where he had tucked them under the couch. A glance at his watch told him it was almost eleven o'clock. He could hear Katie humming as she puttered in the kitchen.

"I guess I'll go," he hollered.

"Oh!" Startled, Katie hurried into the living room, drying her hands on a dishtowel. "Jim, you're awake."

"I wish I wasn't."

"I'm sorry, Jim. I'm just so sorry."

"It's not your fault."

"I know, but..." Katie crossed the room and, sitting at his side, drew him into a hug. "I'll call her and find out what happened."

Pulling out of Katie's embrace, Jim stood. "Don't bother. Is Wayne here?"

"No, he had to go to work."

Jim slipped into his coat. "Tell him I'm sorry about smacking him."

"He knows. Oh, Jim…" Katie wrung her hands and stood up. "Will you be okay?"

"Stop fussing over me, Katie."

"I feel responsible."

"Why should you?"

Katie shrugged. "She's my friend; I introduced you. I don't know."

"Don't worry about it. I don't blame you." Jim patted her arm and went to the door. His hand resting on the doorknob, he turned to look at his cousin. "I just didn't see this coming."

"I didn't either," Katie swallowed a throat full of tears. "I can hardly believe it."

"It's true enough." Jim opened the door to face a world of white brilliance. There was nearly a foot of fresh snow on the ground and more falling. Four inches covered his car. With one impassioned sweep of his arm, he wiped the snow from his front window. As he drove home, he thought about how much a person's life could change in a matter of hours. All his dreams, all he'd been living for, were gone.

When he arrived at his apartment building, he traipsed through the heavy snow that had not yet been shoveled from the stairwell and entered his unit. He flopped onto the sofa, picked up the remote and turned on the television. He flipped through the channels, stopping when he came to a wrestling match. Mesmerized, he imagined he was wrestling with Gavin. It would feel so good to pin him. What kind of guy steals another guy's girl? What kind of girl does that to her boyfriend? Sara Brooks was a mystery to him. One he used to find intriguing, but one he now never wanted to figure out. She was a book he would place back on the shelf, into a corner where he could forget.

Gavin arrived to pick Sara up for the concert. As they approached his car, she noticed two people sitting in his backseat. In the semi-darkness she could not make out the faces. "Is Allie coming with us?"

"No, Mandy and Scott."

"Oh." Disappointed, Sara scooted inside and tossed a greeting to the couple in the backseat. They were kissing and barely acknowledged her. She didn't care. Next to KC, Mandy and Scott were her two least favorite people, but she was not going to let them spoil her date with Gavin.

"I'm glad you came along to the tree farm today and I liked what you said at lunch about opening your own juice and bagel bar someday."

"I just told your family what they wanted to hear."

"You mean it wasn't true?"

Gavin shrugged. "Probably not. I have no idea what I want to do for the rest of my life."

"So you have no plans?"

"Not at this point; there's plenty of time."

"Oh." Sara felt deflated.

"It's not a big deal. I gave a satisfactory answer for your family, didn't I?"

"Yes."

Gavin turned the radio up, putting an end to the conversation. He was in no mood for one of Sara's impassioned sermons. She probably expected him to have high career goals or something, like what's-his-name. But that wasn't Gavin's style, and tonight, he just wanted to hang loose and enjoy the concert.

When Gavin slowed and turned into a parking lot, Sara stared at the neon green sign that said *O'Malley's Tavern*. "I thought we were going to a concert."

"We are. This is where they're playing."

"In a bar?" Slivers of dread ran through her.

Mandy laughed sarcastically. "What's the matter, Sara? I suppose you've never been to a bar before."

Gavin turned into an empty parking space and killed the engine. "It'll be fine. You have your ID, don't you?"

Sara nodded, flabbergasted. "You didn't tell me…"

"It's no big deal. Come on."

Hesitant, Sara glanced to the backseat. She did not want to make a scene in front of Scott and Mandy. They already thought she was childish. Reluctantly, she followed Gavin. Two burly young men stood blocking the door.

"Who are they?" Sara whispered.

"Bouncers. Just show them your ID."

Sara fumbled for her wallet, feeling very tiny next to the men, who seemed even bigger than Moose. Nervously, she held her driver's license out for one of the bouncers to check. He examined it closely and Sara half hoped he wouldn't allow her in, but he waved her past.

Cigarette smoke assaulted her as soon as she entered. Sara glanced around the dimly lit room. There were twenty or so tables, a bar with stools and a small dance floor. Robbie's band was on the corner stage warming up. The room was so noisy that she could barely hear Gavin. She just nodded and followed him to the edge of the stage, where he greeted Robbie. After joking around for a couple of minutes, Gavin wished him luck, then led Sara to the table where Scott and Mandy were already seated. Nodding to the four glasses of beer on the table, Scott informed Gavin that he had bought the first round.

"Thanks."

"Gavin," Sara said under her breath as she took her seat. "The beer…"

"Just drink it, Sara. One glass is not going to make you drunk."

"I know." She shot a look across the table at Scott and Mandy, then lowered her voice. "But I don't want it."

"What's the matter, Sara?" Mandy sneered. "Too much Sunday school in your past?"

Sara blushed while Scott laughed. "Maybe she's not old enough to play with us big kids."

Gavin dropped an arm around Sara's shoulders. "Just take a few sips."

Sara looked from Gavin to her glass of beer. It was humiliating to be thought of as a baby or a Goody-Two-Shoes. Gavin was right. One glass of beer was not a big deal. It was only getting drunk that was harmful. It was probably only after multiple glasses, weekend after weekend, that a person became an alcoholic. It wasn't really that she had a problem with anyone drinking a glass of beer, it was just Uncle Marty and his alcoholism and the vows Sara had made years before. It'd never been difficult to keep those vows until now. She'd never been challenged like this.

Really, Sara Brooks, you should lighten up. One glass is nothing. Tons of people do it every day. Anyway, you know you desire to experience life. You're always saying how you want to soar on the clouds. Gavin's going to be floating away and you'll be stuck with your feet in the mud. With a determined toss of her curls, she picked up the glass and took a sip. She cringed, but swallowed.

Gavin chuckled and winked at her. "It's an acquired taste. Kind of like coffee. Did you like your very first taste of coffee?"

"I guess not." Sara took another small sip, determined to finish it by the end of the concert.

Gavin smiled at her—the special smile that always went directly to her heart. "That's my girl." He leaned back and studied her. "Did I tell you that you look amazing tonight?"

Sara sat up straighter, pleased. "Really?"

"Really."

The band started their concert. Gavin, Robbie and Mandy thoroughly enjoyed the music, but it was not Sara's style. It was strident, with disgusting lyrics—at least the ones she could understand. The band sang a lot about boozing, parties and sex.

Later, when the band took a five-minute break, Gavin flagged down the waitress. She brought another round of beers to their table. Sara's first one was only about a third of the way gone, but she was already beginning to feel the effects of it. "I'm only going to have one," she said quietly to Gavin.

He shrugged, positioning her second glass next to his. "Someone will drink it. How do you like the concert?"

Not wanting to be condescending, Sara took her time before answering. "Well, they are quite talented, but it's not really my kind of music." She took a few more sips of beer, then told him she was going to use the restroom. Gavin watched her cross the room, thinking again how great she looked. He felt a hand on his shoulder and looked up in surprise.

"Hayden! Haven't seen you for a while. What's up?"

"Had to come hear Robbie."

"Take a seat." Gavin grabbed an empty chair and dragged it to the table.

Slightly inebriated, Hayden greeted Scott and Mandy as he straddled the chair. Gavin offered Hayden Sara's second beer. The four talked for a while, catching up on what was happening with each other before turning their attention back to the band.

Sara stayed in the restroom, running her hands under warm water for several minutes. She could hardly believe she was in such a place, listening to such awful music. This night was not turning out as she had hoped. The only positive thing was the way Gavin looked at her. She could see how he cared about her by the look in his eye. That made all this worthwhile. She could put up with lousy company, atmosphere, and music as long as it meant she was with Gavin and pleasing him. "Be a big girl, Sara," she coached herself in the cloudy mirror. "Gavin would never do anything to hurt you."

Sara paused in the doorway and checked the main room. The band had resumed playing and the place was a lot fuller than when they had first arrived. A dance crowd had moved in and every foot of the dance floor was taken. Most of the tables had at least one person sitting at them and the bar stools were all occupied. A few people just stood around, beer glasses in hand, listening to the band. Sara took a few steps into the room, when a man sitting at the corner of the bar put his leg out to stop her.

"Where ya going, little lady?"

Sara took a step back. "To my table."

"You can sit here," he patted his lap. "Or maybe you'd like to dance."

"No thank you!" She took a sidestep, planning to go around him, but he hopped off his stool and stood in her way.

"Pretty thing like you…" His voice trailed off, but his eyes freely roamed Sara's body. He made a move toward her, but Sara stepped away.

"My boyfriend is here," she warned.

"If you get tired of him, I'll be here at the counter."

Sara scampered away, dodging tables and other patrons, and made her way back to Gavin's side. He reached for her hand and introduced her to Hayden. Disappointed that someone else had joined them, she slumped onto her chair, wishing she could tell Gavin about the detestable proposition she had just had. This night was going from bad to worse.

Hayden finished his beer and loudly ordered another round for the table. As the next hour passed, Gavin laughed and drank with Hayden, practically ignoring Sara. She leaned back in her chair, slowly finishing her now warm glass of beer. Scott and Mandy headed for the dance floor. Sara glanced around the room and noticed the man at the end of the counter watching her, so she leaned close to Gavin, took his arm and pretended to be absorbed in the concert.

After what seemed like forever, Robbie's band played their final number. Scott and Mandy returned to the table, bringing Robbie with them. They ordered another round of beer and Sara spent the next thirty minutes listening to the others talk about people she did not know and tell crass jokes. Finally Robbie left, then Hayden.

"Can we go now?" Sara asked.

"Yeah." Swaying slightly, Gavin stood and put on his jacket.

Eyeing him, Sara slipped on her own coat. "Let me drive, okay?"

"Not this again."

"Gavin, you've all had too much to drink."

"I've driven before when I've had more than this."

Sara put her hand out, palm up. "Give me the keys or I'm calling Mark to come get me."

Gavin surrendered the keys with a shrug. "All right, have it your way. Come on, Scott. Sara's going to drive."

They made their way to the parking lot. It did not appear as if any more snow had fallen, but the road looked icy. Sara set the defroster to high and waited impatiently for the windows to clear. While they waited, Gavin switched CDs and turned the volume up. Sara put a hand to her head. "Please, Gavin, I have a headache."

He turned it down slightly, then turned to say something to Scott in the backseat. Scott, however, was already making out with Mandy, so Gavin turned back and grinned at Sara. "Next time, Scott can drive and you and I will have the backseat."

"Never," Sara vowed, backing out of the parking spot.

Gavin chuckled, thinking she was kidding, and sat as close as possible.

"I'm driving, Gavin. Please, I need to concentrate." She clenched the steering wheel and stared straight ahead. The highway was slippery and she did not like the truckers barreling past at high speeds.

Gavin laid his head back against the seat and closed his eyes. He was nearly asleep when the car slid into a curve. He sat up and looked out the window as Sara managed to get the car under control. "Do you know you missed the exit?" he asked indifferently.

"Did I?" Sara had been concentrating so hard on the road conditions that she had forgotten to pay attention to the signs.

"You'll have to turn back."

Sara got off on the next off ramp, but did not get back on the freeway. Instead she opted for backtracking on side roads, where there were no truckers and she could drive slower. Her head throbbed and there was a tension ache in her shoulder blades.

"I can drive," Gavin offered. "This route you're taking is going to take longer."

"No," Sara said firmly. It was hard enough for her to maneuver the icy roads and she had barely finished her single beer. She was not going to turn this car over to somebody who had had a lot more to drink than she had.

Suddenly a pickup emerged from a dark side road. There was the screech of brakes as the driver attempted to avoid hitting Gavin's car. Sara screamed and slammed on her brakes. As their car fishtailed on the icy pavement, Gavin grabbed the steering wheel, attempting to pull them out of a spin, but he overcompensated and they slid for several feet before coming to a stop on the side of the road.

Scott sat up in the backseat. "Dude, man!"

Sara's heart pounded in her throat. "Is everyone okay? Mandy?"

"Fine, we're just fine."

Sara cast a desperate look at Gavin. "Are you all right? What happened?"

"You ran a stop sign."

Trembling, Sara unbuckled her seatbelt and opened her door, but Gavin grabbed her arm. "Where are you going?"

"To make sure the other people are okay."

"They're okay."

"But they went into the ditch."

"Sara, look at me. We've been drinking. We've *all* been drinking, even you." He stared at her, letting his words sink in. She glanced into the rearview mirror. She could see the driver getting out of his truck. He seemed okay. He started walking toward them. Gavin reached over and pulled her door shut. "Get moving, now."

Reluctantly, Sara put the car in drive and gently accelerated. Gavin was right. They couldn't be caught like this—with alcohol on their breath. As she pulled onto the road and put distance between them and the driver of the truck, Sara looked in her rearview mirror. The other man was shaking his fist at them. He seemed mad, but not hurt. That's what was important, Sara told herself. She wouldn't have driven away if he had been hurt.

Gavin brushed her hair from her face. "You're cool, Sara, very cool."

Twenty minutes later, Sara perched on the edge of her bed. She was trembling, literally shaking. Gavin, Scott and Mandy had not seemed too shaken up over the near accident. They just took it in stride. Gavin had wanted her to go to his place after dropping Scott and Mandy off, but she had insisted on going home. She had had enough of Gavin Manes for one night.

As she undressed for bed, she realized her shirt reeked of smoke. Pulling a handful of curls near her face, she grimaced. Her hair smelled, too. Grabbing her pajamas, she headed to the bathroom. Maybe a hot shower would do more than clean her hair, maybe it would wash away the dirty feelings Sara had from the night at the bar. She wanted to forget the crudeness of the song lyrics, the disgusting way some of the people had danced, the way Scott and Mandy constantly made out and Gavin's…Gavin's… Sara stifled a sob. She hated to think that Gavin had treated her badly. He hadn't really, not really.

After a long shower and a few minutes blow-drying her hair, Sara crawled into bed. Turning down the covers, she spied Jim's sweatshirt on the end of the bed where she had tossed it earlier. "Jim…" She reached for the shirt, realizing she had always felt safe with Jim. Safe, secure and pure. "Oh, Jimmy…" Sara pulled his sweatshirt over her pajamas and climbed into bed, wishing that Gavin was a little more like Jim.

She turned off the lamp and lay in the dark. The shower had not really helped. Oh, her hair smelled faintly like lilacs again, but her soul still felt sullied and Sara was confused. Gavin was usually such a charming guy, and drinking one beer really was no crime, so why did she feel so empty? Why was life so hard to figure out and where was a girl supposed to find the answers?

A small voice whispered in her mind, *Run to God.* God? Sara hadn't thought about God or read her Bible for quite a while. Did God really have the answers to her questions? Was He interested in everyday things like boyfriend dilemmas and whether or not to have a beer? Sara flicked her lamp back on and pulled her Bible out of the drawer in her nightstand. Maybe she should give God a chance. After all, He had always guided her before. Of course, life used to be simpler.

Proverbs, the book of wisdom. That's what I need. Sara read the verses on the top of the page. *Trust God from the bottom of your heart. Don't try to figure out everything on your own. Listen for God's voice in everything you do, everywhere you go. He's the one who will keep you on track. Don't assume that you know it all. Run to God! Run from evil!*

Sara looked up, pondering what she had just read. Maybe God did have the answers for her and maybe if she had been listening He would have told her not to go with Gavin tonight. But what if God told her never to be with Gavin again? A lump settled in Sara's stomach at the thought. He wouldn't, would He? She had already given up Jim, surely God wouldn't ask her to give up Gavin, too.

CHAPTER 17

Do not forget my teaching, but keep my commands in your heart.
—Proverbs 3: 1

The next morning, sandwiched between Courtney and a widowed lady from the neighborhood, Sara fixed her eyes on the minister. However, no amount of focusing her eyes could keep her mind centered on the sermon. She kept replaying last night's activities and the disappointment she felt about Gavin's behavior. Was a relationship with him worth all this turmoil? Could she ever grow comfortable in his world? Is this, after all, what she wanted?

On one hand, here was the most handsome man she had ever known; a carefree, fun individual who made her feel like a million bucks—when they were alone, that is. Put him with his friends and he tended to drink too much, tell crude jokes and practically ignore her.

Maybe he's embarrassed because I'm not the easygoing, let-life-happen kind of girl that his crowd is used to. Maybe I just need to relax more and be less uptight. Then, even in the middle of his friends, he'll hold me close and tell me how much I mean to him. How proud he is of me, how he can't live without me.

Courtney tugged on Sara's skirt. Jolted from her reverie, Sara realized the congregation had stood for the benediction and closing hymn. Smiling at her niece, Sara stood and bowed her head for the blessing.

On the ride home, Sara realized she might as well have stayed home for all she had gotten out of church. She hadn't even been able to sing wholeheartedly for wondering if the Lord desired worship from someone as confused as she was.

"It looks like you have company, Sara," Mark commented as they approached the house.

Sara sat up and craned her neck to look past Morgan's headrest to the street in front of the house. Sure enough, there was Gavin's old Chevy parked along the curb. Despite her earlier misgivings, she felt a thrill of excitement. As soon as Mark pulled into the garage and put the van into park, Sara climbed out and hurried to meet Gavin as he nonchalantly walked up the driveway, his hands behind his back.

"Hello," she greeted.

He didn't say a word. He simply drew one hand from behind his back and offered her a single pink rose.

Her breath caught in her throat. "For me? Why?"

Gavin offered a half shrug and his charming smile. "I figured out that you didn't have a very good time last night. I wanted to come by and make it up to you."

"Oh, Gavin..." Sara reached for the rose, her defenses dropping.

"I heard somewhere that the colors of roses symbolize different things, but I couldn't remember which color was for saying I'm sorry. None of the clerks at the grocery store knew either."

"I don't either, but pink is pretty."

"I wanted to get it right, so..." Gavin brought his other hand from behind his back. In it, he held two more roses—one yellow and one white.

"Oh, Gavin!" All thoughts of being angry with him dissolved. Of course Gavin Manes was worth a little trouble. "Last night wasn't *so* bad."

"You didn't enjoy the concert. I figured the drinking bothered you, then the driving incident—"

"It's okay, you don't need to apologize." She couldn't think when he was standing so near with his dark eyes penetrating her own. "You didn't know I wouldn't like the music and..." Really, could he help what his friends were like?

He raised his eyebrows and grinned at her. "So it's not all over? I get a second chance?"

She put her nose down to smell the sweet aroma of the roses, then slowly looked up at him. "Yes. We're still in the 'getting to know each other' stage. It's just going to take some time."

Leaning over the roses, he kissed her. "I like your way of thinking. So, how about some breakfast?"

"Breakfast?" Sara laughed. "I had that three hours ago! We're just about to have Sunday dinner. Do you want to stay and eat with us?"

"Sara, hangin' with your family is not exactly my style. I thought we'd just grab coffee and donuts at the grocery store or something."

"I thought you just came from there." Sara held the roses up to indicate that's where he made the purchase.

"Yeah, well, I wasn't thinking about food then. I was just thinking about you." He wrapped his arms around her waist. "Thoughts of you can drive a guy to distraction, don't you know?"

"No," Sara grinned. "I didn't know." *How thrilling! Had Jim ever been so distracted over me that he forgot to eat?* "Come inside; I'll go change and put the roses in water."

Reluctantly, Gavin followed Sara into the house. He waited impatiently in the entryway while she went up to her room to change into jeans and a sweater. Nicholas toddled from the living room and tugged on Gavin's pants. "No angel," he said.

"I don't know what you want, little guy."

"No angel!" Nicky said, tugging harder on Gavin's jeans.

"He remembers," Sara said, coming downstairs carrying her roses. "He wants you to make a snow angel."

Gavin chuckled and tousled the little boy's blond hair. "Not today, okay? It's almost time to eat." Turning to Sara, he added, "That gives me an idea though. How about if we go sledding? I know a great place."

"That sounds fun. I'll see if Mark has a sled or tube or something."

Gavin helped Mark get a saucer and an inner tube from the garage rafters while Sara hastily made sandwiches with Morgan's Sunday ham. She tossed the sandwiches and a few cookies into a bag, then filled a thermos with hot chocolate. Once they were on the road, Gavin wasted no time pulling out a sandwich to eat.

"This is good," he mumbled, taking another bite. Swallowing, he said, "Did you bring some sodas or water or something?"

"I forgot, sorry. Just the cocoa. Do you want some of that?"

"No, let's save it for after sledding. There's a grocery store up ahead. I'll pull in there."

Sara went inside with him and grabbed a diet cola for herself. "Anything else we need?" she asked, heading toward the express lane.

"I don't think so." Gavin set his cola next to hers and handed the clerk a five-dollar bill. Pocketing his change, he headed toward the exit. Noticing that there was not a clerk manning the small counter where customers could rent movies, he grabbed two packs of gum from a small display stand on the counter and continued sauntering toward the exit.

Tossing one pack to Sara, he stepped outside and unwrapped his own pack. Sticking a piece of gum in his mouth, he realized Sara was not beside him. Turning, he saw her staring at him through the glass doors. He took a step toward the store causing the automatic doors to open.

"Are you coming?" he called.

"The gum," Sara hissed.

"Do what you want, but I'm leaving."

She considered the pack of gum. It was a small package with only six sticks. It probably cost less than fifty cents. She looked toward Gavin. He had already reached the car and was looking at her over the hood waiting, seeming to weigh whether or not Sara was made of the right stuff.

While she debated, another customer left the store without even glancing at Sara. No one was paying any attention to her. With her heart racing, Sara hurried to the car.

"Progress," Gavin muttered to himself as they climbed inside. "That's my girl," he said, leaning across the gearshift and planting a kiss on her mouth. "That really wasn't so hard now, was it?"

She couldn't still the rapid beating of her heart. "Well, actually, yes."

He threw back his head and laughed good-naturedly. With a heavy heart, Sara knew that she had passed some kind of test, but she was afraid it had cost too much.

After a couple of hours spent sledding, Gavin and Sara decided to go to Gavin's apartment. Stomping snow off his feet, Gavin opened the front door. Allison stood in the kitchen, the phone to her ear.

"Just a sec! He's here now." Allison held the phone out to her brother. "It's Robbie."

Sara entered the apartment and slipped off her snow-covered boots. "Hi, Allie. Do you think I could borrow a dry pair of socks?"

"Sure, this way."

Sara followed Allison to her room, stopping in surprise just inside. "What have you been doing? Cleaning your closet?"

199

Allie pulled open a dresser drawer and glanced casually at the clothes spread across her bed. "No, I'm just trying to decide on the perfect outfit for the most important date of my life."

"And what is that?" Sara asked, taking the pair of socks Allison offered.

"Yesterday a lawyer came into the shop and asked me out on a date."

"A lawyer?"

"Well, almost. He's a paralegal, but that's almost the same thing, isn't it?"

"Sort of, almost," Sara agreed. "And he asked you out just like that?"

"He needed something for his sister's birthday. Mrs. Thorton likes us to be personable with the customers. I took him around the store making endless suggestions——"

And flirting big time, no doubt, Sara inserted silently.

"Anyway, when I was ringing him up, he asked me out to dinner on Tuesday night."

"That's great, Allison." Sara nodded, excited for Gavin's sister. This was what Allison needed, a young professional to date.

"I can't believe he asked me. He's got real class, Sara. Not like the jerks I've always dated. I need something to wear."

"Where's he taking you?"

"A restaurant downtown."

"Downtown? It's probably some classy place."

"Probably." Both girls looked at the piles of jeans, sweaters and tank tops on the bed. Allison sank onto her bed. "I just can't find anything. I'm not even sure what a girl should wear when she goes out with a lawyer. What do you think?"

"I'm not sure either, but something nice, Allie. Nice and dressy."

Allison eyed Gavin's girlfriend. Granted, Sara was not exactly her type, but Allie grudgingly admitted to herself that Sara always looked good. "Will you help me?"

Sara thought about it for a moment. This could actually be fun. Sara loved clothes. She adored clothes. "All right."

Sara sifted through some of the things Allison had laid on her bed. "Sorry, but I don't think any of this is dressy enough. Don't you own any nice skirts or dresses?"

"I never wear dresses, except sundresses in the summer." Suddenly Allison bolted off her bed. "I just remembered. Grandma gave me a sweater last year. I've never worn it…" She rummaged through a drawer, then drew out a light gray cashmere sweater and handed it to Sara. "What do you think?"

"Oh, Allison, it's lovely." Sara held the sweater almost reverently, then rubbed the soft material against her cheek. "I've always wanted to wear cashmere…always."

"So it will work?"

"Yes, but what will you wear with it?"

"I'll need a skirt."

"Yes," Sara agreed, envisioning it. "A silky black skirt, mid-calf."

"Yes." Allison thought for a moment, then got a dreamy look in her eye. "Sara, there's the perfect skirt at the store. It's silky, all right, and the hem comes down in various points so some of it is knee-length and some mid-calf. It's very classy."

"All right then," Sara rose from the bed. "Problem solved."

"Not exactly. That skirt costs over two hundred bucks."

"Two hundred dollars!" Sara's mouth fell open. "For a skirt? Wow."

"We only carry top-of-the-line merchandise."

"I guess. What kind of discount do you get?"

"Thirty percent, but it will still be a hundred and forty dollars and I can't spend that kind of money on one skirt."

"No, you can't." Sara understood only too well. She had an overflowing closet, but she always shopped the sales and she had never bought something in an exclusive shop like Charyl's.

"I'd just take it," Allison continued, "but Mrs. T always checks our bags when we leave."

Sara stared at Allison. "She *expects* you to shoplift?"

"I don't think she expects it, she just works to prevent it. We have to record everything we buy and show it to her. I've never dared to snitch anything."

Not realizing what she was suggesting, Sara said, "Too bad you can't just borrow it."

Allison nodded in understanding. "Like buy it and then return it after I wear it. I've done that before in other stores, but Mrs. T has a policy that employees can't make returns."

"You've actually done that?" Sara asked, amazed.

Allison shrugged. "What's the big deal? People do it all the time. They purchase something to wear to a special occasion, then return it."

"They do?"

Allison laughed. "Sara, you are the most naïve person I know. Don't you ever push the limits?"

Sara thought of the silver earrings she had not returned and the stolen apples and how up until she had met Gavin she had tried to walk the straight and narrow. Tossing her head, she said, "I'm not a little Miss Goody-Two-Shoes, you know."

"Then maybe you can help."

"How?"

"Come into the shop tomorrow. I'll find the perfect black skirt for you." Allison winked. "Then, legitimately buy something inexpensive, like a pair of nylons. When I ring them up, I'll pretend to ring up the skirt, too. That way, when Mrs. Thorton glances over, she'll assume everything is on the up and up. I'll slip the skirt into your bag and as simple as that, I'll have my skirt."

"Allison, I am not going to shoplift for you."

"Don't be silly. We won't steal it. I'll just borrow it, like you said. After I wear it, I'll bring it back, hang it on the rack and she'll never know."

"I don't know..."

"Well, if you want, you can pay for it, then return it and get your money back, but they only do store credit, so you'll be stuck with over two hundred dollars of credit."

"What could I get with that?"

"Oh, a dress, maybe. A cashmere sweater."

Sara's eyes grew large. "For two hundred dollars I can get three pair of jeans, a sweater and shoes at a store in the mall."

"That's what I figured. That's why we'll do it my way. We'll borrow the skirt. I'll bring it back after my date. Come on, Sara. You know I have to look stylish. Think about it...a lawyer, Sara. Goodbye to losers like KC."

Before Sara could answer, Gavin stuck his head into the room. "What are you girls doing in here? I was hoping one of you would fix spaghetti or something. I'm starved."

Sara looked at Gavin. "I'll make it." She jumped off the bed and headed toward the door.

"Sara?" Allie asked. "What about it? Will you do it?"

Sara paused at the doorway and looked back at Allison. It would be good if Allison started hanging out with a better class of people. Maybe this first date with the lawyer would lead her into a completely new crowd. Maybe it would lead to new girlfriends and Allie could leave Mandy behind. Sara ignored the battering of her heart and totally disregarded the small voice telling her it was wrong. *I hope I can trust you,* Sara thought. "Promise you'll return it?"

At Allison's nod, Sara agreed. "I'll come tomorrow afternoon. Just make sure your boss doesn't ask to help me."

"She won't. She helps the older women and lets me take on the younger set. That's why I was helping Brandon in the first place."

"Okay then…"

"Thanks, you know, maybe I misjudged you. You're all right, Sara."

Soft, instrumental music, the aroma of jasmine-scented candles and thick, luxurious pink carpeting greeted Sara as she stepped across the threshold of Charyl's Boutique. Squaring her shoulders, she took a quick look around the shop. Allison was behind the marble-topped counter folding scarves while her boss was busy with an elderly lady. Sara strolled over to a rack of dresses and slowly sifted through them until Allison approached, offering assistance.

Sara casually mentioned that she was looking for a new skirt for an important dinner. Allison walked confidently to a rack and pulled out the black skirt she wanted, plus two others. "Would you like to try these on?"

Sara nodded and took them into the changing area. Even the dressing rooms were luxurious, with wood-framed mirrors and pink-skirted chairs. For the sake of performance, she tried on two of the skirts, tarrying a moment in a flowing, burgundy one, turning this way and that so she could view it from every angle in the mirror. Holding her breath, she looked at the price tag, then dropped it like a hot potato.

"A hundred and eighty-nine dollars! Ouch." She quickly changed and strode purposefully out to Allison. "I'll take the black. Oh, and I'll need a pair of nylons, too."

"Right this way." Allison showed Sara where the stockings were, then returned the other two skirts to the rack.

Sara muttered under her breath that even the pantyhose were over priced, but she chose a color she liked and carried it to the checkout counter, where Allison stood folding the black skirt.

Sara shot a glance toward the front of the shop. Mrs. Thorton was still there, patiently helping the other customer with a selection of gloves. Allison rang up the nylons, Sara handed her a ten-dollar bill and Allie gave her the change. "Drop it off at the club," she said under her breath. "I'll get it from Gavin."

Sara nodded, picked up the bag and forced herself to walk nonchalantly toward the front of the store. Allison called after her to have a nice day, but

Sara simply focused on the door and getting outside. A small voice kept pace with her as she made her way down the sidewalk toward her car. *Bring it back. Don't go through with it. Bring it back.*

Sara thrust her key in the lock and, yanking open her car door, tossed the bag across to the passenger seat. "Thank goodness that's over!" At a stoplight, Sara looked at the striped paper bag, hardly believing that she had just walked out of an exclusive boutique with a two-hundred-and-twenty-dollar skirt.

That you didn't pay for!

I'm just borrowing it. That's different than stealing.

Shoplifter. You're no better than Allison and Mandy.

I am too. I'm only doing this as a favor.

Yeah, right. Sara felt the tightening of her stomach. *I don't think that matters.*

CHAPTER 18

Therefore…let us throw off everything that hinders and the sin that so easily entangles; and let us run with perseverance the race marked out for us. Let us fix our eyes on Jesus.
—Hebrews 12: 1-2a

Jim knew he had to study—his first exam was six days away—but he lacked the ability to focus. Vague thoughts of Sara lay always just out of reach and visions of her haunted his restless nights. Andy had dragged him along to church on Sunday morning, but Jim could not recall one word of the sermon. He had spent the hour—indeed, the rest of the day—lost in a fog. His thoughts alternated between sweet memories of the months he had dated Sara to the scene he had witnessed Friday night and the terrible realization that he obviously did not mean to Sara what she meant to him. It made no sense, no sense at all, and this was perhaps the hardest for Jim. He had always been able to rationalize life and put everything into neat compartments. However, this duplicity of Sara had him walking a tightrope between love and hate, stuck between feelings of betrayal and loneliness for the Sara he had loved for so many months.

On Monday, he let routine take over and dictate his actions. He went to his morning classes, then wondered why he had bothered. After lunch he spent ten fruitless minutes looking for his econ book. Andy came home in the middle of the search.

"Did you borrow my environmental economics book?"

"Why would I borrow your book?"

Jim brushed a hand through his hair. "I don't know."

"You probably left it in the library."

"Yeah, maybe."

When he arrived at the bookstore for work, there was a gushing note from Colleen saying she hoped his weekend had been everything he had hoped for and that his girlfriend was indeed very lucky. Jim stared at the note, then crumpled it and tossed it into the wastebasket, wondering if Sara had any inkling of what she had done to his life.

Tuesday afternoon, he ran into Wayne on campus.

"Hey," Wayne greeted. "I've been looking for you. I wanted to see how you were doing."

"How do you think I'm doing?"

"Rotten. I'd guess you're feeling rotten."

The pair stood on the snow-encrusted sidewalk, staring at each other. Jim broke eye contact first, looking across the snowy campus. "I don't even know how I feel."

"Come on, I'll buy you a root beer." Wayne took a couple of steps toward the campus coffee shop.

Jim stood rooted to his spot, envisioning The Beanery, where he and Sara had gone countless times. "I'd rather not. I have to study." Sara had picked the worst possible time to break up with him. Then again, in all honesty, she had not picked the day. He had gone there and surprised her. If he had not gone, he would still be living his dream. If he had not gone, she would still be stringing him along. He gulped and looked at Wayne. "She made a fool of me."

"You're no fool. She kept it secret from all of us—even Katie."

"I should have known. The dwindling e-mails, the stilted phone conversations... Man! How could I have been so blind?"

Wayne laid a hand on his friend's shoulder. "You were in love. Sara's dazzling in both looks and personality. Maybe this other guy fell for her like you did and she got in over her head and—"

"Now you're defending her?"

"No," Wayne was quick to answer. "She treated you like dirt, cheating like she did. I'm just saying—"

"Don't talk about her like that." Jim had no idea why he was sticking up for her.

Wayne sighed. He couldn't defend Sara, nor could he criticize her. "Sorry."

Jim waved off the apology. "It's all right; I know you mean well. Listen, I really do have to study." He resumed walking toward the parking lot, Wayne falling in step beside him.

"Okay, but come over whenever you need to. Katie would love to see you."

"Katie, yeah, well... I'll see. So long."

When Jim arrived home he got three textbooks and a tablet filled with notes and spread everything out on the kitchen table. Craig was in his room with the stereo blaring. Jim shut the bedroom door, then stood facing the work he had laid on the table. He had no idea where to start. He was still standing there when Andy came in carrying the mail.

"You got a package," he announced. When Jim didn't bother to look up, Andy held it out. "From Milwaukee."

That got Jim's attention. He reached for the box with an irrational hope that whatever Sara had sent him would somehow erase the jarring events of the past weekend. He pulled out a chair and sat down as he looked at his name and address written in Sara's bold, flowery hand, then up to the return address, where she had simply put *S. Brooks*. Jim weighed the package in his hand, shooting a questioning look at Andy.

"Too heavy for cookies," his friend said, at a total loss for what to say. He could only hope that Sara was sending a peace offering.

What would a girl send by way of apology, Jim wondered. And whatever it was, would it make any difference?

"Open it," Andy urged, disappearing around the corner to make a pot of coffee and give Jim some privacy.

Jim ripped a hole in the brown packaging, then tore it open to reveal his missing econ book. At first, he stared in disbelief. Sara had not sent an apology, she had simply returned his book. It was thoughtful in a way, but the sight of the book and the painful reminder that he had last used it at Sara's house only minutes before his life erupted made every second of the past few days jarringly real.

A note! he suddenly thought. *She'd have written a note. Something— anything—an epistle on how it had all been a crazy misunderstanding...* Jim reached for the wrapper and carefully sifted through it for a sheet of Sara's stationery. When he didn't find anything, he lifted the book cover, but it only revealed a forgotten sheet of paper with a list of scribbled book titles Jim had penciled weeks ago.

Determined to find something, convinced that Sara—who was never at a loss for words—would have written him, he turned the book upside down and shook it. No paper floated out. Disappointed, he dropped it on the table and stared at it. He found it hard to believe that she had simply wrapped up the book and mailed it without writing a note. Not one single word. No apology, no words of regret, nothing… Jim gave the book a swift shove, which sent it sliding across the table until it fell to the floor with a thud.

"What did Sara send?" Andy asked, coming around the corner, munching on a granola bar.

"Nothing." Jim rose, brushed past Andy and grabbed his coat off the hook. With his hand on the doorknob, he turned and looked at Andy. "She sent me nothing at all."

Thursday afternoon, Sara sat at her desk doing her homework. She couldn't believe the end of the semester was next week. The due dates for her final projects—not to mention exams—were only days away. Why had she not studied more the past week? Well, that was only too obvious. Ever since she had come home from Thanksgiving, life had been a little chaotic. Her love life definitely had priority right now. First there had been the tragic disappointment of the holiday, the mad, surreal weekend with Gavin, then the week of wondering which guy she should concentrate her energies on, then the incredible movie date with Gavin and the heart-wrenching breakup scene with Jim.

Sara felt a catch in her throat. Heart-wrenching was an understatement. Finally, Sara had experienced something truly worthy of a classic novel—the passionate, heated breakup scene—and it was, admittedly, one of the worst moments of her life. Had it really only been six days ago? Six days since Jim had sat downstairs accusing her—*her*—of ruining things between them? So much had happened since then. The wonder of hunting for a Christmas tree and making snow angels with Gavin, the ugliness of Robbie's concert, Gavin and the three roses, Allie and the black skirt…

Sara dropped her head back and sighed. *Why did I do that?* With a sigh, she rose from the desk and looked out the window. It was snowing again. She never would have dreamed that so much drama could happen in two weeks.

And one of the saddest things…she had not been able to talk to Katie about any of it. She hadn't been able to talk to anyone about it. Katie's loyalties would be divided, Morgan seemed somewhat understanding about her love life, but she'd preach a thousand sermons and probably drag Sara home to Dad if she ever got wind that Sara had had to drive her drunken friends home and had actually shoplifted.

Sara wandered to her dresser and picked up a photograph of her and Katie. She missed Katie. More than Jim? No, different than Jim. Boyfriends were boyfriends, but girlfriends were the cement that held life together. Katie would understand that and be willing to give their friendship the chance it deserved. Sara reached for her cell phone and dialed Katie's number. In less than two rings, Wayne answered. When Sara asked for Katie, Wayne stiffly informed her that Katie was at work.

With a harried glance at her watch, Sara sighed. "Of course she is. What a ditz I am. I'm just so anxious to talk to her."

"I can imagine." Wayne wanted to say more, to ask her if she was crazy, but after an audible sigh, he simply said he would let Katie know that Sara had called.

"I'm not a bad person," Sara quickly inserted before he hung up.

Wayne hesitated, picturing Jim—totally devastated. "We don't think you're bad, Sara. We just don't understand it."

"That's one reason I need to talk to Katie. I want to explain."

"Jim's explained, we still don't understand."

"But you've only heard his side of things."

Wayne was growing increasingly uncomfortable. "Listen, I'll tell Katie you called."

"Thanks."

"Well, I'll, um, see you around."

"Will you, Wayne? Would you want to?"

"Aw, man, Sara! You've got me in an awful spot here. It's very awkward to be friends with both of you. You must realize that."

"I understand, but Katie is *my* friend and why should Jim get both of you?"

Wayne paced the small living room. "You've got to accept the fact that he's family."

"Yes," Sara sighed. "Very convenient for him, isn't it? Just tell Katie I'm dying to talk to her."

She flopped back onto her bed, feeling as if the whole world was against her. Well, not the whole world. She had Gavin now. She dialed the number for directory assistance and had the call forwarded to the health club. She asked for the juice bar and waited for one whole minute until Gavin picked up the line.

"It's Sara."

"Hey."

"I just needed to hear a friendly voice."

"Why don't you come down here and do this in person?"

"You know I have tons of studying. I told you that I can't see you much until after I finish exams next week."

Gavin sighed. It was always something with this girl. "Well, can I put in my request for next Saturday?"

Sara chuckled. "Next Saturday? Yes, I'll be totally free from school even before that!"

"Good. They just posted fliers around the club. Next Saturday is the company Christmas party and I want you to come with me."

"I'd love to."

"Good, because there's going to be dancing and I can't think of anyone I'd rather take."

"Dancing? Hmmm…" Like Cinderella at Prince Charming's ball. "Well, you know, we don't have to wait until next weekend. I've been studying hard all week. Do you want to do something tomorrow night?"

"I can't. I'm busy."

"Oh." Wild ideas flashed through her mind. He wasn't taking another girl out, was he? Just because she had told him she needed time to study?

"But, um…I didn't mean for you to think that I would study all through the weekend."

"It's not that. I'm going up to Green Bay to Robbie's brother's house."

"Oh." Sara couldn't deny she was disappointed.

"Just a sec, Sara. I've got a customer."

Sara heard the phone clunk and dangle against the wall. She could just make out Gavin's pleasant, flirtatious voice as he bantered with his customer. It must be a female, Sara was sure of it.

"I'm back," Gavin said.

"About tomorrow, well, I just thought now that Jim and I are officially broken up that you and I would automatically spend weekends together."

"I don't operate that way, Sara. When it's right, it's right and when I'm busy, I'm busy."

And when you're free, I'd better be free, is that right? Of course, Sara would never say her thought aloud. "I see. So, it's important, huh?"

"You're starting to nag, Sara."

She drew in a breath and forced her voice to sound casual. "Sorry."

"Look, it's not that I don't want you to come, it's just our poker night and you'd be a terrible distraction."

"Poker?"

"Yeah, we have a standing game every month. It'd be great to have you along, but I need to concentrate. I've got bills piling up like you would not believe and I need a big take."

"Bills? How do you expect to pay your bills by winning a few dimes and nickels?"

Gavin chuckled. "Dimes and nickels? I don't think so."

"Gavin, if you need money, I'll give you some. I mean, I don't really have very much, but you shouldn't gamble. Besides, what if you lose?"

"I can't afford to lose, but if I do, I might take you up on your offer. Let it go, Sara. I do this all the time. Anyway, poker is not gambling. It's a game of skill."

Sara closed her eyes for a moment, once again unwilling to admit that Gavin lived in a different world than she did.

Friday evening, Sara tried to push all thoughts of Gavin and what he was doing from her mind and called Katie. She was thrilled when her friend answered the phone. "Katie? I can't believe it. We're actually talking!"

"Sara! I'm so glad you called. You have to tell me what's been happening. Jim's been saying some incredible things and leaving out way too many details."

"Yes, well," Sara sat cross-legged on her bed. "I hardly know where to start. Have we really not talked since Thanksgiving weekend?"

"No, and there's way too much I don't understand."

"So much has happened," Sara admitted, wondering just how much of it she could actually tell Katie. "A lot of it hasn't been very pleasant and I don't really understand what went wrong between me and Jim." She glanced at his duffle bag, which she had been stepping over for a week now. His MCU sweatshirt lay draped over the top. It remained a bittersweet reminder of all that she and Jim had meant to each other. "I still can't get over the fact that Jim and I are finished. I had thought we would spend forever together, but that isn't going to happen."

Katie asked a few probing questions, to which Sara gave unsatisfactory answers. Deciding Sara was not going to go into detail about why she and Jim split up, Katie decided to try a new track. "I gather that you have a new guy in your life. Why don't you tell me about him? Is this the one you met at the club?"

"Yes, his name is Gavin."

"Go on," Katie encouraged. After all, she wanted to be fair. If it was possible to juggle a relationship with both Jim and Sara, she would do just that. She listened to Sara's glowing report, then suggested that she and Wayne meet Gavin. She wanted to discover firsthand what this guy was like and how he had managed to send Sara's heart spinning.

"Oh." Sara would give anything if the four of them could be friends, but there were too many sides to Gavin's personality that she did not want Katie and Wayne scrutinizing. "Maybe...we'll see."

"We could get together around New Year's or something."

"Maybe," Sara repeated. "I would love to see you."

"So, what are your plans for vacation?"

"I'm going home for a week. I wanted Gavin to come with me, but he says it's too soon to spend a bunch of time getting to know my family." Sara sighed. "Don't you think that's weird?"

"Well, you haven't been dating very long."

"I know, you're right. Anyway, I won't be home very long because I'm coming back to house-sit while Mark and Morgan go to Iowa over New Year's."

"Well then, we could get together when you come back. We could meet halfway and spend the afternoon and evening together. What do you think?"

"Maybe, yeah. Let's talk to Gavin and Wayne and see what they think."

During the middle of the night something woke Sara. She lay still and listened, wondering if Nicholas or Courtney were up. Nicholas had just learned how to climb out of his bed and she supposed he could be wandering around. There. Again. It must be a tree branch hitting her window. It didn't seem windy outside though. She strained to hear, waiting until the slight clatter hit her window again. It sounded like something was being thrown against the glass. Tossing aside her blankets, she rose and peered outside. In the glow from the street lamp she could clearly see Gavin standing in the driveway. He'd been watching for her and as soon as she appeared in the window he waved. *How romantic,* Sara thought. *Just like Rapunzel!* She waved back and motioned that she would be right down. She grabbed her jacket and slid her stocking feet into a slip-on pair of tennis shoes, then tiptoed down the stairs to the front door.

As soon as she stepped onto the porch, Gavin picked her up and twirled her around. He was a little tipsy and took a misstep, clumsily falling from the porch to the sidewalk. "Come celebrate with me, Sara. I made a ton of money tonight."

"You're drunk." She could smell the alcohol on his breath.

"Not really. Honest. I didn't have a thing to drink during the card game. Only afterward." His words were slurred.

"You're drunk," she repeated, trying to plant her feet on solid ground. "Now put me down."

Gavin lowered Sara to the ground, but did not release her. "Come dancing with me. I know some places that are still open."

"I am not going anywhere with you when you're like this. Go home and sleep it off. Call me later." Sara pushed her hands against his chest, but his hold was too tight and she could not break away.

"Robbie said you wouldn't come."

"He was right."

"You're spoiling all my fun. Have you ever danced at two in the morning?" Gavin took her hand and twirled her around as if they were on a ballroom floor, not a snow-encrusted sidewalk in the middle of a December night. His movements were shaky and his footing unsteady, which only caused him to laugh. "I'm usually better than this."

"Gavin, you need to go home. You'll wake up Mark and Morgan."

"Oh, man…we wouldn't want that to happen." Even in his inebriated state, he realized she was right. He did not want the wrath of big sister on his shoulders. He lowered his voice, trying to whisper, but not succeeding. "So, when will you dance with me? I once told you that if we were dating I'd take you dancing." Still holding her tight, he twirled her around.

"Next week," Sara promised. "At the club's party. You said there would be dancing."

"That's right." Gavin blinked and stopped spinning. "I think I'm going to be sick." He pushed her aside, stumbled back and headed for the bushes.

Gavin returned, wiping his mouth with the sleeve of his jacket. "Sorry. Maybe I will go home." He reached for her hand and held it for a brief moment. "Next Saturday, save every dance for me, okay?"

Sara couldn't help but smile. "Like who else would I dance with?"

Gavin shrugged. "You're a beautiful and enchanting woman, Sara. The men will be lined up to take you for a spin around the dance floor."

Beautiful. Enchanting. "I'll only dance with you," she promised. "We'll dance the night away."

"I'll call you in the morning." Gavin let go of her hand and took a few unsteady steps toward his old Chevy parked in the driveway.

Sara watched while he backed out and nearly sideswiped the neighbor's shrub. She waited on the porch until his car was no longer visible, then crept up to her room. She would call him in a few minutes to make sure he arrived home safely.

Why did he have to drink so much? Sara slipped out of her jacket, kicked off her shoes and, picking up her cell phone, climbed into bed. She was trying to convince herself that the way she felt when Gavin said she was beautiful and enchanting carried more weight than the fact that he had appeared at her doorstep in a drunken state, but did it really?

CHAPTER 19

Do nothing out of selfish ambition or vain conceit…
—Philippians 2:3a

Tuesday afternoon, Jim stood outside Professor Levine's open office door and knocking, peeked in. His instructor glanced up from the papers on his desk.

"You wanted to see me, sir?"

Professor Levine removed his eyeglasses and motioned for Jim to enter and take a seat. Jim nervously perched on the edge of a dark red chair and waited silently. The gray-haired professor studied Jim's face for a moment, then pulled out a blue exam booklet from a top drawer and laid it on his desk.

"I must say, Mr. Hoffman, I was quite surprised by the results of your exam. It's not up to your normal work. In fact, it's way below your average." He paused a moment, letting Jim digest the bad news. When he looked up again, there was kindness in his eyes. "Is there trouble at home?"

Jim blushed, forcing back the anger he felt at Sara for doing this to him.

"Of course," Professor Levine continued, "if it's too personal you don't need to go into details. I was just looking for some explanation."

"It's a girl." Jim's voice cracked so he cleared his throat and started again. "My girlfriend—we just broke up."

The professor slowly shook his head. "Not the best timing for your studies."

"I agree, but it—uh—was inevitable. The timing couldn't be helped."

"It's most unfortunate…"

"Is it possible for me to retake the test?" It was not in Jim's personality to grovel. He would not plead. If the answer was no, so be it, he would live with the consequences. This was just one more arrow with which Sara had pierced his heart.

"What's your schedule look like tomorrow?"

"An eight o'clock for Professor Berg, then I'm finished."

"How about eleven thirty, here in my office?"

"Thank you, sir." Jim rose and shook the professor's hand.

"I think you know the material, or I wouldn't offer this chance to redo it. You need to focus, Mr. Hoffman. You can dwell on the problems with your love life during vacation, but for two more days, you are going to have to focus on your studies."

"Yes, sir, I know. Thank you."

Sheila, the front desk clerk, chuckled to see Sara bouncing into the health club Thursday afternoon. "Someone's in a good mood."

"Do you ever feel as if you could take on the world? I'm simply soaring on air!"

"What's happened?"

"I just finished my last exam for the semester. I know I did great. It feels so wonderful!"

"Congratulations. That's terrific, Sara."

"And what's more…" Sara clapped her hands together. "I have nearly four weeks of freedom before second semester starts."

"Well," Sheila said stacking freshly folded towels, "I wish I could say the same, but I'm a working girl."

"Have you worked here very long?"

"Nearly two years."

"So you've gone to a club Christmas party before?"

"Yes, why?"

"I'm going with Gavin and I've been wondering what to wear."

"People dressed up last year. I don't mean in formals, but nice party dresses."

"Sounds like I might have to go shopping. What a perfect way to celebrate! Thanks."

The next day Sara left a big department store in the mall and headed for a small shop that catered to young women. She had already tried on three dresses and not found what she was looking for. Entering the new shop, she looked carefully through nearly every dress in her size before she eyed the perfect one on display on a mannequin. It was red with shimmering sparkles in it.

"Oh, that's pretty," Sara said aloud to the clerk standing nearby. "Do you have it in a size four?"

"I think so," the clerk headed to a different rack that Sara had not yet seen. "Here you go," she said, handing the dress to Sara. "That's going to look great on you."

Well, of course she would say that, Sara thought as she slipped into the dressing room. She pulled the dress on, then twirled and swayed in the small changing area as if she were dancing, keeping her eye on the dress in the mirror. *Perfect...it is absolutely perfect.* Sara reached for the price tag, held it out at an angle, then dropped it. *Yikes!* Sara studied the dress again from every side, then sighed, thinking how unfair it was that Allison could basically steal a skirt for an important date, but because Sara was honest, she couldn't have the dress she wanted. And this was the dress she wanted. The clerk was right, it did look great—no, it looked fabulous.

Sara stared at the price tag again. *If only Allie was here, she'd figure something out. What am I thinking! I'll pay for this dress or find something cheaper.*

Slowly, Sara unzipped the dress. She had some money in her savings account, but it was barely enough to cover second semester books and the motel bill that was coming due on her credit card. But the dress was wonderful and this date with Gavin was important and she needed the dress *now.* The club party was tomorrow. There would be time to figure out how to pay for the motel and school books later. Maybe she could hit her dad up for some cash. He didn't need to know about the dress, just that she had no money for books.

Her decision made, Sara stepped out of the dress with a smile. Some things were worth sacrificing for and a special party dress was definitely one of those things. She could wear her black heels, so she wouldn't need new shoes. Her silver necklace with the charms would look great and...those earrings she had gotten from Mandy! Sara had never dared wear them after that first afternoon, but they would be perfect.

Sara put her hair up, then took it down, then put it up again, deciding it would be cooler while dancing to have it off her neck. Carefully she applied her lipstick, sprayed herself with her favorite perfume, then stood back to study herself in the mirror. The doorbell rang and she glanced out the window to make sure it was Gavin, then slipped on her coat and went down to greet him.

Gavin was waiting with Mark in the entryway. Nicholas was tugging on his black pants saying, "Boons?"

Gavin looked to Sara for a translation. "I told him you were taking me to a party," she explained. To Nicky she said, "I don't know, sweetie, but if there are any balloons I promise to bring one home for you."

Nicholas clapped his hands. Marked scooped up his son and wished Sara and Gavin a pleasant time. Once they were settled in the car and on their way, Gavin reached for Sara's hand. "Remind me on the way home, we'll stop at a grocery store and get a balloon for Nicky."

"That is so sweet." Sara smiled at him, thinking how his good points outweighed his bad ones. Confident that all would be well, she told him that Katie had suggested meeting halfway. "I'd love you to get to know my friends," she added. "What do you think?"

Gavin shrugged. "Sounds okay to me."

"I'll see what Katie and I can set up." She shifted on the seat so she could sit a little bit closer to him. "I'm really looking forward to the party. I got a new dress just for the occasion."

"Did you now?" He glanced at her with her coat zipped nearly to her chin. "So you gonna show me?"

"When we get there. I'm so excited. I love to dance. I mean, I've only gone to one or two real dances—Jim doesn't like to dance—but I've practiced in my room and when I was growing up my friends and I were forever dancing at slumber parties."

Gavin chuckled. Sara always put her own unique spin on the most ordinary things.

The party was being held in a large hotel near the airport. When Gavin and Sara arrived, he suggested they check their coats, then he draped his arm around her shoulders and steered her toward the elevator. She looked gorgeous, just as he knew she would. The elevator doors were made of large mirrors and as they waited for the lift, he studied Sara from head to toe.

"I like the dress. You look amazing in it."

Sara beamed with delight. "I'm glad you think so."

Gavin ushered her into the elevator. "Me and every other man in this hotel. I told you, they'll be lined up ten deep."

"No they won't." Sara protested, but the thought was pleasing. Imagine, her, the belle of the ball. Just like Cinderella. "It's like a fairy tale," she said softly. "We're like a fairy tale."

"That's what I've been telling you."

They stepped into the room, greeted a few people, and made their way to the punch table. Sara didn't know very many people, but Dean was there, and so was Sheila, the girl who worked front desk in the afternoons when Sara had aerobics.

Sara and Gavin mingled and nibbled on hors d'oeuvres, waiting for the band to begin playing. When it struck its opening chord, Gavin grasped Sara's hand and led her toward the dance floor. They danced to song after song, taking a break now and then for a glass of punch. Gavin was right, a couple of guys asked Sara to dance, but she turned them all down.

"How about getting some food?" Gavin asked near ten o'clock.

"That sounds good."

They moved through the buffet line, then found a small, round corner table to sit at. Sara's hair was coming loose from her silver clips and several strands fell in ringlets around her shoulders.

Gavin wiped his fingers after eating a couple of buffalo wings. "Having fun?"

"The best time ever. Oh, Gavin, I wish this night would last forever."

"I'll never forget how beautiful you look tonight."

"Gavin, you say the sweetest things."

He shrugged. "It's true."

Sara looked into his dark eyes. "Tonight is like a fairy tale come true. I grew up wishing on falling stars and my number one wish was always for the most handsomest Prince Charming to fall in love with me." She looked at him, waiting, wondering if he would tell her he loved her.

Gavin nonchalantly stuffed a cracker in his mouth. He chewed it slowly, then said, "We are like a fairy tale, Sara. Meeting like we did in ninth grade and having all that electricity between us. Then, meeting again at the club. It's like destiny." Gavin was careful not to talk about love. Things certainly had not reached that point. And as long as it was within his power, he'd follow Moose's motto: Keep it light; no commitments.

Several days later, Gavin and Sara sat across the table from each other at a pizza parlor. She was leaving the next day to go home to her parents' house. Neither of them was looking forward to the separation. Sara should be used to it, having been apart from Jim so much, but she couldn't help but wonder if part of the reason things hadn't worked out for them was because from the very beginning they had been separated by too many miles. Now she dreaded the thought of even a one-week separation from Gavin. Gavin wasn't wild about it either—for different reasons. He liked having his girlfriends close at hand.

"Maybe I could come see you—" he suggested at the same time she said, "You know, Madison is only an hour—"

They both stopped talking, then they chuckled. "You're thinking what I'm thinking," Sara said.

"I know I said that I don't want to spend a lot of time with your family, but I could drive over on Saturday just for the day."

"My thoughts exactly. Anyway, my parents want to meet you. We have an extra bedroom. You could stay overnight and leave sometime on Sunday—after church."

"I don't think I'll stay over." The last thing Gavin wanted was to be paraded down a church aisle and have all the old ladies talking about him being Sara's new boyfriend. What's more, he had no desire to spend Sunday dinner around a table being quizzed by Sara's family.

Sara's week at home passed slowly. She was so homesick for Gavin—or maybe it was Jim. The traditional family activities, which she normally loved, brought up bittersweet memories of Jim and she couldn't help but wonder how he was.

The day Gavin visited, her parents gave him a pleasant, if somewhat reserved, greeting. He knew they were sizing him up, comparing him to Jim. He didn't really care what they thought, and as quickly as he could, he whisked Sara away, glad he was not staying longer than one day.

The last night she was home, Sara approached her dad as he sat reading the paper after supper. She knelt on the floor next to his armchair and explained how she was short on money and didn't have enough to purchase textbooks. He gave her a stern look and asked what she had been doing with her money.

Sara gave her dad a small smile. "I don't know. I've hardly bought any new clothes or anything, just one or two things. Life's expensive, Dad.' "

"How's it going living with Morgan and Mark?"

"It's wonderful. And don't get me wrong, they are very generous, but I don't want to take advantage of them. I buy all my own soap and everything."

"I'll tell you what, Sarabelle," her dad had called her that for ages, "I'll pay for your textbooks, but I'm going to make the check payable directly to Milwaukee Tech. Do you understand?"

"Yes, Dad. Thanks. Thanks so much." She gave him a tight hug. "You're the best!"

Mr. Brooks patted her back and sighed. He wasn't sure that was true. If he could prove that Sara was throwing money away, he wouldn't give her any, but Morgan had not complained about anything and nothing seemed remiss. "You're welcome, Sara, but don't think I'm going to do this for you next fall. You need to do a better job of budgeting."

Friday morning, Sara drove back to Milwaukee, excited to see Gavin. She couldn't decide if she should go directly to the club or wait until he got home. She didn't really want to greet him in the club lobby after being apart for six days, but then if she waited until he got home it would be several hours until they would see each other. Pulling off the freeway, she turned into the parking lot of a strip mall and dug through her purse for her cell phone. She called the club and, disguising her voice, asked to speak with Gavin Manes on a personal matter of grave importance. She giggled when he came on the line sounding worried.

Lowering his voice, he said, "Sara, are you back?"

"Yes! I can't wait to see you. Have you had lunch, can you sneak away for your break?"

"I can do better than that. You told them this was important, right? I'll say that my mom needs me home for some family emergency and I need the rest of the day off. I'll meet you somewhere—how about Los Amigos?" Before she could argue about the dishonesty of his proposal he hung up, put a sober expression on his face and pressed the inter-office connection to his supervisor's desk. Ten minutes later, he was pulling on his coat and heading for the parking lot. Not until he was around the corner and out of sight, did he break into a grin and a sprint.

He hadn't realized until now just how much he had missed Sara. He wasn't sure that missing a girl was a good thing. *Get a grip,* he warned himself. *Remember the motto: keep it easy, keep it light, no commitments.*

He pulled into the parking lot of the restaurant. Sara's empty car was parked three spots over. He glanced to the front door, where she waited, hands in her coat pockets, a hat sitting jauntily on her head, a smile lighting her face.

He dashed out of his car, sweeping her into a hug.

"I missed you!" she said.

"Yeah, me too."

"I think this is one of your better ideas," Sara said, laughing merrily.

He winked. "I have plenty more where this one came from. Come on." He took her hand and led her inside, then followed the waiter to a booth along the wall. Gavin didn't even bother to look at his menu, he knew he wanted beef fajitas. He munched on chips and salsa while Sara perused her menu. Suddenly he stiffened, then ducked behind Sara's menu, blindly reaching for his own.

"What are you doing?" Sara asked, closing the large plastic menu.

"Hold it up!" Gavin pleaded. "The club owner just came in with two of the personal trainers. They must be having a lunch meeting. I can't be seen. They think I've gone home for a family emergency."

Sara peeked over the top of her menu. "They're coming this way." Gavin shrank down on the bench, holding his menu close to his face. "Okay," Sara whispered. "They're being seated by the window. What do you want to do?"

"When they pick up their menus we'll leave."

A waiter appeared at Sara's side. "Are you ready to order?"

Sara cast him a beguiling smile. "Could we have a minute, please?"

"Sí." The waiter nodded, then turned back toward the kitchen.

Sara laid her menu down. "Okay, now!" She scooted out of the booth and headed swiftly toward the door. Gavin followed, holding his menu near his face, then he dropped it deftly into a rack by the cash register. They were out the door in mere moments, running to his car across the lot. Once inside, they broke out in laughter.

"That was nerve-wracking. I would never make a very good truant," Sara admitted.

Gavin put a hand on the back of her head and planted a kiss on her lips. "You were cool, Sara. Joe Cool."

She leaned against the backrest, trying to catch her breath. "I have a suggestion to make: takeout!"

That evening, Sara and Gavin decided to just hang out at his place. Allison didn't have plans either, so when Moose, Jared and Robbie called to see what was up, they all decided on an evening of video games and a movie at Allie and Gavin's apartment. Allison called Mandy, who called Scott. Knowing they would soon have an apartment full of friends, Sara baked a pan of brownies while Gavin ran to the store for chips and drinks.

When everyone arrived, Sara was disappointed to see KC walk in behind Moose. During the evening, she managed to keep her distance as best she could in the small, crowded apartment, but she could not stop him from openly gawking at her.

Sara went into the kitchen to get the fresh-baked pan of brownies. Coming back to the living room, she looked at Gavin's group of friends—her friends now. Scott and Mandy were sitting on the floor in the corner. Sara quickly averted her gaze, not believing how open they were with their physical actions. She had always desired a guy to show her attention in pubic—but not like that. Never like that. The others didn't seem fazed by it. Allison sat on the couch paging through a magazine while KC and Moose played a noisy Xbox game. Jared sat on the floor idly watching Robbie and Gavin play blackjack.

Sara walked around the room, offering the warm brownies. KC managed to brush his arm against her. His simple touch made her skin crawl, but she couldn't escape fast enough, with Moose's large body blocking the way.

"We should have checked the paper for a concert," Jared suggested, reaching for a brownie. "There's got to be something good playing in this town."

"Not much," Gavin commented. "I think all the good concerts were before Christmas."

"Well, here we are. Crowded in at Gav and Allie's." Jared got up, stepped over Robbie and got himself another beer. "Any one else?" He brought a handful back to the room and passed them around.

"You're right," Scott agreed, "a concert sounds good. Too bad Robbie's band is not playing tonight. When's your next gig, man?"

Robbie shrugged. "I'm not sure."

"Randy Nichols is playing at the Paramount," Sara spoke up without thinking.

"Randy Nichols? Who's that?"

"You haven't heard of Randy Nichols?" Sara looked around the room, but only received empty looks in return. "He's only the most up and coming contemporary Christian artist."

"Christian?" Scott asked. "You want us to go to a *Christian* concert?"

Sara blushed, why had she opened her mouth? She had to remember whom she was with. This group was never going to accept her if she kept being so…so…Christian. "It's not like it's the Gaither Family," she said in an attempt to neutralize her suggestion. "He's very contemporary. I've heard him on the secular stations."

"Yeah, but *Christian?*" Scott continued. "You trying to get us all saved, Sara?"

"Hey," Gavin said. "She just made a suggestion."

"Not a very good one," Mandy said. "I still remember old Sunday school songs. I don't think I want to hear them in concert."

"It's not like that," Sara said softly. "Never mind, I'm sure it's sold out anyway."

KC laughed. "Like a Christian singer would be sold out! That's a good one!"

Sara opened her mouth, but decided it wasn't worth it. She would just end up digging herself in deeper. She headed back to the kitchen and set the tray of brownies on the table. When she returned to the living room, someone brought up the subject of New Year's Eve.

"We should have a big party, with the whole gang."

"Yeah, but where? Nobody has enough room."

"Certainly not here," Mandy said, eyeing the crowded room. "Troy and Krissa aren't even here and look how we're all crowded in like sardines."

"We have to invite Monica and Karla, too," Allison put in.

"How about your place, Robbie?"

"It's too small," Gavin said.

"If only my folks were going away we could use their house, but they're having friends in," Mandy commented.

"I'll be back in a minute," Gavin said, getting up and tugging Sara after him into the kitchen. He went to the far corner, then quietly said, "We can have the party at Morgan's. You'll be house-sitting."

"Oh, we couldn't. They'd never agree. Morgan's already talked to me about not having more than a couple of friends over. She specifically said, no parties."

"So don't ask them. They'll never know."

"Gavin, I couldn't."

He nodded toward the living room. "You'd make their night, Sara. They'll forget all about that concert thing."

Sara looked over Gavin's shoulder to the group in the next room. It'd be nice to redeem herself, but...

Gavin touched her chin. "Look at me, Sara. If you won't do it for them and you won't do it for yourself, how about doing it for me?"

She looked into his dark eyes, his handsome face, and wavered. She didn't want to disappoint him. She was afraid she'd done enough of that already in their brief relationship. Besides, he was so charming...

"Come on, Sara, for me."

"All right," she whispered. "I'll do it, but do you think it could be a non-alcoholic party?"

Gavin tweaked her nose. "You're funny, Sara. On New Year's Eve?"

Sara smiled lamely. He kissed her, then strode into the midst of his friends and announced that he and Sara would host the party at her sister's house.

CHAPTER 20

What I don't understand about myself is that I decide one way, but then I act another, doing things I absolutely despise.
—Romans 7:15

"Good game." Jim looked over the chessboard at his brother. "You finally beat me."

"It doesn't count," Jason replied, picking up the discarded pieces and placing them back on the board. "Your mind wasn't on the game."

"I was on it."

"No you weren't. You've been brooding over Sara since you came home. I can't imagine spending that much negative energy on a girl."

Jim watched his younger brother neatly line the game pieces on the brown and tan squares. "Then you've never been in love or you'd understand."

"You're right." Jason looked Jim in the eye. "I haven't fallen in love yet, haven't found the right girl, but you did, so if you're this broken up over it why don't you go get her back?"

"Don't think I haven't thought about it."

Jason pushed the chessboard to the far end of the dining room table. "Yeah? So? You just going to let her waltz away without a fight?"

Jim sighed. "Yep, that's what I'm going to do. She chose someone else; I'm not going to fight for her. If she wanted me, she would be here."

"Then let me give you a piece of advice, big brother: get over it." Jason rose from his chair and disappeared down the hall.

Jim whispered his response, "I wish I knew how."

Gavin convinced Allison that she and Mandy needed to help Sara get things ready for the party. Sara spent the morning cleaning—an already clean house—even though Gavin told her no one would care. In the afternoon, she painstakingly put together some of her favorite hors d'oeuvres. Allie and Mandy showed up about five thirty to help, their arms loaded with grocery sacks.

"Boy!" Allison said, eyeing the plates laden with Sara's preparations. "You went through a lot of work. It looks good."

"I'm just about finished with these Mexican pinwheels."

Mandy set her grocery bags on the table and removed the large bag of chips. "I thought we'd just have chips and dip, a beef stick, stuff like that. You didn't have to go through all this work, Sara."

"Maybe not, but when I host a party I like to do it right," Sara said, wiping a strand of hair from her face.

"Well, I'll say it again, your way is a lot of work."

"Maybe, but I had nothing else to do while you were at work and, besides, I love to cook. To me, this is fun."

Mandy rolled her eyes at Allison, who simply shrugged, tossed her coat aside and asked what she could to do help. Sara set Allison to work cutting vegetables, then handed Mandy a package of paper coasters and asked her to set them around the living room and Mark's study.

Mandy stared at the package. "You've got to be kidding. People aren't going to use these."

"Listen, I can't risk getting rings on my sister's furniture. She has all wood tables."

"Then you'd better drape them with towels, because I can guarantee that Moose and KC and Robbie are not going to look for coasters."

Sara looked up from placing the pinwheel appetizers on a large plate and studied Mandy's face. "You're right. We'll cover every end table with bath towels and I'll find a tablecloth for the dining room table. Will you finish putting these on here and I'll go get some towels?"

Not bothering to wash her hands, Mandy elbowed Sara out of the way and began to put the rounded tortillas haphazardly on the plate. "She's really something else," Mandy muttered under her breath after Sara left the room. "All this work and some of those guys are going to show up so plastered they won't even appreciate this stuff."

"I think it's nice," Allison said. "There are finer things in life than what we're used to, Mandy. We could learn a thing or two from Sara."

Mandy snorted. "Yeah, like Sunday school songs."

Allison chuckled. "That too."

"Here we go," Sara reappeared with a stack of towels. "I'll start cleaning up in here, Mandy, if you'll cover the tables."

Taking the towels from Sara, Mandy headed down the hall and entered Mark's office. A Christian CD was playing on the stereo. Mandy grimaced as she listened to the music, but diligently covered the tables and desk, then headed to the living room and did the same there. When she returned to the kitchen she asked Sara what group was playing in the den.

"Do you like it? That's Randy Nichols. Remember, I told you about him?"

Mandy opened her mouth and pointed down her throat. "Gag, Sara. No, and no one else is going to like it either."

Sara blushed. "Well, I wasn't planning on playing that at the party. Gavin's getting the music together."

"Good."

"If you two want to finish up in here, I'll go dig up a tablecloth and cover the dining room table." Sara dried her hands and left the room.

Mandy took over the dishwashing while Allison put the tray of veggies and dip in the fridge. On her way to dry the dishes, she lifted the cover of a crock-pot and peeked at Sara's simmering meatballs. "Mmm...that smells good."

"She has enough food to feed an army," Mandy snapped.

"Why are you making such a big deal out of it?"

"She's so goodie-goodie. Honestly, Allie, I know Gavin asked you, but I still don't understand why you're friends with her. She gives me the creeps."

Sara had located a beige tablecloth in the linen closet and came into the adjacent dining room, just in time to hear Mandy's last statements. She froze and held her breath.

"Give me a break, Mandy," Allison replied. "I'm not exactly friends with her. I'm working off the two hundred dollars Gavin loaned me for my tires. He said I wouldn't have to pay him back if I was friendly to Sara."

Sara gasped and covered her mouth.

Unaware that Sara was in the next room, Mandy asked, "How many weeks of friendship does it take to pay off that debt? I'm getting pretty tired of your little friend."

Angry and embarrassed, Sara stifled a scream and bolted down the hall toward the front door. She tripped over the throw rug in the entryway, yanked open the front door and ran outside just as Gavin was coming up the sidewalk.

"How dare you!" Sara yelled, heading straight for him. "How dare you!" she repeated, beating her hands against a full paper sack he held against his chest.

Gavin looked down at the six bottles of booze the bag held. "The guys are going to expect more than beer, Sara."

"Not that!" She gave him another shove. "Am I so pathetic that you have to buy friends for me?"

Gavin looked from her to the house. "What did Allie tell you?"

"She didn't tell me anything. She's too busy playing nice. I can't believe you paid her to be friends with me."

"That was weeks ago, Sara. I just figured you needed a friend."

"Well, you figured wrong. I don't even like her. Did you hear me?" Sara raised her voice and punctuated each word by striking the bag Gavin held. "I—don't—even—like—her!"

The paper bag split and one of the green bottles fell through, hitting the frozen sidewalk with a crash and spilling its contents at Gavin's feet. He struggled to save the other bottles from sliding through the hole in the sack, but lost another one.

"Sara! Would you help?"

She grasped for a bottle, pulled it from the torn bag and looked at the label on the bottle. "Gin," she said with disgust, then raised the bottle and let it drop.

Gavin watched helplessly as the bottle crashed to the sidewalk. Firmly, he held on to the remaining three bottles. "Do you have any idea how much money you just threw away?"

"It shouldn't be a problem for you, should it? You can just gamble and make some more!" Sara turned on her heels and ran back toward the house. Allison and Mandy, having heard the yelling, were standing on the porch. Sara shoved Mandy out of the way, then flew past her and up the stairs to her room.

"Wow," Mandy said, stepping down from the porch, eyeing the mess of broken bottles and spilled liquor. She was more concerned about this loss than Sara's emotional state.

Gavin stepped over the shards of glass at his feet and looked fiercely at his sister. "How could you tell her about our deal?"

"I didn't," Allison protested. "She must have overheard Mandy and me talking."

He shoved the torn bag with its three remaining bottles into her arms. "Clean it up," he demanded. "Clean up every single sliver of glass." Gavin stepped around his sister and headed into the house. He took the steps two at a time and stopped outside Sara's closed bedroom door. Knocking, he called her name.

"Go away."

"I'm not going away, Sara. I'm coming in." Gavin let the door swing open and peered inside. Sara had turned the rocking chair so her back was to the door, but by the shaking of her shoulders, Gavin knew she was crying. Without saying a word, he walked across the room and sat on the bed. Wiping her tears with the palms of her hands, she turned aside. Gavin glanced around the room, then strode to her dresser, where he picked up a box of tissues. He handed the box to Sara, then resumed his seat on the edge of the bed. She blew her nose and dabbed her eyes, but did not look up to meet his gaze.

"I'm sorry." Gavin genuinely felt bad, which surprised him. He'd never apologized to a girl before—at least not with any amount of sincerity.

"I can't believe you paid Allison to be friends with me. That's lower than low."

"That's not exactly how it happened. For one thing, it was way back at Thanksgiving, when you were lonely. I just asked Allie to be nice to you."

Sara looked up sharply. "She said it was a payback for some two hundred dollars."

Gavin forced out a chuckle. "I didn't buy her off. Come on, Sara. Do you really think I would stoop to that level?"

"It's what she said. I heard her."

"I simply reminded her that since I had loaned her money she owed me a favor. She probably made more of the story for Mandy's benefit."

Sara listened to his explanation, hoping it was true. "Do you know how humiliated I feel?"

"No." Gavin watched as she shredded the dampened tissue. "I'm sorry. It seemed like a good idea at the time—you know, just to help you through a tough weekend. I never meant that Allie should pretend to be your bosom buddy."

"She's hardly been that." Sara's voice was so soft that Gavin barely heard her. Slowly, she lifted her face to his. "What's really sad is that it's true. I have no friends anymore."

"You have me."

"I meant girlfriends."

"You still have Katie."

"Maybe, I'm not so sure. Did I ever tell you that she and Jim are first cousins?"

"I think you omitted that detail."

"Well, they are, and they're very close."

"Oh, well," Gavin shrugged. "She's the one that suggested we get together tomorrow. She and her husband wouldn't be meeting us if she was only siding with Jim."

Sara looked at Gavin. "I think she wants to check you out."

"Don't worry about it. I'll be on my best behavior, I promise." Gavin grinned at her. "Now, about this Allie business, am I forgiven?"

"I guess, but tell her she doesn't have to be my friend anymore."

"So, you really don't like Allie, huh?"

Sara blushed. "I shouldn't have said that, I'm sorry. I like her more than I did at first. Actually, it's Mandy I don't like."

Gavin nodded. Sara and Mandy were as different as black and white. "Well, she and Allie go back a few years. Their friendship is a comfortable, old habit."

They sat in silence for a few moments, then Gavin chuckled. "You sure were mad. Beautiful, but mad."

"I'm sorry about the bottles breaking. Can you get more?"

"I'll call Robbie. I don't have any more money, just enough for our trip tomorrow."

"What happened to your poker wad?"

"Long gone. I paid off my credit card bill. You know what they say, easy come, easy go."

"I'm sorry."

"It's no big deal." His dark eyes penetrated hers, then he stood up, pulled her to her feet and kissed her—a long, passionate kiss.

It felt so good, after being humiliated earlier, to have Gavin show his love this way. Maybe he hadn't ever told her that he loved her, but he showed her every time he kissed her. His kisses were always filled with passion and longing.

Suddenly there was a shriek of laughter from downstairs. Sara pushed away from Gavin and he swore at the untimely interruption.

"I forgot they were here," Sara said.

"I can tell them to leave."

"No," Sara pulled away. "It's okay. Let's go down and find something to eat for supper before everyone shows up for the party."

"Do you want me to go down first and smooth things over with Allie and Mandy?"

"No, I'll just pretend it didn't happen. That'll be easiest."

Gavin stared at her for a moment, trying to figure out the complexities of Sara Brooks. She was intriguing, that was for sure. "If that's what you want."

"For now, yes. I'll see how it goes."

"Okay." Gavin stood up, his thoughts moving ahead to the party and the friends who would soon fill the house. "It's going to be a great night, Sara. I'm glad you agreed to have the party here."

I'm not. I wish it was anywhere but here. "You'll help keep everyone in line and things running smoothly, won't you?"

Gavin saluted her, thinking that he'd keep the music going and the alcohol flowing and in between he'd dance with Sara.

By eight thirty, the house was full of guests. Sara scurried around, offering plates of appetizers, trying to make sure that people were not messing things up and that things did not get out of hand. Several times, she subtly turned down the volume on the stereo—she certainly did not need the neighbors calling the police to report a disturbance. Sara wandered into the living room just as KC was shoving a wing-backed chair out of the way and Robbie was moving an end table. "Careful!" she called.

"We're just making room to dance," Robbie explained.

Gavin entered the room, carrying two glasses. Handing one to Sara, he said, "You need to relax. Stop acting like you're with the Gestapo."

She glanced at the drink in her hand, then to Gavin, a questioning look on her face.

"Don't worry. It's mostly orange juice with a little something mixed in. Nothing that will make you drunk. Just something to help you lighten up and stop policing everybody."

"I'm not that bad, am I?"

Gavin shrugged. "What do you think?"

Sara thought it over and silently acknowledged that she did need to lighten up. How would it help her acceptance into Gavin's group if she agreed to host the party, but then nagged everyone all night? After all, what's the worst that could happen? A spilled drink on the carpet? She took a swallow of her drink. "This is actually pretty good."

"What did you expect from the juice man?"

The front door opened and Moose entered with two girls and a guy whom Sara did not know. "Who's that?" she asked Gavin. "There are so many people here I don't even know."

"Relax. The brunette is Moose's new girl, the others must be friends of hers."

"This makes me very nervous," she admitted.

"See what I mean? You are wound tighter than a spring. Drink up." Gavin nudged Sara's glass and she took another sip, then squared her shoulders, determined to relax and enjoy the party.

During the course of the night, so many people dropped in, sometimes leaving for a while and then returning, that the food ran out. Gavin convinced Sara that nobody cared—as long as there was plenty to drink. Several people brought bottles of alcohol, so Sara figured the ones she had broken would not be missed.

Gavin kept the tunes playing on the CD player and many couples danced. Although KC and a boy she didn't know asked her, Sara saved every dance for Gavin. She finally relaxed and could honestly admit that she was having fun.

Moose and his three friends left around eleven thirty, but a little over an hour later, Moose came back looking for Gavin. He found him and Sara talking and laughing with Robbie and a girl named Crystal.

"Hey, Gav, you too, Robbie, I just found out about an awesome party goin' on over at this friend of Hayden's."

"I'm there!" Robbie said, jumping up from his chair and tugging on his girl's arm.

"Cool." Gavin's face lit up. This party was winding down. The drinks and food had run out and there were only a few people left. "Come on, Sara," he said, rising from the couch.

"Gavin, you can't be serious." Sara stood and held on to Gavin's arm. "We can't leave; we're hosting our own party."

"Look around," Gavin said, turning and swaying slightly from having too much to drink. "There aren't that many people here anymore."

"Listen," Moose interrupted, taking a step toward the front hall. "Robbie and Crystal can follow me. If you decide to come, call for directions."

"We'll be right behind you," Gavin said to his friend's back, as Robbie and Crystal followed Moose.

"I can't believe you," Sara exclaimed, pulling on Gavin's arm so he would face her. "There are still at least a half-dozen people here and we cannot leave before our guests."

"That's not in the rule book, Sara. No one will care."

"Well, I'll care. I'm not going to leave my sister's house with strangers here."

"Come on, Sara. We'll just stay a little while, then come back."

She paused for just a moment. "No, I'm not going. Even if nobody else was here, I still wouldn't want to. But you go ahead."

"You want me to go without you?"

There was no point telling him the truth. That she didn't want him to go without her, that she didn't even want him to want to go. When he was like this, when he'd had too much to drink, there was no telling him anything. Sara nodded. "Have a good time."

Gavin grinned, then he put his arms around her. "You're the best girl, and you're beautiful too." He kissed her, then left her standing in the living room, with another couple dancing and two girls she barely knew giggling excessively in the corner of the room.

The last of the guests left about one thirty. Sara sat idly on the couch and waited up until two in case Gavin came back. When he didn't show, she locked the doors and wearily dragged herself up to bed. Sleep came fitfully and after a few hours, Sara gave up. She pulled on a warm pair of socks and went down to the kitchen to make a pot of strong coffee.

The light above the sink had been left on and, at first, the sight of the kitchen in its post-party disarray was a shock. She'd almost forgotten about the mess that needed to be cleaned up. She shoved aside a stack of dirty dishes in order to reach the coffeepot.

Waiting for the coffee to complete its cycle, she went to stand in front of the sliding glass doors and stared outside. Night's darkness was just beginning to fade, but against its background, her reflection stared back. She shook her head slowly, wondering if she knew who she was anymore. Wondering when it had become so easy to tell lies. Wondering if there was any way to go back.

Sara leaned her forehead against the cold glass door. Back to what? Back to Jim? Impossible. Back to an uncomplicated life? Sara stepped away from the door and glanced around the messy kitchen. But wasn't this what she had always wanted? A dramatic lifestyle, excitement, and, above all, passion? Gavin represented all three: drama, excitement, passion—and how!

I'll get used to it, she decided, heading to the coffeepot. *After all, this is what I always wanted.* She poured a cup of the black liquid, knowing—deep down—that was not exactly true. What she had always wanted, was Jim.

CHAPTER 21

Jesus said, "If your first concern is to look after yourself, you'll never find yourself. But if you forget about yourself and look to me, you'll find both yourself and me."
—Matthew 10:30

Sara sat at the table and nursed her first cup of coffee, not really thinking about anything in particular. After refilling her cup, she did a slow walk through the house. There was garbage to pick up, dirty dishes to wash, empty alcohol and juice bottles to dispose of, all the table coverings to wash and furniture to put back. She sighed just thinking about all the work ahead.

Had it been worth it? Only time would tell. If Gavin's group accepted her better and Gavin himself was pleased beyond measure that she had done it... Sara sincerely hoped Gavin was going to show up and help her clean up this mess. She wondered how late he had stayed out and how early he might come over. It's not like they had all day. They needed to leave by eleven o'clock to meet Katie and Wayne.

Sara started with the garbage. She filled three large bags and piled them next to the door to bring to the dumpster at Gavin's apartment later. There was no way she could leave that evidence next to Mark's garbage cans in the garage. Next, she loaded the dishwasher and hand washed the serving trays and other bulky items. The towels and tablecloth went into the washing machine.

Sara poured another cup of coffee and walked through the house to see if she had missed anything. The living room furniture still needed to be put back and Gavin's CDs packed up. Sighing, she decided to shower and get ready to go. Hopefully by then, Gavin would be here to help with the living room.

She came downstairs at nine thirty wearing blue jeans and a black turtleneck. Her makeup was done although her hair was still damp, but it always took a long time to dry. She tossed the towels into the dryer, then called Gavin. When the call went to the answering machine, she decided he must be on his way over. *Good.* Having drained the coffee, she made a fresh pot, knowing Gavin would want some and she, herself, was operating on precious little sleep. Ten minutes later, the coffee was ready, but Gavin had still not arrived.

She called his cell phone, but got no answer. She called the house again and this time left a terse message about needing to leave in an hour and where was he? Irritated, she went to the living room and wrestled the furniture back into place, then haphazardly loaded his CDs into a shoe box. She put on her black boots, filled a thermos with coffee, grabbed two travel mugs and headed to her car. She had already backed out of the driveway when she remembered the bags of garbage by the backdoor. She hustled back and angrily tossed them into the trunk.

Really, this is the last straw! Jim would never have… Jim! Sara stopped, with her hand poised to slam the trunk shut. She looked up to her bedroom window, where Jim's duffle bag still sat. Today was the perfect opportunity to return it. She hurried back into the house and up to her room. She grabbed his MCU sweatshirt from the floor of her closet and stuffed it inside the duffle bag, then zipped it closed. A lump formed in her throat and she slowly reopened the bag, drew the sweatshirt out and gently traced the broad MCU lettering.

She closed her eyes against the ache in her heart. She longed to pour her heart out to Jim—truly, the best friend she had ever had. She longed to talk to him about everything crazy that was going on in her life. He would listen, let her talk and never judge her. In his quiet way, he would offer guidance, then sit back and let her come to her own conclusions. Jim was truly wise. A sob caught in Sara's throat. How she missed him. Sara laid his sweatshirt aside, deciding to keep it. She had given it to Jim in the first place—he probably didn't even want it anymore, but she did. Zipping the bag, she grabbed its black strap and hurried downstairs. She tossed it into the backseat, not wanting Gavin to see it when he got the garbage out of the trunk. *If* he got the garbage out.

How could he just ignore the party mess? How could he just ignore *her*? She fumed all the way to his apartment where she pounded on the door and repeatedly rang the bell until a sleepy Allie opened the door.

"Sara? What do you want?"

"Your brother."

"I'm sure he's still in bed." Allison shuffled back to her room.

Sara marched to Gavin's closed bedroom door and rapped on it, calling his name at the same time. A groggy, muffled answer came from inside. Sara threw open the door and flicked on the light.

"Wha-a-t?" Gavin yanked the covers over his head.

"Gavin Manes."

At the sound of Sara's angry voice, he peeked out from his blankets. "What are you doing here? And turn off the light."

Sara strode over to the window and opened the blinds. "It's time to get up. It's ten thirty and we're supposed to leave at eleven."

"What for?"

"To meet Wayne and Katie, did you forget?"

Gavin groaned and pulled the pillow over his head. "Whydonyougowithoutme?"

"What did you say?" Sara wrenched the pillow out of his hands and tossed it to the end of his bed.

He rolled over and looked at her. "Why don't you go without me?"

She stared at him. "Go without you? The whole point is for them to meet you. You willingly agreed to come; now get up."

"I have a headache."

"I really don't care."

"Man, what's your problem this morning?"

Sara looked pointedly at her watch. "It's ten thirty."

"You said that already."

"While you've been lying in bed, I've been cleaning up from the party. From *your* party."

"What'd you do that for?"

"Do you think I was going to leave that mess for Morgan to find?"

"Well, no," Gavin sat up. "But I figured we'd clean it up tomorrow. I wanted to sleep this morning."

"Tomorrow? Mark and Morgan are coming back tonight. *Tonight*, Gavin."

"Oh, sorry. I thought you said tomorrow." He looked at her. Boy, was she angry. "Honest, Sara. I'm sorry. I thought it was tomorrow."

She sighed. "Whatever. But you knew we were going to see Katie today."

"Yeah," Gavin rubbed a hand over his face. "But when I agreed to that I guess it didn't dawn on me that it'd be the day after the New Year's Eve party."

"Nobody forced you to go party hopping. What time did you get in, anyway? Never mind; I don't want to know."

Gavin grinned. He loved it when Sara got angry. Her blue eyes blazed and she was full of fire and drama.

"What are grinning about?"

"You." He winked. "Now go make some coffee and I'll shower."

"I brought some with me."

Gavin tossed his legs over the side of the bed. "That's my girl. Fill me a big mug, okay?"

When Gavin came out of the shower, Sara looked at him from her spot at the kitchen table. Even when she was angry, his good looks still got to her. She pushed his cup of coffee toward him with a shrug. "I made a whole other pot. I think you're going to need it."

He took an unhurried sip, eyeing her over the rim of the cup. "It was a great party, Sara."

"Which one?" She looked at him pointedly.

"Ours. Thanks for doing it."

"Yes, well…" She wanted to stay angry, but he was looking at her in that charming way and those dark eyes of his were flashing with spirit and… "You're welcome."

"I mean it. We pulled it off, and Mark and Morgan will never be the wiser."

"I hope not."

Gavin set his cup on the table and, pulling Sara to her feet, placed his arms around her waist. "You're the best, Sara. I'm sorry I didn't help you clean up. Did you do everything? The furniture too?"

"Yes. Your CDs are in the car, oh and the garbage. It'll have to go in your dumpster."

"Yeah, okay." Gavin leaned in for a kiss. "Forgive me, huh, Sara? I mean, I kind of like it when you're angry, but my head hurts and I'd rather not argue."

"Me either."

"Okay then." He kissed her again.

"We need to go," she murmured. "It's a three-hour drive."

"Uh-huh." Another kiss and Sara's knees were turning to jelly.

"They'll be waiting."

"Yeah, okay." He stepped away and looked at his watch. "I should eat something."

"I'm sorry. I should have thought to fix you something."

"It's okay. Put down some toast and I'll take care of the garbage."

They decided to take Sara's car since she had nearly a full tank of gas, but she let Gavin drive. They weren't on the road very long before Sara fell asleep. The short night of sporadic sleep, the energy she had expended first on cleaning, then on anger had worn her out. They were an hour down the road before she woke. Yawning, she looked out the window, trying to figure out how far they had come. "Did I sleep?"

"Yeah," Gavin reached for her hand and squeezed it. "You wake me up, then you get to spend the ride sleeping. Something's not fair here."

"Not fair?" Sara raised her eyebrows. "You don't really want to go there, do you?"

He chuckled. "I guess not. Where did you say we're meeting them?"

"Perkin's Bakery."

"Good, I'm still hungry."

They rode quietly for a while, listening to the radio. Sara thought back over the party. Now that everything was over and cleaned up, she could safely evaluate it. "It did go rather well, didn't it?"

"What's that?"

"The party."

"Yeah, I knew it would."

"It's so easy for you, isn't it?"

"What's easy?"

"Life. You just take it all in stride." *No,* Sara realized. *You just take what you want, without a thought of whether it's right or wrong.*

"I just like to have a good time." Gavin shrugged. "You know me, Sara, always the one for fun, never philosophizing."

"Is that why you don't talk about your faith?" *Or anything else deeply personal, for that matter?*

"My faith? What's there to say? I believe in God. He made the world. He's up there watching over us. There's not much more to it. My goal is to keep things simple and uncomplicated."

"What about Jesus?"

"What about Him?"

"He died for us. For our—our—sins."

Gavin chuckled. "Sins? It's a give and take world, Sara.

Sara stared at him. "I don't think so."

"See, that's your problem. You think too much."

"It's basic theology, Gavin."

"Basic theology. See, Sara, I hate it when you get like this."

"Like what?"

"All preachy and everything. It's a real downer. Honest, I'd rather have you angry and yelling at me." He glanced at her. "You're beautiful when you're angry."

"Yes, you've told me that before."

"It's true. You should look in the mirror some time. Your eyes start blazing and you get this self-righteous tilt to your head and your voice comes out all fearsome and your cheeks turn pink. It's really something."

She smiled. "What good does it do to get angry at you if you enjoy it? I think that sort of defeats the purpose."

"I guess you just shouldn't get mad at me then." He put a hand on the back of her shoulder and indicated that she should snuggle closer. "Moose has a motto. I seriously think you should adopt it."

"What is it?"

"Keep it easy."

"That's it?"

"Well, more or less."

"Keep it easy. Hmm…I'll work on that."

Gavin laughed. "If you have to work on it, it isn't easy."

"You have a point there."

"Man, Sara…" He sighed, trying to keep his eyes on the road. "I have this intense desire to kiss you."

She laughed. Despite everything, there was no denying the way Gavin made her feel. Beautiful, desirable, needed.

"I feel funny about this trip," Wayne admitted to Katie as he pulled onto I-61.

"Because of Jim?"

"Yes. I didn't even tell him we were meeting Sara. I feel like a traitor."

Katie stared out the car window, wishing for the hundredth time that Jim and Sara were still together. "I know, but he wouldn't really want us to ignore her, would he?"

"No, but spending the day with her and Gavin is weird."

"We have to give Gavin a chance, Wayne. Sara is my best friend and I miss her."

"I know; I'm going, aren't I? I just said it feels weird."

"Well, I for one am curious to see what kind of guy stole Sara's heart. You will try to get along with him, won't you?"

"Yes, Katie."

Gavin relaxed, glad that Sara was no longer angry or brooding about the great mysteries of life. A moody girl was definitely a drag. Life was meant to be fun. Gavin's mind moved on to other things. Before long he spoke, "I've been thinking."

"Really?" Sara couldn't wait to hear what was on his mind. Maybe he was finally going to share something significant.

"I'm going to beef up my car engine. Either that or trade it in. I've got to do better at the drag races this summer."

"Beef up the car!" Sara fell back against the car seat. She should have known.

He looked at her, his dark eyes flashing. "Yeah. Unless you're going to let me use this thing. You've got nice pickup." He pushed the accelerator down as he spoke and let the car dart ahead for a quarter mile, before easing up and dropping back to the speed limit.

"Beef up your own car," Sara teased. "I think I'll enter the races myself."

Gavin laughed. He laughed for a long time, then squeezed her hand. "Little Miss Sara Brooks, you've come a long way."

"There they are!" Sara pointed to her friends standing next to Wayne's black car. Gavin pulled into the parking lot, while Sara rolled down her window and waved. Katie waved back and moved out of the way as Gavin rolled past and turned into the parking space. Sara was out of the car in a flash. The two girls were hugging before Gavin had even pulled the key from the ignition. Always confident, he stepped forward and shook Wayne's hand. After a tight squeeze, Sara moved out of Katie's embrace, took her hand and led her over to Gavin. With a flash in his eye and the charming smile he was famous for, Gavin greeted Katie and said he hoped they hadn't been waiting long.

"We just got here," Wayne assured him. Eyeing Sara, he added, "How are you doing?"

"I'm fine." Nervously she approached Wayne. "I was hoping to get a hug."

"Yeah." He accepted her embrace and patted her back. Thinking briefly of Jim, Sara clung to Wayne for just a moment, then stepped back. For a few minutes the four talked and shivered in the parking lot, then Wayne declared that a piece of lemon meringue pie was calling his name.

The hostess seated them at a booth and after ordering, it took only a few awkward moments before they began to talk easily. Katie couldn't quite say for sure, but it seemed as if Gavin was getting her and Wayne to do most of the talking. Wayne finished explaining that even though he'd have his course work done in May, he would have to do his student teaching next fall.

Gavin nodded, as if he totally understood. "I've been thinking I should take a few business classes. Something like that might come in handy when I decide I've had enough of the club's juice bar." He grinned his charming grin. "It's just that I like my free time. You know, for hobbies and to be with Sara." Gavin squeezed Sara's hand under the table and his words sent a shiver of delight up her spine.

"What hobbies, Gavin?" Katie sweetly asked.

Sara's thrill of delight was short lived as she worried what Gavin would say. He wouldn't dare say his hobbies included gambling, racing and drinking, would he? "Gavin loves cars," she quickly inserted. "Like just today, he mentioned fixing the engine in his car. Wayne's a pretty good mechanic, aren't you, Wayne?"

"I know a thing or two about cars. So, you having trouble with yours?"

"Just want a little more power, is all."

While the boys' talk turned to engines and pistons and horsepower, Katie and Sara grinned at each other across the table. They listened for a few minutes, then Sara cleared her throat.

"You guys won't mind if Katie and I step outside for a couple minutes, will you? I have something for her in the car." Sara swung her legs out of the booth and motioned for Katie to join her. "Katie, do you have keys so you can put it in your car?"

"Here." Wayne handed his wife a set of car keys then he and Gavin watched the girls cross the restaurant and disappear out the front door.

"You do realize that was Sara's not-so-subtle way of getting Katie alone to see what she thinks about you," Wayne said with a grin to Gavin.

"I do and when they come back, I'll have to pretend I don't know they've spent ten minutes talking about me."

Wayne chuckled. "And they'll pretend they don't know that you're pretending."

"Girls." Gavin shook his head. "I've never really been able to figure them out."

Once outside, Sara grasped Katie's arm. "So, what do you think?"

"I don't know yet," Katie said with a playful smile. "He's very good looking and nice and charming. He scores ten on all those points, but, Sara, I'm going to need more than forty minutes." Katie put a hand in the air as if taking a vow. "I reserve the right to pass judgment until the end of the day. Fair enough?"

"Fair enough." Sara led Katie to the car. "I really do have something for you." She opened the door to the backseat and lifted the duffle bag out. "This is Jim's. Can you return it for me?"

"Oh." Suddenly serious, Katie asked Sara how long she had had it.

"Since that weekend—since—" Sara couldn't go on, but shoved the duffle bag toward her friend. "Please, just give it to him for me."

"Yes, Sara, of course." Katie walked over to her car and opened the trunk. Slowly, she set the duffle bag inside. This meant she and Wayne would have to own up to seeing Sara, to spending the day with her and Gavin. Jim's lonesome face flashed across Katie's mind. Her dear, sweet cousin, traded in for—Katie glanced back toward the restaurant—for, for… Slamming the trunk, Katie whirled around to face Sara. "Do you love Gavin, Sara?"

"Love?" *Gavin?* Sara knew she loved things about Gavin and she loved how she felt when he kissed her, but truly love him? Like she had loved Jim? "Why?"

"I don't know. I'm just trying to understand. Don't you even want to know how Jim is?"

Sara's gaze met Katie's and she nodded, then quickly shook her head. "No, Katie. I don't. He's not part of my life anymore."

"He could be. He wants to be."

Sara looked at the ground. "Don't, Katie."

"Sara Brooks. I don't understand at all what happened between the two of you. Not at all. You say it was Jim's fault, he says it was yours."

"There is one thing I understand, and you can too: Jim hurt me and I hurt

244

him, and some things are irreversible."

Katie stubbornly looked Sara in the eye. "He loves you."

Tears filled Sara's eyes. "I'm not the same girl that Jim fell in love with all those months ago. I'm not the same girl at all."

"Why not? What's been going on with you?"

Sara looked away from Katie's intense gaze. "That's a story for another time, not today. Today," Sara squared her shoulders and wiped the tears from her eyes. "Today is about us. Our friendship and you and Wayne meeting Gavin. Please, Katie…" Sara searched her friend's face. "Please, give Gavin a chance."

"I will, Sara. You know I will. I just want to make sure you know what you're doing."

Sara wanted to scream that she *didn't* know what she was doing. That traveling Gavin's road was taking her in new and exciting directions, although they were not necessarily ones she would have chosen—not necessarily ones she liked—but of course, she couldn't say that.

There was a movement at the door of the restaurant. Wayne and Gavin came out of the building, Gavin chuckling over something Wayne had said. Just the sight of him set Sara's heart fluttering.

From the bakery they rode together in Wayne's car to Fun City, where they spent a couple of hours riding the bumper cars and playing mini golf and laser tag. Katie and Sara watched the guys in the batting cages, then Sara suggested they use their remaining tokens in the arcade.

"I haven't played a good game of foosball in a while," she said with a smile to Gavin, remembering the night at McGrady's when she had tricked him. He winked at her, remembering also.

"Nobody wants to play foosball with you, Sara," Katie spoke up. "You win every time."

"How about pool?" Gavin suggested, leading the way to an open table and the rack of pool cues. "Sara and I will stand the two of you. And, just to make it interesting," Gavin reached for his wallet and extracted a five dollar bill, "we'll put a little side bet on the game."

Sara's face flushed and she wished the floor would open up and swallow her right here and now. Wayne chuckled good-naturedly and shook his head. "I'm a poor college student, Gavin. I'd better just play this one for fun."

After two games of pool at Fun City, the foursome exited the building and breathed in the invigorating air of a cold January afternoon.

"So, what's the plan?" Wayne asked, leading the group to his black car. After a little discussion, the girls convinced the guys to go to the mall for an hour or so. Katie and Sara had always enjoyed shopping together and they wanted to check out the New Year's Day sales. Wayne and Gavin agreed to hang out at GameWorld and Radio Shack and any other electronic store the mall offered. After agreeing on a meeting time and place they split up, the girls heading at a good clip for the first store on their agenda while the guys moved slowly down the mall.

In the third store, Sara found cashmere sweaters on sale. If there was something she had always wanted to own, it was a cashmere sweater. She stood in front of the display table and fingered them. There were both pullovers and cardigans in five different colors. The half-off sign caught her attention, but she hesitated before finally turning over a price tag to view it. Disappointed, she sighed. She was never going to be able to afford cashmere—not even when it was on sale. Sara ran her hand over the softness of the material, admiring the delicate shades of blue, gray, green, pink and yellow. It really rankled her that Allie had cashmere and she did not. *If only Dad had not written that check out directly to MATC...*

Approaching the table, Katie commented on the pretty sweaters.

"I've always wanted cashmere," Sara admitted. "Allie has one."

"Who's Allie?"

"Gavin's sister. What color would you choose, Katie?"

"You know I've always liked pink, but for you, I'd choose the blue. It'd go great with your eyes."

"Yes, the blue." Sara sighed. "Someday."

"Come on, Sara. It's time to meet the guys."

Sara took one last look at the sweaters, then fell in step beside Katie. They only had to walk a short distance to where the guys waited on a bench drinking coffee.

Wayne pointed to the bag in his wife's hand. "What did you get?"

"A new pair of jeans; there was a great sale."

Gavin looked at Sara's empty hands. "What about you? An hour of shopping and you didn't get anything?"

Sara shook her head. "I can't afford what I want."

"And what is it?"

"A sweater. A beautiful, blue, cashmere sweater."

Gavin reached for his wallet and drew out a debit card. Handing it to her, he said, "There's an ATM over there. 1331's my pin. Take out what you need."

Sara stared at the card. Just yesterday he told her he hardly had any money. Today he was flashing it around like he had oodles of it. She knew he had paid for everyone's pie and coffee, and there was still dinner to pay for.

"Go on," Gavin waved the card at her. "Hurry up. Wayne and I are ready to eat."

Sara reached for the card. She could have used her own card, but she still had part of the hotel bill on it and besides, her dad had drilled into her that credit was for emergencies only. A new sweater—even a cashmere one—did not rank as an emergency. However, Sara had seen Gavin use his credit card frequently. He would probably just say, *Easy come, easy go.* She flashed him a smile and headed for the ATM. Katie followed and watched silently while Sara pushed the card into the machine and typed in Gavin's pin number.

"Do you think this is a good idea, Sara?"

"What?"

"Using his money. It's not like you're married—or even engaged."

Sara tugged the three twenties from the machine. She was not going to let Katie ruin her chance—her only chance—of getting the sweater of her dreams. "It's all right, Katie." She turned and shoved the bills into the pocket of her jeans. "Gavin really doesn't mind and I'm learning to take life a little less seriously and enjoy it more. Really, it'll be okay."

Katie crossed her arms and pressed her lips together. Gavin apparently held sway over Sara's good sense. *Well,* Katie thought silently, following Sara back to the store. *That's one strike against him.*

"I think it was a good day," Sara announced to Gavin on the drive home.

"Yes. It was fun. Do you think I passed inspection?"

Sara looked at him in the dark of the car's interior. It was hard to say what Wayne and Katie really thought. Wayne, who usually wore his emotions on his sleeve, had not given any indication of his impressions of Gavin, although he had been nice and the two seemed to get along. Katie had said plenty, both in favor of and concern over her relationship with Gavin. "I think you passed, but it doesn't really matter what they think."

"Really? Isn't that what this day was all about?"

Sara shrugged. "Only partly. I needed a day with Katie." Whether or not her friends approved of Gavin, Sara felt as if a load of bricks had slipped off her

247

back. Katie and Wayne had met Gavin, she had disposed of Jim's duffle bag, and she and Katie had a chance to discover that their friendship would go on. Basically, her two worlds had met and she was left standing. Sara reached for Gavin's hand, drawing it onto her lap. "I'm very happy right now, Gavin."

"I am too."

Mark and Morgan pulled into their driveway in the middle of the afternoon. Originally they had planned to return later that evening, but the son of their friends had come down with the flu so Morgan had thought it best they return home early. She didn't want to be in the way or risk her own children getting sick.

After hauling the suitcases inside, Mark informed Morgan that he was going to take down the outdoor Christmas lights and shovel the walk again. It looks like they had gotten another inch or two of snow. What a winter! There'd been no break in the cold since that first snowfall.

Mark hoisted the metal ladder so it rested against the porch roof, then climbed up and began unhooking the icicle lights. His head came just above the gutter on the porch roof and as he worked with the string of lights, he gazed across the length of roof, trying to judge just how much snow they did have.

His neighbor to the west, a retired school teacher, was shoveling his walk and greeted Mark with a friendly howdy.

"Happy New Year," Mark hollered in return.

Mr. Trowland shoveled to the end of his walk, then leaned his shovel against his siding and ambled over to where Mark was repositioning his ladder. "Quite the party you threw last night," he said with a good-natured chuckle. "Yes, sir, the neighborhood hasn't had one like that for quite a few years."

"Party? Last night?" Mark paused with his foot in between the second and third rungs. With a sag of his shoulders, Mark put two and two together. *Sara must have thrown a New Year's Eve party.* Mark looked down at his neighbor. "I hope the music wasn't too loud for you."

"No, I could tell you were trying to keep it under control." Mr. Trowland waved a hand in the air. "I understand young folks. Taught high school for thirty-five years. No, I think it's just admirable that you've opened your home for your sister. Have to let those kids have their fun. Well, I'll let you get back to your lights." With a nod, he headed back inside to the warmth of his fireplace and the company of his magazine.

Mark tromped for the house and did not even bother to kick the snow off his boots before entering. "Morgan! I think we have a problem here."

It was nearly midnight by the time Sara had dropped Gavin off at his place and pulled into the driveway. She was so exhausted, she felt as if she could sleep for two days straight. She entered through the front door, noticing the lights left on in the kitchen. Wondering if Mark or Morgan was still up, Sara headed for the kitchen. To her surprise, they were both waiting for her, stern looks on their faces.

Sara smiled. "How was Iowa?"

"It was fine," Morgan answered. "How were things here?"

"Fine. Gavin and I just got back from seeing Wayne and Katie."

"That's nice, Sara," Mark said. "Now, what I'd like is a little explanation as to why the neighbor commented on the party we gave last night."

Sara felt the blood drain from her face. "Neighbor? Party?"

"No lies, Sara," Morgan said. "You promised, no more lies."

"Well, okay." Sara's heart started beating double time and she fiddled with the zipper of her coat. "It's true, I had a New Year's Eve party, but it was just a few friends." She rattled of a half of dozen names, figuring if push came to shove she could claim that all the others were party crashers. "And look," Sara swept her hand around the room. "I cleaned it all up. We bought our own food. Nothing got wrecked; nothing's broken. Really, no harm was done."

"I specifically said no party."

"I guess you did, but you said I could have a few friends over. I'm sorry. I won't do it again."

"Sit down, Sara." Morgan's tone said she wouldn't put up with any arguing. She waited until her sister was seated, then went into a lecture about trust and respect and the fact that Sara was living in a home that did not belong to her. When Morgan was finished, she told Sara that if this type of thing happened again, she might have to send her back home. Sara hated the way her sister made her feel twelve years old. She looked to Mark for sympathy, but he was siding with his wife.

"I understand," Sara said. "I really do. To be honest, I knew I shouldn't do it. I let Allison and Mandy talk me into it."

"Not Gavin?"

"No." She would keep him out of it. She couldn't risk them getting upset with him.

"Sara," Mark said, "you're not a teenager anymore. You should be past the point of peer pressure and letting others talk you into something you know is wrong."

Sara could only nod. They were right. They were. They just didn't understand what it was like to stand with heaven just on the other side of a gully. Sometimes, a girl had to take risks. And it seemed that with Gavin, she was taking more and more all the time.

CHAPTER 22

What good will it be for a man if he gains the whole world, yet forfeits his soul?
Or what can a man give in exchange for his soul?
—Matthew 16:26

Jim's duffle bag sat in the corner of Wayne and Katie's living room for over a week, both of them trying to ignore it. Finally, Wayne mentioned it to Katie. "You're going to have to deliver that one of these days."

"Why don't we have Jim over for supper and give it to him then?"

"He doesn't want to come over. He just wants to be left alone."

"Then you bring it to him."

Wayne shook his head. "No, he'll want to know how she is and you can answer that better than I can."

Katie looked from her husband to the duffle bag and sighed. "Fine, I'll go. I'll do it right now and get it over with."

Katie stood at the door to Jim's apartment and knocked. At Jim's call to come in, she pushed open the door. He sat on the couch, watching a basketball game on television. "Hello, Jim." He nodded a greeting in return. Katie set his bag just inside the door and perched on the armchair. "How are you?"

"Fine."

"Good." Katie looked at the television, trying to build up the courage to tell Jim that she had seen Sara.

After several silent minutes, Jim spoke up. "Did you want something or did Wayne send you over to babysit?"

"Oh, well, you see, I came to bring you this." She rose, retrieved the duffle bag and set it on the floor in front of him.

"You've seen Sara?"

"Yes, Jim." Katie eased back onto the chair. "On New Year's Day."

"It took you nine days to tell me this?"

"Yes." Katie picked at some loose threads on the arm of the green chair. "We weren't sure how you'd feel."

"We? Wayne saw her too?" At Katie's nod, Jim continued, "There? Here?" He didn't know why he was asking, why it even mattered. He'd been trying so hard to put her out of his mind, but the thought that Katie had seen her, knew of her firsthand, was eating at him.

Katie took a deep breath. "Neither. We met in LaCrosse for the day. And I might as well tell you, we met Gavin."

"Gavin?"

"Her new boyfriend." Katie cringed at the words.

"I know who he is."

"Please don't be mad."

"I'm not mad. Although if I was, it'd be because it took you nine days to tell me. In fact, you probably wouldn't have told me at all if you didn't have this," Jim kicked at the duffle bag, "to deliver."

Katie knew Wayne should have done this. She was going about it all wrong. "I'm sorry. We haven't known what to say. It's been a very confusing time."

"Yeah." Jim rose from the couch and wandered to the large window, where he could stare outside. "That's an understatement." He didn't like the way his heart was hammering.

"Jim, is there anything you want to know about Sara?"

"Is she happy?"

"Happy?"

Jim turned from the window and faced his cousin. "Yes. Is she happy?"

"I think she's mixed up right now and chasing after an illusion."

"But is she happy?"

Katie thought about the way Sara's eyes lit up when Gavin was near and the dreamy way she looked at him. Katie turned away from Jim. She didn't want to tell him.

"Katie. Is she happy?"

"Yes, Jim, I think she is."

"Okay then. That's all I want to know." He resumed his place on the couch. "It's all I've ever wanted for her."

One afternoon, a week later, as Gavin cleaned the juice counter, he looked at Sara and said, "I've been thinking. If you were to quit school and get a full-time job, we'd have a lot more expendable income."

"But I'm going to school so I can get the job of my dreams."

"Yeah, but you're not bringing in much money. Think of what we could do if we had more."

"I can't believe you're even suggesting this. I've dreamed of hotel hospitality my whole life. I'm not about to quit now."

"Well, maybe you could just take classes half time and work, too."

"Gavin, I'm already three years behind from first going to nursing school. I'm going to plow ahead and finish."

"Don't nurses make decent money? Are you sure you don't want to do that?"

Sara could only stare at him. "What's this obsession with money all of a sudden?"

Gavin shrugged. "I thought it'd be fun to go away for a few days—down to Fort Lauderdale or somewhere warm. But, of course, there's no money for a trip."

"Even if we had the money, I would not go on a trip with you."

"Why not?"

"We can't travel together, we're not married."

"I don't see what the big deal is."

"You wouldn't," Sara muttered. Sometimes, she wondered if she and Gavin were ever going to mesh their lifestyles. *It's more than a lifestyle*, the still small voice reminded her, *it goes way beyond that*. Sara pushed aside her empty glass. "It really bothers me that you'd even suggest that I quit school. You must know how important it is to me."

"Okay, you don't have to get so mad. It was just a suggestion." Gavin looked at the fire in Sara's blue eyes and knew he had stepped over the line. "I'm sorry." He tossed the rag into a bucket under the sink, then looked back at her. Putting on a smile and all the charm he could muster, he reached across the counter and took her hand. "You'll be the most beautiful hospitality hostess in the entire state and business managers will flock to your hotel just because of your reputation for putting on the absolutely best conventions."

A smile tugged at the corners of Sara's mouth. "All right, I forgive you."

Gavin leaned over the counter and whispered in her ear, "I'd book all my conventions with you—every single one." Before he drew away, he planted a kiss on the corner of her lips. She looked into his face and could only think how lucky she was.

The last Saturday in January, Moose and Jared sat on one of the couches in Gavin's apartment watching snowmobile racing on the television.

"Whoa! Cool!" Jared exclaimed, leaning forward. "Gav! You've gotta see this."

Gavin came from the kitchen with a bag of popcorn and three beers in his hands. He handed a can to each of the others, then plopped down on the other sofa.

"Why haven't we ever tried this?" Jared asked. "Moose, don't you and your brother have a couple of snowmobiles?"

"Yeah."

"There's that park, too, south of your cabin a mile or so," Gavin said, catching Jared's enthusiasm. "It'd be perfect."

"KC's brother has one, too," Moose said.

"What are we waiting for?" Jared asked, jumping up.

"It's too late today," Moose said, pulling him back down. "It'd be dark by the time we got there."

"Yeah," Gavin agreed. "Anyway, I have to pick Sara up in an hour."

Moose looked at his friend and shook his head.

"What?" Gavin asked.

"I can't believe you're still with her."

"Yeah," Jared agreed. "You're getting in pretty deep. Don't you think it's time to pull out?

Gavin shrugged. He didn't want to admit to his friends that for the first time in his life he had no desire to move on. "Not really."

Moose laughed. "Well, well, Jared, what do you know? Ol' Gavin's falling off the Moose Train."

"I'm not." What a scary thought. Falling off Moose's train meant falling in love.

"You'll be hitched before we know it," Moose predicted.

"I never thought I'd live to see it," Jared said.

"You guys! I'm not getting hitched. Now lay off."

Moose looked at Jared and grinned. "Testy, ain't he?"

Jared laughed. Gavin shot several pieces of popcorn at the others. The moment passed and the boys' attention returned to the television. Enthusiastically, they watched a few more races.

"Next week," Moose said. "We'll make a day of it. I'll arrange for the snowmobiles and gas, and map out a route. Jared, you and Robbie bring the food. Gavin, you and Sara get the gang together."

As January gave way to February, Jim decided to start sending out job applications. He prepared his résumé, then spent hours on the Internet searching for small businesses on the West Coast that were hiring. There was no longer any reason to stay in the Midwest. Sara lived only one state away and that was too close. Maybe if he put half a continent between them, he'd get her out of his system.

Saturday morning dawned cold, clear, and windy. Sara dressed in layers, knowing if she was going to be outside to watch—or maybe even participate in—the snowmobile racing she would have to ward off the chilly temperature. As she laced her boots, she wondered if she would really dare race one of the snowmobiles.

Gavin pulled into the driveway, but waited for Sara in the car. Lately, he didn't like the looks Morgan gave him. As if he had corrupted her sister. As if Sara didn't have a mind of her own and the freedom to do what she wanted.

Sara didn't keep him waiting long and when she opened the car door, she tossed a brightly colored aqua scarf at him. Picking it up, he asked what it was for.

"For you to hold at the finish line when I race my snowmobile," she answered cheerily. "You said you always have someone hold a scarf with your colors when you race. I want you to hold mine."

"You're going to race?"

"Yes, don't you think I can?"

Gavin backed out of the driveway, a large grin on his face. "Sara Brooks, I think you can do anything you put your mind to."

They were among the first to arrive at the cabin. The only other ones there were Moose, KC and Robbie. They were in the garage tying flags onto stakes to mark the trail. Gavin joined them in the garage while Sara went into the great room and warmed herself by the roaring fire. Before long, Jared, Troy and Krissa arrived, then Allison and Mandy.

"Where's Scott?" Mandy demanded loudly as she entered the house.

Sara said she didn't think he was here yet. Mandy swore and took off upstairs. Jared and Troy went out to the garage while Allison and Krissa joined Sara by the fire. It was only about ten minutes until Scott arrived with a beautiful blond girl in tow.

"Hey, everybody," Scott cheerfully called. "This is Lani."

Allison was on her feet in an instant. "You brought her here? Mandy's upstairs."

"Ooh, that makes me nervous," Scott said sarcastically.

"Is that Scott?" Mandy's voice drifted from upstairs.

"Let's get out of here," Allison said, tugging Sara and Krissa past Scott and out the door.

They fled to the garage, but they could hear the screaming anyway. Accusations flew from Mandy to Scott and back. The guys exchanged looks with each other, then KC said, "Let the races begin!"

Moose, Robbie and KC each hopped on a snowmobile to drive to the course. Troy, Jared, Krissa, and Allison piled into Troy's Jeep, while Sara climbed into Gavin's car. She couldn't help but think about Mandy. How Scott could flaunt Lani under Mandy's nose was unbelievable. And what happened between Scott and Mandy anyway? Just last weekend they'd been together—together and physically inseparable—as always. Of course, Sara had known from the first time that she met them that it couldn't last. All they seemed to have was a physical attraction, there didn't seem to be anything beyond that.

"Did you know that Scott showed up with another girl?"

"Is that what all the screaming is about?"

"Yes, I'm afraid it might get ugly. Do you think Lani had any idea that Scott already has a girlfriend?" Sara asked as she buckled her seatbelt.

Gavin shrugged. "Scott's a free man. He's never asked Mandy to marry him; he never will. Why should he?"

"But they've been dating so long and…"

"He doesn't love her, Sara."

"You're right," Sara had known it all along. "Still, it isn't very nice."

"If Scott wants to pursue another woman, more power to him."

"So in your opinion, relationships mean nothing until there's an official engagement."

"Sure, that sounds right."

"Like us. Like Jim and I were until—until—oh! You lured me away from Jim."

"Sara, now come on. You and Jim had major troubles—major troubles—ever since I met you. They had nothing to do with me. I was just there to pick up the pieces, remember?"

Sara pressed her lips together. She did remember. She also remembered that it had been very confusing and maybe, just maybe, if Gavin hadn't been so persuasive things might have turned out differently.

"You're no better than Scott," Gavin said.

"What? Me? Like Scott?"

"Yeah, you're dating me, but still thinking about Jim. I thought you'd gotten over him. I thought you were all for us."

"I am."

"You're not acting like it."

Gavin parked the car, the sound of the snowmobiles reaching them from over the hill.

"I'm sorry." Sara fidgeted with her scarf. "It's just…" She waved her arm in the direction of the house. "I don't know why, I don't even like Mandy and Scott, but what he did, just hit me hard." Maybe, it's because it was too much like what she had done to Jim. It was hard to see one's self in light of another's disgusting behavior.

Gavin put a hand on her knee. "I'm not Scott and I'm not Jim and I'm not going anywhere."

"Promise?"

Gavin looked at the tears glistening in her eyes. Here they were, back to promises again. Instead of answering, he kissed her. He kissed her until he was sure she had forgotten about Jim and Scott and everyone except him.

A half an hour later, Scott and Lani showed up at the park. Sara tried not to think about Mandy remaining in the cabin alone. Or maybe she had left, careening down the highway back toward the city.

"What gives?" Gavin came up to Sara, tugging down his stocking cap. "You look all serious."

"Nothing." Sara shook away her thoughts. Mandy and Scott were not her problem. If Gavin and Allison weren't doing anything about it, why should she? "Is it your turn next, because I want to ride on the back."

"Yep. We'll have to carry each other's scarves."

257

Sara laughed and draped her aqua scarf around his neck and tucked his royal blue one around her neck. She positioned herself behind Gavin on one of the snowmobiles. Turning, he winked. "Don't scream in my ears, okay?"

She laughed again and turned to see who they were racing against. Troy and Krissa were on one of the machines and Robbie was on the third. Leaning close to Gavin, she said, "Piece of cake."

He laughed and jerked to a start as Moose lowered the flag.

Two weeks later, on a Saturday morning, Gavin pulled into Mark and Morgan's driveway. The roads were a slushy mess. The temperatures had risen above freezing for the first time in two months and the snow was melting like crazy. It was a regular heat wave. Gavin climbed out of his Chevy in jeans and shirt sleeves and knocked loudly on the front door. He declined Mark's invitation to come inside and instead waited impatiently for Sara on the porch.

"Hi, Gavin. Isn't it fabulous?" she greeted cheerily, throwing her arms out to embrace the sunshine.

Gavin reached behind her to shut the door. "I need two hundred dollars, Sara."

"Two hundred dollars? What for?"

"To pay off my poker debt from last night."

"Oh, Gavin. Two hundred dollars."

"Look, the cards just weren't fallin' my way. Loan me the money so I can get Derrick off my back."

"I can't. I don't have two hundred dollars."

"How much do you have?"

"I'm not sure. Fifty, maybe. I can't believe you lost two hundred dollars. Why didn't you quit earlier?"

Gavin glared at her. "You know nothing about poker, do you?"

"It's *gambling*, Gavin. You shouldn't bet more than you can afford to lose."

"Sara, I do not need a lecture right now, I just need some money. Can you get it from your sister?"

"No, I cannot get it from Morgan. What would I tell her?"

"I don't know. That you need more textbooks or something."

"No, Gavin, I'm sorry. You can have my money, but that's it."

"Well, go get it then." Gavin paced the porch while Sara ran upstairs for her checkbook. When she came back and handed him the check, he shoved it into his pocket and turned to leave. "Thanks. I'll see you later."

"Wait. Where are you going?"

"To find some money."

Sara watched in bewilderment as he spun out of the driveway and headed down the street, wondering how she would meet her miscellaneous expenses over the next few weeks.

When Sara entered the house one evening after having supper with Gavin, Tucker was in his crib screaming. She could hear him all the way downstairs. "Morgan?" she called as she sprinted up the stairs to the nursery. "Where's Mommy?" she cooed, scooping the crying baby into her arms.

"I'm here." Morgan's voice came from the bathroom.

Sara carried the now hiccupping Tucker into the bathroom, where Nicholas was in the tub. Morgan was washing his hair. "Thank goodness, Sara. I thought you'd never get here."

"I'm sorry. I lost track of time. Do you want me to finish that while you take care of the baby?"

"Yes, thanks." Morgan didn't say any more even though she desired to give her sister a good tongue lashing. Things between them had been tense enough lately. Morgan knew that her sister longed only, and always, to be with Gavin. He seemed to have taken over her whole world—with the exception of school. Thankfully, Sara was faithful to her class schedule and her homework, but Morgan couldn't remember the last time her sister had gone to church and she was positive that at times she smelled alcohol on Sara's breath. However, whenever she tried to talk to Sara, it fell on deaf ears. She could only pray and choose her words carefully.

After the children were in bed, Morgan came to the top of the stairs. "Sara, do you want to watch a video or something? I've got the kettle on."

"No, Gavin and I are going to a movie."

"This late?"

"It's not that late, Morgan. Have you forgotten what it's like to be young?"

"No, sorry. It's just that…" Morgan had hoped for so much when Sara agreed to live with them—girl talk and bonding with her sister—but then Gavin had entered Sara's life and her spirit had left the house. "Okay, well, I'll wait up. You can tell me about it when you get home."

"Don't do that, Morgan. We might grab a bite to eat after…" Sara knew that Gavin would want to grab a beer and it would get late.

"Okay, but, Sara, there's school tomorrow."

"I'm nearly twenty-two years old, Morgan, and need I remind you? You are not my mother."

"I know, Sara. It's just that you spend so much time with Gavin and he...well—"

"I don't want to hear any criticism of Gavin."

"All right, but you've changed, Sara."

"Change is not necessarily bad. I'm having the time of my life." She grabbed her coat and purse and pushed past her sister.

"Are you really?" Morgan called after her.

"Am I really what?" Sara whipped around at the bottom of the steps.

"Having the time of your life?"

"Yes!" Sara yanked the door open, stepped outside and slammed it behind her. Morgan had some nerve, telling her it was a school day tomorrow and that she was spending too much time with Gavin. What did she think? That Sara was a teenager?

Morgan knew a losing battle when she saw one. "Just be careful, Sara, please," she said, with a heavy heart. But Sara was already outside and the words got lost in the slamming of the door. Morgan went into the nursery and gazed lovingly at her baby, asleep in his bed. *Dear Lord,* Morgan knelt on the floor, her fingers gripping the rungs of Tucker's crib, and prayed for her sister. *Open her eyes, Lord. Do whatever it takes, but open her eyes.*

It was the second Sunday in March. Daytime temperatures had been hovering above fifty degrees for two weeks. It seemed that after the harsh winter, there would be an early spring. Nearly all the snow had melted and Sara took joy in seeing green grass again.

She and Gavin spent the afternoon at his place, relaxing with video games and a movie. Later they planned to go to a concert of Robbie's, which was billed through a friend of a friend and would be held in a bar in a small town named Hartford. Robbie had taken up songwriting and tonight would be the first time the band would play some of his songs. Several of their friends were planning to attend, except Allison had a date with her lawyer friend, and Mandy and Scott, who had not reconciled, had dropped out of their group. Sara didn't miss them at all.

Gavin was cooking a simple supper of hot dogs when Allison came out of the bedroom, dressed for her date. "Well?" she asked her brother, twirling around. "Do I pass inspection?"

He whistled. "You'll knock his socks off."

Sara rose from the couch to check out how Allison looked. "Allison! You were supposed to return that skirt!"

Allie nonchalantly looked at the black skirt. "Oh, that. Well, I just decided to keep it. I mean, Mrs. T noticed it had sold and I figured it was easier to let her think that."

"But, Allie," Sara's hand flew to her throat where her heart was hammering. She was a bona fide shoplifter. "I never would have taken it if you hadn't promised to return it."

"Relax, Sara. You'll never get caught. It's been months now."

"I'm not worried about getting caught." *I'm worried about the wrath of God.* Oh… "Gavin, tell her she has to return it."

He just shrugged and took the hot dogs from the grill plate. "What's done is done, Sara. No one really cares."

"Well, I care."

The doorbell rang. "He's here," Allison said. "Sara, not a word. Do you hear me?"

"Like I would tell anyone." She waited calmly until the other couple left then she paced the kitchen in a rage. "I'd like to string her up!" She looked at Gavin, who was calmly putting ketchup on a bun. "Your sister has no scruples whatsoever!"

Gavin grinned. "Do you know how beautiful you are when you're angry?" He pulled her into a hug and held her firmly until she stopped stewing, then he kissed her again and again until she forgot all about Allison and the stolen skirt.

Gavin and Sara rode with Moose to Robbie's concert. There was not a lot of leg room in the backseat of his car, so Gavin sat up front and Sara, with her shorter legs, sat in the back. She listened to the guys talk, but didn't say much. They mostly discussed car engines and drag racing.

When Moose pulled into the parking lot of the bar, Sara realized she was much better prepared than the first time they had attended one of Robbie's concerts. The bouncers at the door, the smoky interior, the loud music, she was not going to let any of it throw her this time. She was going to act like going to bars was just a normal part of her life. Which, she realized wryly, it was becoming.

They pushed two tables together in the center of the room. Troy and Krissa danced now and then. Gavin asked Sara, but she didn't feel like dancing—not in this atmosphere nor to the strident music of Robbie's band. Throughout the night the others drank beer, but Sara still had not acquired a taste for it so she had Gavin order sweeter, mixed drinks for her. Over the course of the evening, Sara grew a little lightheaded—although she didn't think she had had that much to drink. After all, how much alcohol could be in a drink that was mostly orange juice?

It was nearly eleven o'clock when the band finished playing. After one more drink with Robbie to celebrate a remarkable concert, Gavin, Sara and their friends left, laughing and joshing all the way to their cars. Jared asked Moose if he had come on Highway 41 or 83. Moose replied 41, assuming it was quickest. This led to a meaningless debate on which route was faster, then whose car was fastest.

"Sounds like you're gunning for a race," Gavin declared.

KC laughed. "All right! Let's do it."

"We'll take 83; you guys take 41," Troy said. "We'll meet at Jared's."

"You haven't got a prayer," Moose said, swinging into the driver's seat of his car. Gavin hopped in next to him while Sara swiftly moved into the backseat behind Moose.

"What's the pot?" Jared yelled, half in and half out of his car.

"A hundred bucks," Moose hollered. Shutting his door, he strapped on his seatbelt, advising Gavin and Sara to do the same, then he revved the engine, waiting for Jared to give the all clear.

In seconds, the two cars tore out of the parking lot. Moose sat on Jared's bumper until they reached the dividing point where he turned east and Jared continued south. Moose wove in and out of cars on the dark two-lane highway. With exaggerated hand motions, Gavin instructed Moose to pass another car.

Sara leaned forward in her seat, peering through the front window, urging the car forward. She cheered silently for them to win, but couldn't help holding her breath each time Moose went into the oncoming lane to pass another vehicle or cut a curve short.

Moose's driving was sloppy at best, his judgments sluggish, but his adrenaline was high and the alcohol in his blood coated his nerves with steel. Feeling confident, he took a lot of chances.

"Here," with one hand, Moose yanked his cell phone off his belt clip and tossed it to Gavin. "Call Troy. Let them know we're coming up on 45 already."

Gavin laughed, looking forward to a little taunting. As he dialed the number, Moose pulled out to pass a semi. Drawing alongside the driver, he tooted the horn, then moved into the lane in front of the trucker. Moose didn't see the curve until his front tires hit gravel. He tried to pull back onto the road, but it was too late. They skidded through the gravel for a few feet before the car careened down an embankment and crashed into a large tree. The last sound Gavin heard before blacking out was Sara's scream.

CHAPTER 23

Do not conform any longer to the pattern of this world, but be transformed by the renewing of your mind.
—Romans 12:2

Gavin waited impatiently for the elevator doors to open. It had been a long night and wasn't dawn yet. He had a cast on his left arm—the ER doctor told him he had broken it in two places—and Moose was under observation due to a severe concussion, but it was Sara Gavin was worried about. No matter how much charm he had used, the nurses wouldn't tell him much. He'd been instructed to go to the operating waiting room where Sara's family was gathered. As the elevator doors opened, Gavin stepped forward fearing the worst.

He only had to walk a short way down the hall. Morgan paced the waiting room while her parents, younger sister and Mark sat in chairs nearest the hall. Another family huddled together on long benches in the opposite corner.

"How is she?" Gavin winced at the weakness in his own voice.

Morgan twirled and marched up to him with all the fury of an angered older sister. "How dare you? How dare you show your face here and ask how she is!"

"Morgan," her father rose and came to her side, "it was an accident. Show some compassion."

Morgan stared at her father. "Dad, the police said they'd been drinking."

"Yes," Mr. Brooks wearily agreed, "and your sister had been drinking as well."

Gavin bravely faced Sara's father, his need to know how she was stronger than his desire to run from her family. "How is she? No one will tell me anything."

"She—" Overcome with emotion, Mr. Brooks wiped a finger across his eyes.

Mark came to stand at his father-in-law's side. "Her face is cut and bruised, she has three fractured ribs and a ruptured spleen. They took X rays, then a CT scan. There was a lot of internal bleeding and no way to repair the spleen. She's in surgery now to have it removed."

Gavin felt as if he'd just been kicked in the stomach. Sweet, beautiful Sara under a doctor's knife. "How long?"

Mark glanced at the clock on the wall. "It'll be at least another hour."

Gavin nodded. "I'll be back." Maybe he could wait in Moose's room. He didn't want to wait here.

Mark put a hand on Gavin's elbow to stop him from leaving. "How's your arm?"

"Fine."

"Gavin?" Sara's mother said. "What about the other boy? What's happened to him?"

"He has a concussion. They're keeping him for observation. His mom's with him."

"And your family?" Mrs. Brook's voice was filled with motherly concern.

"I left a message for Allie." He looked down at his cast. "It's just a broken arm, no big deal."

"Your mother would want to know, dear."

"Maybe." Why was Sara's mom so concerned? It was just a stupid arm. Sara was the one to worry about. Just then, there was the clatter of high heels as Allison came hurrying down the hall, still dressed for her night at the theater. Brandon followed at a close distance.

"There you are! Next time tell me which hospital! I've been looking all over for you."

Gavin was embarrassed—over the fuss, and the commotion his sister brought. He just wanted to shrink into a corner and wait for news about Sara.

He tugged Allison into the hall and found a bench not too far away. Quietly, he told her and Brandon the gist of what had transpired while the Brooks family resumed their prayerful vigil. After a while, Gavin told Allie and Brandon that they might as well go home and try to catch a couple of hours' sleep before they needed to get up for work.

"We'll wait for word on Sara," Allie decided. "What about you? Are you going in to work?"

"No, I'll call when the club opens at six."

They silently waited until the doctor came at a purposeful clip down the hallway, then they followed him to the door of the waiting room. He approached Morgan, the only family member he had spoken to earlier. "Your sister's doing fine. Are these your parents?"

"Yes." Morgan made the introductions.

"She took to the anesthesia just fine and the surgery was quite routine. The biggest concern now is infection. We'll keep a close eye out for that. She'll be here a few days, recuperating."

"When can we see her?"

"She's just been brought to recovery. Once she's awake, the nurse will get you." He informed them that he would be in to check on her later and that someone else would apprise them of her condition and postoperative needs. With a harried goodmorning, he was gone.

Gavin backed away, taking Allison and Brandon with him. "You can go now, Allie. I'm going to wait and try to see her later."

"Okay. Well, I'll see you after work then."

"I'll walk you to the elevator. I want to check on Moose."

It took Gavin twenty minutes to make the rounds to Moose and back. He was sleeping, but Gavin talked briefly to Moose's mom. In all likelihood, he would be released in a couple of hours. When Gavin returned to the operating waiting area, he resumed his place on the bench in the hall. It wasn't very long until a nurse came asking for the family of Sara Brooks. Gavin rose and again, hung on the edges listening to the news.

"She's awake now—groggy, but that's normal."

Tears filled Mrs. Brooks' eyes. "May we see her?"

"Yes. Is anyone here named Jim?"

"Jim?" Morgan spoke up, surprised. "Why?"

"That's the name she's been repeating. I thought if he was here, he should be the one to go in."

"No," Morgan said softly. "No, he's not here."

"All right. Just two of you for now."

Mr. Brooks laid a hand on Morgan's shoulder. "You go in with your mother. I'll wait and see her later."

"Thanks, Dad." Morgan took her mother's arm and followed the nurse. She cast a quick look at Gavin as she passed. Even though she was angry with him, she was sorry that he had to hear that Sara had been murmuring Jim's name.

Morgan and her mother quietly entered the recovery area. It was portioned off into small curtained areas. The nurse pulled aside one of the curtains. Sara lay on her back. Morgan stifled a gasp when she saw her sister's bruised and cut face.

"Oh, baby," her mother whispered.

"Mom? You're here?" Sara's voice was hoarse.

"Of course. So is your father and Nicole. We came as soon as Morgan called."

"I'm sorry, Mom."

"Shhh…" Mrs. Brooks offered soothing words of comfort, as she stroked her daughter's head. They talked quietly for a few minutes, but Sara kept drifting in and out of sleep.

"I'm so tired," she said.

"Just sleep, dear, we'll see you later."

Sara nodded and closed her eyes. Suddenly she opened them and reached for Morgan. "Wait. Gavin and Moose. Are they okay?"

"Yes," Morgan answered. "Moose suffered a concussion, but he'll be fine. Gavin has a broken arm."

"He's waiting to see you," her mother added. Sara simply nodded and drifted off to sleep.

As she and her mother reentered the hallway, Morgan said that she would call Katie. She wandered down the hall to a quiet corner and first dialed information to get the number, then waited for someone to answer.

"Katie? It's Morgan. Sorry to wake you, but Sara's had an accident." Trying to instill as much calm as possible into her voice, Morgan answered all of Katie's frantic questions and explained as well as she could about Sara's condition, the cause of the accident and who else was involved.

Dazed, Katie hung up and sat immobile on the kitchen chair. When she didn't return to the bedroom, Wayne got up to see what was going on. Battling tears, Katie told him. When she finished, he reached for the phone.

"What are you doing?" Katie asked.

"Calling Jim. He'd want to know."

"Are you sure?"

"Yes." As much as he did not understand Sara or what was going on between her and Jim and Gavin, Wayne understood one thing. Jim still loved her. The phone rang four times and then the answering machine came on. Sighing, Wayne hung up. "They're probably all still in bed. I'm going over there."

Katie followed him to the bedroom where he hastily pulled on jeans, a T-shirt and tennis shoes. "Are you sure this is a good idea?"

"Katie, those two are so mixed up. All I know is that if we were estranged and you were lying in a hospital bed, I would want to know."

Katie nodded. "Yes, you're right."

Wayne pounded on the door to Jim's apartment. Not caring if he woke the neighbors, he hollered for Jim or Andy to open up. Eventually Andy came to the door. He'd just gotten out of the shower and his hair was wet. Surprised to see Wayne, he barely got a greeting out before Wayne pushed past him into the room. "Where's Jim?"

Awakened by the commotion, Jim appeared in his bedroom doorway. "I'm here. What's up?"

"It's Sara. There's been an accident. She had major surgery last night." While Wayne finished explaining, Jim backed into his room and got dressed. Shoving his feet into shoes, he looked at Wayne. "Was Gavin involved?"

Wayne nodded. "Yeah, another guy, too. It sounds like they were racing or something, excessive speeding, for sure." Wayne grimaced. He hated being the bearer of bad news. "There's more. They'd all been drinking." He backed out of the way as Jim moved into the bathroom to brush his teeth. "You're heading to Milwaukee, aren't you?"

"Yes."

"I'll come with you."

Jim shook his head. "You don't need to. Besides, you'll miss school and work."

"So will you."

"Yeah, well," Jim ducked back into his room and grabbed his wallet from the dresser. "It's something I have to do. Thanks for the offer, really, but I'd rather just go by myself."

"If you're sure."

Jim wasn't sure of anything except that a lead weight was sitting in his gut. "I'm fine, I'll call Katie when I get there."

Wayne nodded and watched the door close behind his friend. He wasn't surprised one bit that Jim was going to the hospital. He'd do the same.

Once Sara was situated in a private room, her family hovered around her bed. Mid-morning, Mr. Brooks ushered them to the cafeteria for breakfast, with a dual purpose of feeding his family and granting Gavin some time alone with Sara. Grateful, Gavin went to her side and took her hand. Studying her face, he hoped the cuts wouldn't leave scars.

"Sara?" Softly, he called her name, hoping she wasn't still dreaming of Jim. "It's me, Gavin."

Her eyelids fluttered, then opened. With effort, she smiled at him. The pain from her broken ribs and surgery was intense, plus her face hurt, but she was glad to see him. "Your arm…" Weakly, she moved a hand to touch his cast.

"I'm fine, Sara. I'm just worried about you."

They only talked a few minutes before Sara drifted off to sleep again. Gavin moved to a chair in the corner and waited until her family returned. Morgan and Mark wanted to say goodbye to Sara, but since she was sleeping they quietly took their leave. Mark needed to go to work for a few hours, Morgan to relieve the neighbor from watching the children. She and Mark had been the first to arrive last night, in the wee hours of the morning. Mrs. Trowland had been with the children ever since. Morgan peered down at her sleeping sister, praying for God to heal her, both in body and soul.

Gavin stayed until late morning, when Moose called. He was feeling fine, just headachy, and both of them were wanted at the police station for questioning. Sara was sleeping. Looking at Mrs. Brooks, Gavin said, "Tell her I'll be back. After the police station, I'm going to check in with work, then I'll be back."

It was almost noon. Sara lay awake, staring at the ceiling, reflecting on the accident, trying to piece together everything that had happened. Not only everything that had happened last night, but everything that had happened in the last several weeks to bring her to this place. Her mother sat quietly knitting; Nicole sat reading a teen magazine. Sara was glad her mom and sister were occupied, because she needed to think.

There was a motion at the door, causing Mrs. Brooks to look up. "Nicole," she said quietly, yet firmly, "let's go down and get a cup of tea." She stood and gently took her youngest daughter by the arm, with a stern look warning her not to speak. "Sara honey, we'll be back in a little bit. Do you need anything?"

Sara simply shook her head and closed her eyes. In a moment, she heard a dear, familiar voice whispering her name. *Jim.* She must be dreaming again, although the voice sounded so real. Sara opened her eyes a slit. There he was, leaning over, calling her name. "Is it really you?"

"Yes," with a lump in his throat, Jim gently brushed a strand of hair away from her face.

Sara turned away from him. "Don't look at me, Jim."

"I don't care how you look, Sara."

She couldn't begin to explain that it wasn't the physical appearance of her cut, bruised and swollen face that she didn't want him to see. It was all her sins—the lies and drinking and stealing. She felt shamed in his presence.

"What are you doing here?" she whispered.

"I don't know," Jim admitted. In fact, he'd been trying to figure that out for three hundred miles. What they had was over, but that didn't seem to matter to his heart. As soon as Wayne had given him the news, all he wanted to do was rush to Sara's bedside. Now the sight of her lying helpless in this bed, hooked up to an IV, with cuts and bruises on her face, was almost more than he could bear. "I guess I just needed to see for myself how you are."

"I wish you wouldn't look at me."

"You're beautiful, Sara."

"No, I'm not."

Jim decided not to continue down this road. It was no longer his place to tell her she was beautiful. "Are you in pain?"

Sara shrugged. The physical pain came and went. She had a button she could freely push whenever it hurt too much. But the biggest ache was seeing Jim and knowing she could never be his wife. There was no medication to ease that pain. Tears trickled down her cheeks. "I don't know why you're here. It's all over between us."

Jim closed his eyes for a brief moment. He was learning to live with regret, but it was killing him. "I know, Sara."

His simple words made her tears flow heavier. It cost Sara everything to keep her mouth closed and not blurt out that she loved him, that she needed him.

"I'll just sit here with you for a few minutes."

"Don't, Jim. Just go now, please."

Aw, Sara... He tugged a tissue from the box on her side table and offered it to her. The pain of loving her, of losing her, was still incredible even after three and a half months. But she was right, he should go. Why had he even come? So they could talk? About what? He could ask how school was going and tell her about the job interview he had in Oregon, but then, what was the use?

"All right, I'll go, if that's what you want."

Sara nodded, tears streaming down her face. She didn't want him to leave, but if he stayed she was bound to say something she had no right to say. They had already ruined each other's lives, she couldn't entangle him any further in the mess she had made of hers. "Yes, go," she sobbed, "because—because..." She pressed a hand over her mouth and silently screamed, *I still love you, Jimmy, but it's over—hopelessly and irrevocably over.*

"All right." Jim took a couple of steps toward the door, then stopped and turned to look at her. She met his gaze and their eyes locked. He wanted to tell her that he loved her, but instead he told her he would pray for her. She turned away, weeping. With his heart in his throat, he looked at her a moment longer, then turned and left the room. Wiping a tear from his own eye, Jim headed toward the elevator. He pushed the button, deciding to find Mrs. Brooks in the cafeteria and ask more about Sara's condition. Just to know. Just to know beyond a shadow of a doubt that she was expected to have a full recovery and return to an active life.

The elevator bell rang and the doors opened. The young man inside held a bouquet of pink carnations. Jim recognized him as Sara's boyfriend and struggled to keep his anger under control. Clenching his fists, he stood in the man's way. "You know this is all your fault, don't you?"

Gavin looked around. There was no one but himself in the elevator. "Are you talking to me?"

"Yes, you scum. You did this to her."

"To her?" Gavin was puzzled for just a moment longer. "Oh, I see. You must be the ex. Hello, Jim." Stepping out of the elevator, he added, "You shouldn't be so quick to judge a situation that you know nothing about." The doors closed behind him and the elevator continued its ascent to the floors above.

"I know plenty."

"Really? Is that what Sara told you?"

"She wouldn't rat you out."

"No, she wouldn't. Why are you here anyway? You had your chance and blew it."

No longer able to control his rising anger, Jim shoved Gavin against the wall. "So help me, if you don't take better care of her, you'll have me to answer to."

"I'm not afraid of you. And despite what so many people seem to think, Sara's a big girl. She can make her own decisions and look out for herself."

"That's what she wants people to think, but Sara has a lot of needs."

Gavin nodded in satisfaction. "Yeah, I guess that's true, Mr. Boring Boyfriend. Oops, make that *ex*-boyfriend. Apparently Sara needed a lot more than you offered. She's happier with me." He brushed past Jim and strode down the hall to Sara's room.

Jim madly pushed the button for the elevator, then, deciding not to wait, headed to the stairwell and sprinted down four flights. When he reached the landing he leaned over, gulping in air. What did she see in that creep? "Oh, God," Jim prayed from the depths of his soul. "Why do I care?"

I have loved with an everlasting love…

"Maybe you do, God, but I don't want to. I don't want to love her anymore. She belongs to him now."

God whispered His response in Jim's soul. *She belongs to Me and no one shall snatch her out of My hand.*

When Sara's mother returned to the room, she noticed tears running silently down her daughter's face.

"Honey, are you in a lot of pain?"

Sara nodded.

"It's fine to have more pain medicine."

"I know." What Sara didn't know was how to ease the pain in her heart. The pain that came from seeing Jim again, the unrelenting agony she felt over losing him. She thought she had put it behind her, but all it took was a mere ten-minute visit to open the painful wound. She didn't want to compare him to Gavin, but it could hardly be helped. Gavin was more handsome, charming, adventurous and outright open with his affections, but Jim was gentle, compassionate, kind and—probably what was the most important—he lived out his Christian faith every day. "It hurts so bad, Mom."

Sara woke in the middle of the night. Her face hurt, her ribs hurt, her incision hurt, and inside, where the doctor had taken out her spleen, that hurt, too. She knew she could push the button and have medicated relief fill her body, but that also dulled her mind and there was much to think about.

Like how she came to be here and why, like where her life was going, where this relationship with Gavin was taking her, and did she even want to go there? She could easily have died in that car crash. They all could have died. And it had been so stupid, so meaningless and stupid. She couldn't even blame Moose or Gavin. She had been drinking as well, she had urged the car forward, had wanted to win that race, share in that one-hundred-dollar prize. Stupid, stupid, stupid. "I was very foolish," she admitted aloud. "I never should have gotten in that car." Sleep overtook her and she thought no more.

Each day, Sara was better able to focus. She learned to keep her pain under control without relying on medication to such an extreme that she slept for hours on end and lived in a fog. Her mother or Morgan or Gavin were constantly by her side during the day. In the evenings, her dad and Nicole and Mark came. Katie called twice a day. She wanted to visit immediately, but Sara had convinced her to wait until she was home. Her grandparents visited on Tuesday, and Kelly stopped by on Wednesday after aerobics. Allison and Moose were the only friends from Gavin's crowd who came to see her, but as her room gradually filled with bouquets and balloons, stuffed animals and cards, she began to realize that she did have many friends and family who cared about her.

Sara liked having company to help fill the long daytime hours, but she cherished the dark, quiet nights, when she could think. It was after visiting hours Wednesday night when Sara woke. In the room's dim light, she could see a figure sitting in the chair near the foot of her bed. "Mark?"

"Yes, Sara, it's me."

"What are you doing here?"

"You seemed agitated earlier and your mom didn't want to leave you alone. I got permission from the nurse to stay until midnight."

"Oh." A warm, secure feeling flooded Sara's body. "That's sweet of you."

"How are you feeling? Do you need anything?"

In the semi-quiet, with the darkness penetrated only by the small green lights on various machines in the room and a brighter slit of light coming through the partially open hall door, Sara felt drawn to talk to Mark. He was always so levelheaded— really very much like Jim, she realized—it didn't seem threatening to talk to him, only comforting. "Maybe just to talk."

"Sure." He scooted his chair closer to Sara's bed. "What's on your mind?"

"A lot of things, too many things."

"The accident?"

Sara nodded. "Yes, but mostly my relationship with Gavin. I've made a terrible mistake. You know, I used to have an incredible relationship with Jim. He's really sweet and a wonderful Christian. I learned so much from him. Stuff about faith and integrity, and pursuing my dreams. Then, I'm not really sure what happened, but somehow, things went wrong between us. I think I ruined what we had over a stupid misunderstanding. I see now that I was looking for reassurance and love in the wrong places. So when Gavin breezed into my life, I let him sweep me off my feet, even when, deep down, I knew he was wrong for me. I let myself get caught up with his good looks and his charm and, oh Mark, he makes me feel so desirable, but…" Tears slipped down Sara's cheeks and it took a moment before she could continue. "I tried to tell myself that he's a Christian, but he's not. I learned a lot of things from him, too, but they're not *good* things—if you understand what I mean."

Mark nodded, thinking about the lies, and the suspicions Morgan had about Sara drinking. There were doubtless other things, too. He remained quiet though, letting Sara slowly get everything off her mind.

"I know this girl named Mandy. From the moment I met her, I didn't like her. She swears and shoplifts and drinks, but the thing I found most disagreeable was the way she acted with her boyfriend. It was all only physical; they didn't seem to have a true relationship. Not like what Jim and I had, where we could talk for hours about issues and life." Sara took a moment to get her tears under control. Mark reached for a tissue and handed it to her. He knew she wanted to say more. He could wait. Due to his training as a counselor, silences in the middle of a conversation didn't bother him.

"You know what's really sad? I'm turning into a girl like Mandy. As much as I hate to admit it, the relationship I have with Gavin is basically just a physical attraction. We never talk about anything meaningful; he just wants to have a good time. I've finally realized that what Gavin and I have is not very different from what Mandy and Scott had and a very long way from what Jim and I had."

"I'm sorry, Sara, but I'm glad that you figured this out. What do you want to do? Where do you want to go from here?"

"I know it's going to be hard, but I have to break up with him. There's not enough between us to build a lifetime on. And frankly, I don't like where he's taking me. I'm becoming like Mandy in other ways too, and I want to stop before it's too late. You don't think it's too late, do you?"

"Sara, God is a God of second chances and saving grace."

"The thing is, even if I could go back, I don't want to be the old Sara. I mean, I was a very needy, self-centered person. I think that's why it didn't work with Jim and I know that's why I fell for Gavin's charming ways."

"So be a new Sara, a new, improved Sara."

"I don't know how."

"God will show you, Sara. Break off ties with Gavin. Come back to God and let Him make you into His child, then you won't need to find your self-worth in the arms of a handsome man or even as the girlfriend of a Christian man like Jim."

Sara looked at the sincerity in her brother-in-law's face. "Thank you, Mark. I'm glad you were here tonight. I've been thinking about this for days— actually, even before the accident. I know God's been trying to get my attention, but I just kept pushing Him away."

"He can be pretty persistent. And as far as tonight is concerned, I'm just where God wanted me to be." Mark reached for Sara's hand. "May I pray with you, Sara?"

She nodded, closed her eyes and listened as Mark lifted her up to their Heavenly Father. Silently, she asked for strength. She would break up with Gavin, then she would find her way back to God.

CHAPTER 24

When he came to his senses, he said, "...I will set out and go back to my father and say to him; 'Father, I have sinned against heaven and against you...'" So he got up and went to his father. But while he was still a long way off, his father saw him and was filled with compassion for him.
—Luke 15:17-20

Thursday was Gavin's first day back to work following the accident. Having to work with basically one hand, he spilled the first two juices he fixed, but eventually got the hang of it. The preparation took longer, but the customers were understanding and patient. Gavin was grateful that work required more of his concentration than usual, for it kept him from thinking about Sara too much. He was worried about her. The nurses had warned him that although her body was healing, he should prepare himself for a lengthy recovery time. Sara wasn't even going to go to Morgan's when they released her, but to her parents' house. That was an hour's trip—one way! He supposed he could understand that she desired her mother's care, in the quietness of the family home, versus Morgan's divided attention and the noise of her niece and nephews, but sixty miles! Did she think he was going to head to Madison every night after work? And she was so serious all the time! He could hardly get a smile out of her. She said she didn't blame him or Moose, but then what was it? He just wanted her to get her spunk back.

Gavin's supervisor arranged for him to work a shortened shift his first day back, so at two o'clock, he headed for the parking lot, intent on visiting Sara and bringing her out of her slump. On the way to the hospital, he stopped at a drugstore and purchased a gangly stuffed monkey. Driving through the hospital parking lot, he went up and down three rows without finding an empty spot, so he whipped into the lot across the street and pulled into a patient-only parking spot. He grabbed the monkey and trotted for the entrance. He slowed as he approached her room, wondering how many family members he'd have to face. Sara's mother was the only one there. She glanced up and, with a smile, graciously left to give the young couple some time alone.

Gavin sat the monkey on top of his head and whisked up to the bed, a playful look on his face. "I was trying to decide what flavor of juice went best with a missing spleen—certainly not Guava Grapple and I don't think you're quite ready for Pineapple Passion. Kiwi Kiss came to mind, but then this little guy caught my eye and said, 'I want to go play with Sara,' so," Gavin shrugged and tossed the monkey onto her bed, "I figured, listen to the monkey."

Sara smiled weakly, but it quickly faded.

Ignoring her somber look, Gavin pulled a chair close to her bedside. "So, when are they gonna spring you? We've got places to go and things to do."

"Tomorrow."

"That's great." There was a cluster of balloons tied to the front of Sara's bed. Gavin caught the string of one and pulled the balloon down, then let it float up again. "What shall we do to celebrate? I could rent a few chick flicks if you want."

Sara looked into his eyes. "Gavin, I could have died in that accident."

He let go of the string and looked at her. "Way to kill the mood, Sara. Man! I'm trying to cheer you up here."

"I don't want cheering up."

"Come on, Sara. You're going to have a full recovery, the doctors all say so, but you've got to get out of this slump."

"It's true," Sara insisted. "About the accident. I could have died, we all could have."

"But we didn't."

"Seriously, Gavin. I keep thinking about it."

"Stop being melodramatic. You didn't and in a few days you'll be good as new."

"I should not have been in that car. I should not have been with you."

"Where should you have been? In Jared's car? It could just as easily been him."

"No, you don't understand. I should not have been with you. I never should have started dating you."

"Now you're talking crazy. They've got you on so many meds, you can't even think straight."

"I'm thinking perfectly clearly. I've cut back on the painkillers so I can think. It's all I've been doing for days."

"Then think about this, in a few days you'll be good as new. Spring is here. Goodbye snow, hello sunshine. The speedways are going to open soon and then the beaches."

"Please, Gavin. Don't make this any harder for me than it already is. I'm not going to keep going out with you."

"Sara, will you listen to yourself? What about our fairy tale?"

Slowly, Sara shook her head and tears dribbled out of the corners of her eyes. "That's all it is, Gavin, a fairy tale. You and I are from two different worlds and it just isn't going to work."

"Come on, Sara. Think about it: Beauty and the Beast, Cinderella… They never start out in the same world, but they make magic together. *We* make magic together."

Sara studied his face, with its finely chiseled features, the expressive dark eyes, the mouth she enjoyed kissing, and the sweep of his brunette hair. Drawing in a deep, shuddering breath, she said, "I know, we tried, but it isn't the happily-ever-after kind of magic."

"It was one accident, Sara. One lousy accident. You can't give up on us just because of that."

"I'm not. It's just that I want more."

"More? What more could you possibly want? I've given you the world."

"Yes, the world." *A world full of stealing, lies, and alcohol.* "I guess more is the wrong word. I need something different."

"Different as in Jim, right?"

Sara looked up in surprise.

"I know he came here Monday. You're going back to him, aren't you?"

"No, Gavin. I'll never go back to Jim." *He deserves someone much better than me.* "This has nothing to do with Jim and me. It has to do with you and me. I don't fit in your world and to be honest, I don't really want to."

"It's the meds talking, Sara. I know you don't really feel this way."

"Yes, Gavin, I'm sorry, but I do. I've been trying to convince myself since Thanksgiving that you and I could fit together, but we don't."

"Think of all the great times we've had."

"I'll admit, there were some magical moments, but they're not the kind I want to build a life on."

"I never asked you for a lifetime." Gavin stood up and took a step backward. "Man, Sara, maybe that's your problem. You're searching for Mr. Righteous to spend forever with and most guys are simply looking for a good time. Even your precious Jim didn't want to marry you."

Sara held her breath. He could hurt her all he wanted to, she was not going back on her convictions this time. "I've made my decision."

Gavin threw his good hand into the air. "Fine." *I really can't believe this. A girl is actually dumping me, Gavin Manes. I should have gotten out weeks ago, like Moose warned. Before my heart got involved.* "But when you get tired of your perfectly boring world, don't come looking for me. I pulled you out of a pit once before, I'm not about to do it twice." He turned and marched from the room without a backward glance. No girl, not even the vibrant Sara Brooks, was going to make him grovel.

"Take a longer walk every day and start using the stairs tomorrow." The nurse was going over Sara's discharge instructions with her and her parents. "No lifting anything over five pounds or driving for four weeks, no strenuous activity such as softball or aerobics for six weeks. We'll schedule a followup appointment for two weeks from today. Any questions?"

No aerobics. No, never again. She would never again set foot in a health club. There'd be too many memories, some good, some bad. "Hmm? What was that last thing?"

"I wondered if you have any questions."

"When can I go back to school?"

"I should think by Wednesday or Thursday—if it's just for a class or two."

Sara nodded, thinking. "Next week is spring break anyway. I'll contact my instructors and see what I need to do to get caught up."

"That's everything then. By the time you're dressed, I'll have your meds brought up and you'll be free to go."

Sara eased her legs over the side of the bed. Yesterday after Gavin left, the doctor had taken out her stitches. She knew he had been gentle, but it felt like he had just yanked them out. Today, the wound was extremely tender to the touch. "Help me, Dad."

Mr. Brooks took Sara's arm and eased her onto the floor. Looking at his wife, he said, "I'll bring the car around and meet you at the east entrance. Sarabelle, you ride down in a wheelchair now, no arguing."

"Yes, Dad." In the small bathroom, Sara pulled off her hospital gown and gingerly tugged on her sweats and T-shirt. She scrutinized her face in the mirror. The swelling was gone, the cuts nearly healed and the bruising was no longer black and blue, but turning yellow and green. In another week, she would look the same as always, but she knew she would never truly be the same. She'd give anything to be a little girl again—an innocent little girl with too much hair for her face—and be carried out of here, not in a wheelchair, but on her daddy's strong shoulders. Why had she ever caved in to Gavin's charms? *Kiwi Kiss...* Sara traced the outline of her lips. The memory of Gavin's kisses gave way to Jim's. Suddenly, she remembered swinging high into the night sky with Jim laughing at her side.

"Sara?" Her mother's concerned voice came from the other side of the door. "Are you all right? Do you need any help?"

Sara opened the door. "I'm fine. I'll need you to tie my shoes though."

Sara stared out the car window at the spring afternoon. When had the last of the snow melted? When had the crocuses bloomed? And the pink flowers on the ornamental cherry trees, when had they opened? The people on the sidewalks, all the cars...life was going on around her, but she felt as if she would never truly be alive again. She was weighed down with sin.

"When did you say Katie was coming?" her father asked as he turned west onto highway 94.

"The clinic let her off at noon," Sara answered from the backseat. "Mom, what if she arrives before we do?"

"Nicole will let her in."

"Oh, yes." Sara had forgotten. Ever since the accident, she had trouble keeping details straight. Perhaps it had nothing to do with a physical weakness, but the fact that so many other, important issues were crowding her brain. "I can't wait to see her. I have so much to tell her."

Her parents exchanged a look. Sara had said nothing to them about Jim's visit five days ago. She had said very little about breaking up with Gavin, only that she had, but Mrs. Brooks knew that her daughter needed a heart-to-heart talk with her best girl friend. She knew that her daughter would confide in Katie things she did not want to share with her parents or sisters.

Muffled sobs woke Katie in the predawn hours. She glanced across the shadowy bedroom and barely made out Sara's figure huddled under the blankets with her face to the wall. "Sara? Are you in a lot of pain?"

The crying ceased as Sara anxiously wiped her face with the edge of her sheet. "Just a little. That's not what I'm crying about."

"What is it then?"

Sara rolled over and looked at Katie. "Do you really want to listen? I have so much to tell you, but…" Sara swallowed the knot in her throat and willfully held back tears that threatened to spill again.

"Yes, Sara." Katie climbed out of bed, pulling the comforter with her and wrapping it tightly around shoulders. "Do you have a candle?" At Sara's quiet directions, Katie went across the room to the dresser, found a box of matches and lit the jar candle. After the initial brief smell of sulfur, the pleasant aroma of cinnamon-apple filled the room. Katie set the candle on Sara's nightstand, where it cast a small but steady flickering light. Sara drew her knees up, making room on her bed for Katie. This comfortable custom of talking by candlelight in the middle of the night had started early in the first year they lived together in the dorm at MCU. Over time, it had become a ritual whenever one of them had something of a significant nature to share.

Katie waited quietly for her friend to gather her thoughts. Sara was grateful for the nighttime hours and the shadowy room. She wanted to tell Katie everything, but some things she would not have wanted to expose to the daylight.

"You can't tell Jim anything I'm going to say. You must promise."

Surprised, it took Katie just a moment to agree. "I promise, Sara."

"But I don't want you to lie to him. If he comes right out and asks you something, then you must tell the truth, but don't offer any information. And don't let Wayne either." After months spent telling lies, Sara didn't want anyone doing it on her behalf.

"We've always kept each other's secrets, Sara. You can trust me."

Sara studied Katie's face, knowing it was true, building up the courage to begin. "First of all, I broke up with Gavin."

"I'm sorry, Sara." *That explains the tears*, Katie reflected. *So soon after Jim…*

"There's more," Sara interrupted Katie's thoughts.

"I'm listening."

"Please don't judge me too harshly."

"I won't, Sara. You can tell me anything. I'll still love you, no matter what."

Keeping a grasp on a corner of her blanket, Sara occasionally dabbed at the tears that gathered in the corners of her eyes. "I've made a lot of mistakes in the past few months and turned my back on many of my Christian values."

"We all sin, Sara, every last one of us."

"I know, but I kept doing it willfully and getting in deeper and deeper. I've done some things I'm really ashamed of. It all started when I met Gavin. Did I ever tell you that I knew him in ninth grade?" At the shake of Katie's head, Sara filled Katie in on the prior relationship she had had with Gavin and then how they had met again at the health club.

"When I met him at the club, I was growing increasingly unsure of my relationship with Jim, so it was really hard to resist Gavin's advances. One thing led to another, and I'm still not really sure how it happened, but Jim and I broke up and I began dating Gavin exclusively—exclusively and seriously. He practically took over my whole life. It's so clear to me now to see that I fell for superficial things. He is the most handsome man I know, and he's charming, but mainly, he made me feel very desirable. Surface stuff, Katie. I'm ashamed of it now. And as fun as he was to be with some of the time, a lot of the time it was far from fun. I tried so hard to fit in with his crowd and I told a lot of lies to cover my tracks—so many I could hardly keep them straight. I started to drink and…and…" Sara couldn't bring herself to tell Katie she had stolen a skirt and snuck into movie theaters and pilfered apples and other things. "I saw a whole side to life that I wish I'd never seen."

Tears trickled down Katie's cheeks as she wrapped Sara in a tight hug. "It'll be okay, Sara. You'll move on from this. God will help you get past it."

Sara rested her head on Katie's shoulder and sobbed for a few minutes, then sat back and dried her tears. "I hope so, Katie. I want to see God's loving eyes calling me back to Him." Sara remembered that still small voice she had tried so hard to ignore. "I guess He's been there all along, but I didn't listen. I was so caught up in my life with Gavin. Now I want to find my way back. Will you pray for me?"

"Of course, I'll start right now." Katie grasped Sara's hand and fervently asked God to show Sara the way back to Him. When she finished praying, the two friends looked at each other for several moments. "I'm glad you told me all this, Sara. I've felt for the longest time that something wasn't right. Way before you and Jim broke up."

"I was so stupid." Sara shuddered. "It's so sad. I always wanted to soar on the clouds with my Prince Charming. I guess I was doing that all along with Jim, but I wasn't satisfied and didn't realize what I had. Then Gavin came along and promised me the world. I took what he offered, but I still wasn't satisfied. Is there something wrong with me?"

"No." Katie squeezed Sara's hand. "But you might be looking for fulfillment in the wrong places. I'll be praying for you every day."

"Thank you. Thank you for being the best friend a girl could ever have."

CHAPTER 25

Do not cast me away from your presence or take your Holy Spirit from me.
Restore to me the joy of your salvation and grant me a willing spirit.
—Psalm 51:11-12

Daily, Sara gained strength as her body slowly healed. By Tuesday, she could walk around the block—granted, it was a slow walk, but a full one all the way around her parents' block. She began to believe that she would be strong enough to return to classes next week. In anticipation of this, she spent part of each day working on assignments so she would be caught up when classes resumed following MATC's spring break. Since that coincided with the first day of spring break for Nicole, the family planned for her to accompany Sara to Morgan's house to help with the children and drive Sara back and forth to classes.

"Such a bother," Sara muttered when the plans were discussed at supper one evening. Yet she was grateful that Nicole was available and willing. It seemed that God, in His mercy, had made provisions for her long before the accident had taken place. Did that mean He'd been watching over her all along? Did He anxiously wait for her to come back to Him? She wanted to. Wanted to with her whole heart, she was just so unworthy. How did a willful sinner who knew better, but had snubbed God and all His teachings, ever stand in his presence again? Sara was desperate to figure out a way to earn the right to stand before her Lord and Maker. There had to be something she could do...some penance she could pay...help the sick...the poor... If she had some money, she would give it all away, but there was nothing but a few dollars in her purse and a small amount in her checking account. Her savings were nonexistent. Then Sara recalled the story in the Bible of the widow who had given mere pennies, which was all she had, and God had proclaimed her a woman of great faith. *If it worked for her, why wouldn't it work for me?* Eager to take care of this immediately, Sara pushed away from the dinner table and stood too quickly. "Ooh! Ow!"

"Steady, Sarabelle," her father gently warned. "Where's the fire?"

Embarrassed, Sara gently massaged her sore ribs. "There's something I need to do. May I be excused?"

At her mother's nod, Sara gingerly walked to her room, where she wrote a check payable to the church's mission fund, leaving only two dollars in her account. She would place the check in the offering plate on Sunday, with a prayer for forgiveness. God surely wouldn't turn His back on her when she was giving Him everything she had.

Jim waited in the express checkout line with his few items in a blue plastic shopping basket. It didn't hold much, just shampoo, a package of lead for his mechanical pencil, a box of microwave popcorn, and a jar of peanut butter. Simple things for a man leading a simple life. He didn't need much. There were only seven weeks until graduation. The job offer in Oregon looked promising. He didn't want a lot of stuff to cart across the country.

The elderly woman in front of him was tugging her checkbook from the depths of her large handbag. She fumbled with the pen, dropping it to the floor. Jim picked it up for her.

"Thank you," she said with a grandmotherly smile. "Now let's see..." She wrote *March* on the line for the date, then paused and looked at the clerk. "I can't seem to remember the date."

"The twenty-second."

Jim froze. *March 22; Sara's birthday.* Fixedly, he watched the woman write her check while the realization that today was Sara's golden birthday filled him with a dull ache. Twenty-two years old on the twenty-second of March. She had once told him that on her golden birthday she wanted to get all dressed up and go ballroom dancing. *Like a princess*, she had said. He had promised to take her. Even though he didn't like to dance and didn't know how, he had promised. She had made great plans, saying they would take lessons. They never had, then she had moved to Wisconsin…

"Sir?" The clerk's voice broke through Jim's reverie. The elderly woman was gone and the clerk stood waiting.

Silently, Jim placed his shopping basket on the conveyer belt, pulled his debit card from his wallet, and tried not to think about what had happened once Sara had moved to Wisconsin. However, he could not prevent himself from wondering what she was doing on this day—her golden birthday. With fractured ribs and her recent surgery, he was sure that she would not be dancing. He hoped Gavin would make it up to her somehow. He hated to think of Sara not being able to fulfill her dreams—however minor they might seem.

"Do you feel up to going out for a birthday dinner?" Mrs. Brooks asked.

"No," Sara tried to keep the quiver from her voice. "Could you just make baked chicken and chocolate cake? And ask Morgan and Mark and Grandma and Grandpa to come?"

"Yes, dear."

As her mother headed to the laundry room, Nicole dropped onto the chair across the table from Sara. "Gavin or Jim should be here for your birthday. I don't understand why you're not dating either one."

"I broke up with Gavin, Nicole, I told you that."

"I don't understand why." The seventeen-year-old got a wistful look on her face. "He's the dreamiest guy. I think he looks like the actor on *Seaside*."

"There's more to a boy than his looks, Nicole. I learned that the hard way."

"Well, what about Jim? He drove all that way to see you in the hospital. You never even mentioned it to us, but we know he came. Three hundred miles, Sara."

Three hundred miles, five hours. He must have skipped classes…and work. Sara gulped as the reality of what Jim had done dawned on her. *Ten hours round trip for a ten-minute visit. He hadn't even missed classes or work that time I went to visit in the fall.*

"Sara?" Nicole tapped her older sister on the arm. "Did you know that you called for Jim in your sleep?"

Sara's eyes grew large and her hand flew to her throat. "I did?"

"Yes. Gavin was there in the waiting room, but you were calling for Jim.

I thought it was so romantic." Nicole studied her sister's massive curls, blue eyes, pretty face. "You've always been the prettiest of us Brooks girls. You've had guys drooling over you since you were thirteen. If neither Jim nor Gavin are good enough for you, I don't know what you're looking for."

"I don't either." All Sara knew was that there was a gigantic empty hole in her heart and she didn't know what was going to fill it.

As Sara approached the church building on Sunday morning, she lagged slightly behind her parents and sister. The check to the mission board was burning a hole in her purse. She couldn't wait to place it in the offering plate, but she was hesitant to step inside the building—God's house. She wasn't worthy to be here. She had not been to church in over two months. She was ashamed of her unfaithfulness.

"Sara?" Her mother turned at the top of the steps. "Are you feeling up to this? Sitting for an hour on a wooden pew?"

"I'm not sure," she answered, but not for the reason her mother gave.

Mrs. Brooks saw the anxiety on her daughter's face. Morgan had informed her that Sara had been skipping church of late. She also knew about the drinking. "We'll sit toward the back, that way you can slip out if you need to."

Sara gingerly climbed the steps. When she entered the foyer, the minister's wife reached for her hand and gently held it as she wished Sara a good morning. "We've been praying for you. Are you feeling better?"

Sara nodded and moved away from the woman as quickly as she could without being rude. It was bad enough to face God with her sins, did the entire congregation know that she had been drinking the night of the accident?

It was Lent, so the songs and the sermon focused on the road to the cross. *Sinner.* The accusation screamed across Sara's mind. She felt crushed under the weight of her transgressions. She couldn't listen anymore, so she tuned out the pastor's closing words about the redeeming work of Christ on the cross. All she knew was that she had helped put Him there. One of those nails had her name on it. Gratefully, she tugged the check from her purse as the purple, velvet offering bag was passed. As she dropped it inside, she whispered a prayer for forgiveness.

Sara came out of class Wednesday to a slight snowfall. It seemed that winter wanted to take one last stand. Nicole had pulled the car up to the curb. Sara walked slowly across the wide sidewalk and carefully climbed inside.

"How was class?" Nicole asked.

"Fine." In truth, Sara had not been able to concentrate. The satisfying relief she had felt on Sunday with her offering had not lasted. She could not shake her feelings of unworthiness. As Nicole maneuvered toward the main boulevard, Sara stared at the thin layer of snow gradually covering the ground. It was so pretty when it was fresh. Unsullied, clean, bright. *White as snow. Though my sins be as scarlet, may they be white as snow. How can I possibly cover my sins like the snow covers the grass?*

Sara was so lost in thought, she barely paid attention as her younger sister prattled on about the things she had done that morning with Nicky and Courtney. "I kept them entertained while Morgan boxed up some of the clothes that Tucker's outgrown. They're in a box in the backseat. She wants us to run them over to Tina, one of the new mothers in church. Her baby boy is four months younger than Tucker."

"Box them up? Donate them to someone else?"

"Well, temporarily. Tina will give them back when her baby outgrows them."

That's what I'll do. Box up my clothes. I have way more than I need. I'll box them up and donate them to the local homeless shelter. God will certainly be impressed with that. He knows I love clothes. It'll be a true sacrifice. If I do this, I know I'll feel His forgiveness.

After supper, Sara took a box from the storeroom closet, firmly shut her bedroom door, and shoved her closet door wide open. As she sorted through her clothes, she realized this was going to be harder than she thought. *But then, a true sacrifice shouldn't be too easy. Think of Jesus on that cross.*

She took out a few of her shirts and two skirts and, neatly folding them, placed them in the box. A pair of shoes went in next. *That's not enough.* She eyed her wardrobe. *Please, God, make this count.* She pulled out the red party dress she had worn to the health club's Christmas party. She held it against herself and twirled around, remembering how she had danced in Gavin's arms. Then she remembered how much it had cost. How buying the dress had depleted her savings account and had forced her to ask her dad for money. Remembering the half-truths she had told him, Sara jerked the dress off its hanger, folded it and placed it into the box. Then she resolutely pulled open a dresser drawer and removed her new cashmere sweater. The one she had always wanted; the one she had purchased with Gavin's money. She folded the sweater and laid it inside the box. *It still doesn't seem like enough.* With tears in her eyes, Sara placed a few more items in the box, then sealed it with packaging tape. With a wide, black marker she wrote *Homeless Shelter* across the top and placed the box on the floor next to her bedroom door. She stared at it, wondering when she would feel God's forgiveness, because all she felt right now was regret, unhappiness and emptiness.

With the flipping of the calendar page to April, spring arrived in earnest, chasing away the last of winter's snow. Nicole's vacation ended and she returned home. Sara was still not allowed to drive so she studied the local transit schedule and relieved Morgan from the constant need to chauffeur her to class and back. The course the bus drivers took varied from the route she always used and was twenty minutes longer, but it provided time for Sara to think. It didn't seem to make any difference that she had given her money and part of her wardrobe away. Guilt and unworthiness continued to plague her. *I have to do more*, was her constant refrain.

One morning as Sara rode the bus to campus, she noticed a line of people waiting in front of one of the older buildings downtown. She strained to read the small sign that hung sideways over the door. *It's a food bank*, she realized. The vision of the people waiting their turn remained with Sara all through class and as she climbed the steps to her room later that afternoon, she realized that volunteering at a food pantry or soup kitchen would be a physical way to atone for her sins. Giving money and clothes had been too easy. Ladling soup and refilling coffee cups would truly be an act of sacrifice, one God could hardly ignore.

Morgan's pastor put Sara in touch with one of the local soup kitchens and she faithfully worked two Saturday afternoons. The first time she went, she was very nervous, but Mama Jan—as everyone called her—took Sara under her wing and showed her what to do.

"Now, some people," Mama Jan explained, "like you to chat with them a bit, but some are so embarrassed, they'll hardly make eye contact. Those people just want to be left alone."

"How will I know?" Sara asked, positioning herself behind one of the roasters holding vegetable beef soup.

"You'll know, honey. The good Lord, He'll prompt you."

"But—" It was too late. Mama Jan had turned and headed back to the warm kitchen. Sara made sure all the tendrils of her wayward hair were stuffed under the plastic hair bonnet she'd been given, then pasted on a smile as the doors were opened and people filed into the room.

Sara's nerves calmed as she thought of herself as God's hands, tending these needy children of His. Her natural friendliness and spunkiness took over as she wished the people a good day along with their serving of soup. Mama Jan was right. Some people—usually the older ones—paused a moment to say a few words, while others shuffled up, heads bowed, and simply held out their bowl for soup. Sara said good afternoon to them anyway, smiling and offering silent prayers on their behalf.

After the meal had been served to a hundred people, Sara worked in the back kitchen, washing dishes. In her sheltered world, she'd had no idea so many people were in need of daily food. *I have so much*, she reminded herself. She realized how self-centered she had been and made a vow to focus less on the state of her own needy heart and the lack of a Prince Charming in her life, and think more about the needs of others.

Forgive me, Lord.

My grace is sufficient.

You know, Lord, tomorrow is Easter. I'd sure like to know that I've earned the right to claim Christ's forgiveness. If not, I just don't know what more I can do.

My grace is sufficient.

Yes, Lord, I understand. But she didn't really. Grace was a difficult concept to grasp.

Sara followed Mark down the church aisle. The nearer they drew to the front of the sanctuary, the better she could smell the sweet scent of Easter lilies. A dozen potted ones lined the steps and communion table. Sara settled onto the wooden church pew and scanned the bulletin, taking note of what songs they would be singing. She had always loved the pageantry and celebration of Easter. She just wished her heart was clean. All those things she had done to acquire forgiveness seemed paltry now in the light of Jesus' sacrifice.

The choir rose and sang an opening hymn, then two members of the youth group led the congregation in a litany. As the litany came to a close, the pianist played the opening chords to a praise song. With a longing in her heart, Sara sang the well-known words about Christ's salvation being free. After one verse, she stopped singing due to the lump forming in her throat. *Free? But I've tried so hard to earn it.*

Your salvation was already bought. Look to the cross, child. I will freely pardon.

Free is too simple. It has to hurt, Lord.

For by His wounds you are healed.

Yes, Lord, and I inflicted those wounds. Can You ever forgive me?

It's already been done. Not by your sacrifice, but by My Son's. Take it; it's yours.

You must want something, Lord.

A broken and a contrite heart, I will not despise.

Tears slipped down Sara's cheeks. Could it be true? That forgiveness was free? All she had to do was accept it and offer God her broken heart? Yes, she knew it was. It's what she'd been taught all her life. If she hadn't taken her eyes off the cross and been so bound and determined to find her own way, she would have remembered. Sara glanced to the wooden cross behind the pulpit. The light had been turned on behind it, causing it to shine brightly against the mahogany wall. Like God's love for her. Like Christ's salvation. *I accept it, Lord. I do.*

Welcome home, My child.

Is that all I have to do?

My grace is sufficient.

But my guilt and remorse, Lord…

Give it to Me. You're forgiven.

Sara thought back on all the things she had done in the past months and pictured herself handing them to Jesus. *Are You sure You want them?*

As far as the east is from the west, so far are your transgressions removed.

A lightness, such as Sara had not felt in months, filled her heart. She was forgiven. It had been so easy, after all. "Praise God," she whispered, as the congregation finished singing. Gripping Mark's arm, Sara leaned against his shoulder. "I'm forgiven," she whispered. *I'm forgiven!*

CHAPTER 26

Create in me a pure heart, O God, and renew a steadfast spirit within me.
—Psalm 51:10

Katie smiled at Jim across the kitchen table as he told her and Wayne that he had accepted a job in the coastal town of Newport, Oregon. He would spend the summer clerking and learning the store, then take over as manager in October.

"I'm happy for you," Katie said. It was good to see him excited about something and moving on with his life. Graduation was only a month away. Wayne would be graduating also, although he still had to do his student teaching next fall. Then *he* would be looking for a job. She wondered where his search might take them. She used to hope and dream that they would end up in the same town as Jim and Sara. Of course, that was before...

"Jim, don't you want to know how Sara is? It's been almost six weeks since her accident." Five weeks since Sara had broken up with Gavin and bound Katie to secrecy. *Only if Jim asks*, Sara had said. And Katie had promised. But Jim had not brought up Sara's name, not once.

"Why? She's getting better, isn't she?"

"Yes." *That flicker in Jim's eye, what does it mean?*

"Well, then, no, I don't need to know anything else."

"But—" Katie was stuck. Stuck between her promise to Sara and the desire to let her cousin know everything.

"Katie," Wayne gave her a warning look. "He doesn't want to know."

Men! Katie inwardly fumed, then rose to refill their lemonade glasses.

Sara stood on the sidewalk and faced the front door to Charyl's Boutique. It didn't seem possible that four months ago she had actually walked into this beautiful, exclusive shop and stolen a skirt. *What was I ever thinking? You weren't thinking, Sara Brooks, that was the problem. From the day you walked into the club lobby and met Gavin Manes, your brain clicked off.* "Never again," Sara stated aloud. "From now on, I will ask myself what God would have me do." Squaring her shoulders, Sara pushed open the door to the boutique. The same wonderful aroma of jasmine met her; her feet sank into the same luxurious pink carpet. The store owner was nowhere in sight, but at the jingle of the shop's bell, Allison looked up from behind the cash register. Her face paled when she saw Sara.

"Hello, Allie." Sara's greeting was sincere as she approached the counter.

"Sara. I never thought I'd see you again."

"Yes, well," Sara set her pink purse on the counter and tugged out a check from an inside pocket. "I have some unfinished business to take care of." She had had to borrow money from her dad, but she was determined to set things right. "I have a skirt to pay for."

"You can't," Allison protested. "I mean, it isn't even yours and how can I ring up a sale I'm not really making?"

Sara laid the check on the counter. "That's for you to figure out. I just know that I walked out of here with a skirt I hadn't paid for. It wasn't right. This money belongs to your boss. Please make sure she gets it."

"You don't have to do this, Sara."

"Yes, I do."

Allison just shook her head. "If you insist. I think you're crazy, but then I always told Mandy there was something different about you."

"How is Mandy?"

Allison shrugged. "Angry. She and Scott never got back together."

"I'm not surprised. How about you and Brandon? Are you still dating?"

"Yes. Next weekend, he's taking me to Connecticut to meet his family."

"That's nice."

"I know what you're thinking. I don't do it anymore."

"What's that?"

"Shoplift. Hang out with Mandy. Brandon's had a good influence on me. He's changing my world."

Just like Gavin changed mine—only in opposite ways. "I'm glad, Allie." Sara turned to leave, but Allison called after her.

"Wait. How about you? I know we never got along very well, but I felt bad when Gavin broke up with you. I mean, at first, I told Gavin you weren't his type, but he seemed so taken with you. Do you know, he'd never dated anyone as long as he dated you?"

"Really? And he told you that he broke it off?"

"Yes, he went on this whole spiel about how he wasn't ready to fall off the Moose Train and you were getting so serious and all."

Sara smiled. She could let Gavin save face. It didn't matter to her. "It was something like that. Well, it was good to see you, Allie. I hope the trip to Connecticut goes well."

"Thanks. Should I tell Gavin I saw you?"

"If you want. Just tell him that I wish him all the best and every time I see a race car, I'll think of him." Sara stepped into the April sunshine, then stuck her head back inside. "Oh, and that I'll always pray for him."

"Courtney!" Sara called up the steps. "Come see what Auntie Sara bought today."

Sara held the paper bag in front of her and watched her niece skip down the steps. Nicholas followed, thumping from step to step on his rear end. "Wait for Nicky," Sara said as Courtney jumped up and down at her feet. When he reached the bottom step, Nicholas gave his aunt a grin from ear to ear. With a chuckle, she scooped him up and led Courtney into the living room. She gently dropped her nephew onto the couch, then plopped down beside him. Courtney climbed up next to her and stared at the bag on Sara's lap.

"Now, you know how we love to read books together," Sara began to explain. "Well, today I went to a used book store and got some new books to read." One at a time, Sara pulled them from the sack and laid them on her niece's lap. "*Charlotte's Web, Frog and Toad, Corduroy,* and my all-time favorite, *Winnie-the-Pooh.* He's a wonderful little bear."

Courtney looked at the covers of the books. "Where'th the printheth?"

"No more princesses, sweetie." Sara patted Courtney's head. "Aunt Sara is done reading fairy tales. They're just not realistic."

Morgan laughed from the doorway. "And talking spiders and stuffed teddy bears are?"

Sara blushed. "That's different. We can't have Courtney growing up thinking fairy tales come true."

Morgan crossed the room and bent to wrap her sister in a hug. "I'm sorry life's been cruel to you, sis. One of these days your Prince Charming is going to waltz through that door and claim you as his bride."

Sara leaned her forehead against Morgan's shoulder. "That's what would have to happen, Morgan, because I'm not going out searching. God is King of my heart now and I just want what He wants for me. If my future includes a Christian man, God's going to have to bring him to the door with a sign that says, *I'm the one God chose for you.*"

Morgan stood up and smiled at her sister. "You're so funny, Sara."

"I'm not. I'm dead serious."

"And your heart? Has it healed?"

"As far as Gavin is concerned, yes."

"And Jim?"

Sara pressed her lips together and dropped her eyes to her lap. *Jim. Will my heart ever truly be over him?* Blinking back tears, she met her sister's gaze. "When I think back over it all, I realize that Jim loved me more than I thought he did. I wish I'd understood that what we had was true love."

"Maybe it doesn't have to be over, Sara."

"Yes, it's over, but a part of Jim Hoffman will always live in my heart. I like having him in there. I can remember what we had and know that love lives on. Wherever he is, wherever I go, a part of him will always be with me."

While they were talking, Nicholas had tugged one of the new books off his sister's lap. Now he shoved it under Sara's nose. "Dis one. Read dis one."

Chuckling, Sara wiped her eyes. Glancing at her sister, she said, "So much for girl talk." Looking down at the book Nicholas held, she smiled. "*Charlotte's Web.* Do you like spiders, Nicky?" The little boy solemnly nodded, but Courtney firmly announced that she did not. "You'll like this one, I promise." Sara pulled her nephew onto her lap, arranged the book on his legs, placed one arm around Courtney and commenced to read.

Jim stood in his cap and gown with a parent on each side and posed as his sister, Torie, snapped their picture. They stood on the lawn near the president's house, enjoying punch and cake with four hundred and some other graduates and their families.

"Just one more," Torie said, stepping a foot closer.

Jim smiled, but his eyes roamed to a spot where first Greta posed with Andy while Katie took their picture, then Katie posed with Wayne while Greta took theirs. *Sara should be here*, he thought, *posing with me*. For nearly two years, that's the way he had envisioned this day. No matter how hard he tried to put her behind him, she haunted his dreams, she went with him everywhere.

It didn't help that memories of her covered almost every inch of this campus. It would be good when he left. He had already packed his belongings. Tonight, he'd drive to his parents' house, then Monday he would begin the cross country drive to Oregon. Every mile would have him heading west, leaving Sara and all memories of her behind him to the east.

"Jim! Over here!" Katie called, motioning. "We have to have a picture of the three of you." When he reached her side, she took his elbow and positioned him next to Andy and Wayne. Andy groaned, smiling while telling the other two that he hated to pose for pictures.

Wayne chuckled. "Better get used to it. Next month, on your wedding day, there'll be no mercy."

Andy's wedding day. Jim pasted a smile on his face, glad he was going to be in Oregon. Later, when he said goodbye to his roommate of two years, he told Andy he was sorry to miss the wedding, but with the new job and...*and Sara being there...* He knew Sara was going to sit at the guest book. He didn't think his heart could face seeing his friends get married when he and Sara were living separate lives. And he did not want to see her again—not ever. Besides, Gavin would probably be there, too, with that smirk on his face.

*Oh, God...*he silently groaned. *Why can't I just get over her?*

That evening, after a leisurely meal with their parents, Jim, Wayne and Katie lingered at the table, wanting to postpone their goodbyes. Jim's car was packed. When he drove away tonight, it would be the last they would see of each other for several weeks or perhaps even months. They talked for a while about the changes ahead, then, resolutely Jim rose, knowing the goodbyes needed to be said.

As they left the restaurant, Katie hooked her arm through Jim's. "I'm happy you got the job in Oregon, but Wayne and I are really going to miss you."

"The feeling's mutual."

When they reached Jim's car, Wayne held out a hand to Jim, swallowing the lump in his throat. "I'm going to miss you, bud."

"Yeah, me too." Jim turned to Katie for a final hug, then climbed into his car. He started the engine while Wayne shoved his hands deep into his pockets and Katie nervously chewed on her bottom lip.

"Wait!" Regardless of her dress and high heels, Katie hurried after the car as Jim began to pull away. "Jim, wait!"

His window was open, so he simply put the car in park and turned to face her. She crouched down next to him so her face was at eye level with him. "I can't let you go without telling you something."

"What's that?"

"I've been sworn to secrecy. You'll have to ask. Please ask me, Jim."

"Ask you what?"

"About Sara. Ask me how she is. Ask me about her and Gavin."

"I don't want to hear about her and Gavin."

"Jim. Please, ask me."

Jim drew in a deep breath, bracing himself for whatever it might be. With Sara, one never knew. "So, Katie, what's happening with Sara?"

"She broke up with Gavin."

Jim's stomach did a funny flip-flop. "When was this?"

"Right after her accident."

"And you didn't tell me?"

"I couldn't. She made me promise. She said, only if you asked."

"So this is something she didn't want me to know."

"I guess, but, Jim, I couldn't let you move all the way to Oregon and not know. It changes everything."

"It doesn't change anything."

"Yes, it does. You should talk to her. She's different. Calmer, more sure of herself."

If she still loved me, she would have wanted me to know. "Thanks for telling me. All it changes is the way I think about her." Alone. Single. Only until the next guy caught a look at that gorgeous head of hair and heard her sweet voice, laughing and telling one of her stories. There would always be men falling at Sara's feet. Eventually, she'd find the one she wanted.

"But aren't you going to do anything about it? She's free, Jim. It'd be so simple to get her back."

"Things with Sara Brooks are never simple, Katie." Jim reached for his door handle. "I'm leaving now. Heading to Oregon. Gonna put two thousand miles between me and Sara."

"But, Jim…"

"Katie, right now, it's the only thing I know how to do. Go on, Wayne's waiting for you."

"But what do I tell her?"

That I love her like crazy. "If she asks, tell her I got a job on the coast in Oregon, just like I always wanted." With a wave, Jim pulled out of the parking lot. He made it a full block before his eyes filled with tears. "I'm sorry, Sara." He didn't know who he was sorry for. Her, because of her broken dreams with Gavin; or him, because of his broken dreams with her, but he would not go crawling back to her. After all, she had dumped him, not the other way around.

Sara paced the back patio. Tomorrow, she would leave for Greta and Andy's wedding in Iowa. Her heart was all aflutter wondering if Jim was going to be there. She needed to know, needed to prepare her heart. For whichever way. Why had she not asked Katie? Why had Katie not volunteered the information? She reached for the cell phone she had laid on the patio table and dialed Katie's number.

"Hello?" Wayne answered.

"It's Sara. Is Katie home?"

"No, she's shopping with Jenna."

"Oh." There was a long pause.

"So, do you want to leave a message?"

"Umm…maybe you could tell me."

"What?"

"I was wondering about the wedding this weekend. Is Jim planning to be there?"

"No, Sara. He just started his job in Oregon three weeks ago and couldn't ask off."

Oregon. Her heart fell. *He was so far away.* "Okay, that's fine."

"You're not going to call him, are you? I mean, he's starting over. He's doing well."

"No, Wayne. I'm not going to call him. I just needed to know if he was going to be there. Is he really okay then?"

"He's doing pretty good. He likes his job and the little town he's in."

"I'm glad, Wayne. Really, I am. It makes me feel better to know that he's moving on and doing well."

"So…that's all then? You're not going to pester me for his phone number or address?"

"No. Please, Wayne, try to understand. I just want Jim to be happy. I don't expect to be a part of his life again, but I can't forget him so easily either." Sara closed her eyes and pictured Jim standing on the ocean beach in Oregon, watching the sunset. She'd give anything to be standing by his side, but she understood that she had given all that up. Now, his happiness was what she desired. "As long as I can picture him happy and fulfilling his dreams, then I can go on, too."

Wayne remained silent. This calm, unruffled side of Sara was a surprise. Maybe the things she had gone through had changed her, matured her. Maybe Jim would fall in love with her all over again, if given the opportunity. "You seem…better."

"I am, Wayne. I finally have my head on straight and I'm relying on God much more than I ever have before."

"That's good, Sara. I guess we'll see you in Iowa."

"Iowa, yes." Sara smiled. She was looking forward to the wedding of their friends.

"Greta, you look absolutely beautiful!" Sara grasped her friend's hands in the little side room off the church fellowship hall. She had always envied Greta's relationship with Andy. It was so solid, so long lasting, and so authentic. Greta had never even dated anyone else. She'd always known Andy and had always known he was the one for her. As Sara admired her friend's wedding dress, she realized she wasn't the slightest bit envious anymore. When a couple had something as wonderful as Andy and Greta did, it should only be celebrated.

"You look beautiful, too, Sara—very radiant." Greta's sweet compliment was genuine. She had expected Sara to be a little disheartened. Seeing her glowing was a nice surprise. "You look happy."

"Happy is such a relative term, Greta. Let's just say that I'm learning to be content. I'm trying to walk closer with God and let Him guide my path. It's a lot easier this way, resting in Him."

"I'm glad, Sara. I've been praying for you. Are you staying at your sister's for the summer?"

"Yes, a few of the local hotels hire students that are in the hospitality program, so I was able to get a job as a front desk clerk. It's only part-time, but that frees me up to help my sister. Mark ends up doing several teen camps and conventions in the summer. He's all over the country."

The door opened and Greta's aunt poked her head into the room. "Greta, the photographer wants you for a few more pictures. Oh, and it's time for your guest book attendant to take her place now."

"That would be me." Sara gave Greta one last hug, then made her way through the church to the foyer, where she took a seat behind the guest book. While she cheerfully greeted people, she wondered if someday she would be a bride and have a groom look at her the way Andy looked at Greta and Wayne looked at Katie. *Your will be done, Lord*, she breathed, *and help me to accept remaining single for as long as You desire.* A vision of Jim ran through her mind, but she turned it over to God as she had done countless times in the past two months.

CHAPTER 27

Be kind and compassionate to one another, forgiving each other, just as in Christ God forgave you.
—Ephesians 4:32

Welcome to Newport. Population 9,960. "Make that 9,961," Jim stated aloud, passing the sign and slowing to crawl as he entered town from the east on highway 20. "Home at last, Jimmy." He welcomed the smell of the sea and the fresh ocean breeze through his open windows.

Reaching for a tablet of paper, he checked the driving directions for the apartment complex where he had rented a unit, sight unseen, over the phone. Slowly, taking in his surroundings, he followed the instructions. He pulled up to an older fourplex with chipping paint and overgrown shrubbery. At first sight, it was not exactly what he had hoped for, but this place fit his budget. Jim's needs were simple and this place would probably suit him just fine. Anyway, he didn't plan to be home much. For one thing, he wanted to work long hours. It was one sure way to keep his mind off Sara. For another thing, this was a coastal town with plenty of beaches, hiking, and biking trails to explore. No, sir, he would not be sitting home pining away for a lost love.

"You did say it was furnished, right?" Jim asked the landlady, a wizened older woman with watery eyes and thinning gray hair falling around her shoulders. He stuck his checkbook into his back pocket. First and last month's rent, plus the damage deposit, nearly depleted his savings. He wouldn't have money for furniture—even thrift store stuff—until his first paycheck.

"Some," she smiled. "Just the bare necessities. But a single man like yourself, how much can you need?" She handed him the key, informed him which day was garbage day, then ushered him out of her office.

"Thanks." Jim's unit was the top one facing the street. There was no garage, just a carport for his car. He'd be hauling his bike up and down the steps to ensure it did not get stolen. Anxious to see his new home, he took the steps two at a time and hurriedly inserted the key into the lock. Pushing open the door, Jim took a step inside. *Musty*, that was his first thought. He strode through the main rooms, pulling back the faded draperies and opening the kitchen and living room windows as wide as possible. Only after that did he take stock of his new home.

He chuckled at the sight of the end table in the living room made from blond-colored wood, the metal kitchen table with a yellow ceramic top and the old console television. *This place must have been built in the fifties and most of this furniture must have been in here ever since.* There were two kitchen chairs, plus a lumpy green couch and one recliner—which he discovered was broken—but it would be sufficient. He peeked into the bathroom. Just as he suspected, mint-green tile and fixtures. *At least it's not pink!* Then he wandered to the single bedroom.

"Great, just great." He stood in the center of the room, where a bed should have been, and did a three-hundred-and-sixty-degree turn. There was an old dresser and nightstand, a decent-sized closet and a folding chair, but no bed. "You'd think you could have mentioned that!"

Jim pulled aside the woven brown drapes and opened the window. "Great view," he muttered, staring across ten feet of open space to the pale pink stucco wall of the neighboring house. *Remember the low rent, Jimmy. It's good for the pocketbook.*

He spent the next hour moving in his meager belongings. He tossed his sleeping bag and pillow onto the couch, figuring that would serve as a bed for the time being. There were no bookshelves, so he set his stereo on top of the large television console and stacked his books, movies and CDs on the floor. One end of the kitchen table would serve as a desk for his computer, the other end would be for eating.

"As the lady said, how much do I need?" Jim looked around. "Okay, something on the walls and a bed, but for now, it'll do."

He needed to stock up on food and arrange for phone service, but he was eager to meet his boss, see the bike shop and explore Newport. The groceries could wait until after dark, but getting a phone and seeing his boss would have to be done during business hours. Since it was already late afternoon, Jim knocked on his landlady's door and asked where he could find a cellular phone company. Until now, he had resisted the lure of the world of cell phones, but since he needed something, this made the most sense. Otherwise, he'd need an answering machine too, because he didn't plan to spend much time within the walls of his apartment.

Funny, Jim mused as he climbed into his car with his new phone clipped to his belt. Sara had always wanted him to get a cell phone. Now he had one…

He spent the next two hours in the company of his new boss, a jovial red-haired forty-year-old named Rich. If there was ever a person who knew what he wanted, it was Rich. He planned to groom Jim to manage the store so he would be free to head down the coast to Florence and open a second shop. Rich introduced Jim to Ross and Carl, the mechanics. Ross was a big guy, in his early twenties; Carl was a recent high school graduate. They were both knowledgeable about bikes, and besides doing repairs they assisted customers in the shop.

Rich asked Carl to mind the store, then gave Jim a detailed tour of the shop. Afterward they sat in the cluttered office and discussed business matters until the shop closed at seven.

"See you on Monday," Rich said. "Enjoy the weekend."

"I will." Jim waved and headed toward his car. He had three days. Three days of freedom before he became a full-time employed college graduate. It was everything he'd been working toward, everything he'd dreamed of since he was a boy vacationing up and down this coast. So why did he feel so empty?

"I'm just hungry," he told himself as he headed toward Nye Beach. He found a place to park his car and strolled down the sidewalk. His stomach growled relentlessly as the smells of fish and chips and grilled burgers surrounded him. At a touristy beachside café, he ordered a burger, taco and chocolate shake at the walk-up window, then sat at an outdoor table and devoured his supper. Seagulls screeched overhead. Jim tossed the last bit of hamburger bun unto the sand and watched three birds dive for it. He threw his garbage into a nearby trash can, retrieved his sweatshirt from the car, then took a walk along the beach.

His appetite was sated, but there was still an emptiness in his gut. *It's Sara.* He knew it. She would love it here, with her desire for new experiences and natural wonders. She would relish this place, where the tide came and went and the Pacific Ocean stretched toward the setting sun. Jim perched on a rock and watched the sky and a few wispy clouds change from gold to pink to purple to navy. The first stars appeared. They didn't look any different than the ones back home. No different than the ones Sara could see from Morgan's front yard.

Get over her, Jimmy. He kicked the sand at his feet, wondering what his problem was. Even here, two thousand miles away, she was still under his skin. *I need closure, that's what. I need to tell her goodbye, once and for all.* Jim headed back down the beach. When he reached his car, he decided he would write Sara a letter. *I'll tell her about my job and that I'm starting over and I wish her the best.*

He hurried home, got some notepaper, sat at his table and wrote, *Dear Sara.* Then he chewed on the end of his mechanical pencil trying to decide exactly what to say. He didn't want her to think he was begging her to come back or that he still thought about her almost every day. She, obviously, had moved on and probably assumed he had, too.

He made a couple of feeble attempts at a letter, but crumpled each one and tossed them into the wastebasket. Suddenly he remembered receiving his textbook in the mail and how disappointed he had been—angry even—that she had not included a note. Maybe she had tried. Maybe she had agonized over the wording just like he was and in the end decided there was really nothing that could be said. Nothing. Nothing except, *I love you.* A lot of good that would do.

Go to bed, Jim. Things will look better in the morning.

Jim tossed and turned in his sleeping bag. Now he knew why the couch was lumpy. The springs were shot. About one in the morning, he moved to the floor and finally fell into an exhausted sleep. He woke at nine. After showering he realized he had forgotten to go to the grocery store last night and all he had to eat was a bruised apple and a granola bar left from his road trip.

Jim spent the morning stocking up on groceries and a few things for the apartment and learning his way around town. In the afternoon, he took a three-hour bike trip on one of Newport's many biking trails. Saturday, he drove down the coast to Reedsport and ate a late lunch on the dunes. Sunday it rained, so after church he stayed inside, reading and watching movies.

Monday he arrived for work early and stood on the sidewalk under gray skies waiting for Rich to arrive and open the shop. He was standing with his hands shoved into the pockets of his jeans, when a young woman approached the shop door bearing a cardboard drink container that held four cups of coffee.

She flashed Jim a dazzling smile. "We don't open until nine thirty."

"I know. I'm the new employee. Rich told me to come at nine."

"You're Jim, then. I'm Meagan, Rich's stepsister."

"You work here?"

"Only on Monday mornings. I help Rich with his ads for the week and design his sale fliers and other promotional stuff. I have a degree in graphic design and do freelance work."

"That's great."

Meagan laughed, a sweet, silvery laugh. "Just last week I did a banner welcoming our new employee—you."

Jim laughed, too. "I'm flattered." At the sound of footsteps approaching behind him, Jim turned and greeted Rich.

"I see you've met Meagan." Jim was positive he detected a twinkle in Rich's eye as he darted a quick look to his sister. He hoped Rich was not planning on setting him up with Meagan. Jim had no desire to start over with someone new.

Meagan and Jim followed Rich inside. Rich grabbed the cup of coffee that had a capital R written on the lid. Meagan held the container out for Jim. "One of these is for you. I didn't know how you like it so you have a choice. I have mocha, vanilla latté or just plain old black java. There's cream and sugar in the back room."

"I, uh—" How could he tell her that he didn't like coffee? After all the trouble she'd gone through to make sure there would be one of his preference. "I'll just have the plain one, thanks."

The first thing Meagan and Rich did was hang the one-by-three-foot banner announcing Jim as their new employee.

"Do you always do this?" Jim asked as he watched.

"No, but since you'll be the manager come fall, I want to let the locals know who you are."

Meagan smiled at him from the top of the stepladder. She was fairly pretty, with shoulder-length brown hair and eyes to match. She was about five feet, six inches, and carried a few extra pounds, but they suited her well. As he watched her, all Jim could think about was Sara. Next year, she'd be working at a convention center setting out signs to direct people to the appropriate rooms. She'd flash her dazzling smile and stop the hearts of many men. How he longed to have Sara flash her dazzling smile at him, just like she used to.

"Jim?" Rich's voice broke through the daydreams. "You ready to get to work?"

Jim blushed. "You bet. I can't wait to get started."

"That's the spirit!" Rich said, clapping him on the shoulder.

The morning passed quickly, with Jim running the cash register and writing up rental agreements for tourists who wanted bicycles or tandems for the day. Whenever possible, Meagan stood close and chatted with him. Before she left, she made a point of saying goodbye to Jim.

"If you need some company or a tour guide this weekend, you can get my number from Rich. I'd be more than happy to show you around."

"Thanks, but I'll be okay." Determined to remain businesslike, he simply tossed her a wave, then returned to the Schwinn catalogue he was studying. He knew plenty about bikes, from a derailleur to shocks, from road bikes to mountain bikes, but now, spending hours in a shop which was devoted to nothing but bicycles, he realized he had more to learn.

The afternoon passed as quickly as the morning. And so one day turned to another and Jim established a routine. Nine o'clock to work, a brisk walk at lunch the five blocks down to the beach and back, stay late to go over ledgers while the store was quiet. A simple supper at home, then a few hours spent reading or watching a movie or television.

On the weekends Jim explored. He took a new bike path each Saturday until he had covered each one Newport had to offer, on Sundays he went to church, then roamed the beaches. After Memorial Day, tourist season picked up, making everything from the sidewalks to the biking trails crowded. Jim took it all in stride—after all, tourism was their business.

Every Monday, Meagan appeared at the shop, coffee cups in hand. She tended to her work, conferring with Rich on his preferences, but always with an eye on Jim. She cast him numerous smiles, tried persistently to engage him in conversation, and more than once offered to accompany him on a walk or out for a bite to eat. He always thanked her, but told her he was too busy or not interested or whatever excuse he could come up with and not hurt her feelings. Although she was pretty and pleasant to talk to, she held no sway over his heart.

As the weeks passed, Meagan stopped in more frequently than just Mondays. First it was an afternoon for a quick cup of coffee—it seemed she always had a cup of coffee in hand—then a lunch she brought in for Rich, which just happened to be enough for the three of them to share. When she was in the shop, Jim was polite, but distant. He did not want to give her the wrong impression, false hope or encouragement. For what it was worth—which seemed like nil—his heart still belonged to Sara.

One June afternoon, as Jim walked the half mile down to the beach during his lunch break, he spotted a car just like Sara's. For a moment his heart stopped. Of course it wasn't her. *Why would I want it to be?* As his feet pounded the pavement, the question kept running through his mind. *Why would I want it to be?* When he reached the water's edge, breathing hard from his fast pace, he knew the answer. *Because, despite everything, I still love her.* But Sara had wounded him deeply and he had not yet forgiven her.

He turned and began the long trudge back up to the shop. *Forgive and be ye tenderhearted...*

Why should I forgive her, Lord?

Forgive others as I have forgiven you.

But if I forgive her, totally and honestly forgive her, then I open myself up to needing her.

Forgive just as in Christ, God forgave you.

Jim pushed open the shop door and strode to the back office. He firmly closed the door and sank onto the desk chair. Jim knew God was right. There was no sense arguing. He had to forgive Sara once and for all. Completely forgive and let go of his lingering resentment. Jim bowed his head. He'd been stubborn, clinging to his righteous anger and hurt, but as he forgave Sara and asked God to take away the residual bitterness, Jim felt a weight slip from his shoulders.

One morning, Jim woke with a craving for donuts, so after parking his car behind the bike shop, he jogged two blocks to the bakery. He ordered a half dozen donuts to share at work. When he left the sweet shop carrying a bag of raised donuts in one hand and his chocolate-covered éclair in the other, an elderly woman was just coming in. Awkwardly, Jim held the door for her, while trying not to let the custard drip out of his donut. Once on the sidewalk, Jim took a large bite, then turned to set a quick pace back to his own shop. About twenty feet ahead of him was a woman with hair and a body build just like Sara's. His heart did a double beat and instinctively he quickened his pace.

"Sara!" The woman did not turn around. Yellow custard dripped down Jim's fingers. He tossed the donut into a sidewalk trash can, then licked the filling from his fingers. "Sara!" He had nearly caught up to her when she turned and entered a café.

It was not Sara. Of course it was not her. Why would she be here? Jim leaned against a light pole, silently berating himself. He needed to get a grip on reality. He could not keep imagining that Sara was here. There was absolutely no reason for her to be in Oregon.

He turned and headed toward the bike shop. *Would she even come if I asked? If she knew that I still loved her? Had always loved her? Aw...Jimmy boy...that's been the problem all along. You never stopped loving her, but she left you.* Distraught, Jim muttered aloud to himself, "Why? Why did she do it?"

She told you why. She thought you were going to break up with her. She had no idea you were planning to ask her to marry you.

"That's ridiculous!" Jim shoved the front door to the bike shop open, strode across to the counter and plopped down the bag of donuts.

"What's ridiculous?" Rich asked, coming out of the back office.

"Women." Jim stared at his employer. "They're crazy. They're so needy. They need everything explained. If you don't do it all just right, then—" Jim smacked his hands together for emphasis, "*bam!* They throw a curve at you."

Rich smiled. "I didn't think you had a girlfriend. You never mentioned anybody."

"I don't." Jim pointed to the bakery sack. "I brought donuts. Help yourself. I'm going to finish that inventory I was working on yesterday." Jim reached for his clipboard and turned his back on Rich. As far as he was concerned, this conversation was over. But it wasn't so easy to block it from his mind. He kept needing to recount items. After about fifteen frustrating minutes, Jim stormed over to the counter, dropped the clipboard and informed Rich that he'd be back in a few. As he went outside, he met Ross coming in.

"Mind the front," Jim said. "I'll be back soon."

He hustled around to the parking lot, climbed into his car and headed to Agate Beach. After parking, he strode through the foot tunnel to the sandy shoreline. Kicking off his shoes and socks, he waded into the water and let the shocking cold waves lap around his ankles, wetting the bottoms of his khakis.

It didn't make any sense. Why did Sara leave him when they'd been dating nearly two years? They seldom fought, they could talk about everything, they'd given their hearts to each other. They were on a path headed for marriage. How could she not know that?

Did you ever tell her?

Tell her? I wasn't ready to propose. There was too much to figure out.

Did you tell her that you were planning to spend the rest of your life with her? Did you ever ask her to help you figure it all out? Or did pride stand in your way? You left her in the dark; she had no idea what you were planning.

She should have known.

Sara's very needy. The words Jim had said to Gavin came back to haunt him. She was very needy. She had low self esteem and had needed Jim to reaffirm his love countless times. And she was such a dreamer, while Jim was proud of the fact that he was a planner, and a thinker who would figure out their future before asking her to marry him.

Jim shook his head as reality sank in. "I left her floundering, wondering if I was ever going to commit to a forever after. I'm sorry, Sara. It was all my fault."

Maybe it's not too late!

Jim kicked at the sand. It was too late. Hadn't she practically forced him from her hospital room? She didn't even want to see him, let alone date him again. He had ruined it and now he had to live with that realization.

The following Monday, Meagan came out of Rich's office while Jim was sorting the mail. He had a stack of new catalogues in one pile, bills and advertisements in another. Muttering under his breath that Rich never threw out the old catalogues, he squatted onto his haunches so he could clean out the plastic containers under the counter.

"Housecleaning, I see," Meagan said, stopping to talk like she always did.

"Yeah, say, hand me that recycle bin, will you?"

Meagan brought him the green tub and watched as he checked dates. "Four years," Jim said, tossing the outdated catalogue. "Why does your brother think we need that?"

Meagan chuckled. "You should see his apartment."

"I've seen the office."

The bell over the front door tinkled as a customer walked in. Ross approached and asked if she needed assistance.

"I'm looking for a gel seat cover."

Jim froze. That voice! He dropped the magazine he held and stood up in such a rush that he bumped his head on the corner of the counter. His eyes darted to the customer who was now following Ross across the store. She had dark hair, was taller than Sara by at least four inches and was older by at least six years. He rubbed the bump on his head, then knelt to resume his task.

"So where does she live?" Meagan asked softly.

"Who?" Jim said, trying to find the date on a Fuji bike catalogue.

"The woman you're in love with."

"I'm not—how did you—?" Jim stared at Meagan.

She smiled and knelt next to him. "Besides the fact that you turn me down every time I invite you anywhere and always keep a polite distance, it's as obvious as the nose on your face."

"That I'm in love?"

"Yes." Meagan waited for Jim to answer her original question.

"She's in Milwaukee."

"And you're here. Why is that?"

"We broke up last fall. Over some stupid misunderstanding."

"Jim," Meagan raised her eyebrows. "A misunderstanding? Something as insignificant as that can usually be fixed."

"You'd think so, wouldn't you?"

"Have you tried?"

"It's complicated. There was this other guy...but then they broke up...she..."

"Have you tried?" Meagan repeated.

"No."

"If you still love her after all this time, I'd think you'd want to try to resolve the issue and get back together." Meagan rose and brushed her hands together. "You're no use to any other woman until you at least try. You owe it not only to yourself and the woman you love, but to the rest of us eligible girls that are floating around the edges of your life."

Jim cracked a grin. As if there were so many of those. Just Meagan, maybe... "Do you think there's a chance she'd accept my apology and hear me out?"

"She'd be a fool not to." Meagan slipped out from behind the counter just as the customer with the gel seat approached to make her purchase. With a last look at Jim, she added, "Let me know how it turns out."

That night Jim paced his apartment, cell phone in hand. He had already dialed Sara's number once, but had hung up before it could even ring. He didn't want to have Sara hang up on him before he could even get out an apology. That day in the hospital, she'd looked so defeated, yet resolved. Determined not to let him back into her life. Anyway, this was too important to mess up with words spoken hastily. He glanced at his computer. It was also too important for e-mail. That left a letter. He'd tried that before. Of course, that was when he only wanted closure. Now he wanted forgiveness. He needed to admit that it was his fault and he didn't blame her. He also wanted her back. He knew that now. He'd court her all over again if he had to. They'd make a fresh start. Only this time, Jim would make sure she understood he was jumping in with both feet and never climbing out.

He shoved aside some paperwork and sat at his table with a pen and a sheet of notebook paper.

Dear Sara,

Please don't tear this into tiny pieces until you've read it.

There's so much to say, but I guess it basically comes down to this: I'm sorry. It's only recently dawned on me that what happened was my fault. All my fault. I failed you. I never made it perfectly clear that I wanted to spend the rest of my life with you. I still want to. I've never stopped loving you and I can't stop thinking about you.

Can you ever forgive me? Is there any way that we can start over? If I thought you loved Gavin, I wouldn't ask, but I found out from Katie that you're no longer dating him. I'm not foolish enough to think you might be pining for me, but if you still care for me just a little, I'd like the chance to prove my love all over again. This time, I'll do it right.

There's more to discuss, but this is enough for now. If you don't want me back in your life, then tell me and I promise to leave you alone. Either way, I hope you'll forgive me. If you desire what I do, then I think the next step would be to talk face to face. We'll deal with the past in order to embrace the future.

Love, Jim

CHAPTER 28

Then make my joy complete by being like minded, having the same love,
being one in spirit and purpose.
—Philippians 2:2

One July evening Sara went into the kitchen to find Mark at the table
with a cup of coffee, a piece of cake, and several papers spread in front of him.
Casting a curious glance his way as she got a carton of yogurt from the fridge,
she asked what he was doing.

Mark looked up as if noticing her for the first time. "Say, you wouldn't
want to go on a trip, would you?"

Sara chuckled. "Are you trying to get rid of me?"

"No," Mark ran a hand through his hair. "I have so many free miles built
up, I can't use them all."

Sara leaned against the counter and took the lid off her yogurt. "So take
your family on a vacation. Or better yet, just take Morgan. I'll babysit. You two
deserve to get away."

"We are. We're planning a trip in October, but, Sara, I have so much
credit, we won't use it all." Mark held up a piece of paper. "This one expires
September first. It's transferable. I'm making a serious offer here. Take a trip.
On me."

Sara's eyes lit up. "Really?"

"Really."

"But I have no money for a hotel or anything."

Mark chuckled. "No problem. I have vouchers for everything. I can get you a plane ticket, train tickets, a rental car, hotels. You name it, it's yours."

Sara thoughtfully licked her spoon. "Where could I go?"

"You have to stay in the States. I can't get you overseas. Just think of the possibilities. You could go to Florida or Arizona or New Orleans."

"In the summer?"

"Okay, how about the East Coast? New York, DC, Maine, or think west. Colorado or California, maybe."

West? Oregon! Sara's heart rate increased. *Of course I can't go to Oregon.*

"Sara? What do you say?"

"I say…I'll think about it. Thanks, Mark. This is great."

The next day, Sara breezed in from a trip to the grocery store. Setting the bulging paper bag on the table she informed Morgan that she hoped she hadn't forgotten anything. Morgan looked up from scrubbing the sink. "Thanks. Um, Sara, a letter came for you."

"Really? Who's it from?"

Morgan nodded toward the desk. "It's there."

Sara crossed the room. As she neared the desk, her eyes fell on the envelope with her name and address written on it in neat, block lettering. *Jim!* Her eyes flew to the return address. *Newport, Oregon.* Sara's heart skipped a beat and her eyes met Morgan's. "What can it mean?"

"Why don't you open it and find out?"

"Yes…" Sara picked up the envelope and nervously ran her fingers over the seal. After all this time, Jim had written her. What could he possibly have to say? Slowly, she headed for the sliding glass doors and went outside. She sat down on a patio chair, carefully tore open the envelope and drew out the single sheet of paper.

Dear Sara… She smiled when she read the warning not to rip the letter into pieces. As if she would! *Oh Jim…* He still loved her! He wanted her in his life—forever!

Her joy was short lived as she realized he didn't know about all the sin in her life. If he did, he probably wouldn't want her, would he? Could he? Dare she hope that he could love her in spite of it all? God had forgiven her. Maybe Jim would too. If she and Jim were ever going to start over, she would have to tell him everything. Then he could decide if he still wanted her back.

Sara closed her eyes, leaned back in the chair and let her dreams fill her heart and mind. Mixed in with her hopes were prayers. Fervent prayers. She needed God's guidance before she answered Jim's letter. She would not make a move until she was confident she knew what God would have her do.

Two days later, Sara found Mark in the living room watching the six o'clock news and bouncing Tucker on his knee at the same time. "Mark? I decided to take you up on the trip offer. I want to go to Oregon and I want to go as soon as possible."

Jim arrived early to work on Friday. He had his own key now and often came early or left late. He had finally convinced Rich to let him clean out the office and he couldn't wait to get started. His boss was such a pack rat. The room was only eight by ten feet and nearly every square foot was filled with clutter. Paperwork dating from years back, odd bicycle parts, a broken fan, a misplaced pair of tennis shoes—no one could remember whom they belonged to—you name it, it was in the office.

Jim parked his car temporarily alongside the curb so he could unload the empty boxes he had picked up from the grocery store. He didn't plan to store much of the clutter, but the boxes would work for hauling stuff to the dumpster in the alley. Once he had all the boxes inside, Jim moved his car around to the back lot.

Deciding he needed a donut for fortification, he made a quick dash to the bakery and ended up buying a dozen. He set the box on the counter near the cash register, took out an apple fritter and walked to the door of the office. He stared at the pile of clutter and wondered where to start. His gaze landed on the corner, where a stack of newspapers rose over two feet high. "A fire hazard," Jim muttered, deciding they would be the first to go. He tossed them into one of the largest boxes, wrote *RECYCLE* on a piece of white paper and taped it to the top sheet of newsprint. He picked up the box and was heading toward the backdoor when Rich walked in.

His boss took one look at the box. "So, it's begun."

"Today's the day," Jim said, setting the box next to the back exit. "To make it go down easier, I brought donuts."

"That's the spirit." Rich headed for the pastry box, then stood in the office doorway for a few minutes, watching Jim toss odds and ends into a box for the dumpster. "I'll just sit at the desk and pay bills. You won't throw *me* out, will you?"

"Ha, ha. Get in my way and I just might."

Rich eased past Jim, sat on his desk chair and reached for his ledgers. Jim put the radio on and the men settled into work without talking. Jim hefted the box he had just filled so he could carry it out to the dumpster. As he left the room, he glanced back. He'd hardly made a dent in the clutter. With a sigh, he headed toward the back of the store. Just as he was about to push open the alley door, the bell on the front door tinkled, announcing a customer. Adjusting the box, he managed to glance at his watch. It wasn't even nine o'clock.

"We don't open until nine thirty," he called over his shoulder.

"I'll wait then."

Half in, half out of the door, Jim froze. That voice. It must be the woman who had bought the gel seat a couple of weeks ago. *Don't look*, he ordered himself, *you know it isn't her. Just get on with your business.* He went outside, tossed the box into the dumpster, then hurriedly reentered the shop. He couldn't help himself. He looked toward the front door. The woman stood silhouetted against the bright morning sunshine that was streaming in through the glass door and the large windows on either side. She was Sara's height and the hair was all bunchy and wild like Sara's, but her face was in the shadows.

Jim took a few steps toward the center of the store, his eyes locked on the woman.

"I got your letter." Sara smiled and moved out of the sunlight.

Jim's heart stopped. "It is you."

"Yes." Uncertain, she took two more small steps forward. "I came to tell you that I forgive you. And to talk, face to face, like you suggested."

"Sara." Jim's heart was now beating double time. He couldn't corral his thoughts or put together a sentence. He could hardly believe she was here. "Where—how did you get here?"

Sara grinned. "I took a red-eye flight to Portland. Then I jumped on something that looked like a toy plane and flew right into Newport's Municipal Airport. Originally I planned to rent a car in Portland, but do you know that a person has to be twenty-six to rent a car? Can you believe it? Twenty-six! I guess the people that make those rules feel it's safer to travel around in tiny little airplanes than on national highways with people under twenty-six driving." When Sara stopped to catch her breath, Jim smiled. She was the same old Sara with her dramatic storytelling. Man, he loved this woman. "I was hoping to catch you before you left for work, but you weren't that hard to track down. There's only one bike shop in Newport, the taxi driver knew where it was."

"Jim," Rich called from the office. "Is that a customer already?"

"No, it's uh—" Jim's feet were rooted to the floor. He had not moved since Sara had revealed herself. His mind was still sluggish from the surprise.

"A salesperson?" Jim heard Rich get to his feet.

"No, it's Sara, my—uh—my…"

Sara stepped purposefully toward Rich as he came out of the office and extended her hand. "I'm Sara Brooks, a friend of Jim's from back home."

Rich pumped her hand. "I'm Rich. Nice to meet you." He looked from her to Jim and back again. "Are you visiting for a few days?"

"Yes." Sara's eyes rested on Jim. "I hope so."

"Well, Jim, I think that office can wait for another day. Why don't you take the morning off? The boys can manage the store for a few hours. Check in after lunch, okay?"

"Yeah sure, thanks." Jim could not take his eyes off Sara. She was absolutely beautiful. More so than he remembered.

Rich went over and clapped Jim on the shoulder. "Go on, show Sara around." He gave him a nudge forward, whispering, "She's some gal you've been keeping secret."

Jim tore his eyes from Sara and caught Rich's. "She is at that." He turned, approached Sara and ushered her outside. "I can hardly believe you're here. I'm still in shock."

"You're not sorry I came?"

"Not a bit."

"I took your letter to heart, Jim, and I agree. We need to talk person to person, face to face."

"Face to face. Yes, well, you always were full of surprises. Never in my wildest dreams did I expect this kind of answer to my letter."

"We can thank Mark. I'll explain later. First we have more important things to talk about."

"Yes, but not here in front of the shop. Let's head to the beach. There'll be a cool morning breeze. Do you have a sweatshirt or jacket handy?"

"Yes, my suitcase is right inside the door."

Jim hadn't noticed it before, but as he opened the shop door he saw her bag sitting against a tandem bicycle. Sara unzipped it and pulled out a navy-blue sweatshirt. "Recognize this?" she asked, holding it up. Jim grinned. It was his MCU sweatshirt. The one he'd lost last winter. He liked the thought that

Sara had had it all this time. She shoved her purse strap onto her shoulder and held the sweatshirt in the crook of her elbow. "Are we walking or driving?"

Jim debated for just a moment. They could walk down to Nye Beach, but it would soon be crowded with tourists. Agate Beach, just a mile north of town, would be less busy and it offered an endless stretch of sandy beach. "I know the perfect place." He picked up her suitcase to stow in his trunk. "Come on, my car's around back."

As they headed to his car, Jim's heartbeat started returning to normal. He could think again. He wanted to take Sara in his arms and kiss her, but he felt aggravatingly shy. There was so much unfinished business between them. He unlocked the car door for her and held it while she climbed inside. Quickly, he placed her suitcase in the trunk and jogged around to the driver's side. He climbed inside, buckled his seat belt and turned to her. "Coming here took a lot of courage, Sara."

"Not really. I wanted to see you so badly."

"Then why did you kick me out of your hospital room when I came to see you?"

Sara leaned her head back and closed her eyes for a moment. "That was a different time and place. I hadn't decided to break up with Gavin yet. And I didn't want you to see me like that."

"I didn't mind the cuts and bruises, Sara."

"That's not what I'm talking about." Sara turned away and looked out the side window as Jim pulled onto the street. "There are things you don't know, Jim."

Jim took a left turn. "Let's talk about it when we get to the beach. I want to be able to give you my full attention."

"All right. I'll tell you about my amazing brother-in-law and what he all did to get me here."

When they arrived at the parking area for the beach, Jim locked Sara's purse in the trunk. They donned their sweatshirts—Jim chuckling over how big his MCU one was on Sara—then he took her hand and led her into the walk-through tunnel. When they emerged from the passageway, Sara stared at the ocean.

"Oh, Jim! It's fabulous!" She sprinted for the water, kicked off her flip-flops, and ran out a few feet. Surprised at the coldness, she hustled back toward shore, then, laughing, turned and waded back out until the water lapped at her knees. She looked at the horizon, then overhead to the screeching seagulls, then up and down the beach. "It goes forever. This is beautiful."

Jim stood at the water's edge, the waves licking his tennis shoes. "You've never been to the ocean?"

"No. Just what I could see from the taxi this morning." A large wave crested, splashing Sara's shorts. With a shriek, she raced for the safety of the sand. Jim caught her and drew her into an embrace.

"You have no idea how much I missed you." His voice was husky with emotion. "Stay with me forever, Sara."

Her breath caught in her throat. *Not yet, Jimmy…* "I—um—" Flustered, she looked down at her wet legs and the sand sticking to her feet. She shoved her hand up into the oversized sleeve of her sweatshirt and bent to dry her calves, then rinsed off her feet and slipped her flip-flops on.

Jim took Sara's hand and they began a slow walk along the water's edge. There were only a few other people on the beach this early—a young woman jogging, a man playing fetch with his dog, an older couple leisurely strolling. Sara leaned her head slightly against Jim's shoulder and silently braced herself for the discussion she knew they must have. "Jim, before we can talk about the future, we need to discuss the past."

"I agree and I'll start. I was really stupid, Sara."

"No, you weren't," Sara interrupted. "It was me…it was all me and I regret it so much."

Jim looked at Sara with a depth of love in his eyes. "For a long time I was so angry that you had gone out with…Gavin," Jim forced the name from his mouth, "but now I realize that you had no way of knowing what I was thinking. I was so busy trying to figure everything out that I lost sight of the fact that you didn't know I planned to ask you to marry me."

Sara shook her head. Jim's faults were so small in comparison to hers. "No, Jim. I should have understood that you were committed. If I hadn't been so blinded by my dreams and so insecure and impatient, Gavin would never have gotten a foothold on my heart. I went running all wild and made such wrong assumptions."

"Which you wouldn't have if I had talked things over with you and let you in on the planning. You know, it took me until this summer to figure that out."

"But I should have talked to you, Jim. I should have shared my insecurities. I never should have—have—" Tears streamed down Sara's face.

Jim stopped walking and looped his arms loosely around her shoulders. "Don't cry, Sara. I don't blame you anymore."

"You must have hated me. I can't believe what I did and how badly I hurt you. I feel awful that you saw me kissing—" She didn't even want to say it.

"I'll admit, it was a bad time, Sara, but let's put it behind us. I'm willing to accept my share of the blame for what happened. If I had been more open with you and met your needs you never would have been tempted by Gavin's advances."

"Oh, Jim…" She buried her face on his shoulder, wetting his sweatshirt with her tears. "I'm so terribly sorry."

"Come on, Sara, let it go. For us, please. I love you. I always have. From that first winter day I met you." He nodded to the ocean as the waves swelled and rolled toward them. "Like the tide is pulled to shore, I love you. It's something beyond my control. These past months have been unbearable."

His sweet, genuine words caused Sara's heart to swell with love and hope, but she needed to get everything out in the open. Resolutely, she wiped her eyes and slowly resumed walking, waiting until he fell in step beside her. "There's more stuff to tell you. We can't start over until I tell you everything about those months I dated Gavin."

Jim held tightly to her hand. "I'm listening."

And so Sara told him about the countless lies, the stealing and the drinking. She told him about the kind of people she had hung out with and how she had drifted away from God and the church. Jim listened quietly and let her get it all off her chest. When she was finished, he drew her into his arms. He didn't say anything for the longest time, just held her close and let their hearts beat as one.

"I'm sorry you went through all that, I truly am, but I can see how you've grown through the experience. You've been here less than two hours, but already I see a strength in you that was never there before. I still love you, Sara Brooks. I always have; I always will."

She smiled at him, relieved at having told him everything. "Even after knowing all that?"

"Even after." He looked deeply into her watery eyes. "Now, I can only assume since you came all this way that you must still love me, too."

"I never stopped loving you. I tried to bury my feelings, but I never quite succeeded."

Jim placed a hand behind her head and leaned down for a kiss, a sweet, lingering kiss, on the beach, in public for the whole world to see.

CHAPTER 29

May he give you the desires of your heart and make all your plans succeed.
—Psalm 20:4

Jim and Sara continued to talk, walking far down the beach, then sitting for a while on a log that had long ago drifted ashore and settled partway into the sand at high tide. Laughing at something silly Sara said, Jim gave her a quick kiss on the cheek.

"You know, Sara, you wouldn't believe how dull my life has been without you. You're my sunshine, the breeze on my face on a hot summer day, the oasis in the desert of my heart."

Sara laughed light-heartedly, then sobered and looked into Jim's hazel eyes. "You're my anchor."

"That sounds like a drag." Jim chuckled at his own pun.

"Seriously, Jim, you're my security in a storm. My lighthouse, protecting me from the craggy rocks."

"So I'm the lighthouse and you're the sun. I like that." Jim glanced at his watch. "We should get back and grab some lunch. What do you want to do this afternoon while I'm at work?"

"Let's see if they'll give me an early check-in at the motel. I didn't get much sleep on the plane last night. I wouldn't mind taking a nap."

After a lunch of burgers and fries, Jim got Sara settled into her room at the hotel. Mark had made a reservation for her on the other side of town near the airport. Sara was delighted to discover that her room had a view of the ocean.

"Don't stand there staring out to sea all afternoon," Jim warned. "Get some sleep so you don't nod off over dinner tonight."

"Yes, sir," Sara grinned and saluted him. "And you'd better go back to your bike shop and explain to your boss just who I am."

"I will. I'll pick you up at six thirty, okay?"

"I'll be ready."

He kissed her goodbye then rode the elevator to ground level and jogged to his car. What an unbelievable morning. He still could hardly believe that she had come. *What a girl!*

As soon as Jim entered the bike shop, Ross looked up from behind the counter and whistled. "Ooh, Jimbo, Rich tells us you have quite a good-looking lady friend."

At the sound of Ross' voice, Carl came from the enclosed repair area, wiping his greasy hands on a rag. "Yeah, where've you been keeping her?"

Jim grinned and proceeded toward the office, calling over his shoulder, "Sounds like you guys are jealous."

"She got any sisters?" Ross asked.

Jim paused at the doorway to reply. "Yep, but one is married and the one is way too young for you." He entered the office to find Rich sitting at the desk. "How's it been?"

"Slow. Carl and Ross are getting caught up on the repairs."

"Fine. That'll give me a chance to finish in here." Jim tossed off his sweatshirt and set to work as if he'd not been interrupted four hours earlier.

Rich watched him for a few minutes. "Want some help?"

"Sure. You can go through those file folders in that box. Only keep stuff from the past seven years. Everything else goes in the shredder."

Rich grinned. "You're already acting like the boss."

Jim grunted as he lifted the broken fan and headed toward the dumpster. When he came back through the store, Ross whistled again. When Jim returned, Rich was sitting in front of the file box, already sorting the material.

"So are you going to tell us about your morning visitor or just keep us in the dark?"

"It's a long story."

"Well, I'm not going anywhere. This project is going to keep us busy for a while."

"Yeah…" Jim bent over a crate of old bike parts and began pulling them out one at a time and deciding if each item should be kept or dumped. As he and Rich sorted, Jim talked about his and Sara's relationship, making sure to place the blame for the breakup on himself. He didn't realize until he finished the tale that Ross and Carl were standing in the doorway listening.

"You're not going to let her get away again, are you?" Carl asked.

Surprised, Jim looked up. "Aren't you guys supposed to be fixing bikes?"

"Aw, come on, nothing dramatic like this ever happens around here."

"No, I'm not going to let her get away."

The front bell tinkled. "Back to work," Rich said, shooing his mechanics to the repair room while he went to wait on the couple that had just entered.

Jim carried another box to the dumpster. When he came back in, he noticed another customer had entered the shop, but Rich seemed to have it all in hand so he returned to the office. As he stood in the doorway, he realized the office was really taking shape. Most of the clutter was gone, leaving mainly three file boxes that needed sorting. He pulled one onto his lap and started going through the papers in each folder, checking dates. He was glad the task did not require much concentration, because his mind was back on Agate Beach with Sara.

He meant what he said to his coworkers. He was not going to let her get away. He couldn't bear the thought of her leaving on Monday and not knowing when he would see her again. Now instead of three hundred miles, they had two thousand separating them. He chewed on the possibilities and problems. There was no great solution. He'd committed a minimum of two years to Rich. It was in his contract. He was already halfway through the five-month stretch they had laid out for him to learn the business. Plans were well underway for the opening of the new shop. Rich was already spending one day a week down there. If it wasn't for honoring this commitment, he'd move back to Milwaukee and be with Sara while she finished college.

She could move here, but a town the size of Newport didn't have a college. She could commute, but she'd probably have to go as far as Portland to find a school that offered the hospitality program. Even Portland was too far. And he couldn't—wouldn't—ask her to give up her dream. Suddenly Jim looked up from the papers on his lap. He was doing it again. Trying to solve all the problems by himself without including Sara. Maybe, just maybe, she would see a solution that he didn't. They would talk at dinner. He'd present the problem to her, after he made sure she felt the same way he did. That she didn't want to be separated again. He hoped she would agree, because there was no way on earth he wanted to attempt living in different cities again.

His mind made up, Jim tackled the file box in earnest, but something kept nagging him. He was just old fashioned enough to think that before he talked to Sara about where and how to spend their future, he should first ask her to marry him. He closed his eyes as the thought planted itself firmly on his mind and he could no longer ignore it. She was leaving on Monday morning. He couldn't let her go without making some plans, but that meant asking her to marry him first. Well, then, that's what he would do. He'd ask her to marry him. He'd always wanted to. He'd do it tomorrow. *Tomorrow? No, tonight. Tonight? Ask her to marry me tonight?* Jim glanced at his watch. It was nearly three o'clock. *Am I crazy? I have no plan, no ring, no nothing. You can't ask a girl like Sara to marry you just like that. There have to be flowers—tons of flowers— and candles and music...*

Where could he put this together? He didn't want to do it in his apartment. Bringing a girl to a private place like that had always been drilled into him as forbidden. It still seemed like wise advice to follow. The beach had the perfect ambience, but he could hardly have the flowers, candles and music there. A fancy restaurant was a plausible solution, but it was too public for Jim's taste. He just needed a room...a quiet corner... Suddenly he stood up and looked out at the main floor of the shop. *Forget it, Jimmy. You're not going to propose to Sara surrounded by bikes and racks of clothing.* He turned back to the office, when his eyes widened. *The office.* He turned a circle, eyeing it critically. He could get the rest of the junk out of here in no time and stack these three boxes in the corner. Rich already had a CD player in here. He could bring in a few dozen roses and candles...

"Rich! Hey, guys! I'm going to need some help here."

"What?" Reluctantly, Rich approached the doorway. "You're not moving out the desk, are you?"

"No, we only have a matter of hours to turn this room into the perfect setting for a proposal of marriage." He ignored Ross' whistle. "And I have a ring to purchase, candles and flowers to get, dinner reservations to make..." Jim's voice trailed off as he wondered if his best shirt needed ironing.

"What's this?" Rich asked. "You're going to ask that little lady to marry you here? In my office?"

"It'll be my office in a matter of weeks, remember? And yes, if you guys will help."

"That's the spirit!" Rich said, grinning. "Tell us what you're thinking."

Jim laid out his plans. Carl laughed good-naturedly and said he was in.

Ross said his cousin was a florist in town and he'd see if he could get a break on the flowers. Rich reached for the phone and said he'd call Meagan. "We might need a woman's touch."

Three and a half hours later, Jim stood in front of Sara's door, a single red rose in his hand. He was dressed in his khaki pants and a striped dress shirt, freshly pressed by his landlady. He'd been running in high gear since three o'clock. The guys and Meagan had really come through. Now, if he just could calm his nerves. This whole day had been unbelievable. He half expected to wake up and discover he was only dreaming.

Sara opened the door with a smile and immediately noticed the red rose Jim held. "Ooh, how pretty. Thank you, Jim. You're so sweet."

"You look great, Sara."

She glanced down at her creamy, floral skirt and sort-sleeved light blue sweater. "I mostly packed jeans and shorts. I hope this is okay."

"Very okay. You ready to go?"

"Yes. Let me just grab my purse." Sara reached for her small bag and tossed in her room key. Still carrying the rose, she stepped into the hall. "I had the best nap. It must have been all that fresh sea air this morning. I feel so rested. How about you? Did you have a good afternoon?"

Jim pushed the button for the elevator. "I kept busy working on a special project."

During the ride to the lobby he told her about Rich's habit of squirreling away everything that came through the door of the shop and how he'd been dropping hints since May that the office needed to be cleaned out. "It's crazy really. He keeps a neat shop and a meticulous repair room, but that office…" Jim shook his head as the elevator doors opened. They stepped out and Jim took Sara's hand, subtly nodding at the young clerk.

"Oh, Miss Brooks," the desk clerk said, "I have a message for you."

"Really?"

"Yes, here it is." The clerk brought a red rose from behind the counter and held it out.

"Jim!" Laughing, Sara accepted the rose.

He shrugged, trying not to grin, and led her outside. He opened the car door for her and as she started to climb inside she saw another rose on the seat. Scooping it up, she held all three to her nose and smelled the sweet, heady scent. Once Jim was seated and buckled, she leaned over and placed a kiss on his freshly shaven cheek. "I always knew you had a romantic flair."

Jim shrugged and pulled onto the street. "You took me by such surprise this morning, it's taken me all afternoon to get over it. The least I can do is surprise you with a few flowers."

There was another rose lying across her napkin on the candle-lit table at the restaurant. Another one arrived with her menu and yet another with her meal. "Jim Hoffman!" She laughed. "How many more are there going to be?"

He grinned. "Usually roses come in a dozen, so figure it out."

"Six more? Where are they all hiding?"

He just shrugged and cut open his baked potato. So far, his plan was working like a charm. One nice thing about a town this size, people knew people. Ross's cousin knew the head waiter here...yes, sir, things were all going according to plan.

"Would you care for dessert?" their waiter politely asked after he had taken away their dinner dishes.

Sara laid a hand on her stomach. "I couldn't possibly."

"But they have your favorite, raspberry cheesecake," Jim explained. "And I'm sure you want some coffee."

"That sounds very tempting. Just a tiny piece though. What about you?"

Jim looked at the waiter. "I'll have the chocolate torte and some iced tea."

"Very well." The waiter left and returned in a few minutes with their dessert. Another red rose was placed next to Sara's cheesecake.

"Skip dessert and you'd miss getting one of your flowers," Jim said.

"Number seven." Sara looked at Jim over her cup of coffee. What fun this was. He was so sweet, trying to make up for all those awful months they were apart. "I never want this night to end," she said softly.

He reached for her hand and held it on top of the table. "We have two and a half more days, Sara. We're going to make the most of them."

"And then?" She hardly dared to ask. She had not allowed herself to think beyond Monday when she would have to get back on that plane.

"We'll talk about it later. Tomorrow. Tonight, let's just enjoy being together."

When the waiter brought the bill, he also delivered another rose to Sara. She smiled at Jim. "You get the bill and I get a rose. I like this."

"Let's go."

They stepped outside. Sara breathed deeply, pulling the salt sea air into her lungs. "I love that smell. I wish I could bottle it up and take it home with me."

They decided to take a walk along Nye beach. Sara carried her roses and hooked her other hand through the crook of Jim's arm. "Can we stay and watch the sunset?" she asked.

"We can, but that's another couple hours away yet."

"I don't mind. It's so beautiful here."

Just then Jim's cell phone rang. It was Rich informing him the candles were lit, the music was on and everything was ready. "All right," Jim said into the phone piece. Folding it, he clipped it to his belt. "Sorry, Sara. That was Rich. He's halfway to Florence and remembered he was supposed to send a fax out. It's going to the East Coast and they have to have it first thing in the morning. I need to run over to the store and send it."

"All right. Don't worry about it. We can come back for the sunset, can't we?"

"You bet." He ushered her to the car. Before climbing in himself, he said, "Oh, I forgot something." He opened the trunk, took out another rose and gave it to her. "Number nine, right?"

"Jim Hoffman, you are the most creative guy I know. Wait until I tell Katie about this."

"I'm sure Wayne's done his share of romantic stuff. It's not that big of a deal."

"It is too."

When they arrived at the store, Sara left her roses in the car and followed Jim inside. He re-locked the door behind him and did not bother to turn on the lights. Since it wasn't dark outside, they could easily see their way to the office.

"The fax machine is in here," Jim said, approaching the closed office door. He stood behind Sara so nothing would block her view as he slowly pushed the door open. He heard her sharp intake of breath, then with a hand to her mouth, Sara slowly stepped inside the office. There were bouquets of roses sitting everywhere, and in between were tea lights, all lit. Dozens of tea lights. And soft music. And the overpowering, heady scent of the roses in the small, closed room. A banner, Meagan's touch, crossed from corner to corner on the far wall. In navy letters across a pale pink background it said, *Will you marry me?*

"Jim..." Sara did a slow twirl around the room, counting bouquets. "Eleven bouquets," she whispered. "When you said they came in dozens, you meant it."

Jim stood silently, watching her pure surprise and enjoyment. Her eyes roamed to the banner on the wall. "Will I marry you?" Tears pricked her eyes and she turned and moved into his waiting arms. "Yes, Jim. Tonight, tomorrow, next week…just name the day."

"Oh, one more thing." Jim moved to the desk and opened the top drawer.

"Another rose?" Sara asked, still looking around in disbelief at all the flowers in the room.

"No," Jim said, returning to her side. "This." He held out a gold ring with three small diamonds on the center of the band. "Sara Brooks, will you do me the honor of being my wife?"

"Yes, Jim," she whispered, staring at the beautiful ring. It was incredible. She had always wanted a ring with three stones to represent yesterday, today and tomorrow. "How did you know?"

"I called Katie. You tell her everything. I figured she'd know what kind of ring you always dreamed of."

Sara could only stare at him. "You've thought of everything. Are you sure you didn't know I was coming? Mark or Morgan didn't clue you in, did they?"

"No, Sara. I was totally shocked this morning. I planned all this since three o'clock."

"Three o'clock!"

Jim grinned. "I admit, I had a little help from my friends." He drew her into his arms and kissed her. "Sara, I know our love will last forever. It's been tested and tried and never faded. I'm committing myself to you. Never doubt me again. I'll do anything for you, go anywhere you want me to. I'll dry all your tears, listen to all your stories and help make your dreams come true. Just say you'll be with me forever."

"I will, Jim. I know I belong by your side. From now and forever…for better or worse…for richer for poorer… I finally understand that what we have is true love. No other kind could have withstood what we went through. I love you; I always will."

It was after midnight when Jim walked Sara to her door. He carried a vase bulging with roses from the office while she carried the nine single ones she had gotten at the beginning of the night. She slipped her key through the lock, then pushed the door open. Jim reached inside and set the vase of flowers on the nearest counter, then pulled Sara close for a good night kiss.

"Sleep well, my beloved fiancée. I'll be back in the morning."

"You too. We have much to discuss."

Another kiss, then Jim tore himself away and walked toward the elevator.

Sara watched until he rounded the corner, then entered her room, turning on a light as she did. When she turned toward her bed, she smiled. Lying across her pillow were three more roses. Now her original dozen was complete. These were the ones she would somehow get home. She would dry them and keep them forever as a reminder of tonight. She buried her nose in the buds and breathed in the sweet aroma, then went onto her balcony and looked west, where the surf was building and crashing against the shore.

It had been a most perfect night—worthy of a romance novel; better than any fairy tale. Jim had amazed her. Standing on the balcony, Sara recalled every detail of the night. She would have to write it all down Monday on the plane so she could capture it forever—as if she would ever forget this night. It had been so fun when they called their parents, Morgan and Mark, and Katie and Wayne with their news. Eventually, she and Jim had returned to the beach and watched a splendid sunset. One so colorful it was as if God had painted the skies in celebration of their engagement.

In the midst of the night's enchantment, they had readily agreed to put off the discussion of when they would marry and where they would live until tomorrow. They had wanted only to bask in their rediscovered love and the pledge they had given each other. Now, as Sara recalled the way the office looked with his bounty of roses and flickering candlelight, she knew that she wanted to recreate that for her wedding. She would fill the church with red roses and candles—that's all she wanted for decoration. Dozens of roses, dozens of candles and Prince Charming waiting for her at the end of the aisle.

Sara and Jim returned to the beach on Saturday. They spent the first couple of hours playing like carefree children. They purchased two kites and flew them, then spent a long time making an elaborate sand castle. After eating their picnic lunch, Jim told Sara he had somewhere to take her.

"And then we'll talk," he promised. Anxious as they were to decide when to marry, they knew it was complicated and had delayed facing the issue. "Come on." Jim tossed the remains of their lunch in the small cooler they had brought, then pulled Sara to her feet. As she shook the sand from their beach blanket, she took a long look at the rolling ocean.

"Will we be back?"

"Yes."

"Good. I love it here," she said, falling in step beside him. "I could live here, Jim." She looked pointedly at him. "Really, keep that in mind for our discussion. I would love to live here."

"It isn't always like this. The beach is often lost in the mist and they get a lot of rain, even in the summer."

Undaunted, Sara said, "Misty beaches are romantic and rainy days are cozy."

Jim grinned, but kept silent. He would do whatever it took for them to stay together; it sounded like Sara was making up her mind to do the same. When they reached the car, they stowed the blanket, kites and cooler in the trunk. As they pulled onto highway 101, Sara asked where they were going.

"You've seen the lighthouse from the road, haven't you?" Jim asked.

"Yes, it's wonderful."

"Well, it's open for visitors."

The parking lot to the Yaquina Head Lighthouse was quite full, but Jim found an open spot. Sara grabbed her camera and grasped Jim's hand as they strolled among other tourists down the paved path to the base of the lighthouse. Sara looked up to the windows at the top. "Rapunzel," she whispered, "let down your hair."

"Want to climb up?" Jim asked. "It's over a hundred steps."

Sara agreed eagerly. She needed to rest partway up the long circular climb, but the view from the top was breathtaking and worth the climb. "You can see for miles!" she exclaimed.

The gentleman who was spending his afternoon as a volunteer lighthouse host overheard. "Nineteen to be exact," he informed her. "The light was first lit in 1873," he added, happy to pass on a little piece of history.

Jim was standing behind Sara. He wrapped his arms around her waist and leaned down to rest his chin on her shoulder. "I came up here for the first time a couple of weeks ago—right after I wrote you that letter. I thought about how my love was like a beacon, calling to you across the miles. Yesterday, when you told me I was your lighthouse, I knew I had to bring you here."

Sara turned from the view of the ocean and looked into Jim's eyes. "Jim Hoffman, you are the most amazing man. I love you so much."

"Come on, it's time we figure out our future. We can't keep avoiding it any longer."

They descended the steps, took a few pictures, then returned to the car. Jim drove back to Agate Beach, where they spread their blanket on the sand, far from the incoming tide. Jim lay on his stomach, propping his chin on his elbows while Sara sat next to him.

"I'm not going to live apart from you again," Sara stated.

"We're in agreement on that point."

"And I want to get married as soon as possible. This summer yet."

"Sara, it's the end of July. You'll never get the wedding of your dreams planned in a few weeks."

"The wedding of my dreams? That will come true no matter what, because I'm marrying you. I don't care about made-to-order dresses and a fancy catered wedding supper. I can buy a dress off the rack, we can just serve cake and punch and only invite family and our very closest friends. Please, Jim, I just want us to be married."

He studied her face. "Someday you might regret that you—"

"Do you want to wait?"

"No."

"Okay. There will be no regrets. We've had enough of those."

"I have a regret right now," Jim said. "This commitment I've made to Rich. I signed a two-year contract, Sara. It'll be two years until I'm free to move."

"I already told you I could live here. I *want* to live here."

"I don't want you to give up your dream of getting your hospitality degree. I don't know if you've realized it, but there's not a college here. You should go back to MATC and finish. It's just one more year."

"I'm not going to be separated from you again."

"It'll be different this time. We're engaged; we have a wedding to look forward to."

"Jim, do you honestly want me to live in Milwaukee while you stay here? We won't even have weekend visits."

"No, Sara." He sighed. He'd known it would be like this. They were at an impasse. Drawing in a determined breath, he said, "It's not like I'm a prisoner here. People break contracts all the time. There are extenuating circumstances. Rich will understand."

"No," Sara said. "I will not let you do that. One of the things I admire most about you is your integrity. You will not back out of your contract and you will not leave Rich without a manager."

"Then you'll be forced to give up your dream, Sara."

"I won't be giving it up. I'll be postponing it. In two years, we can reevaluate things. If I still want to finish school, then we can move. Until then, I'm going to be living my other dream. I'll be married to the man I love, in this most incredible place. I can probably get a job at one of the hotels here and work at the front desk. I've already learned so much about hotel management. Who knows, Jim, they might hire me to be a front desk manager."

"They don't have conventions out here."

"No, but they have lighthouses and beaches and wonderful people who spend their afternoons filling a room with flowers and candles. I have ready-made friends here."

"What about Morgan and the children?" Jim loved the way he was feeling with the knowledge that he and Sara could be married in a matter of weeks and living here, but he wanted to make sure every base was covered.

"I always hoped we would get married after you graduated, so I never made a promise to Morgan that I'd stay for two years. Besides, Tucker had his first birthday; Courtney is nearly five. Morgan doesn't need me as much as she did before."

Jim grinned and reached for her hand. "I ran out of arguments."

"This is right, Jim; I just know it."

He nodded. "I'll talk to Rich about getting a couple of weeks off. September would be best, because the tourist season slacks off after school starts. We can get married, go on a honeymoon and be back with a couple of weeks to spare before his mid-October departure date."

"A September wedding…perfect! It'll be easier to find an open date at church and get a photographer."

"We'll only have to be apart for a few weeks."

"Maybe Mark has some more vouchers he needs to redeem. I could come back for a weekend."

"Make it a long weekend."

Sara threw her arms around his neck. "We're really going to do this, aren't we?"

"Yes, Sara. In six weeks you'll be Mrs. Jim Hoffman."

Before pulling out of the church's parking lot Sunday after the morning service, Jim cast a long look at Sara.

"What is it, Jim?"

"It's you. In all the times we've attended church together, you have never seemed so involved as you were today. I love the way you sang with your whole heart and you were so intent on the sermon."

"I love the church you've chosen and the pastor's message was so meaningful, but mostly, my whole outlook on worship has changed. I used to go to church mainly because I knew that's what God expected of me, now I go because I want to. I want to bring Him my praises and fellowship with other Christians and learn from the minister. I discovered the hard way how strong the devil is and how we need to stay grounded in God's Word to fight his temptations."

"I'm glad, Sara. You're much more confident and serene than you used to be. I love you even more than I did before."

"I regret so many things, but in a way, I'm glad it happened. I needed my faith challenged. It wasn't easy though; it's like my heart had to get torn up and sewn back together before I could fully understand God's grace. And now I'm also better able to understand human love. I feel better able to love you, Jim."

He reached for her hand and gently squeezed it. "Me too. I didn't need my faith challenged, but my heart needed to be torn up and sewn back together too, so I could become the husband you need." They traveled a few blocks in silence, then Jim spoke again. "I guess it goes to show how God really does make everything work together for our good. When everything seemed so bleak, God was working His will in our hearts."

Monday, Jim and Sara walked hand in hand down the hallway of the airport. She carried her purse and her bouquet of roses. Little beads of moisture filled the crevices of the plastic that was wrapped around the stems. Jim carried a small paper bag.

"This is as far as I can go," Jim said as they came to the security gate.

Sara turned toward him, tears gathering in the corners of her blue eyes. "Our relationship has certainly had its share of goodbyes."

"Not for much longer." They embraced and kissed, then Sara said she must go. "Here," he said, handing her the bag. "I got you something."

"Lunch?"

"No, just a little gift. Open it on the plane."

She threw her arms around him for one last hug, murmuring that she loved him.

"I love you, too. Call me when you get there."

"I will." Tearfully, she stepped up to the security area. She placed her belongings in the gray plastic tub, then with a final wave went through the metal detector. Jim watched until she was out of sight, then with a sigh, turned and headed back to his car.

Once the plane was airborne, Sara curiously opened Jim's gift. It was a hardbound journal, decorated with a photo of the Yaquina Head Lighthouse. *Oh Jim...* She flipped it open to the front page. He had written a note:

To Sara, may this journal be a place for your thoughts or memories, or maybe the beginnings of the great American novel you've always dreamed of writing. Your light in the storm, Jim.

Sara turned the page to see that Jim had written yet another line. *Once upon a time there was a very ordinary boy who loved a girl with wild curls and a great imagination…* With a tearful smile and a deep longing in her heart, she flipped through the journal. The rest of the pages were blank except the very last one. There, Jim had penned one final line. This one simply said, *And they lived happily ever after.*

Printed in the United States
70049LV00003B/73-90